"You'll definitely see elements of yourself and your girlfriends in this terrific novel. Like many close friends, Clare and Sally sometimes lose touch for months, but they can always depend on each other when times are tough. And isn't that what friendship is all about?"
—*Redbook*

"Moody is brilliant at exposing just how emotionally and morally complex a friendship can be. As Clare and Sally survive their own illusions and sometimes desperate accommodations to what fate has in store, they test the limits of loyalty and the latitudes of forgiveness. The course of these paths as they twine and intertwine will enwrap you as well—I guarantee it. This book is a gift. Get it, give it!"
—Diane Vreuls,
author of *Are We There Yet?*

"Martha Moody's first novel, *Best Friends*, bodes well for the future of this talented novelist."
—Josephine Humphreys,
author of *Nowhere Else on Earth*

Best Friends

martha moody

RIVERHEAD BOOKS

new york

THE BERKLEY PUBLISHING GROUP
Published by the Penguin Group
Penguin Group (USA) Inc.
375 Hudson Street, New York, New York 10014, USA
Penguin Group (Canada), 10 Alcorn Avenue, Toronto, Ontario M4V 3B2, Canada
(a division of Pearson Penguin Canada Inc.)
Penguin Books Ltd., 80 Strand, London WC2R 0RL, England
Penguin Group Ireland, 25 St. Stephen's Green, Dublin 2, Ireland (a division of Penguin Books Ltd.)
Penguin Group (Australia), 250 Camberwell Road, Camberwell, Victoria 3124, Australia
(a division of Pearson Australia Group Pty. Ltd.)
Penguin Books India Pvt. Ltd., 11 Community Centre, Panchsheel Park, New Delhi—110 017, India
Penguin Group (NZ), cnr Airborne and Rosedale Roads, Albany, Auckland 1310, New Zealand
(a division of Pearson New Zealand Ltd.)
Penguin Books (South Africa) (Pty.) Ltd., 24 Sturdee Avenue, Rosebank, Johannesburg 2196,
South Africa

Penguin Books Ltd., Registered Offices: 80 Strand, London WC2R 0RL, England

This is a work of fiction. Names, characters, places, and incidents either are the product of the author's imagination or are used fictitiously, and any resemblance to actual persons, living or dead, business establishments, events, or locales is entirely coincidental.

The author gratefully acknowledges permission to reprint lines from "Waiting" by Miroslav Holub, from *Selected Poems: Miroslav Holub*, translated by Ian Milner and George Theiner, published by Penguin Books, 1967. Copyright © 1967 Miroslav Holub; translation copyright © 1967 Penguin Books Ltd.

PRINTING HISTORY
First Riverhead hardcover edition: June 2001
First Riverhead trade paperback edition: June 2002
Riverhead trade paperback ISBN: 1-57322-935-0

The Library of Congress has catalogued the Riverhead hardcover edition as follows:

Moody, Martha.
    Best friends / Martha Moody.
        p.   cm.
    ISBN 1-57322-188-0
    1. Women college students—Fiction.   2. Female friendship—Fiction.   3. Roommates—
Fiction.   I. Title
PS3563.O553   B54   2001   00-053323
813'.6—dc21

PRINTED IN THE UNITED STATES OF AMERICA

20   19   18   17   16   15   14   13

for Jill

In between, the passage grows complex.

DAVID ST. JOHN

One

REALLY, ALL I WANTED in a college was unrest and demonstrations. But I was late. By 1973 no one was demonstrating, Vietnam was basically over, and what good was college now? I wrote this in my letter to Sally, my mystery roommate whose name and address had arrived sometime in August, along with the names of two other roommates who would join us in a quad. I expected her to understand that I was joking because she was from California. She wrote back on fancy Hallmark stationery with a pink band edging the page.

"That roommate wrote me," I told my family at supper. "The one from California." She'd made no mention at all of my demonstration comment.

"Debbie?" my mother asked.

"No, Mother. Debbie's from Indiana."

"Lindsey?"

"Lindsey's from Pennsylvania, Mom. Jeez."

"Sally's the one from California," my father said. "Sally Rose."

"Right." I smiled gratefully at him.

"I don't know how I'll ever keep you girls straight." My mother shook her head.

"You keep your kids straight, don't you?" I was the youngest of four, the only girl. My mother taught classrooms of twenty-six. "Or do you?"

"You can't bait me into another argument with you, Clare Ann."

"Clare," my brother Baxter corrected her. He knew I wanted to rid myself of any cuteness.

"Clare," my mother repeated, exhaling a short laugh. "It's certainly time for you to get away from home, I can see that."

"Me, too." Baxter smiled. He was hoping to move to Amish country to work as an apprentice chair-maker, a plan that caused my parents consternation because their older sons had both attended college, an educational commitment that was, as I liked to point out, at least partly explained by the draft.

My father cleared his throat. "How does this Sally sound?"

"She sounds nice." I paused a moment, aware of the inadequacy of my description. She sounded incredibly straight. *I'm excited, but I'm nervous, too. I have one little brother, Ben. He is really sweet and I'm sure I'll miss him a lot.* She didn't sound California at all. "Amazingly nice," I said. "Almost like . . . Debbie from Indiana."

WE MET AT Oberlin College, just southwest of Cleveland, in September 1973. I was from an Ohio town midway between Akron and Youngstown, a town I referred to as Happyville (to call it Dullsville would underestimate the self-satisfaction of its residents), a place where the banner headline of the newspaper on December 24 read UFO SIGHTING OVER NORTH POLE. I picked Oberlin because it was the only school within driving distance of Happyville still likely to have demonstrations. Sally picked Oberlin because, on a visit from Los Angeles the previous spring, her father thought the professors were open-minded. Neither of these was a bad reason to pick a college. In fact, these reasons are probably typical. You can gussy them up with all the pretty rationales you want, but most major life decisions are whims.

According to my college guide, Oberlin was one of the most expensive colleges in the country, and this thrilled me because my parents didn't have money. If they were willing to send me to Oberlin, I must be worth a lot. I must really be, as my brothers called me, the Great White Hope of Happyville. My mother, who as a teacher had access to my IQ, refused to tell me in case knowing it would swell my head.

My parents drove me the two hours to Oberlin. The quad, at the end of a hall, consisted of a study area flanked by two bedrooms. Each bedroom contained two single beds, two closets, and two built-in dressers topped by mirrors. When I arrived, only one bed of the four had been taken. Its bedspread was an earth-tone floral; above it hung a poster of a cat dangling off the side of wooden bridge. HANG IN THERE, the poster read. A footlocker sat at the end of the bed.

It didn't make sense. Sally Rose had written saying she'd arrive in Oberlin early, giving herself time to adjust to the new time zone, but could these really be Sally Rose's things? Sally Rose was from Los Angeles! I thought Californians had style.

I thought of my own striped Indian bedspread and woven reed rug, my sleek yellow metal lamp and decorative postcards. "I'll go in here," I told my parents, taking the empty bed in the room I'd decided must be Sally's. I imagined someone thinking my side was California and Sally Rose's Ohio. "You're kidding," they'd say, "you're from Ohio? I thought..."

"Hello?" said a voice from the door. I swiveled. It was Sally Rose, wearing a name tag. She was shorter than me, her wavy dark hair shaped like a May basket turned upside down. Her smile was girlish, eager; the description "apple-cheeked" flew into my mind. "Are you Clare Ann?" she said.

"Clare."

"Oh, I'm so glad you're here!" she cried, throwing her arms around me. Then she threw her arms around my parents.

———

SHE WAS SERIOUSLY HOMESICK. There was a phone at the end of our dorm hall, across from the bathroom, which Sally used for hours every night. "Oh, they're okay, Daddy, they're nice, they're just not like. . . . No, I wanted the art history course, but it was filled—yes, I did go talk to the professor, but she couldn't or she'd have to let in everyone who. . . . Benny? Benny, do you miss me?"

"You think she'd mind that everyone can hear," Indiana said. "I for one have heard enough."

"She's really pretty sweet," I said. "I kind of feel sorry for her."

"Maybe she'll quit and we can spread out and each take a room," Pennsylvania said. "That'd be cool."

On her nightstand, Sally had a photograph of herself and her little brother in a lucite frame. I assumed the photo had been taken at a country club, not that I was sure what one looked like. The little brother was adorable, skinny, curly haired and tan, eyes squinched against the sun; he and Sally stood in their swimsuits in front of a stone wall covered with a strange plant whose trunk twined up the wall and sent out branches right and left in perfect horizontal rows.

"What kind of plant is that?" I asked Sally.

She didn't know, some kind of decorative tree.

"It's amazing," I said. I can't tell you how rare it was for me to say "amazing" in those days; I cultivated a jaded air. "I've never seen a plant that symmetrical."

"Oh, it's trained," Sally said, and as I tried to cover my bewilderment, she brought the photo up close and showed me the thin wires stretched across the wall behind the branches. "I think it's called an espalier," Sally said. "Carlos likes to do it. It takes awhile to grow a nice one."

"Carlos?"

"Our head gardener." Sally set the photograph down. "He's very particular. He has the yard all mapped out."

"So this is"—I waved my hand, trying to think of a subtle way to put it—"at your house?"

"By the pool."

"It's pretty," I said weakly.

"It's a beautiful house," Sally said. "We've been there nine years. Daddy built it. I think the landscaping makes it. It does help to have a particular gardener."

"Head gardener," I said, watching her closely.

Sally showed no trace of discomfort. "There are a couple of others, but Carlos is the idea man. He says do this and they do it."

"Very obedient of them," I noted. For all her love of obedience in me, my mother hated the thought of obedience in workers. Sheep! she said. Management always wants sheep! My mother was the most radical person in Happyville; she believed, for example, that it was not unthinkable for teachers to unionize. Once she had been lucky enough to get a death threat.

Sally and I took the same Introduction to Poetry course, and my first paper didn't get the ecstatic response I was used to. For the life of me, I didn't know why. Sally got better comments than I did, but her paper was so organized and simplistic, every paragraph starting with a topic sentence, that it sounded more like junior high school than college. "My sophomore English teacher taught me to outline," Sally said proudly. "I think that's going to help me all through college." She said the same thing later to her parents on the phone in the dorm hall, sounding even more pleased with herself, and then she went on and on to them about how wonderful they were and how much she missed them, until I kicked the study-room door shut, wondering how much self-congratulation a family could stand.

WHEN YOU'RE IN COLLEGE you haven't had that much life. Parents, school, assorted youth activities—that's about it. I remember a girl in my freshman dorm whose twin had been killed in a boat wreck. Someone else told me her story. I used to run into that girl in the dorm bathroom and she seemed perfectly ordinary. She had long brown hair, and she smiled and washed her face in the sink and used organic toothpaste. How could someone look so normal with a dead twin sister? I was in awe of her. I wished something dramatic would happen to me.

I TOOK SALLY HOME for Thanksgiving with my family. God knows why. Ten minutes after dinner, she was on the phone in the front hall, talking to her parents in her clear, unavoidable voice.

"Nice girl," Frank, my oldest brother, home for the holiday, commented. "I didn't know you had nice friends, Clare Ann. I thought all your friends were just smart."

"Cute, too," my second brother, Eric, said. Baxter wasn't with us. The family he lived with in Amish country had left town for the weekend, and he stayed to look after the dogs.

"Such a sweet girl," my mother said as we cleaned up the kitchen. "Immensely mature." Sally was still on the phone with her parents, phrases wafting in to us from the family room.

"I wouldn't call her mature," I snapped. "She just hasn't rebelled yet."

My mother stood at the edge of the kitchen and listened to Sally's voice. "And she likes her parents so much."

"She's rich, though, you know," I whispered. "Can't trust her."

I knew she was rich from the pictures, from how much she'd traveled, the casual way she and her parents talked for hours long-distance, the puzzled look she got when I said I didn't want to skip the cafeteria and join her for dinner out. Early on, when she was at a class, I'd gone through her orderly closet. Her clothes were about the dullest I'd ever seen: corduroy pants with flared bottoms, jackets with wide lapels, flowered blouses. It shocked me when I saw their labels. I'd never seen designer clothes before. Pierre Cardin. Bill Blass. How much could they cost? I sometimes looked at *Vogue,* hoping to find out I looked like a model (people said I looked like Joni Mitchell, which didn't thrill me), and I thought about the prices beside those photos. And what did you get for such riches? Ordinary clothes, boring clothes,

clothes that looked like something you'd buy at Penney's. I was into thrift shops then. I had a green silk blouse with a pussy willow print that I dearly loved, and a skirt made of vertical rays of fabric. I wore Indian embroidered cotton shirts and jeans with torn knees, and I thought I looked ten times more interesting than Sally "Fashion Plate" Rose.

The next day I took Sally to the county nature center. A few tattered leaves clung to the trees, and it was unseasonably sunny and warm. I remember Sally looking up into the trees as she walked, dizzy with excitement. She took photographs of tree limbs against the sky, of a red barn, of a bridge over a brook. "Clare," she kept saying, "this looks like a picture! This looks like *National Geographic!*"

"How droll," I said.

I TOLD SALLY about my dad's office. It wasn't his, exactly: he was business and personnel manager for a group of doctors. I'd worked there after school doing filing. I knew everything about that place: which patients drove the nurses crazy, which doctors cheated on their wives, who sneaked cigarettes. I even knew which doctors didn't like my father—and I hated them, because who dared not like my father? Their complaint was that he wasn't tough. He didn't have the oomph to fire people. I loved it that he didn't have the oomph, that he split his Christmas bonus with the janitors, that he knew Denise McCalley was pregnant and didn't tell the doctors until she did on the day she quit. "So the doctors make a lot of money, Dad?" I used to ask.

"They work extremely hard," my father answered.

I could read that answer. "Maybe I'll be a doctor," I said.

"You could be," he said. "You could be anything you want. You're a capable young woman."

"YOU KNOW," Sally said, frowning, "I've never been to my dad's office."

"He doesn't invite you?" We were writing papers in our room, Sally at a desk engraving a legal pad with her heavy print as I wrote down ideas on scraps of paper and let them drift to the floor beside my bed. I'd been telling her about my father's office and the demented patient who always called me Miss Muffin.

"No. And your dad's office sounds interesting. I'll have to ask Daddy to take me to his."

I had recently realized I said "interesting" in an idiosyncratic way—inneresting—and while I was trying to determine whether to change this, I listened very closely to how other people said the word. In-ter-est-ing, Sally said, which was typical of the way she spoke. She organized her drawers, and in a very unimaginative way: underwear in the top drawer, shirts in the second, jeans in the third. She got a letter or card from home almost every day, and after reading it, she would add it to a bundle she kept in her underwear drawer. I was dying to know what her family wrote, but I would never know, because she tied the ribbon around her treasure so precisely I could never risk removing it.

"It's just a business, though," Sally was saying. "I don't think there are all those strange people around like at your father's work."

"They're normal people," I said with agitation, not sure what I was defending, "they just do strange things."

Sally looked at me a little too blankly, the red spots in each of her cheeks reminding me suddenly of Tootle, the disobedient engine I had read about as a child. There's a whole world out there, I thought, annoyed. Could she really know so little about it?

Sally was Jewish but had gone to Catholic schools. Her father believed in nuns. He had gone to religious schools himself. There were a lot of good things religion could teach you, he said, if you threw out the guilt and punishment stuff. Sally had always worn a school uniform, and she and her father and her cousin Daphne, who was also her best friend, went shopping together for her nonschool clothes. "Daddy wanted to keep me sheltered," Sally told me, "but now he figures I'm old enough to see the world myself." It sounded like a strange upbringing to me: eighteen years in the nest, then an airborne shove cross-country. I'd been taking short excursions by myself for years.

She couldn't set an alarm clock. She didn't know that whites and colors should be washed separately, and her first pink-underwear experience put her in such a tizzy I heard her down the hall speaking in Spanish to her family's maid. *"Ay,"* she said, *"es muy complicado."*

There were nights I sat in the study room of our quad with the door ajar so I could better hear her phone conversation. "Although I don't know why," I told Pennsylvania, who sometimes listened too. "It's impossibly boring."

I had some other friends. Margaret was the daughter of two missionaries. She was born and raised in Guatemala to age fifteen. This left her, as she was the first to point out, with No Cultural References. "Like *I Love Lucy,*" she'd explain, her eyes widening. "I'd never heard of *I Love Lucy* till I was sixteen years old."

"You think that's a loss?" I asked. Margaret did: cultural references were a kind of shorthand, a means of communication. I hadn't thought of that, I admitted. To catch up on her education, Margaret watched a lot of TV. I don't remember any other freshman having a TV in their room, but Margaret did, and it was always on. Soap operas, game shows, sit-coms, *Sonny and Cher, The Rockford Files.* Sometimes she'd hardly acknowledge your presence, she was so engrossed. She made a good argument, I thought, for letting kids get their fill of TV when they were children. But when you got the TV turned off, she was very likable.

AARGH, LARS. SENIOR, avid vegetarian and bicyclist, beard that looked like parsley. Sally met him at a classical guitar concert she'd attended. He started popping up at our quad at all hours with his lean and hungry look, and one Friday night he arrived when Sally and I were tucked in our beds reading. I walked into the study room and opened the door. "It's late, Lars," I said. "We're in bed."

"Lars?" Sally called. "Is that you? Come on in."

It took only an instant to realize that Sally had no idea what she was doing. By then Lars was through the study room and into our bedroom, eager to close the door. "I live here too, Lars," I said, pushing the bedroom door back open. "Remember?" I walked over to my bed, got in, and stuck my book in front of my nose.

What a day he'd had! Bicycling thirty miles out to the reservoir and back, stopping by some friends' for a bulgur and root-vegetable feast, reading Kierkegaard.... On and on he went, perched on Sally's bed, inching closer and closer to Sally's lips and breasts. I set my book down and lay on my side, facing the two of them, hoping to get Lars's attention.

"I've got to go to sleep, Lars," I finally said. "And I can't do that listening to you."

Sally giggled.

I WOULD PEEP OVER her shoulder at her sleeping face, head sunk into the pillow, mouth open, amazed anew that this was a California face. Her lips were pink and shaped like Chatty Cathy's, her dark eyelashes curved like a baby doll's. "Such an open face," my mother had said in wonderment, glancing at my own face with suspicion. I asked Sally questions. Do you know surfers? A few. They're normal boys. Not glamorous. Don't people dress differently in California? Maybe a little. Daphne has two midiskirts. Do you know anyone in the movies? Oh, sure. Screenwriters' daughters and lighting people's sons, and one of the girls in high school, her uncle—

"Are people really, you know, spacey? I mean, like you hear about California, that people latch on to every new fad?"

Sally looked troubled. "Of course, some people do that. They must do it anywhere." I nodded, unsatisfied.

The temperature was in the sixties in Los Angeles in the winter, Sally said; she didn't have a winter coat. Flowering plants and shrubbery ringed her house. Do trees lose their leaves in winter? I asked. Are there squirrels? Thunderstorms? Can you really feel a breeze off the ocean?

There was another girl from California in our dorm, Gwen Myers, whom I'd seen in the dorm kitchen with her back to me, wearing a pair of tattered denim overalls over a ribbed knit shirt, her blond hair twisted behind her neck and draped over one shoulder. Now Gwen, I thought, Gwen is California. While Sally was a pretender, an impostor, a girl with the geography but not the feeling, a person less from a state than from a family, from a world more circumscribed than my own.

THE MOMENT LARS LEFT, Sally bolted out of bed. "He wanted to sleep with me, didn't he?" she squeaked.

"Don't tell me you wanted to sleep with him."

"Oh no! He's dorky."

This startled me, because Sally was dorky.

"Vegetarian," Sally scoffed. "God, there are a million vegetarians in California. You can't open a car door without hitting one." She grinned. "One riding a bicycle!"

I was astounded. This was a whole new Sally, a Sally I could understand. I felt almost tingly with possibility. People became best friends with their roommates, lay in the dark and talked, got drunk together, lusted after guys, shared clothes. Years later, they hoped for their children to go to college together. I laughed out loud, showing Sally I appreciated her, that I knew what she was offering, that I was available too.

That night I chased Lars away, we lay in our beds in the dark and talked.

"Is sex really that good?" Sally asked.

"Oh yeah," I assured her, although I'd wondered, after my high school experience, the same thing myself. The anticipation had seemed a lot better than the real thing. I hadn't met the right person, I told myself. Then I wondered why Sally assumed I would know about sex. I took it as evidence of my obvious worldliness.

"A guy kissed me once at a wedding," she said, "but he was too old. This guy who works with my father, Hank Barresi. We were dancing, and he pushed me to a corner and kissed me, and I was excited because I knew it was coming and I wondered what it would be like, but when he did it I was disappointed. He had Kahlua on his breath and he was sweating, and then right away he put his tongue in my mouth. I might like someone's tongue in my mouth, but that wasn't the right tongue."

I was taken aback. It struck me that Sally, in her way, was franker than I was. And what did Kahlua smell like? I thought it was a kind of liquor, but I wasn't sure.

"Then last summer this guy bothered me," Sally went on. "In Oahu. He was walking past me and he grabbed my breast."

"Just grabbed it?" I said. "Through your clothes?"

"He was walking in the other direction. And there was a huge crowd. It only lasted a second. Then he was gone."

"God," I said. "How icky. Did you see who did it?"

"I saw his arm." Sally laughed. "Pretty hairy!"

"Were you wearing a bra?" I was trying to think if there was anything about Sally to provoke a man to grab her breast. She did have big breasts, but in the weeks I'd known her, she always wore a bra, even to bed. I hadn't worn a bra for years, but I was flat.

"Of course." Sally sounded offended. "I mean, you've seen me."

Not asking for it at all. As I thought this, I realized it was sexist, the sort of notion I'd jump all over my mother for.

"That's depressing," I said. "That someone could just do that to you."

"Isn't that weird? And in front of my parents, too. I was right beside my dad, and Ben and my mother were in front of us. Nobody saw it."

"What did you do? Did you yell or anything?"

"Oh, no. I kept going. What else could I do? It was over, I didn't know who'd done it." She sighed. "You want to hear something else strange? I enjoyed it."

I gulped. Every feminist urge in me said I shouldn't believe what she'd just said. "You did?"

"It made me feel good. I'm kind of big, some guys like that, and the blouse I had on was white cotton with little flowers. It wasn't see-through or anything, but it was a summer cotton. I thought when I got dressed that morning that I looked nice." She hesitated. "So I took it as a compliment."

We paused and thought, Sally doubtless of the way she'd looked in the mirror, the way her torso thinned out nicely below her breasts; me trying to imagine her looking sexy. I could see it, in a robust, farmgirl-in-the-hay sort of way.

I had a funny thought: "Hard to imagine some Oberlin guy grabbing you like that."

We both laughed.

"People are funny," Sally mused. "That's what Daddy always says. 'You can never tell what'll ring your bell.'"

The more I thought about this, the truer it seemed, and not just in the obvious sexual sense. The one course I loved this semester was Introduction to Genetics. Who would have dreamed that I'd love that course? I'd only taken it because it was premed and I wanted to prove to myself that I was as smart as the premeds, even though I planned to major in English. The doctors I knew were too conservative. "That's pretty profound," I said. "Did your dad think that up?"

"Probably. I'm sure he did. He's a smart guy."

"What does he do again?"

"Magazine distributor."

"Oh, that's right. I remembered he distributed something." The adult world of business and money was still a mystery to me.

"Magayines," Sally said, then explained: "I saw a box for a magazine rack once and it said 'magayine rack, made in Taiwan.'"

"A little problem with the more exotic letters."

"Eyactly."

"Amaying."

We were probably closer at that moment than we were at any time during our freshman year. I was as happy that night as I'd ever been, almost as happy as on the warm night in Los Angeles, almost two years later, that I've labeled for years the happiest moment of my life. It's no wonder we've stayed friends. It's no wonder we've done all we've done for each other.

FALL SEMESTER, SOPHOMORE YEAR, I took Introduction to Religion. Sally took it too. She took Introduction to Everything—philosophy, sociology, English, psychology, art history. "I won't know what I'm missing if I don't," she said. Her father seemed to play into this somehow, to encourage her in this endless branching out. She bought and mailed to him, at tremendous expense, copies of the books she was assigned in each course. He then read along with her, and she reported to him each night what her professors had said that day. Sweet, I thought, touching—Sally's father's faith in education, typical of the high-school dropout he was. I'd always thought of education as a game, a slightly silly and disreputable game that I always won. All through high school, I'd barely studied. My first year at college—with the sad exception of Introduction to Poetry, whose professor, Mr. Gifford, never saw things my way—had not been much different, but sitting in Introduction to Religion in a rickety classroom in a rickety building, it hit me that there was a whole world of thought I hadn't realized existed; for some reason, maybe the height of the room, I sensed this as an enormous orb grazing the top of my hair. It was a euphoric moment, one I couldn't replicate years later when I tried. The spooky thing was Sally felt it too.

She and I hadn't talked for months, not since the spring before, af-

ter Pennsylvania and I had moved out of the quad together. "Listen,"
Pennsylvania had whispered, gesturing at Sally down the hall on the
phone and Indiana in the study room sucking, as she always did when
she was reading, on the left sleeve of her sweater, "we're clearly the two
adults here. Why don't we get our own room?" In April, Sally and I
had met one Saturday afternoon for sundaes and I'd gloated—really
gloated, afterward I was ashamed—about how happy I was rooming
with Pennsylvania. "That's nice," Sally had said, but she looked listless, her pupils flat as tacks. Grace Chang, her new roommate, was
okay. Just okay? Maybe not even okay. "You know what?" Sally said.
"I don't know why she'd do this, but I think she went through my letters from home."

"You're kidding!" I feigned shock, hoping I wasn't giving myself
away by a blush.

Sally was nodding soberly. "I know. It's like Daddy says, she's not
quality."

How damning! But Sally was right, to go through someone else's
letters was not quality. I frowned inwardly, wondering where this left
me, a person who wanted to do it, who might have done it but for the
ribbon. But I hadn't done it, had I? There *was* a difference between
Grace Chang and me. Maybe the ribbon was less an impediment than
a scruple.

"This course is exciting, isn't it?" Sally whispered six months later
as we filed out of Introduction to Religion.

Yes, it was exciting, although I never would have expected Sally to
recognize it. "I love it," I said, looking at her in surprise. My forehead
felt suddenly damp. I hated sounding emotional. I couldn't remember
the last time I'd said I loved something. "Daddy took me to a Indian
temple once, off the road, way out in the desert," Sally said, "and I
could feel that—I felt it was a sacred space. It didn't look special, but
it felt special."

I felt a surge of envy. What I would give to visit a sacred space!

———

AS A SOPHOMORE, Sally had a double to herself in the hall where we'd shared a room freshman year; her father had written a letter to campus housing. The doubles in that dorm were two small rooms, originally planned as a study room and a sleeping room, although everybody split them into two separate bedrooms. I noticed that Sally had the same furniture as last year, plus some new things: a stereo system, a microwave, a little TV. Luxuries. I wondered again about her phone bills.

Pennsylvania had a boyfriend who took to staying overnight in our room that year. One weekend I arranged to go home, and several nights I spent in the dorm lobby. I tried to talk to Pennsylvania about it. "There's no reason you have to go off somewhere," she told me, breathing quickly. "Jeff and I don't care if you watch."

When I repeated this to Sally, she burst out laughing. I was startled to see her head back, mouth open, the fillings in her teeth revealed. A real laugh. What had happened to her over the summer? She was a thousand times more relaxed.

When she finished laughing, she smiled. "Would you like to move in here with me?"

WE WERE HAPPY TOGETHER. I had the room that led to the hall, and Sally had the inside room. We kept Sally's refrigerator and TV in my room. We sat in my room evenings after studying, splitting a carton of ice cream. We shared the usual late-adolescent fascination with our parents, the burgeoning realization that they were people too, and we talked a lot about our families, who were, after all, the filter through which we saw the world. By then Frank and Eric were both married, play-acting at adulthood (Frank was very proud of his car; Eric's wife, although they had no children, worried endlessly about school systems), and Baxter was off in his strange woodcrafting world, doodling chair designs on paper bags, wood shavings tangled in his increasingly bushy beard. Sally knew my mother drove me crazy and how much I liked my dad, and I knew Sally's mother counted so little in her life it seemed as if she didn't have a mother—a revelation I found most haunting years later when I had a daughter of my own. At the time, Sally's estrangement from her mother seemed romantic—or maybe I admired it because my mother and I were so antagonistically entwined. My mother could still slip a line in a letter that would anger me for weeks. You're not going to get an A in every course. You looked so tired last weekend. You're just like me, you always think...

Sally adored her father. There was something to this Oedipus thing, we agreed. Sally's dad was just so interesting, she'd say, and so interested. How many forty-eight-year-old men would read along with their daughter's courses? He'd done Introduction to Sociology and Introduction to the Novel; now he was doing Introduction to Religion. He didn't have to do any of this, Sally pointed out. He was a businessman, incredibly busy. Night after night, he'd have meetings or business dinners and not get home till ten. In high school, Sally waited up for him. They'd sit in the family room or on the patio, and Sally's dad would fix her a weak Scotch. "Tell me everything you've learned today," he'd say, and not just school stuff but personal insights, news of the world, observations about the weather. Everything.

"He lets you drink Scotch?" I asked, incredulous.

"I love Scotch," Sally said. "Have you tried it? It tastes like smoke. We'll have to get some." She had no idea that this would be difficult, no thought that in Ohio (as in California) the legal age for buying alcohol was twenty-one. When I pointed this out, she was startled. I was struck, as I would so often be, by Sally's peculiar blend of worldliness and naivete.

She still talked to her parents—but now I knew she was talking to her father, her mother only an absence on the line—almost every night, but maybe for only fifteen minutes. I kept my door cracked and listened with a kind of pleasure, so I could hear the nice things Sally said about me: Clare calls our religion professor a priest in disguise. Clare made us beef Stroganoff in the dorm kitchen. Clare found this new shampoo made with placentas, it's disgusting, you should see....

I WAS WATCHING SALLY as she talked about her brother. She waved her hands, explaining the way he flitted from enthusiasm to enthusiasm like a bee from flower to flower, when I realized: my friend is odd. I had great respect for oddness, for both the force of character it took and the passion needed to sustain it. Once I realized that Sally was odd, the conventionality of her clothes no longer mattered, her enormous towels lost their intimidating aspect, her lips moving as she read no longer hinted at a profound dullness.

I loved her adjectives. One day she was talking about a teacher in her high school who had been in a plane wreck, an experience Sally called "searing"; another day she referred to our senior dorm adviser as "obsequious." "You're a real English major!" I said. Sally smiled her little turned-down smile and walked back into her room, pleased. Her adjectives took possession of whatever she was describing; their precision made them inarguable, tiny facts rather than opinions. And Sally had lots of opinions. She would burst into speeches precariously near dogmatism—about Martin Luther, whom she liked despite his anti-Semitism, or the women workers in the cafeteria line, whom for a variety of trivial reasons she didn't like—and then listen to someone else's opinion with barely disguised impatience, if the person had the nerve to voice an opinion at all. I thought Sally was a radical feminist without having the slightest notion that she was feminist at all; I'd never heard a girl (and I thought of us as girls, although in the campus lingo we were women) present herself with such fearlessness and definition. Certainly I never presented myself that directly. I made jokes, sly asides, sarcastic underminings—I didn't come right out and say things.

In Introduction to Women's Studies our sophomore year, Sally read *The Diary of Anaïs Nin.* Halfway through, she decided Nin was a selfish and silly woman, a real dolt—a thesis that appalled Sally's professor, a female Nin fan, or, as we dubbed her, a "Ninite." As Sally finished each assigned reading, she presented to me the ways in which Nin had revealed herself to be an idiot—occasionally she even let out a whoop and said, "Listen to this!"—and I sat there enjoying her show, anticipating how she'd burst into class and torment her professor. I wished I was in that class. Sally versus the Ninite, three bouts a week. Sally gave me the blow-by-blows. The Ninite would bridle when Sally walked in; was slow to call on Sally; and tried to cut Sally off as she was talking, although Sally was quick to assure me she wouldn't be cut off. At the end of the course, the Ninite wondered aloud if Sally—in her neat red vest, oxford-cloth blouse, trousers instead of blue jeans, knee-high stockings—wasn't threatened by Nin's "unapologetic sexuality."

"Oh, her sexuality's not the point," Sally assured her. "The point is her self-absorption, which makes her sexual focus seem almost masturbatory, and..."

"Then what did she say?" I asked when Sally finished, minutes later.

"She told me I should be a lawyer."

It was only about five o'clock, but it was late October, so our quarters were almost dark. Sally's shadow moved from her room back to mine.

"That's an idea," I said.

Sally chortled. "I think she meant to be withering." I shook my head and smiled, feeling a little sorry for the Ninite. A lawyer. What an excellent idea.

ON SATURDAY MORNING I finally went to a demonstration, letting Sally think I was going to the library. The demonstration was as small as it was listless. I don't remember what it was for. The organizers were three guys I barely knew, and when they raised their arms to lead chants, their stomachs were distractingly hairy. I walked off campus and breathed the autumn-smoked air, feeling adult, mature, a person who could handle the dashing of her dreams.

SALLY HAD SOME new clothes, but still the primmest, dullest ones I could imagine, all made by famous designers. She knew wine; she'd eaten snails. She'd stayed in a hotel in Madrid where President Nixon had stayed. It was wild. She looked so uncool, but she was cool. I was the twerp of the twosome.

She told the Hare Krishna guy to go away. I opened the door for him and I listened as he soulfully showed me his expensive book with its vaguely erotic illustrations. "No, thank you!" Sally said, practically pushing him out the door. "We have to study tonight, and we can't concentrate with you here talking. Good-bye!"

"Another lost soul from Brooklyn," she said as the Hare Krishna glided away. "Doesn't he look like Joshua Goldberg from down the hall? If Josh shaved his head and put on robes." It took me years to realize what she'd been pointing out.

ALTHOUGH SALLY WAS the Jewish one, I was the roommate who discovered the notion of the Sabbath. In our religion class, we read Abraham Pincus, who referred to the Sabbath as a sacred time, and I got so excited by that idea I set out to observe the Sabbath myself. My plan was to not study or do errands on the Sabbath, but to read inspiring things and take walks and think about life. Originally, I planned not to mention this to anyone but simply to worship in my own way, but my first Sabbath morning went so well I couldn't help but tell Sally.

"But it's Saturday," Sally said, astonishment flooding her face. "Aren't you a Christian?"

Then I had to explain, flustered, that my Sabbath was going to be Saturday and Sunday mornings, which I knew was truncated and piecemeal but I didn't think the Lord would mind since I hadn't thought of the Sabbath at all before, and on Friday and Saturday nights I liked to go out, which was important for my mental health, and on Sunday afternoons I did my best studying. The skepticism on Sally's face grew with each word, so it hurt me but didn't really surprise me when at the end of my speech she started giggling.

"I can't wait to to tell Daddy," she said.

Later, she appeared in the doorway. "Daddy wants to talk with you."

My stomach lurched. I walked out into the dorm hallway. Sally following. The telephone dangled on its cord. Sally stood next to me.

"Clare?" a big voice said. "What's the deal with this Sabbath crap?"

I had never had an adult ask me so aggressive a question. I had only heard an adult say "crap" once, at a high school football game. I opened and closed my mouth.

"You know the word 'travesty'? That's what you're doing. It's not evil, don't get me wrong, it won't hurt you, but don't you see you're missing the whole point? Remember the Shabbos to keep it holy. That's a commandment. You don't get to pick, okay? You don't say, well, I've got Wednesday between two and four, so that'll be my Shabbos. That's you penciling in God. When, if you believe in anything, God should be penciling in *you*."

My throat was dry. I hadn't expected Sally's father to be so loud, his tone so definite. But why not? He was Sally's father. I realized that my own father was soft-spoken. "I see, sir," I said.

Mr. Rose laughed. "You need to sir me?" he boomed. "It's God you need to sir. If you believe in God, that is. In a male God, that is."

"I think I believe in God," I managed. Too late, I realized what I should have said to him: Do you believe in God? Clearly the guy was big on questions. Sally was right beside me, grinning in an eager way. Down the hall a door slammed. Our Indian hallmate Nita emerged from the bathroom carrying a towel, shooting Sally and me a curious look.

"Not that you have to," Mr. Rose said. "Heh, maybe God is dead, right?"

"Do you believe God is dead?"

Mr. Rose laughed louder. "Good question! I don't know what I believe. I am open-minded. A closed mind is worse than a stupid one, Sally ever tell you that? Listen, Clare, if you want to do Shabbos, I suggest you do it right. I'll send you a book. My daughter still there?" Relieved, I handed the phone to Sally.

"Well?" she said, back in our room. I was irritated she'd told her father about my Sabbath, but of course she told him everything.

"He's sending me a book."

"He grew up in a really strict household. They couldn't turn the lights on or off on Shabbos. They couldn't flush the toilet. Daddy had to tear sheets of toilet paper ahead of time because you're not allowed to tear things on Shabbos."

This shocked me. I couldn't believe the celebration of the Sabbath could be so bizarrely restrictive. I liked my version of the Sabbath much better. "Do you do that now?"

Sally laughed. "Oh God, no, we don't do anything. We're very assimilated." She threw out her hands. "We have a Christmas tree!"

I never tried a Sabbath again, and Mr. Rose never sent the book.

IN THE HALL, a gaggle of students was discussing Nixon's recent resignation. They'd just moved on from his un-nurturing mother to his repressed id when Sally slammed our door. "I hate psychology," she said. This surprised me, because every other college student loved it, always talking about their birth order or their parents' divorce or their oppressive superego. I had never met so many people who'd been to psychiatrists. The expression "She's a little neurotic" was not meant as an insult.

"You do?" I asked, "Why?"

"It makes things little," Sally said. "It puts everybody in a box. Clare, I swear to you, people are mysterious."

Mysterious. This adjective surprised me. I tried to think of Richard Nixon as mysterious. I thought of the people on our hall—Peter the premed, Karen the flutist, Melanie the angry feminist. None of them seemed mysterious to me. That Sally thought they were gave her—not them—a troubling sort of grace.

"CLARE," she'd say, "that's sick!"—lengthening the adjective into two syllables, one high and one low. To Sally, lots of things were si-ick, often things I might find only suspect or mildly amusing, like Jim Fosdick's endless nattering about once having sex with a dog. "I strongly doubt it," I told Sally when she asked me if I thought it was true. "But why he would he talk about it?" she worried. "Why would he even think of such a thing? Clare, that's—"

"Si-ick," I finished, pleasing us both.

In the wings were guys. I had some wanton ways: a hockey player one weekend, a poet the next. I wasn't a very good flirt (how could I be? With three big brothers, I knew the male mind), so I slept with them and got it over with. My logic went like this: Sex is an enjoyable human activity, I'm human, X is human, why not have sex? There were certainly college guys grateful for a female with my attitude. I was insistent on having sex only in their rooms, never in mine and Sally's, and a few times (this gives me a twinge), I borrowed an off-campus apartment for the purpose. A couple of the guys fell in love with me and showed up in our dorm hall, but the ones I really liked sort of ig-nored me. I thought I must have a complex to only want the ones who didn't care. I reminded myself of my brothers in that regard. Sally eyed all my bedmates with polite disinterest. None of them was good enough for me. "But I have needs!" I told her. I thought of her story of the guy in Oahu. "Don't you have needs too?"

She made a funny fake frown and retreated through the door to her half of the room. "Not pressing needs," she called cheerfully. "Not needs like that."

ON THE FLIGHT back to Oberlin our second semester, the Los Angeles to Chicago leg, Sally sat next to an elderly couple who changed her dreams. They'd been married forty-four years and had five children, one of whom they were flying to Chicago to visit, and they were, as Sally put it, a "unit."

"What do you mean?"

"They were so"—Sally lifted her hands and wrapped them around an imaginary globe—"together. They were two people but one entity. When they passed out blankets, she took one for him and tucked it around his legs. When they got off the plane, he held her purse until she'd stood up. I'd ask them a question and only one of them would answer, and it wasn't as if they were taking turns, it was as if they both knew which person should answer which question. It was wonderful."

"How'd they meet?"

"Grocery store. She was his customer."

"Did they know right off they'd get married?"

"They went out a couple times and then didn't see each other for a while, and about a year later, they ran into each other and it clicked. He said that: 'That time we just clicked.'"

I nodded. Sally had asked the questions I would have asked. "So how'd they do it? Unitize?"

"I asked them that! And she said, 'Oh, we just kind of rubbed along together.' But they've been through a lot, you could tell. The guy owned a print shop and went bankrupt. They had a son killed in the war. The woman had some kind of cancer."

"So are your parents a unit?"

"No," Sally answered without hesitation. "Are yours?"

She had met my parents. I gave her a scornful glance. "What do you think?"

"I haven't really met any units," Sally said wistfully, "except for that couple on the plane." But, knowing Sally's determination, it was not totally surprising when, one February evening, we walked out to the local burger place, got our food and sat down in our booth, and Sally smiled at me and said, "Clare, I'm in love. I've met the man I'm going to marry." His name was George Timmey, but from childhood he'd been called Timbo. Sally had been in line at the bookstore, buying

spring-semester textbooks for herself and her dad, and Timbo asked if
she was a twin.

I saw a lot of Timbo. He and Sally were a strange couple, but logical: the two virgins at Oberlin had found each other. Timbo was from
Kentucky. He had luminescent blue eyes, hair that was short and well
groomed, and a big digital watch—the first I'd ever seen—strapped on
his left wrist. I told Sally he looked like an ROTC cadet. Sally laughed.
It wasn't entirely clear how he'd ended up at Oberlin; his high school
guidance counselor apparently had recommended it. Timbo swam at
the big new college gym, and he ran, and like Sally, he was an excellent
bowler. At home he had three little brothers and two sisters, a brood
he said he chased around "like ducklings." Timbo could see a little
townie kid in the street, bend over to talk with him or her—with ex-
travagant gestures and head-rolling on both sides—then emerge with
the kid on his shoulders. Sally would grin at me, squeeze my elbow in
excitement. "I'm not kidding," she said that first evening, pleased at
my astonishment, "I'll marry him." As if that weren't enough of a
knife: "And guess what, he's from an even bigger family than yours."

He was okay. They'd sit in Sally's room studying with the door between her and my room open, Sally bent over her desk and Timbo
with his papers spread out on the bed. Sex wasn't a problem: they
ended their evenings with some giggling and a kiss or two, then Timbo
shoved through the door into my room, thanked me for putting up
with him, and headed out to the hall—the kind of boy my mother
would like (she was a member of socialism's puritan branch). He lived
in a men's dorm, one of the few single-sex dorms, known as the haven
for jocks. He studied biochemistry and plant genetics and psychology;
he wanted to be a family doctor. Sally thought he was perfect, but I
had my own ideas. He wasn't odd enough for her. The only odd thing
about Timbo was that he'd ended up at Oberlin, and that was an accident, I was sure, not an act of will.

"He's the oldest, too," Sally had said. "That's a lot of responsibility."

"Oh that's right," I said. "I forgot. I'm the spoiled baby." I frowned. "Why did you say 'even bigger than yours'? That hurt my feelings."

"It did? You're kidding. It really did? Really, Clare?"

I nodded.

"I'm sorry," Sally said, sitting up in her bed, hugging her knees to her chest. "I didn't mean to hurt you. He just, well, he *is* from a bigger family."

"I know, but it was like . . . it was like you were saying he was better than me somehow. You know? It's stupid, I know, but . . ." I lingered in the doorway between our rooms, hoping she would say something to make me feel better.

"Oh, Clare. I would never hurt your feelings on purpose. You're my best friend. I don't think anyone except my family has ever known me as well as you. And I think I know you well too, don't I?"

I nodded again.

"Like"—she smiled—"I know about your needs."

We both giggled.

"Clare, I was thinking, you've got to come to California. You've got to visit me this summer." She pushed herself to the edge of the bed and slipped her feet to the floor, as if we were leaving this moment. "Oh Clare, don't you think you could visit?"

But how could I go? How could I? By car would be cheaper, but the only car I could borrow was my mother's, and how could I afford the gas? It thrilled me to think of a plane: up there, disconnected, not in orbit and not on solid ground. I'd never been in a plane; no one in my family had. It thrilled me too to think of Sally's house: the swimming pool, the espalier. But the trip was so expensive, two hundred dollars minimum for a round-trip flight, and I'd be working at my dad's office all summer making sixty bucks a week, with that money earmarked for textbooks and supplies. I chewed the inside of my right cheek, the way I always did when I got edgy. What, was I going to have a summer like every other, filing charts and taking old ladies to exam rooms? "Here's a cup for your urine, Mrs. Snodgrass; be sure you wipe off with the moist towelette first, front to back." I thought of the old man who called me Miss Muffin, the way he liked to sneak behind me and eye my behind. You keep looking, Mr. Buns-for-brains, I told him in my mind. You drive up that nasty blood pressure and have your stroke.

EXAMS CAME, the school year ended, Sally and I packed up our rooms and went home. "Anytime," Sally said. "Just call me. And for as long as you want. The only week that wouldn't work is when we're going to Lake Tahoe." Unlike me, she was looking forward to relaxing with her family.

Was there a part-time job I could get? Kmart? Dairy Queen? Two hundred dollars. Twenty-five extra dollars a week and I could do it.

"I'd hate to see you take a second job," my father said. "You work so hard at school." I had my old familiar sensation looking at him, a flood of gratitude and love. He was always good to me. He told me how he'd gone on a trip to Nashville when he was in college and had a wonderful time. "Don't you worry," he said. "I can save a few dollars a week. Our little secret."

I still had some friends from high school in Happyville, and lots of nights we went out, usually in a group. We sat down by the reservoir and smoked, or visited a bar outside town that was lax about IDs. I drank Scotch, but never much. I didn't have sex with anyone, or even neck. I got home before midnight. My old friends thought I'd become an in-tel-lec-tu-al snob, but I didn't care. I was filling in time, waiting for my real summer, my real life, which would start the second I reached L.A.

To save money, my dad packed his lunches, stretched the time between dry cleanings, walked to work. He liked to buy a candy bar every day to eat on his way home, but for my sake he gave that up. He also gave up doughnuts and elephant ears from the bakery. He kept me posted. By the middle of July he had one hundred and sixty-five dollars, and had incidentally lost eleven pounds. He figured I could go to California the first week of August, when the doctors' office was always slow. In Nashville my father had met a fellow who took him home for a dinner of squirrel stew.

"Squirrel stew!'" I said. "Yuk!"

"Oh no, the sauce was delicious. And believe me, in a bowl of squirrel stew you don't encounter too much meat."

Then, out of the blue, there was a crisis. It changed everything, in a way.

My father always dressed for work very formally in deference to the doctors. When I was a kid, he'd worn a hat. He even ironed his own shirts, and he hardly ever wore one with short sleeves. He had three suits, one blue, one black, one green. I knew the green one was a problem—it had a sheen to the fabric, it just wasn't attractive—but he'd picked it out himself.

One of the doctors' wives, Mrs. Danforth, stopped by the office two days in a row. She told her husband that the first day his office manager (my father, that is) looked like a funeral director, and the second day he looked like a used-car salesman, and she didn't know which was worse. Dr. Danforth told my father, my father came home and told my mother and me, and the upshot of all this quoting was that my father had no choice but to buy, with the money earmarked for my trip to California, two new suits. I accompanied him shopping. And the suits he bought were beautiful, truly. "I owe you one," he said.

I GOT OFF the plane and it was bright, it was glaring, I could hardly see. There were lots of people I assumed were foreigners, Indians in saris and Orientals in too-short trousers, but the people who didn't look like foreigners dressed in short shorts and tight T-shirts or open shirts the likes of which I'd never seen. Every other woman my age was overgroomed, tanned, overweeningly self-conscious, an aspiring starlet. I slouched and shrugged and ambled through the airport. I was wearing a pair of straight-leg jeans and my pussywillow blouse, and I looked fine. I was twenty years old, a month from my junior year of college. Sally met me by the baggage area and hugged me, her grip tugging at the ends of my curtain of hair. "It's not smoggy!" she said excitedly. "I woke up this morning and I said, 'Daddy, it's not smoggy!' That's a sign." She called for a porter, then led me to a big black Mercedes with a Mexican driver in it. "Julio," Sally said, *"Aquí es mi amiga Clare."* She looked at me and grinned, hoping for a reaction. *"Mucho gusto,"* I said, cool as a cucumber, glad I remembered a phrase or two of my high school Spanish. I was still puffed up with pride from flying. *"Mucho gusto a Usted,"* Julio said. Julio was large and middle-aged and wore an embroidered Cuban cotton shirt. I wondered if he'd ever flown. He put my suitcase in the trunk. It looked like a thimble in a sewing kit.

"It's splendid that your dad popped up with the tickets," Sally said. "Where in the world did he get the money?"

I was so taken with her "splendid" that I lost my train of thought. How did he get the money? I had no idea. "Magic!" I laughed, snapping my fingers.

We climbed into the wide backseat. "This is actually something," I said, and a spasm of pleasure crossed Sally's face.

"It's really Daddy's car," she confided. "He doesn't like me to come to the airport by myself." She rolled her eyes. "Fear of terrorists. But it is kind of fun, isn't it?"

Here I am being driven through Los Angeles in a black Mercedes with a Mexican chauffeur, I thought. *Ay caramba.* I put on my new sunglasses and grinned at Sally.

"GUESS WHO I saw today? Ali MacGraw."

"Really, Daddy? Where?"

We'd just finished touring the house. The front entrance hall, backed by a bank of windows, was two stories high, and we were on the balcony above it when Mr. Rose appeared, hand on the polished railing, at the bottom of the stairs. The sun was setting and threw a glare off the window, the stone floor, the stair railing, the gleaming wood table, off everything but Mr. Rose. I couldn't see him clearly. A squat dark figure in a brilliant room. At that moment I remembered a picture book from my childhood and the words "Rumplestiltskin, that odd little man."

"In that flower shop off Sunset. You know."

"Did she look nice?"

"Very pretty. Fresh. Like you." For the first time he noticed me. "Maybe like you too," he said, jabbing the air in front of him with his finger.

"I'm Clare."

"Figured."

There was an awkward pause. "I'm happy to be here."

"You like the house?" he asked. "Sally show you your room?" He spoke as he had on the phone, loudly and definitely.

"She's sleeping in my room, Daddy."

"You sure?" Mr. Rose asked me. "You don't want to try the guest room?"

Sally answered for me. "No, Daddy. We want to talk."

Mr. Rose threw out his hands. "We got this great guest room and no one ever uses it."

"Patricia could use it." Pa-tree-cee-a, she said it in the Spanish way. Sally was grinning at her father: this must be a private joke.

He took a few steps up the stairs, and I could see him more clearly. Thinning hair, black streaked with gray, sideburns that stretched under his cheekbones, dense hair on his arms, pale and watery eyes. He wore khaki trousers, an open-necked shirt, a large watch. "Patricia has a color TV now, okay? Patricia is totally happy where she is. Patricia lives"—he rolled his eyes, flashed a rakish smile—"in the temple of the now."

When he smiled, he was transformed. I could understand why Sally described him as handsome.

"I like that." I smiled. "'Temple of the now.'"

"Sure you do," Mr. Rose said. "What's not to like?" He abruptly turned away from us and strode off down the steps, but called over his shoulder, "Hey Clare!" He was walking so quickly I couldn't have answered him if I'd tried. "You still keeping your wacky Shabbos?"

"WHAT DID CALIFORNIA look like?" my father asked.

"Like you'd expect. Palm trees, dry-grass hillsides, fancy cars. It looks like the movies. The only thing that surprised me was how close together the houses are in Beverly Hills. Huge houses with these tiny side yards. Where Sally lives, though, it's nice. She lives on this spur off Mulholland—that's a road that runs on top of a spine of hills. The guy at the hot dog place said people go up to Mulholland to neck. Sally didn't even know that."

"And Sally's house, it was like you expected? It was a big place?"

"Oh, Dad, you wouldn't have believed it. It makes Dr. Danforth's place look like a tract home. We pulled up in this big black car, like a diplomat's car, with Julio the driver and Sally and me in back, and there's this big black gate with curlicues. It just swings open! Julio opens it by remote control. Like James Bond or something. This wide wide driveway. The house looks like some big gray ship that's crashed into the rock. Sally says it's organic architecture, it won some award. It's supposed to look like it's growing out of the rock. On the other side of the house is the pool and patio, and beyond them the hill drops away, and right there at your feet is Los Angeles."

"Los Angeles at your feet. I'm not surprised."

MY FATHER HAD COME up with the money— magic!—and presented me with the plane tickets. "How—?" I'd asked. "You didn't borrow—?"

"Shhh. It's all set," he'd said. "Don't worry, it worked out. The doctors know and it's fine if you take that week off." The trip was for eight nights, from Saturday to Sunday. I would be leaving in a week. "And here's something for clothes," my father said, handing me fifty dollars. "You'll want to look nice."

"Dad! I can't believe this."

"You deserve it," he said. "Go out there and eat some squirrel stew."

"I have no idea," my mother said when I asked her. "And he won't tell me. Your father can keep his mouth shut."

WE DID THE TOURIST THINGS, sure, but mostly we stayed at the Roses' house, which had been designed by an architect based in New York City. There were roofs at funny angles, balconies whose sole purpose seemed to be holding boxes of flowers. There was the espalier near the pool, in all its useless and deformed beauty. Who would plan a tree like that? Who would have the patience to guide and prune it year after year? "It's like Carlos's damn kid," Mr. Rose said. "It was nothing to start, a baby tree two feet high." A flagstone patio ran across the entire back of the house. The patio held three or four tables with umbrellas, surrounded by chairs, and still the stone expanse looked vacant.

The rooms inside were as big as hotel lobbies, with seamed tile floors, cold on bare feet, scattered with rugs in wavy patterns. Windows as big as aquarium walls faced the patio. Huge abstract paintings hung on the walls. "That's a Pollock," Sally said of one. I'd just learned the word "gouache" and I thought Sally was talking about a painting technique. "Cool," I said.

The closets did impress me. They were equipped with cubicles and wooden cabinets nice enough to show off in a living room. When you opened any closet door, a light automatically came on. Sally's bathroom, just off her bedroom, was bigger than my bedroom at home, with plants and a skylight and a see-through glass shower stall you had to step down to enter.

"Quite a house," I told Sally. How could you eat a Sunday-night supper of leftovers here? How could you yell for your brother to answer the phone? He couldn't even hear you.

MRS. ROSE LIVED in the kitchen. It was only years later that I thought of her as a troll in a cave. The kitchen was expansive, uncluttered, gleamingly clean. Small pots of cooking herbs lined up on the ledge of the window. Mrs. Rose was neat too, and drab. Her hair was a stiff brown helmet. She looked older than her husband and dressed like an older version of Sally, a simple knit top tucked into a pair of belted pants. I wondered what designers she was wearing. "Clare?" Mrs. Rose said, her inflection slightly questioning. Sally had told me so little about her mother that her inoffensiveness took me by surprise.

I noticed the noise of a TV, realized it came from a room across a hall from the rear of the kitchen. I glanced around a door: a dark woman in a light green uniform was sitting on a single bed, smiling at something on TV. Color TV. Patricia. The maids' quarters.

Actually, there were two maids, and they spent a lot of time in the kitchen. The first day I washed my hands in Sally's bathroom, and when I returned a half hour later, the towel was gone. "Did you see my towel?" I asked Sally.

"Oh," Sally answered, "Patricia must have taken it." She showed me where to get a fresh towel, out of one of the illuminated closets. The first morning my bed was made before I came back upstairs after breakfast. But on the days Patricia and Conchita moved around the kitchen—chopping, sauteeing, stirring, measuring—my bed wasn't made till after noon. Mrs. Rose stood in the center with her wooden spoon, turning the pages of cookbooks, pondering. She had a little handheld dictaphone into which she dictated grocery lists. Sally said Conchita often shopped more than once a day. The food we ate!

SALLY'S AUNT AND COUSIN—Mr. Rose's younger sister Ruby and her daughter Daphne—dropped by to meet me. Ruby had been Ruth, and Daphne was Danielle, but (this was a family secret) both had changed their names on the advice of a numerologist. Aunt Ruby and Daphne wore great clouds of perfume and clothes that looked expensive and fluffy, like Barbie outfits or the clothes Eva Gabor wore on *Green Acres*. They yoo-hooed, walked in, then skittered around kissing cheeks. Even I got kissed. I found it peculiar to be kissed by an unknown eighteen-year-old wearing makeup. I told Sally I could picture Aunt Ruby in translucent robes with feathers at the neck and cuff, mules on her pink-toenailed feet. "You're not far off," Sally said.

Later we visited, with Mr. Rose, Aunt Ruby's terrifying house. "It's like walking into a jewel box," Sally warned me. The carpeting was cream, and almost every wall had a painting of a nude or an Oriental screen. The ceiling in the TV room was covered with bronze paper. The canopy bed was huge. The husband, Dr. Fred Finkelstein, was skinny, with a hangdog look and a preposterous wardrobe that included platform shoes and an astrological medallion on a chain around his neck. He was a successful dermatologist. "What a nar," Mr. Rose said out loud when Uncle Fred left the room.

"What's a nar?"

"Yiddish," Mr. Rose explained. "A nar's like a dummy, a lunkhead." I was shocked that Mr. Rose was telling me this in Dr. Finkelstein's own house.

"But he must be a good dermatologist," I said, glancing around the living room, hoping the doctor wasn't hiding in one of the halls. "He must have a big practice."

"Listen, you'd have to be one lousy dermatologist to not make a go of it here. This town lives on skin."

Uncle Fred was a Pisces. As we drove back to Sally's, I said that he was obviously fishy. "Fishy Finkelstein!" Mr. Rose said. "I love it." Sally chuckled too. I was pleased but embarrassed—pleased to be pleasing Mr. Rose, embarrassed that I should want to.

"I HAD TO GET my own towel this morning," Mr. Rose told his wife. "You've got to let Patricia out of the kitchen."

"I have lunches to think about now too," Mrs. Rose said. "With the girls here."

"Let the girls go out to lunch! Let them go down to the Tail o' the Pup and get a hot dog." He turned to me. "You want to eat at a real L.A. landmark? Hot dog stand shaped like a hot dog?"

My eyes darted from Mr. to Mrs. Rose. But he was the force in the family.

"Why not?" I said.

"Sure you do," Mr. Rose said at the same time.

"HE'S SO KIND," Sally said. "Did you know he once sewed a button onto my coat? I was busy studying, and he took out my sewing kit and sewed it on."

She was talking about Timbo. I was trying to figure out when this had happened, how I had missed it.

"I really miss him," Sally said, turning her face to the sea. We were on the Santa Monica pier eating ice cream, and this was the one moment that marred my day, like the half hour or so each night I roamed the patio or leafed through magazines while Sally talked to Timbo on the phone. *Time, U.S. News & World Report, McCall's*—for a magazine distributor, Mr. Rose didn't keep his home very interestingly stocked.

When I was old and rich I'd get subscriptions to, I don't know, thirty magazines. Anything that interested me slightly. And I'd buy hardback books, not paperbacks.

"DO YOU LIKE BASKETBALL?" asked Sally's little brother, Ben. He was ten years old. He ran up and down the tiled hallway, dribbling. "Do you like snakes? I have a pet snake, Charlie." And later: "Do you like ambulances? Do you like to swim?" His little tan face, his sharp nose, his deep brown eyes. It seemed to me he was a ball of eagerness with skin. When he ran, he reminded me of Reddy Kilowatt, a stick figure of electricity, arms and legs sizzling. I wondered if my brothers had been like that before they grew up and got self-conscious. "Clare! Clare!" Ben would shout beside the pool. "Watch me do a cannonball!"

He really liked me. Once he got out of the pool and came over to my chaise, sat down on the concrete beside me, and lay his head across my legs. I ruffled his hair, feeling awkward, thinking how absurdly unaffectionate my family was. Ben's hair was surprisingly coarse, like a terrier's. "You have hair like a little dog," I said.

"Arf!" Ben said, smiling. "Want a soda?" he asked, and sat up. "I'll get us both a soda!" He scampered to the fridge in the pool house.

"What a cute kid," I said to Mr. Rose. It amazed me to hear myself saying this, sounding disgustingly adult. I was only twenty.

"He's a pistol." Mr. Rose shook his head. "Sometimes you hate to see them grow up."

"Mountain Dew or Fresca?" Ben asked breathlessly, running up to me. He was already handing me the can. "I think girls like Fresca," he confided to his dad.

"Are you expanding your business?" I asked Mr. Rose. Sally had mentioned that her father was expanding. My father always wanted the doctors to hire more doctors.

"Sure," said Mr. Rose. "I've had my seven fat years, so now I got to stay big enough to swing the seven lean ones. That make any sense to you?"

I smiled politely. It did make sense, vaguely.

"You read the Bible at all? Or did you give that up when you gave up Shabbos?"

I looked away, embarrassed.

"Joseph," Mr. Rose announced. "Remember him? Joseph of the coat of many colors? He had those dreams, seven fat cows, seven thin cows, seven fat ears of corn, seven thin ears—this ring a bell at all?"

It did, sort of. I rallied. "So you've been having dreams, huh?"

Mr. Rose threw his head back and laughed. "I don't dream," he said when he'd calmed down. "Not my nature. I don't dream, I scheme." He tapped the side of his head with his index finger. "I've always got a plan. Remember that, Clare. I've always got a plan. Seriously, you and Sally are smart girls, you both should read the Bible. Great stories. I even read the New Testament, you know that? Not that I like a God that wishy-washy."

"You leave a copy in my nightstand?"

Mr. Rose laughed again. "No wonder my daughter likes you. You've got spunk."

IN THE MORNINGS, Mrs. Rose sat in a robe at a table in the big master bedroom with an array of pens and stationery in front of her. Ben rolled around on the king-size bed, did a somersault off it, rolled himself up in the abstract-patterned bedspread and asked if we could find him. "Wild child," Mrs. Rose said calmly, working on a letter. "Come out, wild child."

She had pen pals she'd been matched up with through a pen pal service. That day she was writing her friend in Ireland. "She lives in a house with a dirt floor," Mrs. Rose said. "They just got their first refrigerator two years ago. They don't call it a refrigerator; it's an icebox. It can hold"—Mrs. Rose raised her eyes as if reading something in her memory—"two pints of milk, a couple pounds of cheese, half a chicken, and a wee bit of butter. They're thrilled with it."

"Have you been to visit her?"

"I'd love to visit her," Mrs. Rose said. "But the problem is getting away." Her eyes cast around the room in a sort of helplessness, settling briefly on Ben. "How could I get away?" she asked.

It was poignant to me that she thought of herself as essential, when everyone else barely noticed she was there.

For dinner the evening after our hot dogs, we ate Caesar salad, bouillabaisse, and pecan pie with two nut layers. "Your mother's an unbelievable cook," I told Sally as her mother went to the kitchen to supervise the coffee.

Sally looked pleased. "She's good, isn't she? She does have a lot of help."

"Your wife cooks like a gourmet chef," I told Mr. Rose over brandy.

"She should," he said. "She has enough help."

"You're a good cook," I told Mrs. Rose in the kitchen.

"Thank you, dear," she said, twisting off a bit of green herb and sniffing it. "The kitchen's sort of *my* place, do you know what I mean?"

"Let's go out tomorrow night," Mr. Rose said, bursting through the kitchen on his way to get a can of soda. "Enough of this home-cooking crap. Aren't I a man of simple tastes? I want a steak."

Later, he asked me, "What do you think of the sofa, you like the sofa?"

"I do."

"And the granite in the gate, you notice that? That's Italian granite."

"I'll have to notice it."

"It's not just any granite. It's not just veneer granite. It's an inch thick. You believe that? An inch!"

"Impressive."

"You like the art? Esther picks the art. I don't know from art. But Esther's daddy was an art professor, he was one of those German Jews, know what I mean?"

I stared back blankly.

"Snobs. Intellectuals. German Jew girl marries a Pole like me, the parents go apeshit. But Esther wanted me. Anyways, she picks the art. It's good art. Museums want it."

"Really?"

"I don't scrimp on quality. That's what my mother used to say, don't scrimp on quality. In the end you get what you pay for, right?"

"So I hear."

"Yeah, it's a decent house," Mr. Rose admitted. He leaned back in his chair and intertwined his hands behind his head. Something sexy in that gesture, dangerous. He crossed his legs, his ankle on his knee. Could guys at Oberlin ever look like that? Or my brothers? Mr. Rose narrowed his eyes. "It's not a perfect house, though."

"What would make it perfect?" I asked, and took a sip of Scotch.

"View of the sea. I mean a real view, not some blueness in the distance. I grew up in Brooklyn, my family lived in an apartment building with a shower down the hall, but you could climb on the roof of our building and see the Atlantic." Mr. Rose reached under his shirt and scratched his shoulder. "Next house."

I tried to imagine what had kept him from getting a view of the sea this time. Surely not money—a house by the sea couldn't cost more than this. In fact, the seaside places Sally and I'd seen were surprisingly small.

"But this is a nice neighborhood," he said. "Good place for a family. Some of those beach places are a little..." He held out his hand, palm down, and rocked it back and forth.

I thought of Venice, where Sally and I had walked the boardwalk, dodging street performers. Racy, I thought. Druggy. Loose. I nodded.

"Earthquakes," he said. "Fires. Landslides. You're safer farther inland."

FOR ALL THE HOURS Sally's father was reputed to work, he was spending a lot of time away from work this week; only three or four hours a day at the office. He was taking a breather, he said; he liked to meet his daughter's friends. When he went to work, he wore knit shirts and big-buckled belts, the same things he wore at home. He was the boss, Sally said, he didn't have to dress for work. He didn't even have to go in every day.

Cocktails around back, outside the living room, on the wide flagstone patio with a low stone wall around it, overlooking the city.

We were talking about Oberlin and Sally's psychology course. Mr. Rose, like Sally, was anti-psychology. "All that explaining, that analyzing. I hate that. It's like no one understands anymore that what is *is*. Why try to explain it? It's like what turns people on. You can never tell what'll ring your bell. It's a mystery, a human mystery. I like people being mysterious. I wouldn't want it any other way."

Sally looked at me and grinned.

"So, I don't know," he continued. "The stuff you're reading, it's okay, but it's too analytical. But it's typical, I've got to say, it's typical of your school. All those Oberlin pansies you got there staring at their navels."

"Daddy! They're not pansies."

Sid winked at me. "I love it when she argues. Are you arguing with me, sweetheart? You're not, you're disagreeing. I want an argument, okay? I don't want a simple denial, I want counterpoint."

"I don't know why you call the men at Oberlin pansies. You don't even know them."

"How about that goofy professor of yours? What was his name, Mr. Biff? The one who drooled over your papers. What was his favorite poet? Hart Crane." Sid lifted his fingers in his air and twittered his fingers—"'Oh the youthful exuberance, the wordsmithing, the exquisite curiosity Hart Crane brings...' Listen, I talked to my educated buddy: Hart Crane was a fruit. That Mr. Biff's not married, is he?"

"Mr. Gifford," Sally said. "No, I don't think he does happen to be married, but you have no proof—"

"No poof? No poof?"

"Daddy!" It was the same two-toned intonation as her "si-ick," high-pitched then low.

"A lot of professors aren't married," I said. "That doesn't mean they're not normal."

"Point," Mr. Rose conceded.

"So what if Mr. Gifford is homosexual?" Sally asked, changing her tack. "Is a person's being homosexual relevant to what he thinks or teaches or does?"

"Better point," Sid said. "I like that."

"You were making an inflammatory statement with no inkling of what you really wanted to say. You were teasing me. You were leading me on."

"Moi?" Sid reached for a carrot stick and chomped on it. "What do you think of this kind of conversation, Clare? You think it's at all interesting or useful?"

"Socratic method, I guess," I mumbled, feeling foolish.

But Sid was pleased. "That's exactly right, Socratic method. We learned about that last year in Intro to Philosophy, right, Sal?"

"What I can't figure out is if you want your kids to argue and question things, why'd you send them to Catholic schools?" I asked.

Sid raised his eyebrows. "Excellent question. Two reasons: first, the teachers are better, and second, I like the discipline. Children require discipline until they're old enough to decide things for themselves."

"So Sally's old enough now. Being at Oberlin." I couldn't think of a more nonreligious school.

"Of course. Sally's an adult."

Sally shifted in her seat, looking flattered, and took another sip of Scotch.

"Now, getting back to your English professor—excuse me, your *poofe*ssor—let me try this one on you. I personally believe that a homo can't in an essential way understand the world. Because the world is heterosexual. Yin and yang. Black and white. Not—" he paused, his face screwed up, a fleck of carrot at the corner of his mouth—"not *gray.*"

All cats are gray in the dark, I thought. I didn't say it. "It takes some intelligence to argue," Mr. Rose had said the night before at dinner. "Any idiot can disagree." I didn't want to to sound like an idiot.

Patricia arrived with drinks and a tray of food. "Señora Rose made these specially," she murmured, pointing to the stuffed crescents.

"I should be nicer to fruits," Sid said, stretching out his arms and cracking his knuckles, "I really should. It's just I deal with so damn many of them in my business."

"In magazines?" I said, surprised.

"Oh, God, they're all over magazines," Mr. Rose said. "You wouldn't believe."

I frowned and ate a pastry. I loved magazines, I read them all the time, but I had no idea homosexuals were big in magazines. I wondered if I'd be able to pick out which articles they'd written.

"What do you think of this Timbo guy my daughter's in love with?" Mr. Rose asked suddenly. "He quality at all?"

"He's quality," I said, so quickly I surprised myself, and when I looked at Sally, she was beaming.

"WAIT A MINUTE, wait a minute," Mr. Rose said. "Both of you, lean in." He staggered a couple steps closer to us, the camera over his face, knees and hips flexed, toes out. Sally and I were seated at a table on the patio, the espalier behind us. Instead of "cheese," Mr. Rose exclaimed, "Big future!" We grinned. The flashbulb sizzled. Sally and I were frozen in the moment.

"Great," Mr. Rose said. "That's a keeper."

That evening Sally and I stayed seated at the patio table, our only light what seeped out through the windows, and talked about life and got plowed. We had a bottle of vodka, an ice bucket, and a pitcher of fresh orange juice, and when the orange juice and the ice were gone, we drank the vodka straight. We talked about Sally's major (English; she was thinking about law school), my major (English too, but what was I going to do with it?), the guys I'd known, my brothers, Sally's brother, how our parents met. The air was warm, there was a wonderful planty smell, and the shadow of Timbo barely touched me—he was at home in Kentucky, only a name, not a presence. It was Sally and me, me and Sally. Revelations bumped and brushed in the night air. About two A.M. we wandered across the patio to look at the city below, and I remember wanting to push myself over the low wall and fall, fall—not that I was suicidal, not that I would hurt myself, simply as a form of immersion in the night and in the place. The night was perfect, and I had such faith: enough faith to believe, even fleetingly, that the air would enfold me.

The next day I flew home to Ohio.

"THE MAIL'S SLOW. We didn't get your postcard."

"I didn't send one."

"Surely you noticed the smog."

"Smog?"

"Is he a millionaire? From the looks of that house, he surely is."

"I didn't think to ask him, Mother."

"How much help do they have?"

"Enough to keep the grass mowed."

"Are their servants legal? Do they have their green cards?"

"Green cards? I don't know what color their cards are. Their uniforms are light green, does that count?"

"You know what they say! Behind every great fortune, there's a great crime."

"Mother, please? I'm trying to read the paper."

I could close my eyes and summon up that magic world, Sally and me in her Kharmann Ghia driving down one of those famous canyons, windows open, music spilling from the car. I could close my eyes and summon up that world.

———

IN LATE AUGUST 1975, ten days after I returned from Los Angeles to Ohio, Timbo was killed by a drunk driver. Sally flew to Kentucky for the funeral. Timbo's mother, it turned out, was odd. "What do you mean, odd?" I asked over the phone. Oddness to me was positive, but clearly Mrs. Timmey's oddness wasn't good.

"It's a funny thing," Sally said. "You talk to her and you realize she's odd, and that makes you think, what is odd? What is it about a person that makes them odd?" Sally sounded exhausted, her voice raspy and soft with an undercurrent of tears. I could picture her swollen eyes, her damp cheeks. It was the first time, I realized, that Sally seemed adult to me.

Timbo's mother had never stopped talking, about anything that popped into her head. There was no internal censor. "George really liked you," she had told Sally. "Although maybe it's better you two never got any further, because you're Jewish, aren't you? That wouldn't work with our family. And you're from California, the godless state. People go to naked encounter groups in California. The sin." What was she saying? Sin was everywhere these days. You had to throw yourself on Jesus' mercy for forgiveness. Timbo's family wasn't going to press charges. Who knows? Maybe George's death was God's punishment.

"Punishment?" Sally had said, incredulous, goaded into speech.

"Don't you know?" Timbo's mother had said. "Didn't you hear?" George had a rubber ring around his privates. His fly was open. He was driving down the road fondling himself when the other car crossed the center line and hit him. One drunk, one onanist. Didn't it balance out? Never, never did George's mother think her family would come to this.

"Oh my God," I said, shocked. I don't think I was very consoling. "Sally, that's so weird."

Our first night back at Oberlin, Sally said, "I should have slept with him." We had the same room we'd had the year before, the bathroom and phone still steps away.

"Sally," I pointed out, "would it have made any difference? You sleep with him in May, he wouldn't be masturbating in August? Maybe he'd be masturbating more."

"But that ring..." Sally said.

I too found the ring an icky touch, although unlike Sally I had heard of such things, from my brothers and their jokes.

I thought of my sweet friend Sally, her memory of Timbo sullied, and Timbo's stupid mother talking, talking, pouring out her sticky grief. A wave of fury hit me. Why did Timbo's mother feel compelled to tell Sally—or anyone—exactly how Timbo died? Why should any-one have to hear about the ring? "Who else did she tell?" I demanded. "Did she stand up and give a speech about it at the funeral? 'He was a nice boy, my son, but he got what he deserved.' Any loving mother would have kept quiet. Hasn't she heard of death with dignity?"

For an instant Sally looked stunned. The thought that someone could willfully, and with good intentions, withhold something hit Sally the way it had hit me—as a kind of revelation. The Oberlin cul-ture praised honesty, openness, letting it all it hang out. "She didn't have to tell me," Sally repeated wonderingly. "She didn't."

I was furious. "Of course not. But everybody's so open these days," I said angrily. "Everybody's so up front."

"You're right." Sally leaned forward with a sudden urgency. "Why *did* she tell me? I wouldn't tell something like that if it were my son."

"Of course you wouldn't," I scoffed. "What's the point? She told you because she couldn't stand knowing it herself. She had to dilute the nastiness."

Sally blinked. "If she had any inner strength, she wouldn't have told me."

"Of course. She has no inner strength." I paused, then spat it out. "She's not *quality*."

A COUPLE OF GUYS from Timbo's old dorm had been at the funeral, so I assumed they knew. The word must have spread through the dorm, then leaked onto campus through girlfriends, classmates, friends of friends, acquaintances, professors. I heard about it in psychology class, only the ring had metamorphosed into a whole contraption, a blowup thing like a blood-pressure cuff, and the accident had been solely Timbo's fault.

"Guess the moral is, don't diddle and drive," someone said.

"Shows what a frustrated id will do."

"Sad. Did he have a girlfriend?"

"Yeah, but..." Laughter and shaking of heads. My face blazed, I bit the inside of my cheek. These were my classmates? These were people I was supposed to feel close to? I'd thought this college was supposed to be liberal.

In our dorm there were debates in the halls. Both males and females participated. What, really, was wrong with a penis ring? What was wrong with masturbation? Didn't everybody masturbate? Should the fact that Timbo was wearing a masturbatory aide diminish his death in any way? The debates often deteriorated, going from principles of freedom into talk of things the ancient Greeks did, or the Chinese metal masturbation balls mentioned in *Our Bodies, Ourselves,* or the true meaning of the lyrics to "Layla," which ostensibly no woman understood. Eventually, people dissolved into their rooms, less edified than stirred up.

"I hate that," Sally said. "I don't want to hear about masturbation every moment of my life." For a while, to escape the talk, she took a circuitous path—through a fire escape door and stairwell—to and from our room. Then one day she got angry. She held her head up and walked right past them.

"Nobody ever says anything to you, do they?" I asked.

"Are you kidding?" Sally answered, her tone scathing. "They wouldn't have the balls."

Balls? I thought, smiling to myself. Did Sally really say "balls"?

MARGARET—MY FRIEND with no cultural references—accompanied Sally and me to the Campus Restaurant for breakfast. "Do you like bacon?" Margaret asked Sally, then quickly put her hand over her mouth. "Oh. I'm sorry."

"What are you talking about?" Sally said, although I'm sure she knew.

"Clare told me you're Jewish," Margaret said in a confiding tone.

"And?"

Margaret seemed to realize at this point that she'd said something wrong, and her voice took on a mild whininess I'd heard before. "Well, pork, pork," she said, and went on about the Bible and its dietary laws, which was something she knew about from Sholom Aleichem and *Fiddler on the Roof.* I felt sorry for her. It had been hard to be raised in Guatemala with nobody around but missionary Baptists and native Catholics, no TV, no movies, no cosmetic ads. She'd never heard of Max Factor!

"Half the students at this college are Jewish," Sally said. "Do you see people eating bacon in the cafeterias? Do you see many men wearing yarmulkes?"

Margaret believed more in the images she got from movies and TV and reading than in what she could look around and see. This was her sublime goofiness, one of the things that made her, for me, such fun to be with. But I could see it drove Sally crazy.

"People away at college are known to deny their backgrounds," Margaret said. "I'm sure the Jewish students don't eat bacon when they're home." Her voice became almost belligerent. "And I bet a lot of them wear skullcaps, too!"

Sally shot me an incredulous look and asked Margaret, "Do you have any idea what my father's like? I'll help you. He's fifty years old and he grew up in a kosher home in Brooklyn. When he was a boy, he never thought of eating a cheeseburger, because that's meat and dairy combined. And now he lives in Los Angeles and he's a businessman. Do you have a mental picture of him?" She was reaching into her handbag. "Does he have a long beard? Does he wear a 'skullcap'?"

Margaret, stunningly, continued to miss the point. "Is he in the diamond business?" she asked eagerly.

Sally laid a photograph on the table. Her father was standing in the sun on what I recognized as their patio, the espalier behind him. He wore a white shirt with the collar open, his face lit up with his most radiant smile, the smile he gave his daughter. "How does he look?" Sally asked.

Margaret picked the photo up and studied it. There was no mistaking her surprise. "He looks...normal."

Sally snorted and took the picture back. The waitress arrived. Sally ordered a ham and cheese omelet, which I'd never seen her eat. Normally she didn't care for eggs.

SALLY AND I SAW a bad cop-action movie, where a villain was shot though the door of a bathroom stall. I heard about that scene for weeks. I thought Sally would never get over it.

Especially after Timbo died, Sally was always thinking how much something would hurt, how frightened a victim must feel. The person being hurt was always her. Ironic, because her parents never once even spanked her.

Sometimes she wouldn't run down the hall to answer the phone at the appointed time her father called and I would feel compelled to get it. "She okay?" Mr. Rose would ask.

"She's fine," I'd say. She's washing up/in the shower/finishing a sentence in her paper, will be out in a minute.

"Tough thing," Mr. Rose said once, and I knew he was referring to Timbo. I agreed.

"You hear about the ring?"

I almost dropped the phone. Did Mr. Rose really have to mention the ring? Did everybody in God's creation have to talk about the ring? Was it really that big a deal? My heart sank to hear that Sally had told even her father about it; but of course she told him everything. I realized that Mr. Rose was amused. I felt a kind of hopeless grief for Timbo, whose death evoked more titillation than tragedy.

"Yes," I said shortly.

"She should have slept with the guy," Mr. Rose said.

"Oh, I don't know," I said, exasperated. "I don't see how that would have made any difference."

"For Sally!" Mr. Rose said. "Now she'll never know. Now she'll always wonder: What would it've been like to sleep with Timbo? Remember, Clare, and I tell this to Sally too: you're only young once. Once. And you said he was quality."

WHEN I TOLD my mother, I started, "It irritates me, because everyone—" My mother jumped on this, because for once the thing irritating me wasn't her.

"What? What?" she said.

"Well, when Timbo was in that car wreck, he was wearing…" I stopped. How could I do this? I wouldn't. I was better than that. I had inner strength.

"What?" my mother said.

I scrambled: "He had an engagement ring in his pocket. He was probably going to ask Sally to marry him."

"Ohhhh," my mother sighed. She sat down at the kitchen table, wiped her hands on a towel. "Maybe it's best," she said after a pause. "They're both so young."

I RELAYED OUR CONVERSATION to Sally. "And guess what else she said? She said maybe it was for the best, since you were both so young."

Sally winced.

"And she wonders why I don't want to come home over Christmas."

"Come home with me," Sally said. "Did you look in the paper? There're always ads for people to drive cars cross-country. All you'd need is plane fare back. You could stay all January. We could both do our winter term out there."

"I REMEMBERED SOMETHING," Sally said as we drove west. "I was about seven or eight, it was before Ben was born, and we went up to Lake Tahoe. Daddy took me swimming. We went to a store beside the lake for ice cream, and there was a tabloid paper in a rack on the floor. I read the headline and I thought I was going to die. I mean, it was awful. I couldn't breathe, and I didn't want Daddy to know I'd read it, and I was trying to get between him and the paper so he wouldn't read it too."

"What was the headline?"

Sally hesitated. "MAN FEEDS SON TO PIGS."

I recoiled. It was pretty horrific. Especially to a seven-year-old.

"I used to lie awake in bed at night thinking of that headline. And I'd been excited to be able to read, but then...it scared me." She hesitated, then started in a lower tone. "Please don't tell Daddy how upset I am about Timbo."

My hands almost fell off the wheel. "Doesn't he realize?"

"Daddy doesn't understand about me and Timbo. He thinks it was a"—out of the corner of my eye, I could see Sally's mouth twist—"crush. That's the word he used. And I don't even want to say it, but I think he thinks how Timbo died was funny."

"It was tragic. The fact that people think it was funny makes it more tragic."

"I know," Sally whispered, her eyes glistening. She watched the road for a while. "I figure other people I love will die. I figure this is the worst of it, because it's my first time." She swirled her hand in the air in front of her, an uncharacteristically chaotic gesture. "From now on, I'll expect this grief."

I loved driving west. I loved the sky opening out and the land flattening, the very landscape an echo of my own widening horizons. I was going to California, California! It staggered me that my life, without my planning it, was leading me again to such a wondrous place. It must be fated that I should drive cross-country, in Stan Guardino's dark blue BMW, a novelty car for 1975, a car that provoked all kinds of stares and honks. "You don't need to drive," my father had said. "I'll buy you a plane ticket." But no, I wanted to drive, to eat with my best friend at truck stops and stay at cheap motels with fake log walls and erratic heating and tepee-printed curtains.

"L.A.," Mr. Rose would say when I got there, "you look L.A." And I did, I knew I did. Ben let me play with his pet snake, and Mrs. Rose fussed a little less in the kitchen; Patricia had had to go back to Mexico to help out her sick mother. I acted as a sort of shield between Sally and her father, and in gratitude she let me drive her little Kharmann Ghia. I drove up and down the canyons, took corners fast, drove all the way down Sunset from Olvera to Pacific with my sunglasses on and the Who on the car radio. I could drop Sally off downtown at her winter term project, working with a woman lawyer who specialized in estate planning and trusts, and have the car all day.

My winter term project was to experience Los Angeles. I'd found a sponsor in the sociology department; I didn't even have to write a paper. I saw Warren Beatty in a terrible rush. And Dennis Hopper, draped by two dissolute girls, playing what looked like hopscotch on the sidewalk.

Mr. Rose liked to repeat that truism about youth being wasted on the young, but in my case, that was not to be. I loved slamming on my brakes and smiling sheepishly at the drivers beside me. Once I spotted a guy beside me at a red light and noticed his pleasure as I glanced over, glanced again: he had a neon green streak in his hair. He smiled; I smiled. The light changed, he lifted his hand, and we went on.

"I'm glad you're here," Sally said. "It makes things easier."

"You're a good friend to us, you know that?" Mr. Rose said. "When you're done with that pinko college of yours, you should move out here."

At the end of winter term, we came back to Ohio. My father mailed me plane fare, and Sally and I flew back together.

I hadn't realized Ohio was so gray. The trees, the roads, the sky. The worst was the sky, a sheet of clouds almost white, variationless. Walking out in the middle of the day, you couldn't tell where the sun was. What was I doing here? Me, Clare Mann, young, smart, and allegedly free. Ohio was nothing but my dues to pay this winter and the next, my junior and senior college years. Then I would be gone. A little puff of gray on a gray landscape.

Years later, Sally and I saw the movie *Prizzi's Honor*. In the climactic scene, if you haven't seen it, the husband and wife who each have a contract to kill the other meet in their mutual bed. She has a gun and he has a stiletto. It's hilarious, they're like two barracudas, and the question is who'll get it first.

I knew Sally wasn't looking. There was a gunshot, then a whizzing sound and a thwack.

"What happened?" she whispered, face squinched. "Did she hit him?"

"Missed."

"Did he hit her?"

"Yes. She's dead." I waited until the image of her neck pinned to the wall left the screen. "You can look now," I whispered.

"That was a good movie," she said afterward. "I'm glad you made me see it." I remembered that comment later, thinking of the other things I'd forced Sally to see.

I grayed things up for her, yes. Then she grayed things up for me.

ABOUT OUR SENIOR college year I remember two things, a dog run and Dan.

The Dan story isn't very interesting. It doesn't matter how we met, his last name, the color of his hair. He was an associate professor of chemistry at Case Western Reserve in Cleveland, but he lived in Oberlin because his wife (yes) taught French there, and it was cheaper to live in Oberlin than in Cleveland.

He used to appear in the hall outside my classes; in his car, driving slowly down the street; in the lobby of the library behind a newspaper. He was everywhere. One of the things he liked to do was throw me up against a wall and kiss me. Another was to open his passenger-side door and say, "Get in, little girl." I got in. I crouched on the hump in the middle of the floor and unzipped his pants and did things, and then he twisted my body onto the seat beside him and dove his fingers between my legs and moved me with such vigor that I bounced like a puppet. We did this even in daylight, and once parked in front of the Oberlin bank while Sally was inside cashing a check. We didn't have a lot of places to go, other than his car and my house. Sally and I lived in a rented house then, far off campus.

I'd been understanding enough with Sally—letting her cry over Timbo, letting her sulk—that she returned the favor, and although I later learned she thought my affair with Dan was crazy, she never at the time let on. She would go into the kitchen and make her methodical tea (Earl Grey, made using a tea ball), discreetly shutting the door as Dan and I rolled off the couch in the living room. She told me, before he showed up, that I looked nice, although how I must have really must have looked was *loca,* running to the front window hoping to see him, throwing myself on the bed in despair that he might not show. He didn't always. For all the times he surprised me from the shadows as I left a movie theater, there were whole evenings of plans when he simply didn't arrive. Marriage was unpredictable, he said.

I thought at the time that my loving Dan was a tribute to Sally, because I really did love him, madly, especially his hands and eyes; I lusted after him and enjoyed every libidinous moment in a way I never had before. In fact, I could have an orgasm simply thinking about him, as I did several times in physical chemistry class. I was proud of all I felt for him, this intimacy, this letting go, which maybe I couldn't have experienced without knowing Sally. She was my first real female intimate, so I had been primed for a male. "Get over here," I'd say on the phone, "I want to jump your bones." Or words to that effect.

Our two-bedroom bungalow was at the south edge of town, and I could afford it only because Sally paid three-quarters of the rent. We were the only two Oberlin students I knew with a house to ourselves. In size and atmosphere, our house was very much like a lakeside cottage (wood paneling, mildew), but I thought it was fabulous. Its only drawback was a dog run next door with barking day and night, a problem our landlord tried to solve by giving Sally and me white-noise boxes to keep in our bedrooms. The white noise didn't work for Sally. "I hate static," she said. She talked to the neighbor who owned the dogs, Mr. Morgan, at least every other day, suggesting solutions from muzzles to canine hypnosis. She liked to catch Mr. Morgan in his driveway when he got home from work, before he could disappear into his house and take care of his sick mother, a shriveled woman who, on nicer evenings, appeared in a wheelchair on the porch as her son worked in the yard. "Maybe it's like *Psycho,*" I said. "Maybe she's dead." But she wasn't dead, she actually cackled, and I had the feeling her son was afraid of her, running across the lawn to her whenever she made her screechy noise.

"I doubt she can hear the dogs," Sally said. "He could move the run over to her side of the house."

Mr. Morgan had three strands of long hair he combed over his bald head, a round belly, and a giggle. He worked as a clerk at the state liquor store in Wellington, ten miles down the road, and although I suspected he drank, Sally was less convinced. "They're dogs! I tell you, dogs!" Mr. Morgan would say, giggling. "Dogs bark!" I remember watching from inside our house as Sally arrived home, got off her bike and locked it, and Mr. Morgan, spotting her, scurried behind his house to stand plastered against the back wall, arms out, palms flat on the bricks. But Sally had spotted him too, and soon she was behind the house with him, bobbing her head earnestly as Mr. Morgan made desperate gestures toward the house. They must have talked for twenty minutes, or Sally talked and Mr. Morgan gestured, as the evening came and the backyard darkened.

"He's moving the run," Sally said when she got back, her cheeks red with triumph. "This weekend."

And he did, although it was rainy and cold, and the job involved a dump truck, several other men, and a flat platform on wheels to move the kennel, which was the size of a small garage. I felt a rueful compassion for Mr. Morgan, running from side to side of his house, pointing, shouting, glancing over his shoulder to our windows. Sally had gone to the library to study. That night I didn't notice much difference. The barking was slightly more distant but still there.

"Well?" Sally said the next morning.

I told her my opinion.

"You don't think it's better?" She looked incredulous. "It's definitely better. I went right to sleep. It's not perfect, I admit—but it's certainly better."

"Boy." I shook my head. "Remind me never to cross you."

"Oh, you won't," Sally said cheerfully, slicing her banana. By then she was certain she was going to law school. She dreamed of becoming a judge.

At the beginning of the year, we biked to campus, but that became difficult as the weather got colder. In the snow it was impossible. As rich as Sally was, she didn't have a car at Oberlin; no student had a car at Oberlin. During the week, when I had classes, I would have liked to study at home during the day, but home was too far away, and I ended up staying on campus in the big new library, taking occasional breaks to visit the snack shop. Sally and I studied in different places in the library. Sally really studied, at a carrel with her head down and her books out, and I flopped on one beanbag chair and then another, getting up and walking around every ten pages or so, or closing my eyes and imagining molecules, or imagining Dan and trying to work up an orgasm. I thought Dan and I were meant to be together. I thought that, when we were having sex, our bodies dissolved and flowed into each other so that we were truly one. I knew this was not molecular, but still. His marriage was of no consequence. Divorce now, divorce later, it didn't matter. Ultimately, we would be together.

We'd move to California and I'd get a California driver's license and register to vote, two requisites to meeting residency requirements for a California med school, and Dan would get a job at one of the gazillion universities there. We'd have an apartment with a view of the sea and a shared car, maybe a secondhand Saab. No reason not to go to med school: I had the grades, I had the interest. Freddy Finkelstein's house amazed me. If this was what a career as a dermatologist could offer, what about a career as an eye doctor or surgeon? Any other jobs seemed boring. Dan's job seemed unbearable—not the research, which he liked, but the teaching, all those bored kids sitting in rows in front of him thinking about sex. At least that's what I thought about.

"I worry about you sometimes," Sally said one evening.

"Why?" I shot back, my question antagonistic enough to warn her.

She looked at me regretfully, as if I shouldn't be making her say it. "Because he's married, Clare. I don't think married men tend to leave their wives."

"Oh, plenty of them do. And if it's an empty marriage—"

"Does he mention leaving?"

"We don't need to talk about it. It's a nonissue. We're fine. Listen, Sally, you know the way you were sure you and Timbo were going to work out"—this was a little mean, but I had to defend myself—"that's the way I'm sure Dan and I are going to work out."

Sally's lips, slightly parted, closed. "You know you can't—" she started.

"Be sure of anything," I finished, recklessly. "Of course not, I know that. Who knows what's going to happen to anyone?" I waved my hands, dismissing all arguments. "Dan and I are fine, I feel it. The universe wants us to be together." I felt a little silly saying this, but who else could I say it to?

Sally raised her eyebrows, but she changed the subject. She started talking about her next paper, a critique of *The Sun Also Rises,* which she thought had a wobbly view of women.

"Listen to you!" I said. "Talk about a born opponent."

Sally went home with me again for Thanksgiving. Things seemed better for my folks. My mother had a Pendleton suit and set out a tray of shrimp for appetizers, not the tiny shrimp she usually bought but shrimp that required more than one bite to eat. The whole atmosphere at home was better, the way a little extra money makes it—freer, looser, more fun. No one was agonizing. Everyone was there for Thanksgiving dinner, Sally, my brothers, their wives, my little nieces and nephew. We had three kinds of pie, including a pecan pie with nut halves instead of chips. I had suspected my parents had been surreptitiously sending money to Eric, whose wife had just had a baby and who had until recently been out of work. The funds from Mom and Dad must have stopped, I thought, and now Eric was acting proud. He bought flowers for the table and kept lifting his baby in the air and kissing her, showing off how lovey-dovey he was. Well, good. He was married, he was twenty-seven. I was glad my parents were free from the onus of Eric. He wasn't my favorite brother. The one time I'd ever had an accident with my mother's car, Eric had rushed right home and told my parents. When we were kids, he liked to get me in the tree house and run off with the ladder.

"I think they quit sending Eric money," I told Sally.

"Really? I think your dad got a raise." Sally grinned. She was always happy to see my family doing well. We were very open with each other about the generalities, if not the specifics, of money.

I was going to California again over Christmas our senior year. I'd been planning to do what I'd done the year before for the accommodating Mr. Guardino, drive another car west, but Dad pulled me aside at Thanksgiving and said he'd have a round-trip airplane ticket for me this year. "Could you go after Christmas?" he said. "Your mother and I would love to have you at home for Christmas."

"Sure," I said. I'd save five or six days by not driving. I would have all of January in Los Angeles, hanging out with Sally, visiting med schools, maybe driving down to Mexico or up the coast to Half Moon Bay. We had no college projects to do this winter term. And why not spend Christmas with my family? This would be my last year in Ohio.

Sally was planning to attend law school in California. She wanted me to go to med school there. She and I could share a rented house and continue our Oberlin life in a fresh venue. At times I resented her dreams for us: Would she still be paying more rent than me? Did she think I'd always be happy with a bicycle for transportation? In my dreams, I shared an apartment with Dan, with Sally across the street or down the beach, somewhere close but not oppressive. Dan and I would have a queen-size bed. We'd have Sally over for dinner and I'd cook delicious food, even if I hardly ever cooked now. Sally and I always ate together at a co-op, where we were bread bakers together on Thursday afternoons. There wasn't a night we didn't eat dinner together, then ride our bikes or walk back home.

One night in the shower, I had a revelation. I went over it in my head a while until I could phrase it properly, then popped out to deliver it to Sally. She was in our living room, watching *The Mary Tyler Moore Show* on TV.

"I've been thinking about college," I said, perching on a chair, tow-

eling my wet hair, "and I think the first year I learned about independence, the second year I learned about religion, the third year I learned
about Los Angeles, and this year I'm learning about sex."

"What a progression."

"Isn't it?" I grinned, pleased with myself.

Sally considered a moment. "I think the first year I learned to be
away from home, the second year I learned about friendship and love,
the third year I learned about death, and this year I'm learning about
justice."

"Wow," I said. I went whole days forgetting about Timbo. "You
certainly sound more serious than me." I reviewed my own list in my
mind. Independence, religion, Los Angeles, sex. Not everyone would
call it progress.

"Well," Sally said, "I'm more linear."

"Right." I nodded and padded away, the towel wrapped around my
head.

MY FATHER DROVE to Oberlin to pick me up after each semester, and always in the evening, after work. But in December, Dad arrived by one in the afternoon.

"What happened?" I cried, distressed. "You're so early. I'm not
even packed. They didn't say the weather would be bad, did they?"

"Oh no, no," my father said. "Just thought I'd get here early."

I was expecting Dan any minute.

"Can I help you pack anything?" my father said. His eyes landed on
a table next to a chair. "Is that our table?"

"Yes, Dad, but I'm not taking furniture home now," I said, surprised that the end of my college days should already be looming for
my father. "I'll be back in seven weeks. All I'm taking home now is
clothes."

"Where's Sally?"

I glanced out the front window: no turquoise Volvo, thank God,
no Dan. "She's on campus," I answered. "She had to turn in a paper."

That was partly true: Sally was actually on campus so Dan and I could have time to ourselves.

I fixed my father a cup of coffee with lots of milk and sugar, the way he liked it, and then switched on the TV because my father liked game shows, but there was nothing on but soaps. "Everybody still coming New Year's?" I asked, and my father's eyes seemed to cloud. He took a second to answer, and I realized something was wrong.

"What's up, Dad?" I said—but at that moment I saw a flash of turquoise out the window and heard a car door slam.

"What's up, pussycat?" Dan said when I got outside. (This was the sort of thing he said.)

"My dad's here."

It startled me to see Dan straighten up, tuck in his shirt, tuck back his chin. "Onward and upward," he said, taking a deep breath.

"This is my friend Dan," I told my father at the front door. My father was aware I had a "friend," although he never asked specific questions. I always suspected my father thought not asking about men kept me from noticing them.

"Mr. Mann," Dan said in his deepest voice, holding out his right hand, and it must have been at the same millisecond that Dan, my father, and I all noticed the wedding ring on his other hand.

"Are you a student here, Dan?" my father asked, and Dan, slipping his hands in his jacket pockets, said no, actually he taught chemistry at Case in Cleveland, but he lived in Oberlin because, because... Dan faltered. Another minute and he left.

I turned from shutting the door after Dan to my father fiddling with the TV dial, and it was only an instant before I realized I was safe. My father wouldn't say a word. I loved my father. "I'll hurry and pack," I said.

"Fine, fine," my father said, settling himself in a plaid armchair to watch a rerun of *Gilligan's Island.*

I never saw Dan again. I wasn't sure how to write him, whether a letter addressed to him at Case Western would reach his hands. The secretaries there might open his mail. I finally did write him in March.

A neutral letter, something a former student might write: Hi, how was he, I was doing this, I thought of him whenever I saw a... He didn't write back. Sally saw him twice in downtown Oberlin during her final spring semester, once looking in the Army-Navy store window and once coming out of the bookstore. He ignored her both times, and so completely it was clear he was pretending he hadn't seen her. Neither time was he accompanied by his wife. "I bet they get a divorce," I told Sally. "You wait." I was almost as sure as I'd been in November that Dan and I would end up together. Some things took years; I could wait.

But now, in the car heading off the state route below Oberlin and onto the freeway, my father cleared his throat. Gray, gray, that horrible Ohio gray, and although it wasn't yet five o'clock, the sun was setting. Patches of ice shimmered on the road. "I lost my job," my father said.

I looked at his profile, the landscape slipping behind it. "You're serious."

A pause. My father cleared his throat again. "I was fired."

"Fired! You're kidding! But you do everything for them, how could they—?" But then I stopped, thinking how he'd said nothing to me about Dan, how the kindest thing I could do was to say nothing, to let him reveal what he wanted in his own way.

He didn't reveal much. We made it home without talking about his job again, and I ended up entertaining him with the story of Sally and Mr. Morgan, the doggy neighbor, recasting the story not as a morality play—the way Sally presented it—but as a comedy, with a big emphasis on Mr. Morgan's "They're dogs, I tell you, dogs! Dogs bark!" Mr. Morgan was a silly and distant enough figure that we could laugh at him: his defeat was not at all like my father's. My father, that kind and enormously ethical man.

"I STILL HAVE THE TICKETS," my father announced. "You might as well go."

My mother erupted. "You have the tickets! I thought you'd turned in the tickets! She's already said she's staying here."

"You're kidding, Dad," I said. "You still thought I'd go to California for January?"

"I want you to go. I know how much you like it there. I thought the tickets could be your Christmas present."

"You can't give your daughter airline tickets and your sons screwdriver sets for Christmas," my mother said. "I'm sorry."

"No way I'd go, Dad. No way in a thousand years. Turn them in for a refund. Please. Promise you'll turn them in?"

My father sighed. "If I have to, honey. If I have to."

I BORROWED MY PARENTS' car and went to visit Baxter. He was living in the mother-in-law suite of a rambling house out in the country, with a family whose wife was cousin to the man who was teaching him woodworking. The family wasn't Amish, but Amish farms encircled theirs.

I was driving down a sweeping hillside on a county road surrounded by winter fields when an apparition appeared at the side of the road: a massive man in a plaid flannel shirt, with a dark beard almost to his waist and wild long hair. It was Baxter, waving.

He introduced me to his landlords as "the family brain," walked me around the barns, drove me to his workshop, and showed me the nailless construction he particularly liked to do. His teacher and boss was a weathered, thin-lipped man maybe twenty years older than Baxter, slight enough to look as though he bought his pants in the boys' department. He barely spoke; his eyes were hooded and intense. "He's an artist," the man said of Baxter, running his finger over a seam in one of Baxter's chests, and Baxter's face split into a grin so delighted I was embarrassed for him.

I was spending the night and Baxter insisted on giving me his bedroom—he'd sleep on the couch in the sitting room. "Give you a drawer," he said, pulling out a small drawer from the top of his bedroom cabinet and dumping its contents into a larger drawer farther down. There was the flash of a blue-and-white-striped brief falling out of that drawer, nothing Baxter could wear, or maybe it was a piece of women's underwear? But Baxter pushed the bottom drawer shut and it was gone.

"Do you have friends here?" I asked.

"Oh, sure," Baxter said. "I'm fine."

I could have looked in that drawer. Baxter slept heavily, and in his apartment nothing squeaked. But I remembered my father watching *Gilligan's Island*. I gave Baxter the dignity of his secrets.

ONE DAY LATE that winter, I was at the supermarket doing my mother's shopping when I ran into Dr. Danforth, one of the doctors from my father's old office. He was heading down an aisle and I called after him, belatedly realizing as he turned that maybe he was trying to avoid me. This got me mad. Dr. Danforth had always been my buddy when I worked at the office. I didn't like his wife, but I liked him. And he was my father's favorite doctor. A real gentleman, Dad said.

"How are you, Clare Ann?" Dr. Danforth asked.

"Fine," I said. "I'm at home and I'm taking some courses at the branch."

"Oh, you're not finishing at Oberlin?"

"I'm done there. I'll get an Oberlin degree, I'm just finishing up some credit hours."

"You're getting an Oberlin degree," he repeated. "I'm glad. Your father's very proud of you. More than you know. Very, very proud of you. He'd do anything for you."

"I'm applying to med school," I said.

"I see." Dr. Danforth nodded. I thought he might offer me a job at the office or a med school recommendation, but he didn't. "Well, it's very good to see you," he said in a quizzical but final sort of way. "You look well."

You look well, I thought, walking away. That must be a doctor compliment. You do not look eaten up with cancer, you do not have blue fingernails, there are no maggots crawling out of your nose. You look well.

Screw you, you slimy old doctor, I thought as I reached my parents' car. I kicked a wad of dirty ice out of the wheel well. You'll die a long time before I will, Dr. Danforth, I thought.

ASTONISHING HOW QUICKLY my life—along with my parents' life—changed.

I got a job as a waitress in a twenty-four-hour diner and moved back into my old room. My father started working in the hardware department at Sears. After a few weeks, it was clear he wasn't right; he didn't eat, he left buttons on his shirts undone, he forgot which days he was scheduled to work. I heard one of his coworkers, a guy not much older than me, refer to him as "the old man." "He's very stressed," my mother said, "and it's stressing me too." Actually, I got him to the doctor. He had cancer of the stomach with metastases into the liver, and the estimate was three months to live. At this point my mother insisted they sell their house, because my parents had no health insurance and the bills were staggering, and my mother didn't want to be left a widow in debt. I don't think my father was at that point capable of making big decisions. The money I earned as a waitress helped pay the rent on a one-bedroom apartment, where my bed was set behind a screen in the corner of the living room. I went to one med school interview but started crying in the middle of it, and after that I withdrew all my applications.

I don't know which seemed more dreamlike, the waitressing and the doctors' waiting rooms and that tiny apartment where my mother fixed creamed everything on toast (cheap, and my dad could keep it down), or the trip I made back to California. The trip was a present—ostensibly to Sally—from the Roses: a flight back to California with them and Sally to celebrate the end of our college life. "Go for me," my father said. "I insist." I had eight days off work. The Oberlin graduation had gone well: my father was not only alive (it had been three months and three weeks since his diagnosis), but he hadn't needed his wheelchair once, and at dinner the evening before the ceremony, he'd enchanted Sally's mother. "He has such kind eyes," she told me more than once. Between Mr. Rose and my father, there was a certain wariness. Sally had told me once that sick people made her father nervous. Mr. Rose directed his conversation to everyone but my father, throwing his credit card on the table like a trump card. Later he slapped my father on the back so hard I winced.

"Oh thank you," my mother said. "Oh my, this has just been lovely." For a socialist she loved fine dining.

"YOU HAVE TO BE a doctor," Sally said as we sat, in the middle of the afternoon, in a dark California bar. We were twenty-two, finally legal in a bar.

"Why?"

"Because you're smart, you're compassionate, and deep down it's what you want to do. It's your calling. Like the law is a calling to me."

"That sounds sort of religious."

"Well."

"But I don't do religion, Sally. Remember when I was going to observe the Sabbath?" We both laughed.

MRS. ROSE WASN'T COOKING much. She spent most of her days in her bedroom, curtains closed except for a seam of light, drafting letters to her pen pals. "It must be interesting to be a waitress," she told me, "meeting people not like you."

California seemed different to me. I didn't like it as much anymore. On and around Mulholland, you never saw people in their yards. And their yards weren't really yards, they were landscaped areas, terraces or flowerbeds or trees surrounded by vegetation, not expanses you could tromp around in. You did see gardeners who looked Mexican, although Sally said they could be from Central America. You saw Chinese houseboys on the streets walking dogs, and occasionally you saw a jogger, usually wearing a sweatband and dark glasses, either a celebrity or disguised as one. That summer the fence around Sally's family's property was topped with swirls of barbed wire.

"I don't know why Daddy put that up," Sally complained. "Talk about ugly." There had been robberies. The neighbor on the east had moving picture cameras installed above his doors. The neighbor on the west had dogs.

And Ben? He got older. He got friends. He missed Sally's and my Oberlin graduation because he had to stay in Los Angeles for school. I think that was the first year of the camera. He wanted underwater equipment so he could take pictures of his buddies in the pool. "It'd only be two hundred dollars," he whined to his dad.

Sally's father insisted that I call him Sid, telling me, "You're a college graduate. I didn't even finish high school. You're a hell of a lot more educated than me. And wait till you're a doctor, huh? Wait till then!"

He sat beside his pool and spouted his ideas about the world. Being in Ohio had reminded him he was glad to be out of the east, because easterners were hidebound—"But you could use another expression."

"They told me I couldn't do business out here," he said, "but I showed them."

"Why?" I asked. "Is magazine distribution mostly based in New York?"

Sid gave me a curious look. "A lot of it is. And I have to go to New York sometimes, but I try not to make it a habit. They think they have everything, they don't seem to understand that our business is entertainment, and what's the entertainment capital of the world?"

I was expected to answer. "Here."

"Here." Sid nodded approvingly. "You betcha. All the pretty girls come here, all the studs come here."

There was smog but a breeze by the pool, a wonderful green smell. Ben was launching off the diving board into his cannonball and Sally was sitting on a deck chair reading *Chilly Scenes of Winter,* her feet propped on another chair. The palm trees were high, exultant, not droopy and sheltering like the trees at home. Patricia, back with the Roses, her mother in Mexico dead, picked up and refilled our glasses.

"It's not that the brains come here," Mr. Rose went on, considering. "It's more the meat."

What Sid would really like to do, what he'd always dreamed of doing, was something with the Bible. "Maybe a movie," he said one night over dinner. "A movie of those great old stories that have survived thousands of years."

"What, like Adam and Eve?"

"And the flood, and Abraham and Isaac, and Daniel and his dreams. And the whole David saga, wow. Those are great stories. Got everything in those stories. Sex, violence, greed, jealousy. Family betrayal. I'd like to see a movie of the real stuff. Not that Ten Commandments crap."

We ate more of our wonderful meal, the only meal Sally's mother cooked all week, and then Mr. Rose started talking about taking his family to Israel, and not just Israel but the whole Middle East, to see the places where the Bible stories had occurred.

"Like the mountain that Moses came down with the tablets, what was that? Mount Sinai. You've seen that movie, haven't you, Clare? Old Charlton. Or the spring Bathsheba bathed in. Remember? David liked the looks of her, so he sent her husband off to battle. It worked, too. Sacred places, right?" He nodded at Sally. "That's what your Elascu guy talks about." He was referring to the book he'd read with Sally for her religion course. "And who knows if they're the real places, right? But you think they're real, so they're real."

Every time I tired of Sid, every time he seemed stupid or tasteless, he popped up next with something dazzling. *You think they're real, so they're real.* The notion was so expansively wise, world-accepting, not like, say, the narrowness of my mother. Are you sure you're all right? she'd hector me. Why are you losing so much weight? And those foolish things you're doing—why would someone with an IQ like yours ever leave a van in drive?

I seemed to be eating fine in California.

I'd thought that everyone got narrower as they got older, more stubborn and convinced of their own rightness. What a relief to know Sid, whose mind was getting larger! I understood his reading Sally's course books in a new way. He wasn't an overly possessive, hokey father: he was a man trying to enlarge his mind.

"I KNOW HE IMAGINES me in front of a jury," Sally said, "and the irony of it is, if I go into estate law, the last thing I'll ever want to see is a jury."

We laughed. That day we were sharing some sort of low-fat blended fruit drink at a juice bar, feeling very virtuous to not be eating ice cream.

"I don't know what my parents expect from me," I said.

"I'm sure they expect what all parents expect," Sally said. "Perfection." She gave a peculiar smirk, a flash of bitterness toward her father that was so quick and unexpected I think I laughed again.

ON THE FLIGHT BACK to Ohio, I discovered Dunhill cigarettes. Back then you could smoke on a plane. There was a half pack left in the seat pocket on the plane, and I opened it and savored the remains. They were in a long maroon box, the cigarettes arranged double file with gold foil folded over them. On the outside was an "In Service to Her Majesty the Queen" seal. I felt so adult pulling out my

pack of Dunhills, tapping out a cigarette, and lighting it with my
abalone lighter. I imagined how I looked: cool, aesthetic, the tiniest bit
jaded. I looked L.A.

Before I left, in a bar in the airport, Sid told me he had forgotten I
was from Ohio. I was looking like a California girl.

"Really, Daddy?" Sally had said, turning to me with a grin, and I
waited a moment for him to elaborate. When he didn't, I had to ask:
"Why do I seem like a California girl?"

He shrugged. "You know. Charming but neurotic."

What a relief to be in California, where neurosis could be charm.
At home they seemed to think I was insane. "Maybe I'm a little neurotic." I was happy he found me charming.

"And there's more than that," Mr. Rose said after a pause. He was
newly full of these dramatic pauses, like Marlon Brando playing the
Godfather. "A good shopper." Me? I thought. Shop? I shopped thrift
shops.

"A nice dresser, looks after her appearance. A worrier." He took his
longest pause, brought his fingertips to his forehead with both hands:
"*Aspirations* to deep thought."

Now this was insulting. I laughed a little falsely. "Aspirations, huh?
Not the real thing?"

Mr. Rose gave me a sly grin. "It's good to aspire."

Idiot, I thought. Creep. My eyes met Sally's across the table, and
very clearly, I saw my own father, reclining on his hospital bed, reaching for a glass of Coca-Cola. My strongest urge, suddenly, was to be
home.

EIGHT YEARS LATER, at the end of my residency, I took a
course in the management of a medical practice. One of the speakers
depicted for us the typical medical-practice embezzler: a trusted employee with more than seven years in the firm, someone you'd never
suspect, someone with access to money and records of money, some-

one who feels extra money is justifiably owed him, someone with extensive family debts—a sick child, kids in college, a new house.

My father, I thought. My father embezzled the money that got me to California.

Everything from those distant days suddenly made sense: my father's passivity in the face of his firing, his taking a job at Sears instead of looking for another practice management job, Dr. Danforth's cool behavior toward me in the supermarket, my mother's angry stoicism. My father was long dead by that time, so I didn't hold my new knowledge against him; he had more than atoned. Ah, I thought, another packet of corruption. Then I got frantic. Is the stain really everywhere, in everybody? Is everyone impure? Even my wonderful, gentlemanly father? I remember getting up from the meeting, notebook under my arm, beeper heavy in my white coat pocket, avoiding all the residents I usually palled around with. I felt the same stunned way I had when my father's nurse touched me on the shoulder to awaken me, when my first thought was to close my mouth because I must be drooling. It wasn't until I shut my mouth and swallowed that it sank in. "I'm sorry," the nurse said. My father's back was quiet, quiet.

"Oh my God," I said to nobody, eight years later. I stumbled to the door of the conference room. As if my father had died all over again.

I asked my mother about it once. "I was just thinking about something from years ago. Remember when Dad lost his job at the doctors' office? Did the doctors at the group think"— I was careful how I phrased this—"did they think Dad had taken any money?"

"Maybe there was some talk about that," my mother said, her spine suddenly stiff. She was stirring something on the stove. "It was just that, talk." She splashed the contents of her pot into the colander, steam rising up around her. Her jaw clenched in an angry way. "They never proved anything."

"It was like talking to your mother about cats," I told Sally later (Sally's mother had a phobia). "Verboten."

"Oh, Clare. If he did it, he did it for you."

I'M WELL AWARE that some people hate cottage cheese. I think it's the lumpy texture, the little curds floating in their not-quite-milky sea. Me, I love the stuff. In fact, for my first two years of med school, it was almost all I ate. That and lettuce and—but only in season—tomatoes. A typical dinner was a bed of lettuce topped with a scoop of cottage cheese, drizzled with lemon. Occasionally, I topped this with sprouts. That was a typical lunch, too, and I didn't eat breakfast. Grocery shopping took me minutes. I did take a vitamin pill. It never crossed my mind that my eating was a problem, and when I got on the wards in the third year of med school, I started to get hungry; once again I ate hamburgers and spaghetti and chicken, the things people usually eat. Looking back at pictures from my first years of med school, I realize I was terribly thin, thin even by Los Angeles standards. Although Sally lived in Sacramento then, she never mentioned my weight to me—she watched, with perfect equanimity, as I made my low-fat salad during my visits to her house (in her honor, I would eat plums from the tree in her yard), and I didn't recognize my thinness as suspicious. It's my underlying belief that over time the human spirit tends toward sanity, just as the human body tends toward health, so minor aberrations are rarely ominous and only mildly interesting. And major aberrations are just that. Major.

I spent a year in that little apartment with my mother, watching my father die, and when that ordeal was done, I was twenty-three and resolute. I was going to med school, no matter how I had to swing it. By then the only schools I could possibly afford were state schools in Ohio; I was also truly poor, so sources of funding opened up. Scholarships assume virtue in destitution. I used to tell people, in all honesty, that 80 percent of the money I'd made waitressing had gone to pay my father's medical bills, and this fact had an effect on medical and hospital people. I don't think I ever felt so wanted. I remember one woman in an admissions office putting her hand on top of mine and squeezing. "Don't worry, we'll get you there," she said. "We'll get you your dream!"

Golly, I felt like saying, me? Gosh darn, what'll they think back in the holler!

Which is not to say I wasn't grateful.

AT SALLY'S LAW SCHOOL in Sacramento, there was a large women's restroom near the main teaching auditorium, and one day early that fall, Sally walked in and found a cluster of her women classmates hunched around a sink over tiny mirrors, fingers at the sides of their noses. What in the world? she thought. She knew what they were doing only because Daphne had explained how it was done, and my God, why oh why did these law students, *law students,* think they were immune to the laws of the land or even the laws of natural consequence? Didn't they know cocaine would make them stupid? Or, if not exactly stupid, then careless? Daphne and her boyfriend, high on cocaine, had once walked out of a Sambo's restaurant without leaving a tip.

"Right there," Sally said. "Right in the middle of the bathroom, not even hidden in a stall."

"You should come to Ohio," I said. "I've never seen anything like that in med school."

"It's si-ick!" Sally said. "I can't use that bathroom anymore. I'm not going to stand there and be an indifferent witness. I have to use a rest-room upstairs by the administration office."

"You'll know it's bad when you find someone doing coke in that one," I joked.

Sally didn't laugh. "Si-ick!" she repeated. The tiny house she was renting was far from the school, on the edge of some farmland. It was her haven. She felt so alone. She couldn't wait for me to visit.

I DID WELL the first two years in med school in Akron—the aca-demic years, the years of histology and biochem and physiology. My grades were the best. I was known as the weird chick who threw off the curve. Several of my professors encouraged me to try research. But I wasn't interested in cannulating the ureters of rats. I wasn't interested in doing what I knew I could do well. I was looking forward to my third and fourth years, in the hospitals and with patients. I'd never been a people person, but I wanted to be a people doctor. This desire was only partly in memory of my father. I wanted to be able to sniff at someone and tell—as I'd heard was possible—that his diabetes was out of control; to feel a breast lump before anyone else knew it was there; to say the one true thing a patient would always remember.

"You sound like King David," Sid said when I explained this. "He wanted something more."

"King David, huh?" I said drily. "Nothing like a little self-aggran-dizement." I remembered his insulting remarks to me in the airport.

"There's nothing wrong with self-aggrandizement," Sid protested. "Keeps you thinking big!" He wagged his finger at me. "You think I could keep growing my business if I didn't think big?"

I MADE TWO FRIENDS in med school, Andy Braverman, who was stationed at the body catty-corner from mine in the anatomy lab, and Gillian Watkins, who actually pursued me as a buddy because she liked the way I asked questions.

Andy is now a private-practice general surgeon somewhere in West Virginia—we've lost touch—and Gillian took an even loopier route to ambulatory AIDS than I did, starting out in pediatrics and then doing medical missionary work in Zaire before coming back to the U.S., moving to San Francisco, and opening up her own practice. Not pediatric AIDS, although she is trained as a pediatrician, but adult AIDS. "Why don't you do the kids?" I asked her once. It wasn't because the kids were too depressing; the kids had enough advocates, and she wanted to deal with the promiscuous and the drug abusers, patients people blame for their disease. "It's like lepers, you know?" she said. "I would have loved to work with lepers." Religion may be involved here: it's not something Gillian discusses. We see each other at various conferences. After Zaire, she says, the AIDS in San Francisco seems so tameable. "I mean, God," she says, "at least you've got antibiotics. You've got support groups. You have hospices! No one gets left beside the road to die."

I WAS IN LOS ANGELES so often the visits blurred. One trip I took a bus out; one trip Mrs. Rose stayed in bed with the flu; several trips were paid for by Sid or Sally. I went to Sacramento too, visiting Sally's little house, but that was a duller, pallid California, one that seemed suspiciously Midwestern.

There was a record producer whose son was a friend of Ben's, whose dim and narrow Malibu house (brown curtains on all the windows, letting in the narrowest chinks of sun and sea) Sally and I visited one year around Christmas. We were picking up Ben, who must have been about fifteen, from a visit. The producer's wife was in hot pants baking cookies—there were baking sheets cooling around the kitchen—and the producer (whose name I'd heard, whose acts I knew) sat in the living room in a special chair that surrounded him with music. His wife, to get his attention, had to hit him on the knee. Neither one of them knew where their son and Ben were. "Maybe they're in the cabana," the wife said. "Honey, would you check the cabana?"

"Can't you check it? You're the mother."

A timer went off in the kitchen. "Oh!" The wife threw up her hands. "Duty calls."

The producer scowled and uncoiled from his chair. I smiled at him, showing him we were grateful.

"We'll wait outside," Sally said, and announced, "I don't like them," as we sat in the car, our windows rolled down and the sea breezes wafting through. You could smell the sea, hear it, but not see it: the producer's house and the houses flanking it formed a sort of wall.

I had my sunglasses on, as I always did in California. "What's not to like?" I said—Sid's expression, my own little joke.

"I'm sure the parents use cocaine."

I was shocked. Parents, using cocaine? At the same time, I was struck by the naïveté of Sally's language. Any with-it person would say "snorting coke" or "doing blow." Still, she had recognized something I'd never thought to look for. "How can you tell?"

"The way they act. They don't even know where their son is! He's their only child, it's not like they have a gang of them. And their house is always dark and the husband's always brooding and the wife's always . . . up. In a weird way. I was over here last year, and she was making angels out of paper cups and cotton balls."

"At least she's industrious," I hazarded.

"Well. In a useless way."

Sally seemed less happy that year—less easy at home, less enthralled with her family and life. She said several times that she was eager to get back to her house in Sacramento and the stray cat she'd adopted.

"A cat!" I exclaimed. "What does your mother say?"

"Does she come visit?" Sally retorted. She had not found any soul mates at law school. I hated to think of Sally as a young woman needing a pet. I vowed that I would never get one.

SID SAT ON HIS throne, the big maroon leather chair in the den. The TV was always on now, usually sports. Sally wasn't there. Maybe I had a Scotch. Later I switched to brandy. "You imagine what it was like growing up in a place like that?" Sid said. "We had nothing. Not even a closet. My mother's clothes used to hang on a nail on the back of a door."

I nodded. It didn't sound so terrible. They had an apartment. They ate. It crossed my mind that Sid had no idea how sparely I'd been living these last few years.

"My father had one pair of shoes. One pair. I remember shining those shoes up. I had to have them done by the Shabbos, Friday night at sundown. If I didn't have them done right, he'd beat me, but he'd wait till Shabbos was over. You imagine me sitting in shul all day Saturday, knowing that when services were over, my dad was going to beat the crap out of me? I was the only one didn't want services to end."

"It's hard to imagine you were beaten," I say. "You treat your kids so—"

"I know. Jews don't usually beat up on their families. We're not known for that. My dad was an exception. Of course, most Jews don't drink, either."

"What about your mom, did she try to protect you?"

"It was like she wasn't there." Sid's eyes bored into me. When I didn't look shocked or sympathetic, he sighed and sat back in his chair. "She was nice, don't get me wrong, but she was scared. Women didn't resist back then. You were married, that was your lot." He shook his head and smiled. "Old days. Long ago." He peered into his drink, shaking his ice cubes, and when he looked up, his gaze was almost shy. "Sally tell you I set up a scholarship fund, help some of the kids who work for me pay for college?"

"You did? That's wonderful, Sid." Now that I was older, I saw a point in virtue. A year before, I would have thought the scholarships were something Sid did for himself. But so what if they were? I thought of Rabbi Hillel's famous comment, which Sally had taught me: "If I am not for myself, who is for me?"

"Sally didn't tell you?" Sid asked, his tone chastened. "Not that money will save them. Money helps, but it's not the end of the world."

"If I am only for myself, what am I?" Rabbi Hillel had gone on.

"I thought she'd spread that around." Sid pouted. "It's a good deal.

Three full scholarships last year. I'll have to remind Sally to start brag-ging on me."

Rabbi Hillel's final question: "And if not now, when?"

"She always brags on you," I said, and at the time, I almost didn't register the quick and hopeful glance Sid gave me at those words.

I don't know, looking back, what happened to me each time I got to Los Angeles. I don't know why I, a legend in my own mind for my intelligence, became mute and stupid. But I did. I remember telling Sid about all the fishing magazines I'd noticed in a store. Trout-fishing magazines, fly-fishing magazines, bass-fishing magazines.

"Oh, everything." Sid laughed. "You name it."

"It amazed me that people buy these magazines. I mean, *American Fly-Fishing?*"

"I figure on some of my products I've only got only five thousand customers, but if a magazine can sell for twenty-five bucks a pop, and if I target the right five thousand..."

I was already calculating, oblivious to the unlikelihood of any mag-azine I'd ever seen selling for twenty-five dollars.

BEN HAD BEEN a kid when I met him. My brothers got taller and taller and gawkier and gawkier, then, suddenly, overnight it seemed, they turned into men. But Ben never became a man. He never made that click where the knob turned and the adult came into focus. Each time I saw him, he looked not less boyish but less centered. His parents had a darkroom built in the corner of his room, and then one year, he had a four-by-five camera, one of those little boxes the photographer has to peer into with a cover over his head. He looked so thin and seri-ous, hunched over his camera. He made his own prints, and then he made his own prints not in silver but in platinum, which had a fragile aged quality. That year he persuaded me to pose for him, because, he said, I had the most beautiful wrists he'd ever seen.

Sid hooted across the den. "Wrists? Benny, did you say wrists?"

I was turning red. I had never thought of little Ben as a sexual being. I kept glancing at my wrists, wondering what he saw in them. I'd
never really noticed them before.

"They're beautiful," Ben said urgently, and for a second, I thought
he was going to take one in his hand and fondle it.

"You really want to take a picture of my wrists, Ben?"

"I want to capture them."

"They are nice wrists," Sally said, now beside me looking down at
them. "Sort of bony."

"Wrists," Sid said. "Think there's a market?"

Something about their attention made me uncomfortable. "Of
course they're bony! Whose wrists aren't bony?"

"So let him take a picture," Sally said, and her intonation, flat and
weary, sounded exactly like her father. I can't tell you how many times
and in what circumstances—years later—I was to imagine Sally's father saying those very same words.

"YOU SPENT THE WHOLE weekend in bed?" Sally said from California. "That's not good."

That was a time when living seemed like too much work. "Oh," my mother had said at Thanksgiving, "I suppose your life seems important to *you*."

"Come out over Christmas again," Sally said. "I'll talk to Daddy. I'll make it happen."

Make it happen: Sally's California-ese.

"I feel guilty spending his—"

"Clare, he can afford it. And he likes you. He loves for you to come out. And if you're there, it'll take the heat off me."

"Tell him I owe him one, okay?" I realized my eyes were watering. I was speaking words my dad had used to me.

"I DON'T KNOW," I said at the Roses' dinner table, "this has been a rough year for me. It's been two years since I lost my father, and still—"

"What," Ben said, sniggering, "he vanish down the aisle at a Kmart?"

Ben? This was sweet little Ben? It took me a moment to absorb his

words. Had he really said them? He was well aware my dad was dead.
I thought of Ben five years before, running down the hall, laying his
head across my legs as I sat beside the pool. He still had the same curly
hair and dark eyes, but he looked different, with black jeans, a black
shirt, a dangling earring. By then the room was in an uproar.

"You have no idea," Sally's mother said to Ben, clutching the edge
of the table. "You cannot imagine."

"My own son," Sid said. "May God strike me dead right now if I
ever, ever thought I'd hear my own son talk like that." He raised his
hand as if to strike Ben but ended in an strange collapse.

"Benny?" Sally implored. "What are you thinking? You can't have
meant such a cruel thing."

I never thought of Ben the same after that. I was less angry with
him than his family was. His mother was right in saying that he had no
idea. He didn't. I don't think anyone who hasn't had a parent die can
really know what it is to lose one. Why should Ben even start to understand? He was fifteen years old, he lived in a house the size of a department store, his family was healthy. He hadn't been through
anything, really. I should have been direct, I should have said "My father died" instead of saying I'd lost him. I'd always hated eu-
phemisms—why did I use one?

If anything, Sally and her parents thought more of me afterward.
Because I didn't blow up or disintegrate or any of those things. I han-
dled it. They all apologized, even Ben. I remember his exact words.
Sorry, that was a butthole thing to say. That's exactly what he said the
next morning. Between me and the family, there was no rupture.
Now, between Ben and his father—that was the rupture.

"What, he vanish down the aisle at a Kmart?" And what, exactly,
was so frightening about that remark? The scary thing about Ben's
crack was not its disrespect to me, its disrepect to death. Nor was it the
vague class-consciousness of where I might have "lost" my father. The
disturbing thing about Ben's crack was that, in nineties lingo, he
dissed the father—mine, ostensibly, but the real insult was to Sid. It
would mean nothing to me, Dad, Ben was saying—or they *thought* he

was saying—if you, you old guy, just walked away. Disappeared, va-
moosed, vanished without a trace. Good-bye.

"HE HAD TO BE taking something, don't you think?" Sally's aunt
Ruby leaned forward in her deck chair and looked straight at me.
"Young people are bound to experiment. I'm sure he didn't mean it.
Ben's a good boy. What did you take, Daphne, was it LSD?"

Daphne, perched on a deck chair and naked except for a glittery
bikini bottom and an ankle bracelet, was bent over painting her toenails. I had never before seen anyone sunbathe topless, and certainly
not in front of her mother. Daphne's brown breasts grazed her knees;
it was hard not to stare. "It was psilocybin, Mom. Mushrooms."

"Oh, that's right. Mushrooms." Aunt Ruby rolled her eyes. "She
was very odd. Came walking into the family room saying she was stuck
inside a toaster. She thought the sofa was a giant heating element. Oh
my! And then you brought home that boy."

"I've managed to almost finish law school without taking drugs,"
Sally said. "Does that count for anything?"

"Oh Sally, you're an innocent," Aunt Ruby said. "You have the innocence of springtime, may it never leave you."

"I don't think I'm such an innocent," Sally snapped. I looked away
from her, out of tact, and was surprised to see Daphne rubbing a cheek
with the back of her hand, smiling at me with an air of conspiracy.

AFTER HIS APOLOGY, Ben followed me to the kitchen. That day
he wore a bandanna knotted around his forearm and a white T-shirt
with the sleeves rolled up.

I smiled to show him I accepted his apology. "You have more
looks," I said, nodding at his bandanna.

"I'm aesthetic," he answered, dropping his wrist.

I knew there were gays in the world. At college they'd held gay
dances, in high school I'd gone to a David Bowie concert (the "Ziggy

Stardust" tour—Ben was impressed) where two nuzzling guys in front of me had blocked much of the view. But it hadn't yet struck me that people I didn't think of as gay could be gay, and so I missed Ben's inference totally. I thought he was talking about himself as an artiste. "Better aesthetic than athletic," I said.

"Are you an aesthetic supporter, Clare?" Ben asked in a plaintive tone.

"Oh, absolutely," I said. "I read a poem a day."

Ben looked at me dully, then turned away.

When I left L.A. the next week, he was in the adolescent drug and alcohol rehab unit of a hospital. Drugs of abuse, the intake form read: alcohol, amyl nitrite, marijuana. Sally was incensed that her parents hadn't suspected. "He's at home with them every night," she fumed. "Don't they watch him at all? Don't they look to see who his friends are? I can't be the only one in the family who looks after Ben." It struck me that in the past she would have been angry only with her mother, but now she blamed her father too.

Sally and I stopped to visit Ben on our way to the airport. "I'm afraid this visit hasn't been the respite you needed," Sally said, and I said well, that's life.

"What do you think of my institution?" Ben asked, drawing out the "u," nodding at the walls. He smoked unfiltered Parliaments and touched his tongue, in a gesture that was surely practiced, to remove bits of tobacco. By that time I had quit smoking, and it startled me that Ben had started. Behind his smoke cloud, he looked as sweet and young as ever. He was only fifteen. His chin, I noticed, was weak. I had lost my father, and now Ben's family was losing their son.

I FLEW BACK TO OHIO, Ben got out of rehab, the Rose family minus Sally went to counseling. "Daddy says she seems like a sharp therapist," Sally said. "She doesn't do any weird stuff."

"Weird stuff?"

"Oh, you know, past lives, acupuncture, hypnosis."

Oh my, I thought. California.

"I'm going home this weekend," Sally said.

"How can you go home? Don't you need the law library?"

"I'll study more next week. What else can I do? It's *family*."

And later in the conversation: "It's one of those adolescent things, I'm sure. He'll snap out of it."

How can you know that? I thought. I knew adolescent things, binges and slamming doors and long car rides with friends talking about idiot parents, but I had been through that. I had rebelled. Sally hadn't.

When she hung up, even the click was brisk. It's *family*.

BAXTER CALLED ME. "I'm moving away on you, sis," he said.

"Moving! But why? Where?" He was well established as a furniture-maker. He now owned half the shop; he and his partner got orders from as far off as Chicago.

"Sometimes you just have to move on," Baxter said. "I'm going south."

"Alabama? Florida?"

Baxter laughed. "Southern Ohio. Hocking County. Gonna build me a cabin in the woods."

"But why, Baxter? Are you going to build furniture down there?"

"Sometimes you have to move on," he repeated.

THAT WINTER HAD SOME serious ice. When I drove home from the medical school library, it was always dark. Some days I drove cautiously, thinking about family, sometimes Sally's, sometimes mine. What exactly had happened to Baxter? Why did my mother care more about the people who needed the Emergency Food Bank than about me? Was I really morally obliged, as my brother Frank suggested, to give my old car to Eric (whose wife had had three children in four years) when I bought a new one? Other nights I drove recklessly, thinking Los Angeles was nice, but wouldn't you miss icicles hanging on the stoplights like Santa's beards, or pine trees so stiffly encrusted with ice they looked like giant toilet brushes? And could you slide off the road in Los Angeles, your car spinning to face the direction you'd started? Could you say "Whoo," check your mirrors, be sure no one had seen you, then, grinning, carry on in your new direction?

WHEN SALLY GRADUATED from law school that spring, I wasn't invited. Not that I could have gone—I was starting my third year of med school with clinical rotations, a daily grind with teams of interns and residents in the hospital, and I had no money. But still I believed that the invitation and the means to go would come, that one day I'd open my mailbox and there would be an airline ticket to Sacramento. It didn't happen. "Daddy wants just family," Sally said. "He thinks that'll make it easier for Ben."

Sally started work in July 1980 as an associate in a medium-size law firm in downtown Los Angeles, living at home with her parents and Ben until she could find the proper condo. We were both twenty-five. Sally had abandoned her early focus on estate planning—too much venality, she said—and signed on to her new law firm as a generalist. She was convinced her niche would reveal itself.

An older couple named Waluskey bought a double-wide trailer and moved it into a park near Palm Springs. When the trailer's roof developed a leak near the front door, the Waluskeys sued for the cost of a new trailer plus pain and suffering. Sally's firm, which did insurance defense work, represented the insurer of the trailer's manufacturer. Getting rid of the Waluskeys was Sally's first solo task.

Sally didn't want the case to settle; she wanted it to go to court. Because it would be fun, because the complaints were absurd, because she hated the Waluskeys and their stupid contending and alleging. She believed the Waluskeys had caused the trailer's leak themselves by adding a porch with a roof outside their front door. It was their own damn fault.

"Daddy says he'll come to the trial," Sally said. "He says the Waluskeys won't know what hit them."

ACCOMPANYING HER GARDENER LUIS to a nursery to choose some shrubs, Aunt Ruby, getting out of a pickup truck, toppled off a pair of high-heeled mules and sprained her ankle. It was a scene: Aunt Ruby's pastel jeans and sweater covered with mud, Luis struggling to pick her up, Aunt Ruby shrieking. Someone at the nursery thought an assault was going on and called the police, one of whom upset Aunt Ruby so much with an anti-Latino comment that she swatted him with her handbag and ended up booked for assault. Sally was just home from work when Uncle Freddie phoned.

"So here's F. Lee Baileyette," someone cracked when Sally arrived at the jail.

Years later, when Sally had pruned Aunt Ruby and Daphne like limbs from her family tree, I used to think of her—brisk, efficient, a little peeved—arriving to bail out Aunt Ruby. "Here's my girl!" I imagined Aunt Ruby saying, or something similarly sweet. She had such faith. Ruby was disorganized, she wasn't the smartest woman in town, she was silly—but she did love Sally. I haven't seen Ruby for years. Or Daphne either, with her rolling eyes and perky breasts.

"She took him to the store with her," my mother said, shaking her head. "As simple manual labor. As a pair of arms. As if he's not even a person."

"Mom," I said, "he's a gardener. Carting plants is his work. And Aunt Ruby hit the cop when he insulted him."

"When, oh when, will people stop thinking they can find happiness on the backs of the indigent laborers of this world?"

This was a bit much even for my mother. I burst out laughing. "Are you crazy?" I asked.

"Crazy!" she raved. "Crazy! What is that family doing to you? What has happened to your conscience?"

SALLY'S MOTHER SWATTED imaginary bugs, her robe billowing around her. "Wicked Waluskeys," Sally's mother said with a swat. "Wretched Waluskeys, pesky Waluskeys..."

It was early fall. Sally had sent me a plane ticket, bought with her new salary. She and I were beside the Rose pool in deck chairs. "Apparently Daddy's very good at what he does," Sally said, ignoring her mother. Ben, wearing a funny tight pair of swim trunks, was emerging from the water. Whorls of pubic hair peeked out at the top of his thighs. "Very good. Or so they say. They! I mean so he says." She snorted a puff of air out through her nose, like a dragon, and I blamed her displeasure on Ben's suit.

BY SEPTEMBER, I was feeling like a real doctor. During my internal medicine rotation, I met an elderly black woman, Mrs. Sidebottham, who was dying of ovarian cancer. She was my patient. I was the only one at the hospital who talked to her and her family, who wrote notes on her, who gave one damn about her belly pain and constipation. I was proud that I, a lowly third-year med student, should have my own patient, even if she was a patient no one else wanted. Mrs. Sidebottham was a medical failure, dying of a disease no one could cure or even palliate, refusing to leave the hospital for a nursing home or hospice. According to certain people, she was a drain on the system.

"Sit down and read to me, girl," she'd say, gesturing to her Bible. "I like the way you talk." She told me what chapters to read, and when I was done, she'd harrumph and cross her hands over her belly and close her eyes, as if she were cradling a secret.

Mrs. Sidebottham's belly got bigger and bigger, her skin thinner and thinner. Her veins stuck out like road maps. One day she stopped asking me to read. Two days later she stopped talking. When her arm scraped the bedrail, a piece of skin the size and shape of a credit card peeled off.

"You gives us hope," one of the daughters told me. "None of the other doctors ever gives us hope."

I pointed out I was only a student doctor. But really, I thought, could a little hope hurt? My father lived three months longer than predicted.

"That's all right! You don't have to be a complete doctor. You're the only one comes by here, anyway."

Eventually it became clear, even to me, that Mrs. Sidebottham was dying. She went to hospice three days later. "You got the family to agree to that?" the attending said, looking over his spectacles with new respect. "Good job." He shuffled through his stack of file cards for the one stamped with Mrs. Sidebottham's name, then scrawled a black "X" across the front.

"I CAN'T BELIEVE IT!" Sally said. "I'm so upset I can't see straight. You remember the Waluskeys and their allegedly defective trailer? The insurance company ordered me to settle with them. Five thousand dollars to get the Waluskeys off their back! Just pay them off, they said. Isn't that criminal? Can you believe the greed? Is that all there is in the world? Greed and lies?"

"You really can't blame them for suing, Sally. It's their home. They bought it new and they were disappointed. That patient I was following died," I went on. "Remember I told you about her? Mrs. Sidebottham. She went to hospice and she died there. I saw the obituary in the paper."

"I don't know if I can stand it," Sally said.

"Stand what? Death?"

"No! The greed and the lies."

"Aren't you going a little crazy over this one case?" I asked.

"Didn't you tell me she had cancer everywhere? Aren't you going a little crazy over this one case?"

"Sally," I reproached her. We both fell silent. Neither of us apologized. We said our quick good-byes and hung up.

I walked into the kitchen, heels (I always wore heels to work now, not wanting to look sloppy) echoing on the linoleum floor. I poured myself a glass of water and sat at my kitchen table in front of a framed photograph, left by the previous tenant, of a beech forest in winter. If I didn't have Sally, I had no one. Frank and Eric thought I was standoffish and weird, I thought Baxter was weird, my mother believed I'd abandoned my principles, and my old anatomy partner, who'd had a two-year crush on me, had written me a letter telling me I should get therapy to overcome my "fear of intimacy." And now Mrs. Sidebottham was dead. Suddenly I saw my whole career in front in me, years of work and fatigue and encouragement, and the patients dying just the same. All dying, every one. No matter what I'd do, I couldn't save them.

Well, that's life, I thought. It ends. And that's friendship: every friendship has its wobbly moments. Live with it, I told myself. Get used to it. I remembered Sally years before in the car driving west, swirling her hand in that chaotic gesture, saying from now on the deaths would be easier. And I had a true friend, right? Yes, one true friend. A friend of immeasurable value. Because who else but Sally could ever love my prickly nugget of a soul?

SALLY MET HER HUSBAND FIRST. She met him that autumn in a disco. His name was Flavio, age twenty-nine, born in Spain and raised in Israel, South America, and Hong Kong. His father was an importer; Flavio worked in the family business.

"A disco? You were at a disco?" In 1980 there were still discos.

She went there in the evening sometimes, with people from work. She even danced, did I believe that?

"Wow," I said. So Sally was friendly with people from work. I felt a stab of jealousy. "Does this Flavio look like that guy I danced with that time we drove to Tijuana?"

Sally laughed, almost giddily. "He's not disreputable, he's handsome!" I could almost feel the heat of her flushing cheeks through the receiver.

"I'm eager to meet him," I said. "Flavio. I can't imagine."

"You can't imagine," Sally eagerly agreed.

I flew out. He was better and worse than I expected. He was obscenely good-looking, like some TV star almost too perfect to make it to the big screen. He looked as though he had been worked on: nose fixed, hair coiffed, an exercise trainer coaxing the shape of his rear. He had an accent, and a sidelong stare well aware of its effect. Dark hair, olive skin, blue eyes. This was before colored contacts. I told Sally that if he were a dog, he'd be Best of Show.

"Even in Los Angeles they stare," Sally confided. "People come right up to him: Are you an actor? Should I know you? I've never been around someone physically beautiful, and it's fascinating. The beautiful do have an effect."

"Doesn't it make you, like"—I hesitated, not wanting to be unkind—"jealous?"

"Last week a woman asked me if I was his publicist."

"The nerve."

"I said no, I'm his girlfriend. That shut her up. Then I gave her my card. And I'm his lawyer too, I said."

Sally had never been beautiful, but now she was close. Her hair in its customary wedge had a new sheen, her eyes danced, even her teeth seemed radiant. She looked like one of those girls on the cover of a fitness magazine trotting along with a bicycle, brimming with youth and health. Next to her I looked tired and hard. Like a waitress, maybe, or a night clerk at a twenty-four-hour gas station.

Good breeding stock, I thought. They could have gorgeous children.

But Flavio made me nervous. Talking to him, I was always conscious of his looks, of my looks, of trying not to stare at him, not to flirt with him, to act natural. So of course I was never natural. I remember one afternoon especially, walking along the sidewalk in Venice. Sally stopped to look in a T-shirt shop, and Flavio and I moved on. He was talking about something harmless, his sister who lived in London and dreamed of meeting Lady Diana Spencer, whom she was sure the Prince would marry, because Lady Diana had the only good hair in London. Ah, I teased Flavio, how did those Londoners cope? I looked behind for Sally; we'd gotten too far away from her. Did I perm my hair? Flavio asked, or were my waves...natural? He might have gestured to my head, he might have actually reached for my hair and touched it. Still, the closeness of his hand made me breathless.

There was a crowd around a street comedian, and I moved into it. Flavio followed. More people came, pushing Flavio and me closer together. I saw people—both men and women—glance at Flavio. The ordinary-looking ones eyed me with curiosity, even despair. The more attractive ones looked right past me, daring Flavio to look back. The comedian was raunchy. I wasn't sure how much Flavio, with his charmingly limited English, understood. It was warm. I felt like I could faint.

"What is 'come'?" Flavio asked.

It was too much. He was playing with me. He was playing with everyone: Sally, me, Sally's parents, Aunt Ruby, Uncle Freddie. Suddenly I hated him, his looks, his confidence, the cockiness that made him dare to ask such a question in "innocence." "We've got to find Sally," I said, pushing back out through the crowd, willing Sally into my line of vision.

"Flavio!" Sally was waving. "Clare! Look at this cute T-shirt I found for Daddy!"

The T-shirt was gray, with a pseudo-academic seal: PSYCHOTIC STATE.

Flavio smiled warily. "Oh, this is a joke," he said.

"WHAT DO YOU THINK of him?" I asked Aunt Ruby.

"Ooh, isn't he adorable? I could just eat him up. But I have to say, he isn't the young man I would have picked for Sally. I thought she'd find a *nice* Jewish boy. Maybe a dentist. Or one of those little urologists, they always dress nice and neat. But this one..." Aunt Ruby waggled her eyebrows suggestively.

"Sally wants something better," Sid cut in. "She's not like you, Ruby. She'd never settle."

"Freddie's a fine husband," Aunt Ruby retorted. "You can just stop about Freddie."

Ben, passing through the room, grabbed a handful of pistachios from a bowl. "You talking about Flavio again? All I can say is, guy looks like a fruit to me."

It was impossible to look at him—the perfectly tousled hair, the cheekbones, the very white whites of his eyes—without getting a clear sense of his sexual worth, a disquietingly transactional vision of his relationships with other people. So just what did Sally have? Was she that charming, that smart, that rich? She was my best friend, but I'd never thought she was that ... what? That valuable?

Could I ever capture a man like Flavio? Would he ever glance from Sally to me and think: "But wait, I am with the wrong woman"? I had fantasies about him. He knocked on the door of the guest room late at night, he pulled me off the sidewalk into an alley behind a Dumpster and pressed me up against a brick wall.

"Are you sleeping with him, at least?"

"I made a mistake with Timbo," Sally answered with charming obliquity, both she and I remembering that not sleeping with Timbo had once been her mistake. She gave me a coy smile. "I'm a quick learner."

"MAYBE SHE'LL MARRY HIM." Sid and I sat in his family room drinking brandy. I enjoyed drinking brandy with Sid. It made me feel fully adult.

"Maybe," I agreed. "You think he's quality?"

"He looks good, he's Jewish. He's got money." Sid shrugged. "Hard to say. What's quality? But then again, what's not to like?"

I laughed.

"What about this guy you're seeing, this former anatomy partner of yours. You going to marry him?"

"Nope," I answered quickly, thrilled as ever by Sid's blunt questions. "We're splitting up."

"Why?"

"I'm not in love with him."

"What do you need love for? You tell me this kid's from a nice family, he's going to med school, he's ambitious. What's not to like? He
good in bed?"

I shrugged. "Creditable."

"What the hell, Clare, why not marry him? You're old enough."
Sid waved his snifter. "Listen, marriage is an arrangement. This love
stuff is way overrated. I'm not kidding. I'll tell you something, I've
never loved Esther."

I gulped a sip of brandy.

"It's true!" Sid threw his hands out, the bowl of the snifter balanced
on his fingertips. "You ask her. It's no secret. Of course, we don't talk
about it, it's not something a woman wants to hear, but I certainly
don't love her. It's funny, you know, I could say she's a good wife and
mother, but"—he gave a short laugh—"you know her. She's a nice
woman, but she's vague. I met her at a dance party at the Brooklyn
JCC, has Sally told you that? She was beautiful. Beautiful. And high-
class, sure; her father sold paintings to the Carnegies. You know what
we talked about that first night? Nuns. They fascinated her."

I nodded. The cruelty of what he was saying started to creep in on
me, like dampness seeping through a coat. I wondered if Esther, in the
kitchen, could hear him. I pictured her opening the freezer door, hiding behind the noise of the compressor.

"Because, you know, her father used to sell Catholic art. Those
Mother-of-God paintings, you've seen those. Esther had been all over
Europe with her daddy. Any of those broomstick-up-the-ass intellectuals could have gotten her, but I got her instead." Sid glittered with
self-satisfaction. "And you know why?" He leaned over the arm of his
big chair confidentially, looked up at me with a crooked smile. I
braced myself, fearful that he was about to confide some sexual secret.
"She thought I was a genius."

"A genius!" I made the mistake of laughing.

"You don't think I'm a genius? Well, maybe not a genius, but you
have to admit I'm pretty smart. I've gotten places. Look at this house.
This is a big house, right? And we're not in Idaho, where an acre of

land is two cents and a piss in the wind. We're talking real estate here. How'd I do it? You ever think of that? I told you where I came from. I grew up in a tenement, I got five cents for shining the neighbor's shoes, I dropped out of high school and worked for the kosher butcher." Sid set his snifter on the table, undid the top button of his shirt, reached in to scratch his neck. "Listen, you heard of niche marketing? You know what that is? Targeting a product to a certain group. Finding out just what people want and giving it to them. Lots of little groups, lots of products. Strawberry chewing gum for the strawberry lovers, licorice chewing gum, spearmint... you get the idea. Listen, I invented niche marketing. Or maybe I didn't invent it, but I was the first one to apply it to my field."

I wasn't sure I completely followed him. "You mean to distributing magazines?"

"Distributing, publishing. You talked about it yourself, all those magazines you saw for fishermen. See, I go for the small groups, the special interests." I pictured again all the magazines I'd seen at newsstands: *Bodybuilding Today* or *Youngstown After Dark,* topics that apparently appealed to someone. "I'm proud of my little business." Sid smiled at me, his teeth gleaming. For the first time I wondered if the teeth were fake. "Of course, it's not so little."

"WE'RE COMPATIBLE," Flavio said, pouring me more wine from a carafe. The lukewarmness of this declaration startled me: he wasn't saying "We're in love" or "We're soul mates," things I'd heard Sally say about him. Sally was in the restroom. The restaurants he and Sally frequented were different from the ones she and I went to: these places were young, funky. The waiters and waitresses sneered and had aggressively stylish haircuts. They made all Sally's and my restaurants seem out of date, faded, Sid-ish. But Flavio seemed right at home in these places.

There was a fussiness to Flavio, I noticed, which relieved me because I'd always found fussiness unattractive. He poured wine in an

overcontrolled way. Some—not all—of his shirts had darts. He wore
belts tipped with metal ornaments and large watches with all sorts of
dials.

"I have no home, you see? And Sally"—Flavio lisped slightly on her
name, it came out "Sa-wee"—"has too much home." The remark startled me, not that I agreed with it, but it did suggest resources of intro-
spection and judgment I wouldn't have guessed Flavio had. What do
you know, I remember noting, surprised, the guy thinks. When to
look at him, you'd believe he never thought at all.

"IT'S SIMPLE," Sally said. "I want him."

"You mean sexually? Like lust?"

"Of course, but not just that, I want *him*. All of him, all the time. I
want the two of us to be a unit. I want to marry him."

Wasn't this the same thing she'd said about Timbo? She wanted to
be part of a unit.

There was something in Sally's face that I was to recognize later in
the faces of athletes before a competition, a ferocious resolution, an intense concentration that said *I will not be denied.* It was a frightening
look, an intensely private look, as if I and any other outsider were mere
impediments.

"Sally, you just met him," I objected weakly.

"When you know, you know."

"Is he quality?" I asked, half joking, and Sally cast me a look of such
disappointment that I vowed never to criticize Flavio again.

"SALLY'S LIKE THE MOST spiritual person I know," Sally's
cousin Daphne confided.

"Spiritual?" I asked. This adjective had never come to me in thinking about Sally.

Daphne was working part-time in housewares at a department
store. She wore earrings dangling with tiny pots and pans. "She's a very

old soul, don't you think? Someone like her's not going to get waylaid by lust. I think Flavio's a pretty old soul too, but with men it's harder to tell. I can't look at them with a pure spirit eye. That sex stuff"— Daphne wrinkled her nose—"it gets in the way." She held out a skillet for me to inspect. "See those concentric circles? They distribute the heat. You won't get any scorching, guaranteed."

"Maybe I should buy one," Sally said over my shoulder, returning from a foray into linens.

"Don't you dare!" Daphne scolded. She swung around and thwacked the skillet down. "I'm getting you a whole set for your wedding." And she did.

IN THE PHOTOS from Sally's wedding, I hate to say it, I look smarmy. I'm grinning too much, my arm over the back of a chair is calculated, overrelaxed. I'm standing too close to Sid, to Aunt Ruby, my head is cocked in a sickeningly perky way. I was Sally's maid of honor in a hotel wedding with over four hundred guests. The wedding was actually scheduled to coincide with my spring break. I went to all the parties. I stayed with Sally at her parents' house. I drove the dresses to the hotel with Aunt Ruby, tossing the keys to Sid's navy Jaguar to a valet, asking the doorman to reach into the backseat for Sally's gown. While Sally and Flavio and Sid and Esther had discussions with the photographer the day before the wedding, I sat beside the pool with the out-of-town guests. "Patricia," I'd say, gesturing toward one of Sally's young cousins, *"por favor, un helado por la chica."*

"Now what's over that direction?" someone would ask. "Is that the San Joaquin Valley?"

"San Fernando," I'd correct. Every insult I'd felt in being left out of Sally's graduation was canceled ten times over. I was the fifth Rose.

"Twenty thousand dollars if you two just go out on a boat and elope," Sid had said. "Fifty thousand if you don't invite me."

"Daddy!"

"A hundred thousand if you don't tell me until it's over."

"Daddy! That's si-ick!"

"Thank God I only have one daughter. At Ben's wedding I can sit there and drink."

"TO MY BEAUTIFUL, wonderful bride," Flavio said, lifting his glass. It was the dinner for out-of-town guests the evening before the wedding. A modest supper, only seventy or so attendees, held in the private dining room at a dark Italian restaurant. I smiled at Sally. She reached across the table and touched my hand. Sid was smiling, Esther was smiling. And Flavio, standing over Sally: I had to admit he looked sincere.

"God," Daphne said loopily, her long hair even bigger than usual, curling over the tops of her arms, "doesn't it make you want to get married?" I didn't even answer. Daphne didn't bother me on this trip. She was a bridesmaid, true, but I was maid of honor.

FLAVIO'S FATHER AND SID both approved of nuns. Sid pointed out with pride that two nuns, former teachers of Sally's, would attend the wedding. "You must introduce me," Flavio's father said. He was short and lined, like a thin Aristotle Onassis, with long tobacco-stained fingers. He'd been hidden in an Italian convent during World War II, and his lifelong business was imports-exports; after dessert one evening, he swept from his pocket a wooden box containing cigars that were really, truly Cuban. "You're kidding," Sid said, examining the little gold band. "You smuggle these from El Salvador or something?" Flavio's father only smiled.

The mother was blond and glamorous, with a peculiar lisp that was either an accent or a speech impediment. She was Shpanish, she said, and when I looked blank, she spoke louder: from Shpain. I volunteered to speak Spanish with her. "I like English," she said. "Ish more practical." She nodded at Flavio and Sally, who were cooing at each other down the table. "Shpanish ish the language of looove."

I got such a kick out of that. Unlike other lines, this one for me maintains its innocence. About Flavio's mother I remember little else.

"We're delighted with her," Flavio's father said at one point. "We were not sure Flavio would marry."

"That's impossible!" Daphne cried. "He's so handsome."

"We are delighted with her," Flavio's father repeated.

At some point I started wondering exactly what the export-import dealings were—if Flavio's father was an arms dealer, for example, or a shipper of plutonium or chemicals, or a smuggler of drugs. "What exactly do you import?" I asked him flat out at the wedding reception, where he and I, at the head table, were separated only by his wife. The wife raised her eyebrows and leaned back, clearing the space between us for his answer.

"Have you heard of tchotchkes?" Flavio's father said.

I had. It was one of those colorful and useful Yiddish words I'd learned from Sid. "You mean knickknacks?" I asked. "Little souvenir-y things?" To impress him with my knowledge, I gave examples: ashtrays stamped with pictures of Niagara Falls; dome paperweights you turned over to sprinkle snow.

"Exactly," Flavio's father said. "That is my business. My business is tchotchkes. I have factories in Taiwan and Hong Kong."

"Oh my," I said, chuckling. I chuckled so much I could tell I was exasperating him, but because I was drunk, I didn't care.

A bathtub-size vat of shrimp. Mountains of flowers. Four hundred and fifteen rented chairs slipcovered in black or white with contrasting bows, and three open bars. Two ice sculptures, the larger a ship with sails on a wave-tossed sea.

"What's the ship stand for?" a short man with a cigarette holder asked Sid. "That the boat your grandparents came over on?"

His wife elbowed him. "I like it," she assured Sid. "Something different from the usual swan."

There was an orchestra in the main dining room and a string quartet in the foyer, not to mention the roving mariachi band from East L.A. whose members seemed to be mysteriously changing, a band that

Ben, in charge of the music, had insisted upon as *auténtico*. And in the center of this was Sally—no, she wasn't in the center, she was whispering to Flavio behind the potted bougainvillea, she was nodding as Esther gesticulated at some guest, she was standing very close to me watching the guests pile up hors d'oeuvres. "This is a big wedding," she said in a wondering tone.

"You should have gone for the boat."

Sally laughed and shook her head. "You know Daddy!"

And the thing was, I thought I did.

Ben had a friend at the wedding, a young man named Ray, who wore a poorly fitting suit and lank bangs that half covered his eyes. As Daphne and I stood waiting for Sally and Flavio to cut the wedding cake, Ben and Ray were nudging each other and laughing. "We can tell about Daphne," Ray said, "but what are you, Clare?"

"I'm the maid of honor," I said.

Ben and Ray broke into a fresh round of guffaws. "No, not your role in the wedding, essential as it undoubtedly is," Ray said. "We mean, what are you? Homo? Hetero? Bi?"

"Hetero," I said quickly. I stood on my tiptoes to get a glimpse of Sally, hoping Flavio didn't shove cake in her face. "How old are you, anyway?"

"God," Daphne said, sighing, "you can just see it. Soul mates."

Ray jutted out his chin and shook the bangs from his face. "I'm sixteen. I've, like, got my license and everything."

Sixteen. The same age as Ben. People definitely grew up faster in California. "What about you?" I asked.

"Oh, Ray's definitely gay," Ben said. "Gay Ray." He turned to Ray for confirmation. "Right?"

Some older people around us were wrinkling their foreheads and inching away. Daphne frowned at Ray and shushed him. At Oberlin my junior year, I had participated in a "happening" that was actually an art class project. My classmates and I stood in a soccer field and knotted ourselves into various positions, and people who walked by us looked both curious and uncomfortable, although I felt cool and unthreatened. Ray and Ben reminded me of myself doing that project, and I thought of the giddy superiority they must feel.

"I don't know what I am," Ben said.

"You like guys, face it, you're a guy guy," Ray said. Sally and Flavio were motionless, like ornaments, facing the cake, Flavio behind Sally with his left arm around her shoulder, his right hand clutching her wrist. Sally held the knife. I realized they were posing.

"But I like girls too," Ben said.

Ray giggled. "Maybe you're a lesbian."

"I hope he shoves it in her face," Daphne said. "That's so cute when they do that."

Flashbulbs clicked. Sally turned her face to Flavio and smiled. "Excuse me, guys," I said, moving away.

Later, Sally and Flavio were dancing, the other occupants of the head table had drifted off to mingle, and I was the only person sitting when suddenly a woman was standing beside me, juggling her plate and a drink and chatting away. She was wearing a straw hat with feathers sticking over its brim. I missed the beginning of what she said. "They're not all blue, but most of them are," she continued.

The wedding, like the slipcovered chairs, was black and white with rose accents, and it wasn't until years later that I had any idea what this woman was talking about. At the time I thought she was an ingrate, making to me, a member of the wedding, snide remarks about the reception and its cost.

"I guess that's where the money is!" she said cheerfully, her immense head bobbing. Her nose resembled a beak. I was tempted to reach up and dislodge a feather.

"And if you think about it," she went on, "what is it but entertainment, and what's wrong with that? This whole town's built on entertainment."

"Excuse me," I said. "Little girls' room!"—wondering if she'd recognize this as an insult.

There must be lots of money in tchotchkes, I thought in the bathroom. Two rich kids: a marriage of tchotchkes and magazines. My wedding would be nothing like this. Maybe I'd elope to Las Vegas, save myself the ignominy of a church chapel and a tacky reception hall. Magazines and tchotchkes. It made you shake your head. And yet how better to make money than on things people used every day? I looked around for ideas. Toilet paper! Lipstick! Hairpins! There was a purity to it. It wasn't like money made on cattle futures or loan-sharking. It was respectable money. My hair, which I'd had tied up, had half fallen around my shoulders. I hoped I'd look presentable in the wedding pictures. Now I looked looped. "You little alky, you," I said to myself in the mirror, wagging a finger. As I walked back out the bathroom door, I fell off my shoes.

THE NIGHT BEFORE the wedding, Sally and I lay in the dark in her bedroom and talked. She'd thought she'd never get over Timbo, that she would be a kind of premature widow, an excellent lawyer consumed only by her cases. She'd written off her whole sexual being. And then, out of the blue....

"He's so good," she said, propping herself up on her elbow. "Can't you see how good he is? I told him about Timbo, and he cried. He didn't laugh, he cried!" She sighed. "Am I lucky. I'm blessed! There's no other word for it. I'm blessed." She reached out and touched my arm. "You'll be blessed someday too."

I thought about my former anatomy partner, who'd told me as we stood in line for a movie that he might someday love me more than his own mother. "Your mother?" I'd answered, astonished. "I'm competing with your mother?" I'd had to let him down, and fast.

I thought about Dan, my chem-professor lover, who, according to a former French major Sally had run into, was still married, still teaching in Cleveland, and now had two children.

Sally fell asleep, her breath coming calm and easy. It impressed me that, on the eve of her wedding, she fell asleep before I did. She seemed to be suffering nothing; no anxiety or regrets or self-censure, when here I was seething with all of them. It struck me once again how different Sally and I were. At Sally's inner core there was a kernel of faith, while at mine there was a kernel of anger. In a funny way we complemented each other. "I love you," she always said over the phone. And she did. I loved her too. I was not an endless drag on her, I was a help. I kept her from too much faith. Thinking this, I finally fell asleep.

SALLY AND FLAVIO were still dancing. Arthur Murray had given them their money's worth. At one point I collapsed on a chair beside the dance floor, and there they were six feet from me, entwined, barely moving. They didn't see me. Sally reached her right hand up and cupped the side of Flavio's face, murmuring something. Flavio dipped his face into her hand and nuzzled her, his hand moving over her breast. She moved closer and he kissed her hair, and then she pulled back a bit and looked up at him, her face so open and radiant that tears came to my eyes. What a creep I was to doubt them. They rotated, and Flavio's face came into view, his head cocked and wistful, his eyes gazing at some inward picture. I thought at that moment I could read his mind, that he was thinking of their future together. I stood and slipped quickly away before they turned again and Sally could see me.

I stayed for three days after the wedding, helping the guests gather up their belongings, driving people to the airport, sitting around in the evening watching videos with Sid and Esther. I hoped I hadn't made a fool of myself at the end of the reception, doing some sort of jitterbug with Flavio's cousin, but no one mentioned it. I didn't even remember Flavio and Sally's leaving the reception for their honeymoon.

Who would I visit now in Los Angeles? Where would I stay? When Sid drove me to the airport, he hugged me—something he'd never done before—and as my plane moved off from the gate, I was startled to see him waving from the waiting-room window.

IN THE MONTHS AFTER the wedding, I got postcards, an occasional airmail letter, a call when Sally and Flavio got back to Los Angeles, which she at least considered their home. She quit her new job, which to me was astonishing, since I knew how focused Sally was. I wanted to ask her if she'd lost her ambition, but I didn't dare. "I'm a wife," I imagined her saying, chastising me in a surprised tone. I gathered that she considered the energy she threw into wifedom equivalent to the energy she'd thrown into law school, although I never asked her this directly. I couldn't; I never saw her. Her wifedom was certainly not conventional, no dinners at home or redecorating, no children or carpools. The places they went were amazing, and for what seemed to me extravagantly extended periods—six weeks, two months—or decadently short ones. They once flew to London for a wedding and were back in three days. I got missives, words from the front: Hong Kong was very very busy. In Paraguay, bugs the size of matchbox cars skittered across the sidewalks, smuggling was the major industry, and everything was named for the dictator. Morocco was bustling and calm, relaxing and sinister, and the people they stayed with were Americans who dressed in Arab clothes. The Nepalese were cheerful and welcoming, although the altitude gave Sally headaches. Everywhere there was some business, everywhere Flavio or his father or his cousin had contacts, and they stayed at people's houses or at the company apartments and visited English-speaking clubs and attended far-flung bar mitzvahs. Somewhere in this time I heard the word "Eurotrash," and I wondered if Flavio was that. No, I thought, he seemed to work hard, whatever he did. Sally said he'd often have meetings all day, and she was stuck with the wives and daughters or, better, by herself at a hotel, which she could use either as a base to go out and explore a city or as a retreat. Their life was unimaginable, beyond glamour. I bought a world atlas. I imagined going on a trip with them to see what it was like. I told Sally once—when she called me from Rio on my birthday, the connection eerily clear—I'd love to simply *be* her for three weeks. "It's busy," she said—not the adjective I'd expected, and the precision of Sally's adjectives was something I admired.

WE AGREED LATER that it had been lost time for us, those years she was with Flavio.

"Years?" Sally said. "I wasn't with Flavio for years. We were married twenty months."

I swore it had to be longer.

"Wouldn't I know?" Sally said. "It was twenty months. Twenty months and two hundred thousand miles. Don't you remember, I got married in March 1981, less than a year after I got out of law school, which was right before you started your last year in med school and met Mark Petrello? And you were only married a few months. You were through with him before Flavio's and my first anniversary."

"Can that be true?"

"Sure it's true. On our only anniversary, Flavio and I were in Los Angeles for once, and we ate out at Trumps, and I remember telling Flavio your getting married and divorced seemed like a dream to me, because I hadn't even met your husband."

"Well, your life seemed like a dream to me. Every time I opened my mailbox, you were somewhere different."

"One hundred and eight planes in a year. I kept track. I wrote you to keep myself sane. It seems like a dream to me now, especially with, well, especially now that Ben—"

I hurried to interrupt her. "I wonder what happened to Flavio's sister. You think she's met Princess Di yet, now that Di's come down in the world?"

THE ONLY OTHER PERSON from college with whom I kept in contact was Margaret. She'd gone to chef school after graduation but found that the "important" restaurants didn't want to hire women, so she'd gone to work at a head shop in Cambridge and pursued a degree in library science. She stopped to see me as she drove from Massachusetts westward to a new home and job. She stayed with me three nights, bringing with her in her maroon Gremlin two cats, innumerable plants, a futon, and a boyfriend named Roger. "What's his story?" I whispered as he skulked off.

Margaret shook her head. "I know what you're thinking. I myself thought wow, this fellow looks like Charles Manson! And I was in Guatemala for Charles Manson. But he's really very gentle, Clare. It's just..." She pursed her lips and looked around her. "Vietnam, Clare. In a word, Vietnam."

He hit her, I'm sure; she had a bruise over her right cheekbone, which she blamed on an open door. She referred to their twisty rings made of wire coated with colored plastic as "commitment symbols"; they each wore it on their left hand.

They were headed for Salina, Kansas. Windy, Margaret said. Sort of desolate. Did I remember *Bonnie and Clyde*? That kind of landscape. She hoped to find a farmhouse to live in, because having people on top of him drove Roger crazy. She'd be working at a Pioneer Museum, cataloging papers and artifacts. And what would Roger do during the day when she was gone? Margaret frowned. "I think he'll try his hand at making furniture. He'll miss me. It'll be hard." She looked at me with a modest smile. "He says I keep the wolves from his door."

———

SALLY AND FLAVIO BOUGHT a condo in Los Angeles, a place I visited exactly once, shortly after their first and only anniversary and after my divorce. I was already depressed, and their condo depressed me more. It was in Brentwood, allegedly a posh area, but it had stuccoed walls and an outside staircase, and the number 5 in their neighbor's address marker hung upside down. There were a lot of runners in their complex, people passing their windows wearing sleeveless T-shirts and headbands and fancy sneakers. A neighbor's car had a bumper sticker that mystified me: MY OTHER CAR IS UP MY NOSE. I asked Sally about it. "Cocaine," she said. I laughed and shook my head. It seemed like the only appropriate response.

One night we ate dinner at Sid and Esther's. The food was excellent, better than anyone's mood. "Tell me about Nepal!" Esther said. Sally talked at length, but Flavio sat silent and hunched over, peering down the table.

We had the double-layer pecan pie for dessert. "Tell me about Hong Kong!" Esther said. "I've always wanted to visit Hong Kong." I got up to use the bathroom. Ben hadn't eaten with us; he and a gang of his friends were in the kitchen. Esther, Sally had told me, let them smoke pot in the garage, so she would know what Ben was doing. "Let's get high and go to Chuck E. Cheese," I heard someone in the kitchen say, and then there was a general movement toward the door.

NOW, ABOUT MY HUSBAND. His name was Mark Petrello, and he was an emergency room attending doctor, a hotshot who had finished the residency program and been hired on to teach. He was thin, about two inches shorter than me, and he strutted around like a bantam rooster. He reminded me of Prince, the singer, who was popular at the time; in fact, before I fell in love with Mark, I referred to him in the ER as "the Princeling," a remark everyone who worked there found wildly amusing.

We fell for each other in July, the first month of my final year in med school. I was doing a month in the ER, and a major head trauma came in. The patient had fallen off a platform and landed in some kind of industrial shredder; basically, he had no face. I had no desire to see this and was scurrying out of the trauma room when Mark Petrello, who was in charge of the case, commanded, "I need you." I thought he meant me and turned around, realizing too late that he was talking to a paramedic, and then I was simply mesmerized, standing there, looking at Mark Petrello at the head of the bed, the bloody not-a-face in front of him, realizing that he was going to try to save this guy, wondering how in the world he'd do it. The first thing you do in resuscitating someone is to establish an airway, either through the mouth (this patient's mouth was unrecognizable) or through the nose (the nose was gone). What would Mark Petrello do? Desperation welled up inside me: even the Princeling could fail. But he extended his arm in front of him and pointed, and then he really did look like Prince striking a pose. Only Mark Petrello said, "Trach kit."

Twenty seconds later, the guy was breathing through a hole sliced in his neck. Mark Petrello had saved a life. I melted. I knew this was the sort of moment ER docs like him lived for, that he'd just done what any quick-thinking doc would do—he'd been prepared for it, even; the radioed message from the ambulance had told him it would need to be done. Still, it moved me. Sexually, I mean. From that moment, Mark Petrello was my man. And, boy, did we know it.

We were married in less than eight weeks. I think we got married so fast because we were both afraid the other would get away, or our feelings would go away, and Mark's very job, day after day with the almost dead and dying, gave him a sense of perpetual urgency. We got married at City Hall in September 1981. Mark and I were holding hands. We'd brought no witnesses, no family. All that mattered was each other. On the stairs up to the judge's chamber, Mark pushed me against the banister and kissed me. My hands were all over him. The judge had the decency to look amused. His secretary was our witness. "Good luck to you both," the judge said, shaking our hands. He told me I was a radiant bride, probably a generous comment. I was a hot bride.

We checked into a downtown hotel and didn't emerge for thirty-six hours. I missed a rheumatology clinic, an allergy clinic, and a tutorial on lupus; I also missed (as I pointed out to Mark, indignantly) several meals. Since I'd met him, all my appetites had returned. "So eat me, baby," he kept saying, stroking my hair. "Eat me."

His idea of fun could be strange. He and his ER buddies rented gory movies to laugh at their special effects. "God," they'd say, "another rare levo-liver"—meaning a liver on the left side of the body, instead of on the right. "Oh no!" they'd shout. "Another Beefheart Syndrome!"

"Don't you see enough of that blood-and-guts stuff at work?" I asked, incredulous. Sally, who still read the "Movie Guide for Puzzled Parents" in *McCall's*, would die if she were forced to watch these movies.

Mark slumped on the couch, the remote control slipped between his legs. "Sick, isn't it? You like being married to a sicko, sweetheart?"

We consolidated our things into his apartment. I dropped all my inquiries to residency programs in California, because I intended to stay right where I was. And there was no question that, as Mark Petrello's wife, I would be admitted by the internal medicine residency at the university.

Maybe in the future, Mark and I both thought, maybe after my residency, we'd move to California. Mark would be a published hotshot then, a valuable commodity for any trauma center, and I could work some reasonable hours at Kaiser, leaving me time to raise kids. Mark had a friend in California who was an hour from the mountains, an hour from the desert, and right beside the sea. That sounded idyllic. Certainly not a landscape we'd find in Ohio.

I CALLED MY MOTHER after we'd been married three days. Satisfyingly, she wept. "But you're my only daughter!" she said. "Couldn't you have let me be there?"

I called Sally a week later, when I knew she'd be back in Los Angeles from another trip to Hong Kong. "How was Hong Kong?" I said.

"Okay," she said. "Hectic. How are you?"

"I'm married!" I said. "Just like you!"

It was only after I got off the phone that I wondered at myself. *I'm married, just like you!* What a goofy thing to say. Was that really why I'd gotten married, to be just like Sally? And if not, why had I gotten married, exactly, and in such a dramatic, precipitous way? Why wasn't I changing my name?

THE FIRST HUMILIATION with Mark was when I started rethinking trimethoprim sulfa. Trimethoprim sulfa (trade names

Bactrim or Septra) was and is the antibiotic you use almost instinctively to treat a urinary tract infection. It works, but it's not always a harmless medicine. "I saw someone else with a Bactrim rash this week," I told Mark. "And Pete Hemphill had a patient whose white count dropped to eight hundred. Did you know Bactrim elevates serum creatinine? It decreases the tubular secretion of creatinine, so in a way it's artifactual, but—"

"God," Mark exploded, "you really are a baby flea, aren't you?" Internists have the reputation for being obsessed with minutiae. Other docs sometimes call them "fleas"—the last ones off a dying dog.

I was furious. "You knew that," I said. I walked around our apartment, attacking the blinds with a dust cloth. "You knew that." I wanted to stir up dust. I sneezed and my eyes watered. "So what do you want me to be? A stupid ER cowboy like you?"

The next humiliation: I was looking at our water bill, which for some reason came addressed to Dr. and Mrs. Mark Petrello, not to Dr. Mark Petrello like our usual bills, and it struck me that we should have a joint checking account.

"Why?" Mark said. "I can pay the bills. You don't have any money."

That was true. I was still in med school; I wouldn't have any money until I started my residency next July. "But we're married," I said. "Married people have joint accounts. It's a married thing to do."

Mark gave me a cold look. "Are you going to want alimony too?"

HE WAS A GOOD ER doc, he told me once, because he was always thinking about what he should do next. Let's say he had a woman in ventricular fibrillation, the heart wiggling like a bag of worms. First, of course, Mark would shock her, then shock her again, and in the meantime he'd be running in bretylium, and he'd be thinking in the back of his mind that the woman could go flatline, in which case Mark would give her atropine, then epi, then maybe an external pacer, and there was always the possibility after a pulse was restored that the woman would be hypotensive, in which case Mark would run in fluid, then dopamine, then levophed, then if that didn't work, Mark could even stick a needle in the heart, drain off any fluid that might be compressing it. A whole tree of possibilities grew in Mark's brain in seconds, and one of the branches, surely, was the branch he would need to climb. He could make decisions quickly. He didn't have doubts and regrets. If A didn't work, he'd try B. If B didn't work, he'd try C. Et cetera. "What if you get to X-Y-Z?" I asked. "What if you can't think of anything else?"

He laughed. "Sweetheart, haven't you heard of death?"

THE FINAL HUMILIATION was an ER nurse, Leslie, who lifted weights and ran and liked to talk about high-protein drinks and the gun she kept in her car. Mark slept with her probably twice a week. I knew it was twice a week because about that often Mark came home smelling like lavender. Why such a hip chick wore lavender, I'll never know.

We were all together at the ER staff Christmas party. There was a loud band, but I wasn't dancing. I was drinking. The Princeling was dancing all over the place. He danced with most of the ER nurses, then with a homely girl from transcription. Leslie the Lavender Lady was standing near my table.

"Are you going to dance with the Prince?" I asked. I was drunk.

"Maybe I should," Leslie said, "maybe he needs a faster woman."

My hips and thighs—always my problem areas—seemed to get bigger and heavier until I was simply a lump sitting in the chair, and it didn't surprise me at all when skinny little Mark, my sprite, after dancing with Leslie, came over and looked down at me with what could only be contempt. "Clare," he said, "look at you. Have you moved one centimeter since we got here?"

Our marriage lasted six months and sixteen days. I was lucky to get out that fast. I wouldn't have gotten out that fast on Sally's power, because all she did during our phone conversations was listen and sigh, and occasionally throw in a word or two about where she and Flavio had come from or where they were off to.

My oldest brother, Frank, visited for a weekend; he had a new sales job and traveled around the state. Friday night Mark got home late, smelling of lavender. Saturday I worked half the day and Mark, who was supposed to be home with my brother, disappeared. "Gotta do some errands," he called, swinging out the door. He got home hours later with no packages, no explanations.

"You take care of those errands?" Frank asked Mark levelly, and there was a cool eye-to-eye between them.

The next day Mark was working. "Are you sure you want to keep living in this situation?" Frank asked me as we sat in the kitchen eating bagels, and then he infuriated me by saying that no one in my family expected my marriage to last.

"That's because I didn't invite anyone to the wedding," I said.

"No," Frank answered patiently. "It's because you don't sound happy on the phone."

"I sound happy."

"Listen to yourself," Frank said. "Do you sound happy? Even Baxter's worried," he added.

We sat in silence for a while. "Why didn't Baxter tell me if he thought I'd made a mistake?" I finally said.

"You know how you are, Clare," Frank said. "What can anybody tell you?"

It struck me, suddenly, that Mark lived his life the same way he practiced medicine. Single didn't work, so he tried marriage. Marriage didn't work, so he tried Leslie. If not A, B; if not B, C. Those quick decisions, that desperate confidence.

"Honestly, I'm surprised," Frank said. "I never thought you'd listen to me."

Sweetheart, haven't you heard of death?

MARK CAME HOME with news, a tidbit he dropped on me as he twirled his finger through a jar of peanut butter and nibbled from it. "Remember that guy who'd fallen and shredded his face off? You remember him, don't you? It was right when we met."

I felt suddenly sick. This would not be good news. "Sure," I said, sitting down on a kitchen chair.

Mark turned toward the refrigerator. "We got any of that marshmallow cream? You finish it?" He was often like this after work—wired, hungry.

"You know I don't eat that stuff."

"Oh yeah, right, Miss Cottage Cheese." He was coiled over the open fridge, hands braced on one of the shelves. "Anyway, they brought him through in a body wagon today." Deaths at home were brought by van to the emergency room, so a doctor could declare the person dead. "I declared him. Suicide. Guess what he did?"

"I don't want to guess."

"Come on, guess. It was appropriate." Mark opened a bottle of pop and lifted it to his lips.

"He shot himself in the head."

"He shot himself in the face. Right below the chin and pointed up." Mark lifted his finger and jutted out his jaw to illustrate.

"God."

Mark's eyes narrowed. He hated it when I went wimpy; which to him was a kind of moral flaw, a failure of nerve in the face of obstacles. He had often said that he'd want to be alive as a paraplegic, as a retard, as a disembodied head sitting on a table. What happened to the body didn't matter, it was the alive that counted. "*I* don't really understand it," Mark said, pointedly emphasizing the "I." "He was home, he had a mouth, he had an eye left. The plastics people had all kinds of plans for him."

I thought of the guy the way I'd seen him. What kind of plans could the plastic surgeons have? How many operations? What peculiar results? "Maybe he just couldn't stand it anymore."

"Guess not, sweetheart." Mark swung his leg over a chair, wrapped his arms around the back of the chair, and faced me.

"I want a divorce," I said.

For a split second, Mark Petrello looked surprised. Then he took a swig of pop, and in the time it took to lift and lower his bottle, his swagger had come back. "You're right," he said, shrugging. "Sorry."

"Me too," I said.

I don't think I emerged from the marriage much different. A little sadder, maybe, a little more bitter, but not essentially changed. It was years later, when I was a practicing doctor, single again but this time with a new baby, that Mark Petrello made his difference in my life. At that earlier time, I realized only that I'd experienced one of those disastrous marriages people refuse to talk about. I didn't know then that Sally's marriage to Flavio would be the same.

WHEN I WAS VISITING Sally and Flavio just after my first divorce and their only anniversary, Ben Rose hit me with a confession. We were sitting by the pool at Sally and Flavio's apartment when Ben leaned over, whipped off his sunglasses, and looked me in the eye. "Would you think it was awful if I told you I think I'm gay?"

I was so startled by his removing his sunglasses (was that his idea of sincerity? how California) that I'm afraid my response was flip. "Awful you'd tell me, or awful you are?"

Ben blinked. He still looked very young. Although he was almost eighteen, his beard wasn't fully formed, and I often wondered if he really had to shave. "That I am."

"Are you?"

Ben nodded. "I think so."

"I can't say I'm surprised, Ben."

"You're not?"

"No."

"You're really not?"

"No."

"Not a little bit?"

I could see he was disappointed, which irritated me. Did he think that my being "nice," my being from Ohio, precluded any knowledge of the world? "I've always had the notion that normal people can be gay, Ben. I mean, it's always been possible to me that anyone I know could be gay. And on top of that you seem, well, you seem gay." I thought of Ben's friend Ray at Sally's wedding and Ben and Ray's behavior.

Ben frowned and put his sunglasses back on. "I seem gay?"

"The clothes. Your friends. Like Ray at Sally's wedding. Remember, I met him?"

Ben nodded solemnly, brow furrowed. He gazed out over the pool. "I've always wondered how people know," he said.

"People just know." I remembered the bandanna tied on his arm. "It's a style thing, don't you think? And, well, a person has to think that somebody might be gay. It has to cross their mind."

"It doesn't cross Mom and Dad's mind," Ben said, his voice forlorn. He turned to me again. "Can I tell you something else? This is so weird. I don't know if I should tell you. I mean, you're Sally's best friend and all, and . . ."

"What?" I said, shrugging. "I'm open-minded," I said. "I'm almost a doctor. I'm divorced. You can tell me anything, I won't be shocked."

"But this is so weird, man, it's weird. I just realized it myself, and it's so weird." Ben was fidgeting, twisting in his beach chair.

"What? What can be that weird?" I kept my tone light, making sure he'd tell me.

"You know Flavio, Sally's husband? He's gay too."

I WASN'T HAPPY with their apartment. There were objects in it that I blamed on Flavio: a bed with a wrought-iron headboard recycled from an old fence, a triangular table with painted leopard-spotted legs. Hipper-than-thou furniture, Sally used to call it. I remembered the crack she'd made about the parents of Ben's Malibu friend, that their white cat was less a pet than an accessory. And now she had a lava lamp in her living room. Isn't it interesting, Aunt Ruby said, laughing, when I mentioned it, love's blind and it's tasteless too. Didn't I know that?

"I never thought I'd see you with a lava lamp," I told Sally.

"Oh"—she rolled her eyes—"it's camp. You know."

Of course I knew. "Did Flavio even have lava lamps where he grew up?" Wherever that was, I was thinking.

"Buenos Aires. We were there two months ago. Sure he did. Buenos Aires is incredibly cosmopolitan. There were stores open at two in the morning."

"Stores full of lava lamps, no doubt."

But Sally didn't laugh. Her marriage, she seemed to be saying, was no laughing matter. When she spoke again, her tone was light but cautionary. "It's a minor compromise. And that's what marriage is about, right? An endless string of accommodation and compromise."

It escaped neither of us that I'd been divorced twenty-nine days.

OF COURSE BEN had no proof. I made sure of that right off, asking for details, confessions, sightings, anything. But there was nothing, only Ben's vague "feelings." "That's a horrible thing to say without proof, Ben," I said. "I hope you don't ever say it to Sally."

"Why is it horrible?" Ben whined. "You're the one who said normal people could be gay."

"Jesus, Ben," I sputtered. "Not normal married people. If you're gay, you should never get married. It's too confusing. You're potentially hurting your mate too much."

Ben sank peevishly into his chair. "He wears very gay-looking shirts."

"He's European!" I burst out. "Or whatever he is. It's a different style."

"You said that was how you could tell. It was a style thing, you said."

I understood, for the first time, how maddening Ben could be. I understood Sid wanting—as he had the day Ben asked about my father disappearing in a Kmart—to strike out at his son.

"SO WHAT DO YOU think of Flavio now?" Daphne asked, blinking, and I wondered if she was the last person in America to wear false eyelashes. Daphne had recently been dumped by a boyfriend. She was in her mid-twenties, still living with Uncle Freddie and Aunt Ruby.

"He's okay," I said. "Actually, he reminds me of Chad in *The Ambassadors*." This was true—I'd never trusted Chad—but I immediately regretted saying it, because why in the world would Daphne know anything about Henry James? It was surprising enough that I did.

Daphne blinked again. I felt guilty. "*The Ambassadors* is a novel by Henry James," I explained. "Chad is a character with lots of charm."

"I don't read," Daphne said sadly.

"Oh, Daphne, only English majors read Henry—"

"Self-help," Aunt Ruby broke in, "you read self-help."

"See?" I said, trying to bolster her. "That's better than reading pornography or something."

Daphne broke into a high-pitched laugh. "Not on this side of the family!"

I wondered if Uncle Freddie's family was into pornography.

"It's all videos anymore, that's what Sid says," Aunt Ruby announced. "It's a different thing, what people will watch in the privacy of their own homes." She wiggled her fingers in the air beside her head. "He's always thinking, that brother of mine."

I tapped my head with my index finger, imitating Sid's habitual gesture. "He always has a plan."

I STARTED LOOKING for clues. First, the money. "I don't know, some friend of his," Sally said. The plan was to buy a block of apartments in Punta del Este, a resort area in Uruguay, then sell them in Europe as time-shares. South America was a hot destination for Europeans. "It's a big investment," Sally said. "I'd have to talk to Daddy about pulling something out of my trust fund. I asked him, 'Can't we at least go down and look at the apartments?' But Flavio doesn't want to go, which is ridiculous, because we go everywhere. He's got some old Israeli friend down there, and Flavio thinks this friend could manage the property." Sally shot me a skeptical look. "Right now this

friend is maître d' at a beach club. It's not like he has management experience. And you know how these real estate deals can be."

I didn't know, but I nodded. "And you'd be absentee landlords," I
pointed out.

"Extremely absentee. I'll tell you, it makes me glad Flavio has money
of his own, because if he didn't, I might worry about why he married
me." Sally's matter-of-factness surprised me, but she'd always been a matter-of-fact girl. The interesting thing was the way she said it, as casually as
if she were mentioning the threat of a plane crashing into her house.

"I'M VERY AWARE of compromise," Sally said. "I never told anyone this, but Flavio had a drug problem."

My head shot up. Sally nodded. "Before we got married. That was
part of the deal: if I married him, he had to give up drugs." She looked
at me calmly. "And he has."

"What did he do?"

"Mostly cocaine. He was a significant user. He could afford it."

"And he just . . . gave it up?"

Sally nodded again. "Completely. It hasn't seemed to bother him.
Sure, he's lost touch with some friends, but—"

"And you trust him, you're sure he's—"

"Of course I trust him. He's my husband. And my part of the deal
is I can't ask him about it. Oh, I could, that's nothing we've articulated, but I won't. I don't need to."

"You're that confident in him."

Sally smiled and shrugged. "I married him, right? I married him."

And I married Mark Petrello.

SECOND, THE SWIMSUIT. We went to the beach at Santa
Monica, not the classiest beach in the world, but one Flavio seemed to
like, and he found us a spot. He stripped off his shirt and revealed the
skimpiest of black swimsuits. His buttocks were clearly visible through

the fabric, and his genitals hung overtly. He lay on his side, resting one foot on the other knee, his equipment spilling across his thigh. Sally had packed sandwiches and was unloading the cooler, prattling on about the string bikinis they'd seen in Brazil and the topless bathers other places, while Flavio, stretched out on his side, ignored us—or indulged us, his sunglasses on and his legs obscenely spread. A balding man in sunglasses and a swimsuit walked slowly past. Flavio rolled onto his stomach. The man walked back past us. I didn't want to look, but it seemed as if Flavio was watching him over his shoulder. The man passed us a third time, this time lifting, ever so slightly, with the tip of a finger, his sunglasses from his nose. I turned to the cooler and started burrowing in the sandwiches, afraid to see if Flavio had lifted his sunglasses too.

Flavio didn't leave his spot beside us for a good ten minutes, enough time for him to eat a sandwich, for me to lose and then regret my suspicions. When he did leave, it seemed perfectly plausible that he was only using the restroom, and he came back in a reasonable period of time. When he sat down, he told us a very funny joke about a man obsessed with breasts.

"Your English is improving, Flavio," I said.

"Isn't it?" Sally beamed, her mouth full of sandwich. "We practice."

"SO WHAT'S YOUR COMPROMISE? Flavio gives up coke so he can marry you; what do you give up for him?"

"I told you, Clare, I don't ask. I let him go out for hours in Rio, and I don't ask what he's up to. I'm sure it's nothing bad. And if he wants to tell me, he'll tell me. But he doesn't have to." She glanced at me and smiled. "It sounds a little hokey, but it works."

"He doesn't come back smelling of lavender, does he?"

"What?"

"Nothing," I said.

———

LAST, THE MAGAZINE.

Sally and Flavio's condo in Brentwood had only one bedroom but two bathrooms, which seemed typically Californian to me. One bathroom—the master bath—was huge and skylighted and off the bedroom; the other, tiny and windowless but still containing a shower and a potted plant, was tucked off the living room next to the front door. I slept on the living room sofa, beside the coffee table with the lava lamp, so obviously the small bathroom was mine.

One night I woke up to hear a door shutting softly, and in a second I spotted the light under the bathroom door. Someone was using my bathroom. The door to Sally and Flavio's bedroom was closed, and I wondered for a moment if it was Sally, doing some private duty (she had always been fastidious about her bodily functions), but then I heard a heavy rush of urine that was surely a man's. Flavio, I thought, and I rolled away and almost drifted back to sleep. But Flavio didn't come out, no one came out, and after several minutes, I wondered if it really was Flavio, and what in the world he was doing. The idea of a perverted burglar crossed my mind. I rolled over carefully and curled up facing the bathroom, waiting for the door to open.

There were some big breaths from the bathroom, a rustle, a flush, then the light went off. The door popped open quietly. It was Flavio, creeping back to his and Sally's bedroom. Next I heard their bed creak, and in a moment or two I heard murmuring and then the rhythmic thumping of their bed against the wall. Newlyweds, I thought. Then I thought of Mark and how six months ago I'd been a newlywed too. I started to get teary, and then I had to pee in the fiercest way and got up.

I was standing in the bathroom trying to decide if I should flush or not—if the proof of my being awake might embarrass them—when I noticed a rolled-up magazine wadded behind the toilet. I picked it up instinctively—I'm neat, I like to keep even my friends' places tidy—and saw that it wasn't an ordinary magazine, not *People* or *Time* or any of the magazines Sally liked to read. It was a porno magazine, very thick, with heavy pages and glossy color photos, and the photos were of men and men. Doing things, inserting things, sucking on things. I couldn't believe it. I saw myself in the mirror, and my mouth was actually hanging open. I rolled up the magazine and put it back, wadded in the dirty crevice where I'd found it. So this was what Flavio was doing. This was why he'd come out to this bathroom.

I was awake until morning. What had Flavio's father said at the wedding? *We were not sure Flavio would marry.* Ah yes, I bet they weren't sure. What tricksters men were, what liars. Mark coming home smelling of lavender, Flavio smelling of men. Brazilian men, Thai men, American men. Sally wouldn't even notice. She'd be so happy to see him with undilated pupils, alert but not hyperalert, hungry but not ravenous. She'd taken a risk for love, believing she had him figured out. Flavio's looks weren't a problem because Sally wasn't jealous. Sally's money wasn't a problem because Flavio had money too. Flavio's drugs weren't a problem because he had given them up. The only problem was one Sally didn't see.

Should I be the one to tell her?

I'd almost decided I had to when Flavio padded out to the kitchen. I lay still in my sofa bed and spied. Flavio made the morning coffee and sat at the kitchen table reading the paper. His lips moved as he read; after all, he was still learning English. Then he set the paper down and stared toward the guest bathroom, and if he'd looked dreamy or libidinous or even content, I might have told her. But his look was only despair. His face became so clouded it was not even handsome.

Later that day, I flew back home. My only moments alone with Sally were in the airport restroom. "So are you happy?" I asked, waving my hands under the blower.

Sally brought her hand up to her chest and laid it there, fingers extended. "Oh God, yes," she said. "I can't believe it. After Timbo I never thought I'd really...but now...."

She used to be so articulate. "He's everything you want?" I asked.

She nodded. "He is, Clare. He is."

Before I started down the tube into the plane she turned around. Flavio had his hands in his pants pockets and his head cocked, looking out the windows at the runways, but Sally was waving at me. "Bye, Clare!" she called. "Love you!"

"Love you too!" I called back, wiggling my fingers. Then Sally, in a gesture that broke my heart, kissed the tips of her fingers and blew the kiss to me.

WHEN PEOPLE LEARN that Mark Petrello and I were once married, their response is invariable: Mark Petrello? You were married to Mark Petrello? (Pause) Wow. I can't see you two together at all.

"I was his first wife," I say, a remark that both pleases and saddens me, because my best memory of Mark is when we first made love, when he cried, literally cried, big fat tears, and I cradled his head on my chest and stroked it. What had his eyes seen? Victims of traumas, accidents, shootings. I wondered how he thought of a head, if it seemed fragile to him, he who had seen it so damaged, crushed, pierced, shattered, while to me, despite my anatomy course, it still seemed like a human head, heavy and substantial. Mark's tears wet my chest. Oh, I loved him. And there's no question he loved me. He wanted to be alive, remember? More than anything, alive. Without qualification. And with me, at the beginning at least, he felt alive.

It's hard to give up a memory. No matter what comes after, it's impossible to forget a small moment of happiness, to admit that it was a fluke, an isolated moment in time with no chance—because our lives are not circular—of reeling around again.

This is nothing I've talked about with Sally—it isn't our way, to share with each other our private moments with men. On the phone, we are very practical. I'm sure Sally has intimate memories of her time with Flavio, and it's because of this that I always cut her some slack. I let her voice catch when she mentions him, I don't say what a waste product he was and how he betrayed her, although he was and he did. A disastrous first marriage no one wants to talk about, a marriage like mine. Still, we're less betrayed by others, it seems, than by our own hopes and dreams.

THERE WERE SEVERAL POOLS at Sally and Flavio's apartment complex, including a small one near their apartment that was rarely used. One Sunday afternoon shortly after my visit, Ben came over, and he and Sally and Flavio went out to sit by the small pool. Sally, tired and jet-lagged, fell asleep in a deck chair. When she awoke, Ben and Flavio were gone—probably inside getting a snack, Sally thought. She was warm and wanted to swim, but there were leaves in the pool, so she went to the maintenence shed to get the pool net. Inside the shed she found Ben and Flavio, snacking, as she put it, on each other.

THERE ARE QUALITIES THAT survive an internal medicine residency, but meekness is not among them. I didn't think meekness survived law school, either, which is why it surprised me when Sally, after her split with Flavio, moved back into her parents' house. Ben had never left. To me, Sally's move seemed like madness; I could understand it only as the message (largely for Ben's benefit, I thought) that family mattered over all.

If I had to pick an adjective for Sally's state then, it would be "seething," but it's hard to say what Ben's was. He was about to finish high school. He had no plans for his life and no apparent interests. When I asked him about his four-by-five camera, he said he didn't know where it was. Most of the time he was holed up in his room watching TV. He was required to come to dinner with the family, a meal Esther produced with little of her past fanfare and one that Ben—making a point, I suppose—pretty much refused to eat. "Is the brisket all right, Ben?" Esther asked, her tone somewhere between despairing and beseeching.

Ben made a disgusted face and snorted.

"Don't talk back to your mother, Ben!" Sid snapped, although Ben had not said a word. "And eat your dinner! Your mother made a nice meal for us!"

Through all this, Sally ate like a machine. She wasn't working, so she was getting chunky. Comments she made about her father reminded me of things I'd said when I lived with my mother after my father's death. "It's not like I'm fifteen anymore," Sally would say, or "Doesn't he think I can have a night out by myself?" She had developed a new allegiance to her mother, the victim, Sally said, of a dominant man. She told me that once her mother had dreamed of being a U.N. translator, but instead she'd made the mistake of marrying Sid.

I visited the whole brood for a week after I finished med school. It was then 1982. Esther cooked and drank and wrote her letters, Sid came home from work at lunchtime, and Sally and I slept in her old room. It was the same room she'd had since high school, the same Yes posters and velour-covered throw pillows and clown music box that played "You Are My Sunshine." "Sally," I said, "you ever getting rid of this stuff?" No, Sally said. Since she wasn't planning to stay here, change would be too much work.

I was relieved that she wasn't planning to stay. She wasn't herself here. She'd let her hair grow to the middle of her back and was wearing it in a ponytail that must have been easy but was terribly unflattering, and even her designer clothes looked sloppy. She wore pants without belts, shoes without socks, sleeves rolled up, shirts with the top three buttons open in a way that, on the right person, might be racy but on Sally looked like lack of effort. Ben looked as bad as she did. His curly hair was matted and his jeans were studded with gray smears where he'd stubbed out his cigarettes. No drugs, Sally assured me, but maybe he missed them.

The Roses had wilted, I thought. They'd become like anybody else, any sad and bickering little family. My magical L.A. nights with them were gone. I remember sitting in the family room one night with them watching *Love Boat* on their huge TV. It was a huge TV, but it was *Love Boat*. Esther and Sid fell asleep in their chairs.

"Welcome to the real world" was Sally's new phrase that year. Had I heard about Ben's psychiatrist and the underwater aversion therapy? Welcome to the real world, Ben. Did I know that Sid expected Sally to move back home permanently, like some socially scarred daughter? Welcome to the real world, Dad. Did I know that Esther believed she didn't drink too much? Welcome...

It's not the real world, I thought, not the real world at all. What a luxury Sally had to not be working, to be thinking about her life, figuring out where she wanted to go with the law. I want to go with the law to Hawaii, she said once, to a nice little cabana, I want to stay up late with the law and drink those drinks with the little umbrellas.

"You could do that here," I said, looking across the patio to the espalier.

"You think this is paradise? Welcome to the real world, Clare."

Where had this bitterness come from? It was troubling because it seemed mistargeted, not directed against Flavio or Ben, the men who had directly betrayed her, but at her father. I could see that Sid had his faults—he was loud and bossy, he treated Ben and Sally like children (after all, they were both living in his house)—but still, I liked him. "Can you imagine," I asked Sally, "seeing your only daughter's life ruined by her husband? By her husband having an affair? By that affair being with your other child? By that other child being your *son*?" Really, it was unreal ("a nice turn of phrase," Sally remarked), and I thought Sid had handled it well. He'd found the lawyer, suggested the annulment (California was a joint property state; a divorce would have

meant giving Flavio half of Sally's assets), and brokered a peace between Sally and Ben, a peace that seemed to have backfired, because
now his two children were united against him.

"Daddy's no angel, Clare," Sally said.

"I'm not saying he is, it's just that in these circumstances he's trying, he—"

"He deserves to try," Sally snapped.

"I'M GETTING INTO FILM," Sid said. I tried not to be alone
with him—afraid of what he'd tell me about Ben, what questions he'd
ask about Sally—but he cornered me. Sally wasn't often where he was
anymore: she was busy in the kitchen, reading in her room, taking a
long shower.

"Movies! How exciting! You mean you're making them?"

"I'm not making them, I'm bankrolling them. Little movies.
Videos, even. We're not talking *Raiders of the Lost Ark*. But I got film
school graduates working for me. You believe that? Film school graduates!"

"And you're making what, training films? Films for the army or for
companies?"

"Yeah." Sid looked amused yet pleased. I thought my perspicacity
had surprised him. "Training films."

"Maybe you'll graduate to bigger films." I was eager to impress
him. "Maybe you'll do a Bible movie," I suggested, remembering how
he loved those stories.

"Oh yeah, oh yeah," Sid said. "A Bible movie. Knock people's
socks off. Show 'em what the Bible really is."

There was one conflagration. Ben was seeing a therapist, a motherly
looking woman who came to the house and Ben's room—with its
Queen posters and drawn blinds and sweaty smell—two times a week.

Ben met his father in the upstairs hall. "You're bugging my room!"
Ben shouted. "I want all bugs out, and I want to see Dr. Morrison in
her office."

"You're crazy," Sid said.

"You think I don't know a bug?" Ben yelled, heading down the stairs. "I want a car. I'm calling her, I'm going to her office!"

"Who's paying her?" Sid bellowed.

Ben's voice was ice. "You made me this."

He went to Dr. Morrison's office, and Sid spent time with the door closed in Ben's room. I was in Sally's bedroom, petrified, mesmerized, wondering if I should repeat the conversation to her. She was taking one of her endless showers. It was a tribute to the house's size and insulation that she emerged from the bathroom with no idea what had gone on. "Your father and Ben had a fight," I whispered. I had been looking under the chairs in Sally's room to be sure there were no bugs here, although I wasn't sure exactly what a bug would look like.

"Really?" Sally said out loud, toweling her wet hair. "Was Daddy riding Ben again?"

SID NEEDED A LAWYER to help him change the name of his corporation.

"I'm sure he's got lawyers," Sally muttered. "You can't have a business like he has and not have lawyers."

"Sally, why don't you do it?" I objected. "He wants you to do it. He wants to use your expertise. And it can't be hard." I was frustrated by her sulkiness.

"Of course it's not hard," Sally snapped. "That's not the point."

I wasn't sure what the point was, but I didn't press it. Sid had told me the current name of his company, Crown Publications, was too limited. "It'll be Crown Communications. That's better, don't you think? You can't forget about videos these days. We want to leave the door open to everything."

I thought Sid sounded savvy. A distributor has distribution channels, so why not use them for other items?

I know, in retrospect, that I was an idiot, that my credulity was almost greater than a reasonable person could understand. And I was smart! I was a doctor! But I never put things together. I never asked Sid more about his work, or Sally about her anger.

Part of me didn't dare question. I saw a family so close it drew together even after betrayal. If I wanted to stay an honorary Rose, I had no choice but to keep quiet. Other than my med school graduation, my family, scattered across Ohio, met once a year at Christmas. My mother phoned only to harangue me, Frank and Eric to solicit medical advice or ask how much I'd chip in for this or that present. Even Baxter didn't communicate with me anymore. He lived in his log cabin now, surviving on odd jobs and barter. To reach him, I had to phone a neighbor. "I'm a hermit," he said. "That's just what I am. Don't tell Mom."

But in Los Angeles, in that huge house on a spur off Mulholland, I felt part of a big wide world that made me happy. Even on that miserable trip, I could walk out the sliding doors and onto the patio, in front of the espalier, to gaze at the city below. It was only because of Mark Petrello that I'd ended up doing my residency in Ohio. Afterward, I would move out here.

"WE DON'T HOLD MUCH hope for him," Sally said after lunch. "He's very anti-gay."

"He's a write-off," Ben confirmed. "He doesn't want to accept that his only son isn't going to be out there producing baby Roses."

"He's from a different generation," I said. "He probably never had any exposure..."

Sally and Ben exchanged glances.

"His business," Ben said, leaning forward to me but looking at Sally, as if asking what he should say, "his business is full of gays."

I remembered that from before. It still surprised me. "That's what he told me," I said. "I mean, magazines! It's not a business you associate with gays, not like decorating or fashion design or something."

Sally and Ben looked at each other again. "Let me tell you," Ben said, "he makes a lot of money off guys like me."

"From magazines? Really? Are gays a good target audience? I guess they would be. You think of them as educated, they have money, they like to read—"

"Clare, stop it," Sally said, and I was so startled I did.

"Oh Sally, did I tell you?" Ben asked. "I found another bug in the curtains yesterday. I didn't make a peep, and I tossed it out the window. We'll see how fast he catches on. See why we hate him, Clare? See?" A waiter walked past. "Oh, look at that tush. Yum yum. Couldn't you just eat it?"

Sally gave an exasperated sigh. "No," she said. "I could not. And I don't need to hear if you could, either."

WHEN I GOT BACK to Ohio, I found a letter from my brother Eric. I knew as I slit the envelope that he wanted something. He had fallen for a fellow Glow Music clerk and had gotten her pregnant. He planned to leave his wife and children. Together he and his new woman—an angel, the love of his life—hoped to open a drive-in restaurant, if only they could get the start-up funds. In the course of the letter, Eric mentioned the names of his girlfriend's children.

"Ginkgo is a boy?" Sally said after a pause.

I picked up the letter again, cradling the phone with my shoulder. "Tahini's a boy too. They're both boys. If I remember right from what Eric told me at Christmas, Tahini's dad was a black guy, and Ginkgo's dad was from Korea or somewhere."

"Tahini is a food. It's Middle Eastern," Sally said. "It's sesame paste. You use it to make hummus."

"I don't think either of the fathers were in the picture when the kids were born. The names are totally hers."

"You can eat ginkgo, too. Ginkgo nuts. They grow on the ginkgo tree. Are you sending money?"

"God, no. Would you? Eric may never speak to me again. Not that that's a loss."

"Sad," Sally said. "But it's interesting, isn't it? All of a sudden you're a doctor, so he thinks you're rich and he can ask you for anything. Still, he's your brother." Before I could answer, she'd moved on, her voice full of sudden mirth: "I wonder what she'll call Eric's baby. Something all-American. Toast? Tahini, Ginkgo, and Toast, there's a threesome."

I couldn't imagine the Sally I'd known in college possessing the sharpness—the fury, really—to come up with "Toast." She was more like me now. It was a loss but it was funny.

Tahini, Ginkgo, and Toast, I repeated. Pretty soon we had the giggles.

"Still, he's your brother," Sally repeated.

THERE WAS NO GOOD reason for me to sleep with my ex-husband. Whim again. It started with a party at an ICU nurse's apartment where everyone drank too much and even doctors who wore antismoking buttons on their white coats cadged cigarettes and shared gruesome and hilarious stories about death. Mark and I started on either end of a sofa, then he laid his head in my lap, then we went back to our old apartment. I had quit the pill after our divorce, a renunciation of the world of men, but birth control didn't cross my mind that evening. The next morning we were both irritable, less with each other than with ourselves. Eight weeks later, I confirmed that I was pregnant.

IN SOME WAYS I loved my residency. I adored the adventure of it, scurrying to the books to read about something I'd barely heard of, the quandaries of care, the peculiar personalities, the physical exams. I liked going to the residents' lab late at night and staining sputum. I loved finding a spleen. I didn't mind examining people with lice, although a lot of the residents would make the ER nurses give the louse-ridden a Kwell bath before they'd even talk to them. I liked being the calm in the center of the storm, being tough, doing what someone else might not do. I'm the baby of four kids, remember, and the only girl: at times I'd felt like the add-on, the accident (which I probably was). But as a resident, I felt essential. One of my attendings referred to me in writing as "particularly useful." I will carry that compliment to my grave. I would be happy if it were on my tombstone.

Having said I loved my residency, I should explain that not everyone loved me. I was only modestly popular with patients, which surprised me. After my father's experiences, I thought what every patient wanted was honesty and attention, two things I could certainly give. Yet there was something about me—I sensed it—that made people nervous. I often said the wrong things. I told the daughter of a nursing home patient admitted with pneumonia that I didn't order blood or sputum cultures because they were expensive and what they might show didn't matter—true, but I shouldn't have said it. A woman with secondary syphilis asked the attending doctor to take me off her case. All I had done was say to her, in what I thought was a friendly way, that what she had was probably enough to make her swear off sex forever. I knew what I was talking about, because I'd just encountered something similar myself.

"YOU CAN'T KEEP IT," Sally said instantly.

"What do you mean?" I said, hurt.

Her voice came through the phone like gunfire. "Do you want to marry Mark again? Is that why you did it?"

"It was an accident! I didn't mean to get pregnant! I wasn't scheming. Sally, you're hurting my feelings."

"You could put it up for adoption. There are lots of deserving parents."

"I want to keep it! If I decide to have it. If I have it, I'll keep it. I'd be a good parent." Wouldn't I? I had an image of myself walking through the L.A. airport with my bundle of baby, a huge grin on my face, going to meet Sally. "I won't even tell Mark, he'll never think it's his. I'm a doctor, I can afford it."

"Clare, every baby deserves a father. I mean that. I feel that strongly. Where would you be without your father?"

I GOT HORRIBLY SICK. I had a fever, bleeding, pain. I crawled to the phone and called the life squad myself after I woke up on my bathroom floor. The resident in the ER described my vaginal discharge as "repulsive" ("No offense," he said a heartbeat later, patting my knee), and the ultrasound of my pelvis showed no fetal heartbeat. I underwent an emergency D and C, then stayed in the hospital for intravenous antibiotics.

I wasn't treated for this at University Hospital, where I was a resident. I was treated at the private hospital next door. I begged the life squad to take me there, where no one would know me. When I was getting sick, I was too embarrassed to go to my gynecologist, and I wasn't about to go to the University Hospital ER and sit in one of the pelvic rooms, my roommate potentially one of those notorious women who leaned out the door in a hospital gown, asking each passing doctor to hurry up and do their exam. This may have been a mistake. Everyone at the private hospital seemed disgusted with me. Even the women bringing meals to my room circled lavishly around my bed. I remember being in the ER, already burning with shame, when the attending doctor asked me why I didn't ask my recent partner to use a condom. "I didn't know him very well," I said, startled into truth, "and I knew I was already pregnant."

"This something you do often?" the doctor asked.

I bit the inside of my cheek, hoping I didn't cry. "No."

"Well, the baby's dead. There's no choice." I winced a little at his wording—"choice"—did he know I'd thought about an abortion?

I swallowed hard and nodded.

"Hell of a way for it to die." But no, he didn't really say that. I imagined he said it. You know: I said it to myself.

———

THE MAN WHO MADE me sick was a musician on tour with a female folk singer I'd never heard of but whose concert I was dragged to by a fan of hers, a female resident like myself. The singer had long blond hair she swooshed around, and behind her hair I caught glimpses of the drummer's chiseled, diffident face. It really was a striking face, a beautiful face, and after the concert, as my friend waited for an autograph, I walked back toward the drum kit and asked the drummer where he'd be playing next. I didn't mean this suggestively, but since he clearly thought I did, I started to believe it too.

My resident friend went home, and the drummer and I went to a bar. The people around us exhibited the same reactions—the despairing glances toward me, the defiantly seductive looks at him—that I had noticed in Venice when I went for my walk with Flavio, which made me realize the drummer was as handsome as I'd thought. As Sally had said, the beautiful do have an effect. Noticing this made sleeping with him inevitable, for how could I turn down the opportunity—which I might never have again—of sleeping with a beautiful man?

I left his hotel room after three A.M., feeling sore between my legs and tainted. He was sound asleep and didn't stir. That he'd never remember my last name was a relief; it was quite another thing when he forgot my first.

ON THE OTHER HAND, no one knew. I got back to my residency rotation a week after I got out of the hospital, telling everyone simply that I'd had an infection. I might have mentioned burning with urination, if anyone pressed me for details. A diabetic woman had just come in with a kidney infection and died, so kidney infections were on everyone's minds. People were actually pretty sympathetic. My senior resident skipped me halfway through the admission rotation, on my first call night, so I admitted two patients while the other two interns each had four. A med student offered to fetch me a Coke from the machine downstairs. My attending had work rounds sitting instead of standing. All these things were big enough deviations from the norm that they truly meant something. I was grateful.

"OH, GOD," Sally said. "You're in the hospital right now?"

"Right now."

"You lost the baby," she repeated. "I'm so sorry."

Tears came to my eyes. I braced myself for what she'd say next: how it would work out, that a baby wouldn't have been good now, that maybe I secretly hadn't wanted a child, that what happened was for the best.

"I'm just so sorry," Sally said.

"**KAPOSI'S,**" Freddie Finkelstein said. "I said, Jeez, that looks like a Kaposi's. You see them sometimes out here, on the legs of some of those old Greeks and Italians."

"Did you biopsy it?"

"Sure I biopsied it. And the path report came back Kaposi's. You notice how I'm saying it: *Ka*Posi's. Those people who say Kap*o*si's, they're all wrong. And then a month later I saw another lesion, just the same, little purple-black raised papule, this time on the back of a male hooker. I knew he was a hooker because he listed escort service as his occupation. I mean, what kind of guy lists escort service as his occupation? And I biopsied this one, and it was Kaposi's too. So I'd seen two in two months, and this is one rare cancer, even in your old Mediterraneans, and these patients were two young homosexual men. So I wrote a letter. *California State Medical Journal,* July 1982. Want to see it?"

AIDS was first identified because doctors like Freddie noticed strange things and reported them—Kaposi's sarcomas in the young; pneumocystis pneumonia in the apparently healthy. A pattern emerged. "So you were a hero," I said. It was 1984. I was still an internal medicine resident in Ohio then, seeing my first cases of AIDS, usually male homosexuals who'd been diagnosed on one of the coasts and had come home to the Midwest to die.

Freddie smiled slightly, trying, not totally successfully, to look modest. "I try to notice the unusual. My father had a saying: You don't look for things, you don't see them."

"Was your father a doctor?"

"Tailor."

I told Freddie about the cases of Kaposi's I'd seen, about the hairdresser whose bed I'd sat on as I gave him the news. "It looks like you may have AIDS," I said. The diagnosis was harder in those days: in 1984 the agent causing AIDS hadn't been identified, some people didn't think it was a virus, and there was no single blood test for the disease. "AIDS?" the hairdresser replied, his face blank. "Is that related to psoriasis?"

I left Freddie feeling that glow I feel when someone has pleasantly surprised me. I told Aunt Ruby how I'd enjoyed the visit. "He's a smart man, my Freddie," she said.

I told Sally about it. "That's interesting," she said, her voice belying her words. "He's such a nar."

Such an idiot, she was saying. "Not a total nar," I said.

Sally shrugged. "He's puerile. Look at Daphne," she said.

But this was unfair. Parents shouldn't be judged by their offspring. And Daphne wasn't that bad. In high school she'd been Sally's closest friend. "Look at Ben!" I felt like saying. Ben had left his parents' house. He was living somewhere, with somebody, doing one drug or another; his parents saw him only in extremis, when he came home and asked for another try at rehab. But Sally had made up her mind about Freddie, and once Sally had chosen her adjective, there was not much I could do.

A year after the annulment of her marriage to Flavio, Sally moved out of her parents' and opened her own law office, for women. To do this, she borrowed money from her father. Her first client was a woman who had been rear-ended. The second lawsuit went to trial, Sally's first ever, and she won big for her client. Then came malpractice claims, slip-and-falls, someone's Dominican maid burned by an overactive pilot light. Sally expanded her ad in the phone book, inserted a photograph of herself looking friendly. She brought in a female tax lawyer because some women, having won lawsuits or gotten settlements, didn't know what to do with their money. Word of mouth about the practice was phenomenal. Within eighteen months, she'd hired two associates. "I'm the avenging agent for the aggrieved," Sally told me over the phone.

I misunderstood her. "The avenging angel?" I said.

"Agent," she corrected me. "Believe me"—her tone was almost maniacal— "I'm no angel."

DURING MY RESIDENCY, I liked the middle of the night best. Maybe I'd get my last admission at one or two A.M., and after that I'd wander the halls and check on my other patients. It's amazing how many people in a hospital are awake, or half awake, or aroused by the shadow of someone at the door at three A.M. I liked to sit on people's beds and talk. About their test results, about my residency, about grandkids, welfare, shooting up heroin, about how before the valley was flooded to make a lake they'd go out on their front porch and yell sheepy-sheepy-sheepy. I've never been crazy about people, but in the middle of the night, they improve. I used to head to the overnight call room after four, knowing but not really caring that I might get beeped again. I felt a kind of euphoria, thinking here I was in Ohio, in the middle of the country, dealing with rich and essential things, life and death and rue and hope, while Sally was in L.A. making money.

I ADMITTED ROGER at about two in the morning. We'd gone through all his history, his lifestyle and habits and weight loss, the cough ("As if I have TB! Really!"), the shortness of breath, the toll on his decorating business, and then I held up a hospital gown for him to put on.

Roger dropped his wrist. "It's a little chi-chi for me, darling."

"God," I laughed, "you are such a type."

"It makes people comfortable," Roger confided. "Then they can peg me."

We looked at each other and smiled. It was, although we didn't know it, the beginning of a friendship. It was also the beginning of my career.

"ANYTHING INTERESTING LATELY?" I asked Sally on the phone.

"Oh, the usual. But this is unique: I met with a woman who wants to sue her plastic surgeon for making her breasts too big. She has a case."

"How do you stand it?"

"It's fun, Clare. Every day I'm arguing. It's fun! And I've almost paid Daddy back, did I tell you? Then I'll feel as if I'm truly"— she hesitated—"free."

I WONDERED ABOUT the drummer. I wondered if I could be infected too. I checked my back in the mirror for purple-black spots; I waited for a fever, a cough. But I stayed healthy. I had gotten out unscathed.

THE SECOND YEAR of my residency, six months after my episode of pelvic inflammatory disease and in the midst of my first celibate phase, a tall and amusing intern joined my team. He was a Cleveland Indians fan who had been his high school bowling champ, and I married him. This was nearly two years after my divorce from Mark Petrello. I thought I was doing everything right, because with Mark I'd been driven by lust and desperation, while with Ted I found companionship and fun. With Ted lust was not an issue, although it ended up being an issue for him. Ted was crazy for me. The month I met him, I led my team to two excellent diagnoses: the first a fun one due to some neat-staining cells in the urine, and the second a bigger winner that impressed even my physician superiors and turned a patient everyone thought was an impossible whiner into a vindicated sufferer of a rare metabolic disease. Both of these diagnoses awed Ted Standforth. "You're unbelievable," Ted used to say. I loved being unbelievable. There's no better aphrodisiac than being desired. Even Baxter liked Ted, inviting us to his cabin; my mom thought he was a prize; Sally—over the phone—approved immensely. We had a wedding at my in-laws'—Lizzie and Phil's—church in July 1984, followed by a reception with delicious church-lady-catered food and a clown to entertain my nieces and nephews. Ted and I paid for the wedding, but my mother-in-law planned it: I was too busy being a resident, and my mother, caught up in her teaching and the Portage County Alliance for Progress, didn't have the inclination. All I did was buy the dress and show. The only question I recall Lizzie Standforth asking was what kind of flowers I'd like in my bouquet.

"But Clare, dear," she said when I'd responded, "tulips are spring flowers." This was a revelation to me.

"You know," I told Ted, "for someone so smart, I sure do miss things."

"Why should you know about tulips?" he countered. "Wasn't your mother too busy rabble-rousing to garden?" That was Ted, always ready with an excuse for me.

He was an only child—his older brother, an Air Force pilot, had been killed in some training accident—and, as I told Sally, Ted was as close to his mother as Sally was to her father. Ted's father didn't talk much. I could see the hypothetical disadvantages of marrying a guy so attached to his mother, but what man would treat his wife better than a man who loved his mom? (Actually Ted made this argument.) Lizzie's phone calls and fretting over the menu and pulling at Ted's tie all touched me, in that inarticulate, stumbly way I get touched, and the only mar in the wedding was my mother pursuing the minister into the church kitchen to talk about repressed Central Americans and the Refuge Movement, an entity she always discussed in capital letters. Did I say that was a mar? It wasn't. It gave Sally and me a chance to poke each other and giggle, and as we pulled out of the church parking lot with Ted and me in the backseat and Sally driving, I felt overwhelmed with serenity and pride, thinking how even though Sally had her fabulous business, even though she was rich, even though both her parents were living, it was *I*, Clare Mann Standforth (I would use Ted's last name socially, at least), who would have a happy marriage.

BEN CLEANED UP, briefly, in the name of gay pride. He moved out of his druggie friends' house and into his own apartment. He got a job with a producer who had done only PBS specials but was planning to unleash upon the world its first serious gay film. Ben's task was to call potential investors, mostly gay males. Ben had a very sincere prewritten appeal, which I heard and found persuasive. It made you sorry you weren't gay, weren't part of that special, talented, misunderstood world. Michelangelo, Walt Whitman, Socrates: Hadn't all the best artists and thinkers been gay? "At least he's not a Scientologist," Sally said cheerfully. The Scientology headquarters on Sunset was a place we often passed, giving us both a wicked frisson.

"You got any dirt on stars who are secretly gay?" I asked Sally at my wedding.

Sally gave a tinkling laugh. "I'm sure I will!"

THE WOMAN IN CHARGE of the wedding food called me on our honeymoon to report that Ted's mother was having palpitations. I wasn't supposed to tell Ted, because Lizzie would worry if he worried, but somebody should know. "Doesn't she have a doctor?" I asked. I'm on my honeymoon, I was thinking. With Lizzie's *son.*

"She doesn't want to bother her doctor," the woman said. "Can you talk to her?"

"Well, okay," I said, glancing toward the bathroom door and hoping Ted didn't emerge. I can see now that in this interchange the seeds to the destruction of my marriage were already being sown.

"I BELIEVE IN NATURAL consequences," the well-groomed woman whose wayward husband had infected her with AIDS said to me years later. I was hit with a flash of recognition: I believe in natural consequences too. It was a credo I'd always known, articulated for the first time.

"Natural consequences," I said. "Yes."

"My ex's time will come," the woman pointed out, "and he'll be all alone. Me, I'll have plenty of support."

She was right. She died in a hospice surrounded by her children, her obituary listing AIDS as the cause of death. Her husband was found dead in a motel room with no identification, and it was three weeks before a daughter claimed him. And now Ted, the man I married back in the infancy of the eighties, is a happy man, with four daughters and a thriving wife, but to achieve this independence, this adulthood, his mother had to step aside.

BEN'S SOBRIETY DIDN'T LAST. He ran into an old friend in West Hollywood and resumed his druggie ways. One night he was sitting with Sally at a restaurant near his apartment, talking about megavitamins, and six days later someone dropped him on his parents' doorstep, passed out, with a note pinned to his shirt saying he should be checked for seizures. By then the gay producer had fired him—reluctantly, over the phone, via Esther. Sid's internist, like me, didn't know what to make of the seizure comment. The internist ordered an EEG. He suggested several rehab facilities, three of which Ben had already been to. A friend of Esther's had a friend whose daughter, a former prostitute and heroin addict, was now a floral designer in a fancy shop. Esther and Sid sent Ben to her rehab.

THE WAY TED AND I planned it, I'd get pregnant within three or six months and have the baby either at the end of my third and final year of residency or just as I started in practice, when my workload would be light and a baby manageable. It was unspoken but understood that when I did get pregnant, we'd move near Lizzie and Phil, or they would move near us, so I could practice medicine and have a reliable sitter. But we'd been married seven months and nothing was happening, my periods arriving every fourth Monday as always. We started timing things, and since I'd read that sex every other night was more likely to result in pregnancy than sex every night—something about the sperm counts dipping with too-frequent sex—we were now on a schedule of sorts, which was difficult with our varying calls spent overnight in the hospital. Some nights I'd drive in from home to the hospital, or Ted would, and we'd have ourselves a quickie in the senior call room—a private room with a lock on the door and one twin bed changed daily by housekeeping. It started to seem like I spent a lot of time in that call room, waiting for Ted, waiting for sex, half hoping my beeper would go off and interrupt me; as I said, lust was not an issue with Ted. In fact, with our new every-other-night-need-it-or-not schedule, lust was even less of an issue, and I began to wonder if I wasn't getting pregnant because I wasn't lusty enough. I knew this was hardly scientific, but the thought nagged. So it felt like fate one day when I opened the third drawer of a bureau sitting in the corner of the senior call room and discovered a cache of dirty magazines.

There were a bunch of *Playboy*s, many *Penthouse*s, and a few specialty magazines devoted to breasts. Some of the magazines were musty and missing covers, all looked well thumbed, and every once in a while, a new issue would show up, stuffed surreptitiously into the center of the pile. It was mildly titillating to think that the magazines had been around for years, and about what they'd been used for, and to wonder which of the other residents, presumably male (I was one of only three women in my group of fifteen), knew about and replenished them. I wondered if the male residents ever mentioned them to one another, a kind of open secret, and I wondered if Ted knew, although I didn't want him to know I knew. I wanted him to think my increased lustiness was due to his appeal alone. It seemed like I'd jinx my chances for pregnancy if he knew what I'd been reading before he showed up.

It was the reading I found interesting. The pictures didn't do much for me, being mostly busty women, but some of the *Playboy* articles were sexy, and the *Penthouse* letters, detailing all sorts of sexual adventures, were my favorites. I loved the deliverymen arriving and the girlfriends surprising girlfriends and the cucumbers and the swing apparatus that lowered a woman up and down. I wondered how I'd gone so long without reading more of this; boy, what I'd been missing!

The last magazines I'd seen like this had been when I was ten or twelve and stumbled upon my brothers' stash, and magazines now were much juicier. On the nights I was to meet Ted—and on other nights—I started to go to the senior call room early, and I hated to be beeped away.

TED AND I WENT to L.A. to visit Sally. I had only three months left in my residency. It was 1985, and I was thirty years old. I was still, despite the magazines, despite the schedule, not pregnant. Ted had never been west of Chicago, so this was a big trip for him. He seemed to me ridiculously worried about what to wear. He didn't want to look like a guy from Ohio, so he bought a pale yellow sports coat. As we headed out the door to the airport, I noticed he wasn't wearing socks. "You have to wear socks," I said. "I'm not going to California with a guy who doesn't wear socks." Instead of arguing or glaring at me, which I would have accepted, Ted went sheepishly to put them on.

When we got there, it rained and rained, which disappointed me, because I wanted Ted to be as taken with Los Angeles as I was. I wanted him to dream, as I did, of finishing our residencies and moving here. Into the sun, far away from Phil and Lizzie; or, of course, they could move to California too. I had to stop myself sometimes from pointing things out. In California they: all have pools; hate cigarettes; call one another by their first names; have numerology shops just sitting there, like beauty parlors; don't wear sundresses in the winter, even though it's warm. I also had to stop myself sometimes from lapsing into California-ese, which was less a vocabulary than a delivery, a deadpan yet showbizzy way of speaking, filled with pauses for imaginary double takes, zoom-ins, applause. The hotel clerk at the Beverly Hills Hilton spoke in California-ese when I pointed out that we wouldn't pay more than we'd promised for the room. "You're right," he said. A intense gaze into my eyes, a pause. "We'll make it work for you." Another woman approached him to ask directions to the pool. The clerk held up his hand in her direction. "Momento," he said. "Please stand by." He could have been talking to me or to her. He was a pro, he knew how to work both cameras.

ON OUR SECOND NIGHT in Los Angeles, we left our hotel and drove to Brentwood to pick up Sally (she lived in another condo now and had a new Mercedes sports car too small for three), then on to Sid and Esther's to pick them up for dinner. It was dusk and drizzling, and at first the house seemed empty, but suddenly Ben was in front of us, standing in the darkened living room. His hair was tied back in a stubby ponytail, and he wore jeans with a pressed fold down the leg and a black T-shirt that read in gray script DON'T YOU WISH. He clapped his hands over his head and swung himself around in a circle, announcing: "Say it proud, I'm gay and I'm loud."

"I don't think that's quite right," I whispered to Sally.

"It's right for him," Sally replied. She told us that Ben was three weeks out of rehab and had recently been taking a designer drug of some sort, which he viewed not as a drug but as a "reality alternative."

"Looks like he needs a reality check," Ted said.

Watching Ben dance, I realized that another person was present, a small white face looking out of the corner. The friend got up and starting dancing himself. He had a whole row of studs in each ear. He and Ben danced separately and silently, oblivious to each other.

Eventually, Sid and Esther arrived, and we stood around talking about heading out to dinner while Ben and his friend continued to dance. I was disappointed that Esther didn't cook anymore; I'd wanted Ted to experience one of her meals.

"Is Ben coming with us?" Esther asked, glancing at him and the friend in a troubled way.

Sally shrugged. "Ben, are you coming?"

Ben didn't answer. "Of course they're coming!" Sid said heatedly. "I can't leave them here! What kind of things would they do on my rug?"

We did all get to a restaurant, but the evening was strained, and midway through, Ben and his friend went off to use the restroom and never reappeared.

SALLY LOOKED FROM ME to Ted in confusion. "But it's only been seven months."

"Eight periods," I said.

"But Clare, that's . . ." She blinked in a way that irritated me, because she was not stupid.

"Do me a favor," I interrupted. "Don't judge until you've been through it. Really, Sally. Don't ever judge." I realized my voice was shaking. Ted, frowning, reached for my hand.

DO WHAT YOU LOVE, they say, and what did she love about it? Oh, everything: the phone calls, the demand letters, the negotiations, the poster she'd made that reduced the defense lawyer to tears, the frizzy-haired clients sitting on the edge of their seats and bouncing as they poured out their woes. "Sometimes I think I'm the only one who listens to them. The only one. Not their husbands, not their mothers, not their best friends—nobody listens but me. It's kind of moving."

I thought of Roger, my patient with AIDS. What do you think? he'd asked. Honestly. Are we talking one year, two years, no years? "I feel that way too," I told Sally. I thought of my female clinic patients sitting on the exam table with their gowns open, exposing a breast as casually as an arm. "Isn't it amazing what people will tell you? You can ask them about their sex lives and everything."

Sally laughed. "You hear more about sex lives than I do. I hear about money." But then we said at the same time, "That's just as private."

That was probably the best conversation we had. The rest of the week Ted and I waited for her at her office, or waited for her at a restaurant, or wandered around on a short leash as she talked into her portable phone. "She used to be fun," I told Ted.

"She's pretty consumed with work," Ted said.

"It's her brother," I corrected him. "He's draining her." I thought of Ben as a boy. Between then and now there was a world of loss. "And she feels bad for her parents. She thinks they've worked hard all their lives and had a lot of hope for both her and Ben, and now..."

"It's tough to lose a brother," Ted said, reminding me that his brother was actually dead. "I don't care if it happens like it did to me or if it's seeing him turn into a drug addict or what. It's tough."

"We'll be lucky if we get a son to lose," I mumbled.

"What?" Ted asked sharply.

I don't remember my response, but I do know we missed making love that night, which upset me because I wanted to be pregnant. At that point, not being pregnant was making me tense, tense, tense.

"I WAS THINKING," Roger had said. "Thousands of years of sexual repression, ten years of fun, and now this."

"At least you had the fun in there somewhere," I said.

"True," Roger conceded. "But I hoped for more fun."

OUR LAST NIGHT IN L.A., Ted rode to Spago with Sally in her Mercedes convertible, and Sid drove me and Ben. We were visiting the restaurant because Ted had heard of it. I sat in the front with Sid while Ben lolled in the back.

"You think this new disease is some sort of a punishment?" Sid asked me. "You wouldn't tell me, would you? You can guess what I think. Even the Israelites, when the Sodomites wanted to have sex with their men, the Israelites sent out a young virgin instead."

"That's true?" I said to Sid. "They sent out a virgin?"

"Jesus," Ben interrupted, "can't you guys shut up and let me sleep?"

"Read your Bible. God made day and he made night. He made man and he made woman. Opposites, two sexes. That wasn't our decision, okay? That was God's thing. He made opposites, and two guys, I'm sorry, two guys aren't opposites."

"Can it, Daddy-o," Ben said in a weary voice.

I'd realized increasingly in the last three years that, as a doctor, I had authority, and sometimes I took it up in ways that surprised me. "On the face of it, two guys aren't opposites," I said, thinking this was the first time I'd disagreed out loud with Sid, "but maybe sex—by that I mean gender—is really a superficial characteristic, and what's more important is the internal—"

Sid made a disparaging face and rolled his eyes toward the backseat. "Oh, come on. You've seen those vacant friends of Ben's. You think any of them have an internal life? You think they think about anything more than their next screw? That buddy of his from the other night is no higher than an octopus. I think that guy's nothing but a nervous system with skin."

I winced. It seemed pointless to argue.

"You and Ted think there'd be any future to the human race if we all were gay?"

"There are a lot of fine gay people," I said.

Sid didn't seem to hear me. "I can't believe I ended up with a fairy son. You think it's genetic? I used to, but I tell you, those genes can't be mine." Sid's voice dropped. "We've got to get him back in rehab."

Pathetic, I thought, how in thrall to his son Sid was. I thought of my mom and all the money she gave my brother Eric through his divorce. You'd think an adult my mother's or Sid's age would have learned how to let a child go.

"Look," Sid whispered, glancing into the backseat, "he's asleep."

Ben was out. Benzos or narcotics crossed my mind. I wasn't hugely sophisticated about the effects of other drugs—when we got an overdose at the hospital, we drew blood and waited for the tox screen. "You never stop being a parent," Sid said. "You'll see. Why can't Sally find someone like Ted?" I smiled a little for Sid. I felt bad. When we reached Spago, a valet opened the door for Ben, and he fell out.

But it was California, so the valet scooped him from the ground and propped him back in the car.

IN A RESTAURANT near the zoo in Columbus, Ted and I sat near a baby with a mother so simpery and self-satisfied that I had to leave the table. In the bathroom, I wondered if Ted's mother had been like that. There were limits. *My little darling, my bonito baby, Mommy's sweet mushroom.* Mommy's sweet mushroom: really. I wasn't even sure I wanted a baby anymore, but now I wanted one more than ever, just so I could be better than that moony woman. My baby would be better-looking too. "Come on," I said to Ted when I got back to the table. "We don't need to eat. Let's go do it in the car."

He was shocked. "But it's Sunday!" (We were still on our alternate-day schedule.)

It had struck me that the reason we weren't getting pregnant was that there was no spontaneity, no lust. But now we were going to have lust. "Listen," I whispered, reaching over the table and grabbing him by the front of the shirt, "be a real man. Give it to me hard and fast." And he did.

MY FRIEND ROGER with AIDS came back in, admitted to my team. He'd been doing relatively well, keeping his weight up, warding off the pneumonia, but a week or so before his admission, he came down with diarrhea. "You can't decorate with diarrhea," he said. "You can't do *anything* with diarrhea. I've lost twelve pounds."

The intern I assigned to Roger was afraid of him, so I spent a lot of time with him myself. It turned out Roger had an intestinal parasite called cryptosporidium and there was medicine to treat it, but even so, Roger's diarrhea didn't slow down.

"What do they look like, the little beasties? The cryptosporidia?" Roger asked. "Are they round or blobby or what? Do they have eyes? I'm visual. I think if I could see them, I could get over them. That's what I did with the pneumonia, those little teacups"—Roger had had pneumonia from pneumocystis, a parasite that indeed looked like a teacup—"I used to picture them breaking. Every teacup just sort of splitting in half."

And so I robed Roger, put him in mask and gloves, and snuck him to the lab in the middle of the night so he could see his cryptosporidia. "Wow," he said, peering in the microscope. "Far out."

"You going to visualize their destruction?"

"Of course. I think I'll picture them exploding."

It had always amazed me that Roger had gotten over his pneumocystis and that he hadn't gotten it again. I wondered if his visualization technique really worked. "You may think I'm crazy," he said primly, standing up from the microscope table, adjusting the tie of his mask over one ear, "but we all have our ways."

TED BOUGHT THE SPONTANEITY theory. He pursued me, grabbed me from behind in the shower, leaned me over the trunk of the car in our garage, rolled me off the sofa downstairs. "I'm an animal!" he'd bellow. "An animal!"

For my part, I was visualizing a nice round egg and hundreds of happy wiggling sperm.

One night I beat Ted home. "We got some photos from Sally," I told him when he walked in. I didn't want to tell him my other news.

We were three weeks home from our vacation, and I thought the photos would make us both happy.

"God, California," he said, shaking his head, leafing through the rest of the mail, "what a bunch of lost souls they are, huh?"

Who was Ted to be a moralist? His mother was as lost a soul as I'd ever encountered. She called Ted to ask about his dental appointment; did the new shirts she'd bought him fit, did he really think the blue was a nice color? "You get your sperm count yet?" I asked.

Ted gave me a look. "I forgot."

"Well, stop forgetting, honeybuns," I said. "I started my period today."

"Shit!" Ted banged the kitchen table with his hand. Up until now he'd been remarkably forbearing about our reproductive woes, but now he was starting to fray. I knew it hurt him that his animal instincts had gone bust.

"So much for spontaneity, huh?" I said. So much for visualization, I was thinking. We both had our disappointments, but I wouldn't have said what I said next if he hadn't made his crack about my Californians. "Listen, Ted. I have my periods like clockwork, and I have Mittelschmerz"—the medical term for the pains some women get when they ovulate—"so I'm ninety-nine percent sure I have eggs."

"And that's supposed to mean?"

"Just get your sperm count, honey." How baldly did I have to put it? I've been pregnant before, you idiot, I thought—not that it was Ted's fault he didn't know. It was far too late to tell him about my lost pregnancy, and now I was stuck with my lie. I *can* get pregnant, I thought. But I also knew that might no longer be true, that the infection might have left its scars. I could never mention this either.

"Listen." Ted was breathing fast. "Every obstetrician I've heard of says to try for a year before you get worried. And we haven't tried even eight months!"

I waved my hands. "I guess I'm in a hurry, Ted."

Ted shook his head. "You're unbelievable," he said. The words he used to say to flatter me hit me like a blow. Ted knew not to look at me. He was peering around like he was looking for an exit arrow on the floor.

THE NEXT TIME I was on call, late at night, I walked into Roger's room to find a picture done in pen and ink sitting on a little easel. I shot Roger an inquiring look, then bent over to look at it. Irregular purple spheres, blotchily stained: a drawing of cryptosporidia.

"How perverse," I said.

"Would you expect anything less?"

"What's that gray stuff in the background, fecal matter?"

"Exactamundo. I think it looks like paisley, don't you? And you know"—he threw up his hands—"paisley is the moment!"

"You are too much," I said, knowing this would please him.

"You flatter me, darling."

What a strange little man he is, I thought. It struck me, suddenly, the effort he must put into his cheerfulness. I was walking down the dark hall away from him when I was overwhelmed by grief, realizing he would die.

"COULD WE JUST FORGET about this for a while, this child stuff?" Ted asked. "I think it's hurting our marriage."

I looked at him. He was haggard and worn, not at all the happy man I'd married.

"You're right."

Relief flooded his face. "Oh, God, Clare, I'm glad you said that. I thought if I had to drive in one more time to the hospital to, you know"—he could never be explicit—"I thought I'd go crazy or something."

I smiled. "It's that bad, huh?"

"Oh, no, not that it's bad, it could never be bad, not with you, but it's so enforced. It's like there's a gun to my, you know."

I snorted ruefully. "I know."

"It's not joy, you know? It's not normal."

"I know." I felt as if my heart were actually breaking, blood filling the spaces around my lungs. He was right, we must stop it, for the sake of our marriage, our sanity. Yet at the same time, it hit me with an overwhelming certainty that I would never miss my period, or vomit in the mornings, or waddle, or clutch at Ted's arm during labor. I'd had my chance at motherhood, and I'd blown it. I'd slept with a carrier of disease, a man I'd never seen again. I would never have a child.

"YOU MUST HATE US patients with AIDS," Roger said. He was still in the hospital.

"Why?" I said, startled. "It's just a disease."

After a pause, Roger spoke. "That's a very comforting thing you said, although I doubt you realize it."

I thought he was being sarcastic. I had been flip. I remembered the woman with syphilis whom I'd offended. "It's a horrible disease," I corrected myself.

"No, no, darling, what you said first was ideal. It's just a disease. You're very matter-of-fact about it, and I and all my fairy friends appreciate it deeply. I was talking to Mr. Fender down the hall." He was another gay guy with AIDS, also a patient of my team's. "My, he's in a sad state, isn't he? He must weigh under ninety pounds. As I said, I was talking to him, and we agreed that you have a knack. Maybe you should specialize."

"In AIDS? I don't think there's an AIDS specialization." I have to admit I was distracted, trying to figure out how Roger could have heard about, and talked to, Mr. Fender, when both of them were supposedly in isolation. "Well, maybe infectious disease. But I have to do my three years in a rural area." I'd taken federal government money for med school, and working in an underserved area was my way to pay them back.

Roger smiled sagely. "We'll wait for you," he said.

———

"THAT ROGER, that guy with AIDS, he told me I should be an AIDS doctor."

"An *AIDS* doc? All those gay guys? All that death?"

Ted was going into gastroenterology, cut-and-dried and incredibly lucrative. Peering down a little tube at ulcers, tunneling up a colon to snare polyps. While he did his GI fellowship at University, I would be in practice in the boonies, where I'd been wooed by an eager hospital. We had bought a small house in the far suburbs, from which we could both commute.

"I actually like it."

Ted gave a shiver.

"You can be useful. Those people are kind of…they're embarrassed, in a way, and they're sad and they're angry, they know they have something bad but they don't want to be isolated like lepers, they're…" Ted was looking at me with something like astonishment. "Well, they're lonely," I finished.

"How can you be lonely when you've had sexual congress with two hundred people? Have you seen the numbers of those gay guys' estimated contacts? They're incredible."

"You sound like Sid." I hesitated a moment to let that sink in, to both myself and Ted. I remembered the ladies who'd brought me my meals when I had my pelvic infection, the way they'd circled far around my bed. "You can be lonely," I said. "You can have sex ten times a day and still be lonely."

"Well, that's true," Ted said. We were lying in bed; his arm was wrapped around me. "That's true," he repeated, and he sighed.

I STILL LOOKED AT the magazines in the call room, but they were changing. A raw element was slipping in. The women were less beamingly healthy, their poses more demeaning than seductive. Actual sex acts were depicted, in ways that did not always look consensual. I opened up one centerfold and saw bruises. I hurled the magazine back in the drawer. Who was responsible for this? Which one of my fellow residents was supplying this room? It seemed to me that all men did was cause pain, and it struck me then that Ted was angry, angry with me, and the magazines could even be his. Couldn't they? Some fantasy of a bruised and battered woman to make up for the way he saw me.

But Ted wouldn't like that stuff. Not Ted.

Still, I wasn't a hundred percent sure. So I was very aware when, during a week Ted was out of town, between Monday when I was admitting officer of the day and Thursday when I covered for Hank Smalley, a new nasty magazine appeared under the others, beneath the torn *Penthouse*s and *Playboy*s.

So, I thought, it wasn't Ted. I should have been relieved, but instead I felt agitated, wondering if it was Neil Youngman, who was always so proper, or nice married Harold Kennedy, or Strindburg with his mustache and leather pants, or dorky Grant Grant. It could be any of them, I realized. Any of them could be men whose thoughts ran toward inflicting pain on women. All the tiny slights I'd suffered at their hands became ominous. Strindburg had laughed when I'd mixed up the lab values on two patients. Grant had said that my latest haircut looked like I'd been run down by a lawn mower. Kennedy had called me a princess. God knew what any of them really thought of me. God knew how many of them used this drawer.

IN MAY, THE PENULTIMATE month of my residency, I was hit with an overwhelming fatigue, the worst I'd suffered since my spell in med school when I didn't have the energy to eat. Each day I got home from work, flopped on the sofa, and didn't move. Ted was used to my making dinner—I would at least heat something up and improve it, like sautéing onions to add to jarred spaghetti sauce—but now I didn't do a thing. "There's a Hungry-Man in the freezer," I'd say. "Put it in yourself."

"Okay," he'd say, and I'd know by his tone of voice that he wasn't going to heat up a Hungry-Man but instead one of the frozen meals his mother had made, ostensibly for both of us (because we were both working and I was so busy) but really for Ted, as sabotage.

"Are you ever going to eat again?" Ted asked one night.

"I don't want one of those dinners, thank you." We both knew what "those dinners" meant.

Still, Ted stayed cheerful. "Should I get you some Lean Cuisines?" (Ted did our grocery shopping.) "Some Hungry-*Woman* meals?" His grinning face leaned over me.

I didn't smile. "I'll have a yogurt."

"That's not dinner."

"Who are you to say what's dinner? A bowl of rice is dinner in lots of the world."

"You want a bowl of rice? We have rice. I can do rice."

I couldn't stand it. "How can you be so happy all the time?" I screamed. "How can you always act like everything is fine? Are you really totally oblivious to the pain and suffering in the world? And

you're a doctor, a doctor of all people should know. It's like you're
wrapped in a happy cloud or something. You're spooky. You're depressing. I can't believe you ever lost a brother."

When I was done yelling, I closed my eyes and felt smothered with
sleep. Then I had a thought and smiled. Weren't fatique and emotional lability frequently unrecognized signs of early pregnancy?

ROGER WAS BACK. Toxoplasmosis in the brain this time, and
only weeks after his cryptosporidia had been controlled. Toxoplasmosis is a parasite found in the feces of cats; litter boxes are a common
source. "I told Herbert I hate cats," Roger complained. "I know
they're always cleaning themselves, but..." He rubbed his fingers in a
gesture of disgust. The mention of Herbert was my first hint that
Roger had become monogamous. "*Feh,* as my friend Morry would
say."

"You knew there was a risk," I pointed out. I had told him explicitly during his last hospitalization to stay away from feces.

"Everywhere's a risk. It's amazing! Last week I met a man who got
a fungal infection from a potted cactus he brought back from Arizona.
A two-inch cactus in a ceramic Indian moccasin. He scratched himself
watering it under the faucet, and the next thing you know they're
threatening to amputate. And he doesn't even have AIDS. A little potted cactus! I mean, some things seem guilty and some seem just plain
innocent, if you catch my drift."

"Nothing's innocent for you," I said.

Roger ran his hand through his thinning hair in a gesture of impatience. "Damn it. I hate this fear."

MY PERIOD CAME on a Monday, and so heavy it leaked through
to my skirt. I stood in my slip in one of the hospital's public restrooms
and rinsed out the skirt. I would have used the sink in the senior residents' call room, but that would have involved an elevator ride and

two walks through the hospital halls. A woman with a cigarette dangling from her mouth came in clutching a baby and pushing a toddler in a stroller. "This ain't no Laundromat, you know," she said.

"I'm sorry if this disturbs you," I said, "but I'm a doctor and I just had a miscarriage in my clothes." This was extremely unlikely, but I wanted to punish her. "Would you like to see it?" I asked. She gave me a horrified look and backed out the door.

THE NEXT WEEK there was another new magazine. I came upon it on a slow and sunny Sunday afternoon when the team on call was sitting outside on benches. I was the admitting officer of the day, and the ER didn't need me at the moment, so I went to the senior call room to get away. I opened the drawer purely out of custom. I'd noticed that none of the magazines affected me anymore. The new ones were too rude, and the established ones were full of tired scenarios. Also all of them, I thought, were disrespectful of women. I hadn't really thought of this before, but now it was obvious.

The fresh magazine in the middle of the pile had a very odd cover. A woman's naked upper torso stretched diagonally across it, a rope knotted around her neck. Her head was tilted back so you couldn't see her face, her breasts were askew, and strands of blond hair fell over her shoulders. She did not look totally conscious. What now, I thought, irritated, what new sicko thing has someone left here to be discovered? I flipped open the magazine to the centerfold. Two men in cowboy boots and jeans were crouched over a naked woman with a branding iron.

I couldn't breathe.

I didn't want to, but I leafed through other pages. Other scenarios, other pictures.

I flipped back to the table of contents. "Branded, Our Cowboys Leave Their Mark." "Sexual Suffocation, 'Tie One On for Me.'" "Female Genital Mutilation, an African Custom 'Comes' to America."

I am not one hundred percent sane. I have my neuroticisms, my borderline eating disorder, my competitiveness, my fear of intimacy, my tendency to emasculate men who want me. Still, I'm normal. And there was nothing in this magazine a normal person could respond to with anything but repugnance. My God, I thought, who looks at this stuff? And there must be an audience (clearly there was, even among my colleagues). There must be someone in a store who sells this stuff, another someone who buys it, who leaves it hidden in a public place, titillated by the thought of someone finding it. And perhaps the person who finds it is titillated too. A depraved chain. What goes around comes around. I read through the titles again. I'd thought I was so worldly. I'd thought seeing a boyfriend snuggling up on a hospital bed next to the woman whose nose he'd broken was the worst thing a person could see. The notion of sin, not a familiar one, floated into my mind. "They put all sorts of garbage into the environment," I could hear my mother saying, irately, "and why? Because of greed, money, because they just don't care." What kind of cynical businessman would publish this stuff? I glanced at the small print at the bottom of the title page. Crown Communications, Los Angeles, California.

I left the call room and wandered down the hall. I could be one of those magazine women, battered, dazed, naked, not quite human anymore, stunned into an abject meekness. The magazine burned in my hand; I almost dropped it. Instead, I punched the elevator button, pulled myself together, rolled the magazine up and stuffed it in my pocket. I would take it to my locker and lock it away. I would save it to show Sally.

Could Sally know?

Alone in the elevator, I realized that when the doors opened, I'd walk out into an essentially rearranged world, a world in which Sally and her family were no longer benign, California no longer wondrous and expansive and mine, a world in which money was indeed, as my mother always said, a reflection of evil. The ache of this was more than I could stand, and as the little bell rang and the elevator doors slid open, I thought of that night on Sally's patio, years ago, when in my euphoria I almost plunged into the warm dark air.

I exited the elevator and stood frozen in the hall. People in scrub suits and white coats bustled past me. Where could I go? What could I do? My strongest urge was to go back to the call room, walk inside, and slam shut that evil drawer. But it was too late. The drawer was open, and I'd opened it.

Two

YOU CAN DIVIDE your life by decades, by duties, by passions, by fortunes, by griefs. Especially by griefs.

I didn't phone her.

I couldn't.

Sid's magazine, flat and studied, sat beneath the paper liner in the bottom of my underwear drawer, where Ted would never find it. The branding iron was surely real. The scar was real, the pain was real, the fear was real. The "dead" woman on pages thirty-four and thirty-five was faked, or she'd better be faked, for if she wasn't, this was more than I could stand.

Was it possible Sally didn't know? *How* could that be possible? "He has to have plenty of lawyers, in his business." She had to know, had to. She knew and she didn't want to tell me.

But maybe not.

I saw, a week or two later, a new patient in the residents' clinic. Her name was Selina Gilbert. She'd been referred from the emergency room, where she showed up a week before with a head laceration requiring twenty-six stitches. She mentioned to the med student who stitched her up that she couldn't stop peeing, and he checked her blood sugar and found it was three times normal. The med student told Selina Gilbert to stay away from sweets and booze and to show up at my clinic, and, surprisingly enough, she did.

Selina Gilbert was a hooker and a drug addict, and her head laceration was from her pimp. A month before, I wouldn't have recognized this, but a whole dark world was newly visible to me, as if my eyes had adjusted to night. Astonishing how naïve I'd been, how eagerly I'd accepted everybody's explanations. Never again.

"Anybody in your family with diabetes?" I asked.

Ms. Gilbert didn't know her parents. She'd been raised by an aunt. A veiled reference to the aunt's boyfriend: probably abused, I thought.

With new-onset diabetes, you look for an infection. Sugars go higher with the stress of an infection, and a tendency to diabetes can be unmasked. I asked her the usual infection questions: head congestion, rash, fever, cough, abdominal pain, burning with urination, vaginal discharge. She did have a discharge, she said. What was it like? It's nasty, she said.

I did her basic exam, then went off to find the clinic nurse, Lillian, to help me with the pelvic. "I know that girl," Lillian said, peering at me from behind her curtain of bangs. "I've seen her on the street up by my sister's." Lillian had been the medical residents' clinic nurse for twenty years; she was notorious for disliking the female residents and for embarrassing male residents with unwanted gifts—rock paperweights she painted herself, tie clips made of safety pins and beads.

"Really?" I said. "She's got new-onset diabetes. And she has a vaginal discharge. I'll need help to do her pelvic."

Lillian shot me a look. "Hadn't you better be sending her to gynecology clinic? We don't hardly do those here."

"Come on, Lillian," I said. "Just call down to the emergency room and get a Pap smear kit and a gonorrhea culture plate. Please. Knock on my door when you have them."

I saw my next three patients, and Lillian didn't knock on my door. Selina Gilbert, bored, had left her exam room and was leaning against the wall. My last patient didn't show. Selina Gilbert's pelvic was my final task of the day in clinic.

"She's soliciting our patients," Lillian hissed.

I looked at Ms. Gilbert. She was back in her street clothes, a cropped T-shirt and shorts and sandals with straps that wrapped around her ankles. I'd seen Daphne in sandals like hers. "You've actually heard this?"

"She doesn't have to to say anything," Lillian retorted, stalking away.

"Ms. Gilbert, I'm going to the ER myself," I told her. "You go back in the exam room and take your bottoms off."

When I got back from the ER, Lillian was sitting in her smoke-filled office, handbag already hanging from her shoulder, leafing through a *Family Circle*. I stood in her doorway.

"Oops, four o'clock," she said, glancing at her wrist. "I'm off at four."

I stood there. "Excuse me?"

"I have a life, you know," Lillian stood up and stuffed her magazine into her handbag.

Down the hall, Selina Gilbert's head popped out of the exam room. "You got a bathroom for me?"

I pointed her toward the restroom. As she walked away, I noticed, below the sleeve of her examining gown, a healed gash on the back of her arm. An oblong, symmetrical gash that looked almost as if it had been placed there.

I turned back toward Lillian. "Can't you see she's a victim?" I whispered. "And you're just victimizing her more."

"I wouldn't call her a victim." Lillian was looking beyond me to the hall and the receptionist's desk. It was clear that she was dying to leave.

"I'll do the pelvic myself," I said. I started to walk away, but it didn't seem I'd said enough. I went back to Lillian's door, blocking her exit. "You think she's any less a person than you are? You think she's some kind of animal because she's had a lousy life? You think she should just suffer with her discharge, serves her right? God, I don't want to know what you think." My voice was as disgusted as I'd ever heard it; it almost frightened me. "You remember one thing, okay? If you read about her in the paper and they've found her body some-where"—I was shaking my finger—"or if she has some kid who dies a horrible death, or if you open some porn magazine someday and see her bound up and being beaten, well, well—you can say you did your part." I was feeling shaky toward the end of that sentence but recovered my stride to repeat, "You did your part."

The door to Ms. Gilbert's exam room slammed. Lillian rolled her eyes; I heard her mumbling as I walked away. As I pushed open the door to the exam room, I saw, against the late-afternoon light slamming through a window, the silhouette of Lillian, fleeing. "Let's do it," I said to Ms. Gilbert. "Legs up." She did have a horrible discharge, so thick I could hardly locate her cervix, and when I palpated her uterus and tubes, her brown eyes, staring straight at the ceiling, welled with tears.

IT WAS AT THIS time that I had the revelation about my father, that he'd been an embezzler, for me. I didn't tell Ted. I couldn't. He was too happy.

I called Sally. I could tell her about Selina Gilbert, about my dad. We could discuss those things, at least. She could make me feel better about those things.

"Oh, Clare," Sally said once I had finished. "What a nightmare. You must be exhausted."

Exhausted? No, that wasn't right. "I'm beat. I feel like I'm seeing all sorts of things clearly for the first time, and I hate what I'm seeing."

"All sorts of things?" Sally asked, the sliver of hesitation in her voice filling me with unease.

"Everything," I said. Could she sense, somehow, that I knew about Sid? Did that mean she knew about him? I wanted to close my ears. No, I wanted to close my mind. I clutched the phone tighter to my ear. "I feel like, I feel like—"

"Wait a minute," Sally said. There was silence, then several whomping sounds. "I'm on the portable phone on the patio with the paper, and I just saw a hornet."

Did she really believe her father distributed magazines? Could someone who attacked hornets with a rolled-up newspaper be that naïve? "Did you get it?" I asked.

"I think I only enraged it. Hold on, I'm going inside. Now, what were you saying? Something about how you felt?"

I took a big breath. "I can't explain it."

"You're disillusioned," Sally announced firmly.

Her sureness was somehow offensive. I stood, with tears running down my cheeks. "I suppose so," I managed after a moment.

"Have you thought about that word? Dis-illusioned? In a way, losing illusions can't be bad."

"If you say so."

"No, really. Dis-*illusioned*. Do you get it? Do you see my point?"

"You don't have to argue at me," I said. "I'm not sitting on one of your juries."

"It's a useful way of looking at it," she persisted. "Dis—"

"Sally!"

There was a long silence. I was not going to be the one to break it.

"I thought I might make things easier for you, give you a different way of looking at things," she said at last.

She did know.

A FOOL. I'D BEEN a simpering fool, worse yet, an uninteresting fool, seduced by the most predictable of blandishments: money, ease, power. *"Hemos guardado un silencio bastante parecido a la estupidez,"* quoted Margaret, my Guatemala-raised friend, newly free of her abusive spouse, the Vietnam Vet from Hell. Loosely translated, the Spanish means: Jeez, we kept so quiet you'd think we were stupid.

"Damn straight," I told Margaret on the phone. I was saying "damn" a lot, a tough word to confront a tougher world.

The quote, Margaret explained, was a snippet of liberation theology, a Jesuit thing. "God," she said, sighing, "I love Jesuits. They're serious. They're sexy."

Characteristic of Margaret, that mixture of politics and giggly lust. There weren't a lot of Jesuits in Kansas. There Margaret collected and ordered, for her museum, stories of pioneer women, their diaries and letters, matter-of-fact accounts of snakebite and hunger and death. "It's amazing," Margaret said, "you realize how privileged we are. Even the Guatemalans I grew up with seem privileged compared to the pioneers."

"You couldn't touch a pioneer woman with a branding iron," I muttered.

"What?" Margaret said.

I almost told her, but even now there was that silliness in her. I

thought of the old days, when she was surprised by Sally eating ham.
Now she was excited by Jesuits.

"I'm not right," I said. "I'm tired." I'd lost my intellect, my sharp
edge. I wanted my old self back, the fearless self I'd been so proud of in
high school. The self who knew it knew everything, that there was
nothing it couldn't handle. "I'm going out to see Sally this month," I
told Margaret. "That should help."

TOO NEAT, TOO CLEAN. As if the force of her appearance
could scrub things away. She was wearing a navy top and a white skirt,
the gold chain of her handbag biting into her shoulder. "Clare!" She
threw her arms around me.

My face was briefly smushed against her shoulder. When we separated, I looked at her again. Amazing—after Timbo, after Flavio, after
her brother and Flavio, after her father—how untouched she looked.
The radiant cheeks, the starry eyes, the curls lying flat on her cheeks.
Maybe it was stupidity. Maybe it was obliviousness bought at some in-
calculable price.

"You look tired, Clare," Sally observed, giving me a rueful smile.
"Are things okay with Ted?"

"Fine." I bit off the word.

"I bet you're glad to be done with residency. The things they put
you through! How was your flight?"

She took my carry-on, she moved us down the concourse. At the
baggage claim, she spotted my suitcase before I did. She had the rest of
the day off, she told me, but first thing tomorrow, she had to take a
deposition. "What is it?" I asked.

"It's a guy suing my client. She hit him from behind, so she's liable,
and he had some injuries, but he wasn't wearing his seat belt, and in
California that automatically cuts down the award. It should be fun."
She hummed a little. "You can see me in action."

THE AWKWARD THING, I found, was not knowing how to bring it up.

"Do you feel like splitting an onion brick?" Sally asked. "Or that hot spinach dip is good."

I didn't want to eat. What we were doing in a restaurant? I wanted to talk about the evil in the world.

"I don't know, Sally, it overwhelms me. And not simply evil—carelessness and lack of caring. That Lillian I told you about didn't care at all about my patient's infection. She didn't care! And she's a nurse."

Sally frowned. "But you took care of your patient, right? It all worked out."

"Yes, but nurses are supposed to care! Why would someone become a nurse if she didn't care?"

"You seem very unhappy," Sally said cautiously after a moment.

I cast my eyes around the restaurant, the customers looking as sleek and self-satisfied as honking seals. "How can I not be unhappy? After what I've seen?"

"Is it your father?" Sally said gently. "Clare, he wasn't a murderer. I know what he did was wrong, but he did it for you."

"It's not my father," I said bitterly.

She didn't seem to hear me. "And sooner or later," she went on, "you have to separate what you're responsible for from what you're not. He was the embezzler, not you. Why should the guilt be yours?"

I looked at her. *Ask me,* her eyes seemed to be saying. *I need you to know that I know.* I gripped the edge of the table, steadying myself for what I had to say. "Sally, do you know what your father really does?"

"Yes," Sally answered, so quickly I was speechless. She took her napkin off the table and smoothed it in her lap. When she looked up, the tilt of her chin was challenging, even angry. "As a matter of fact, I do."

"THIS IS DR. MANN," Sally said. "Okay with you if she sits in?"

Everyone nodded. The plaintiff looked at me and smiled. Twenties, long hair, a soft face and a cheap shirt and tie—he looked like a nice guy. Sally took a thick folder of papers out of her exquisite briefcase.

Sally smiled apologetically at the plaintiff. For the record, would he state his name? Age? Address? Place of his birth? Parents' names? Places of their birth? Oh boy, I thought, settling in my chair, thinking of Sally's deliberate ways, this is going to be a long one.

"IT'S FINE," I SAID. "The flight was good, and Sally was right there to meet me, and we had lunch at a new place, and then we came back here to unpack, and tonight we go to Sid and Esther's for dinner. Esther's cooking." Did any of this matter? But it was the sort of thing Ted liked to hear.

"Good. It sounds like you're having a relaxing time." I was to be away a week, the longest we'd been separated. Since I'd given up on getting pregnant, being away from Ted didn't matter. I couldn't imagine missing him. "I want you to rest, Clare," he was saying. "Three weeks from now, you're going to be starting your new practice. You won't get to sleep in late then! I know you're exhausted. When I saw you drop that coffee mug—" I had dropped it while talking about Sally.

"I just dropped it, okay?" I said tersely. "It wasn't a statement."

"You could have scalded me!" Ted said. "That coffee was coming at me like hot lava!"

"People can have emotions, Ted. People are allowed to have emotions."

Sally set the teapot on the burner and looked at me from across the kitchen.

SHE THOUGHT AUNT RUBY said photographer.

Five years before. Sally had known for five years. Aunt Ruby, after Sally-the-fledgling-lawyer got her out of jail, had invited her back to her house. "You know," Aunt Ruby said at the door, reaching for Sally's hand, "you turned out pretty good for a pornographer's daughter."

"What? Did Daddy get a camera too? I knew Ben was taking pictures, but—"

"Ben's taking pictures?" Aunt Ruby raised her eyebrows. "You're kidding, I never thought your father would let either of you near the business. I don't even know where the offices are, somewhere in the Valley I think, but your dad's like some Mafia guy that way: keep my family out of it. Which you have to give him credit for. Even Freddie gives him credit for that."

"What are you talking about?"

"The way I look at it, Sally, and I've told Sid this, it's not savory, it's not ideal, but there's nothing intrinsically wrong with it. It's the old American bugaboo about sex. There probably wouldn't be a market if Americans weren't such Puritans. It's like Vegas. You go to Vegas, and there's some showgirl with her boobs hanging out and wooo, hot stuff. I ask you, what's the big deal about breasts? Why in the world should breasts be kept under wraps?"

"Market for what? Aunt Ruby, what are you talking about?"

"Of course, I don't want boob shots on my coffee table. Freddie's good about that, if he looks at the stuff he never brings it home. And Sid, well, after what he's seen, I'm sure he'd have no interest. What's that saying about the cobbler's children? They go barefoot. Is that right? I'm not sure it fits, but you see my point."

"What are you talking about? Aunt Ruby, what—"

SHE'D BEEN LIKE ME at first, shocked and angry, confused, but since then she'd thought about it a lot and talked it over with Sid. Some of the things she'd realized surprised her.

First off, he was good at it. It was a business like anything else, and there were lots of unexpected angles. The politics of cover art. Targeting age-groups. Identifying outlets. "He's good at organization and financing," Sally said. "And what sets him apart is he gives his artistic people free rein. You wouldn't believe the people he has working for him. Film school graduates, photographers who put on shows at art galleries, prop people who used to work at *Vogue*. And they're all reasonably happy. It's a living, it's a little bit what they hoped for.

"Clare," she told me, "this stuff is as old as time."

And he paid everybody. "It's not as if a woman comes in and rolls around naked and leaves without a penny to her name. And the performers are not necessarily educated. How else are they going to survive?"

And then there was the whole matter of the First Amendment.

"See, the other thing he's good at is niche marketing. He has a magazine for shoe fetishists, he has a magazine for people who like to see women smeared with food. You could almost say it's therapy. Can you imagine thinking you were the only person in the world who dreamed about a naked woman covered with blueberries? Think how isolated you'd feel. The magazine lets you realize you're not alone."

She brought up Timbo. "Isn't it odd our culture can't talk about sex directly, despite all the breasts and legs used to sell cars and beer? Think about Timbo, crashing a car when he was masturbating! He was a victim of sex. And maybe adult magazines, by bringing things out in the open, make people less likely to be victims."

And the scholarship fund! "How many publishers of adult magazines fund scholarships? I met one of the recipients a month ago, a black guy who studies physical therapy. He was very pleasant. He wore a bow tie."

"DO YOU TRUST your doctor?"

"Do I trust him? Oh sure, I've seen him for years. My parents saw him, my sister sees him."

"And you would say he was truthful, he told the truth?"

"Dr. Olsen? Oh yeah, he's always been truthful, he's always told me the truth. Found my mother's cancer. Told me to quit smoking!"

"Were you wearing your seat belt?"

"Yes."

"Are you sure? You couldn't have forgotten in the excitement of the accident, that you weren't wearing it?"

"I was wearing my seat belt."

"That's definite in your mind?"

"Yes."

"That's always been definite in your mind?"

"Look. I was wearing my seat belt."

Sally sighed and took a sheaf of papers out of her briefcase. "Are you aware that Dr. Olsen, in his deposition, referring to his office records of your visit to him after the accident, stated that you told him you were not wearing your seat belt?"

"IT'S DRECK, BASICALLY," Sid said. "You know that word? It means trash. Worse than trash." He brought up the topic, not me; Sally must have told him, in a whispered conference in the foyer, that I knew. I'd sat silently through the whole meal, thinking of the scathing remarks I'd planned but unable, somehow, to say them. We were back in the dining room with the peach enameled table, where the Pollock had once hung on the wall (replaced by a super-realistic painting of a girl and a dog), where I had, years ago, first tasted bouillabaisse and chardonnay. The conversation was overpolite, off, and the first hint of passion were in these words of Sid's.

"I admit it, it's dreck! That's why I hit it off with Flavio's father: he made tchotchkes, I made dreck. I got into it through the back door. I distributed magazines, I really did, I had those trucks piled up with the latest issues. We'd go back and reclaim the stuff that wasn't sold, and here's what I noticed: the blue stuff didn't come back. *Look, Life,* you name it, *Ladies' Home Journal,* there were always leftover issues. But not the blue stuff. The lightbulb went on, okay? I started with a mimeographed newsletter, believe it or not. Some of my outlets sold it from behind the counter. *Girls Galore,* sketches and stories. I had a buddy who could draw, and I thought up the stories myself. The first advertiser I had was a tobacco shop. This was fifty-seven. Things were pretty innocent back then.

"But hey, basically, it's a stupid business. You're not catering to people's higher interests. Even the stories you tell—if you happen to tell a story, and a lot of times you don't—are stupid stories. Here comes the delivery man delivering flowers, oh look, the girl at home likes him, oh look, he likes her too, she's sticking this out, he's sticking that out, the flowers are everywhere, et cetera. So maybe the delivery guy's a black guy, or maybe he's a girl, or maybe the girl's a guy and he's delivering groceries, cucumbers maybe, or there's two delivery guys and one girl, I don't know. Eh. You can think it's disgusting, or you can just say, well, that's what people like to think about. Why not? Better than imagining your house burning down, or losing your money, or the next Vietnam War. I don't think what people read is what they do, by the way, not really. You ever read those letters in *Penthouse*? Sure you do, everybody's read those. You don't think those are true, do you?"

I could see what he was trying to do, readjust my moral landscape, change my thinking. He was disappointed in me, I supposed, finding me Midwestern and puritanical despite my irony and sharp tongue.

Sally was leaning slightly forward, watching us, catching first my eye, then his. Esther was poking the tines of her fork through a tiny hole in a cloth napkin.

What do they do? I wondered suddenly of Sid and Esther. In the privacy of their bedroom, or on the stairwell, in the laundry room now that Sally and Ben were gone—what do they do? Surely Sid wasn't content with the usual. I thought of passive, listless Esther and voluble Sid. I imagined performances involving servants, the curtains, candlesticks.

"Clare?" Esther repeated. "You'll take some pie, won't you?"

Her best pie, my favorite, the pecan with a double nut layer. "Too rich for me," Sid was saying, waving it away.

"A tiny piece for me, Mom," Sally said.

I looked at Esther's hands across the table, cutting the pie. The slight tremor, her head dipping as if accepting a blow.

He hurts her, I thought, and felt sick. He's a sadist. "I'll have a nice big piece," I said for Esther's sake.

Sid leaned back expansively, clasped his hands behind his head, and stuck his elbows in the air. "Hey, let me ask you this: Is it worse than owning a company that makes the bigger, better bomb?"

SALLY FIXED ME DINNER the next night, an elaborate meal—chicken and mashed potatoes, baby carrots with dill, muffins studded with bits of red and green peppers—and I took this as an act of contrition. We sat at a table in her condo near the sliding glass windows, using cloth napkins and placemats. A bud vase with a single rose stood in the center of the table.

She didn't seem to know about the violence. "Blue magazines," she'd said, and once, with a smile, "girlie magazines." We talked again about my father, the extra money he gave me for clothes, the big shrimp at Thanksgiving.

"If he did it, he did it for you," Sally said, holding out the basket of muffins.

It wasn't quite right. It didn't square with my knowledge of Sally that she should be so accepting. But, as she said, Sid was her father. Honor thy father and thy mother—Bible stuff again. Although I couldn't really say that Sally honored her mother. Mostly, she ignored her.

Sally told me about Ben's new apartment, which he shared with three male friends in a complex in Manhattan Beach. "It's very spartan," she said. "Two chairs and a table in the living room."

"I love your adjectives," I burst out, surprising myself. I'd left the magazine in the bottom of the suitcase, under a camisole and a denim skirt. What adjective would Sally use for it? Disgusting. Vile. Unbelievable. Evil.

"It *is* spartan," Sally went on. "It surprised me that with four gay guys, well, after Flavio, it surprised me that the apartment was so, that it wasn't more..."

I could have helped her.

"That it wasn't more decorated," she finished finally.

"Oh," I said, letting her feel foolish. It seemed unlikely that every gay male had an aesthetic sense, although that was my stereotype too. I thought of my patient, Decorator Roger. I adore pornography, he'd said.

"They seem like decent guys," she said, anxiety in her tone. "Not substance abusers."

"That's promising."

"Not that I can tell for sure." With her fork poised, she looked at me across the table. Then her gaze dropped to her lap, and she smoothed her napkin again. "What does bother me about Daddy, what I found out later, is that he does a lot of magazines for gays."

"What?" This startled me. For no good reason, Sid's producing porn for gays had never occurred to me. I thought of Flavio's magazine behind the toilet.

"It's about a third of his business. I asked him. It's not that I'm anti-gay, you know that; what bothers me is that Daddy's anti-gay. You know how he talks. Yin-yang, the Israelites sending out the virgin. But he makes a lot of money off gay sex. And he expects to make more and more, what with AIDS. He says people buy smut if there's repression or danger, and AIDS is danger."

Sid's cynical expectations surprised me, but of course made perfect sense. And why not market to gays, a bigger group—I hoped—than heterosexual sadists. Smut, Sally had said. Maybe that was what people in the trade called it.

"It doesn't seem right that he should make money off of people who repel him," Sally said firmly, but her voice quivered a bit at the end.

Who better to make money off of? I thought, but didn't say it.

"Before, I could tolerate things, I didn't like them, but they were tolerable. But after I found out about the men's stuff..." Sally hesitated. "After Flavio moved out, after I'd found out all about him and his—" She winced, unable to say it. "I found some magazines Flavio had tucked under our mattress. You know. And I looked through them, and two of them, two of them—"

"Crown Communications," I said.

Sally nodded. "Crown Publications, back then. Daddy, I said, how can you publish this stuff? And he said I publish it, I don't enjoy it. But that's not the point, I said, don't you see how hypocritical it is? And he said honey, it's a market. And I said is everything a market? And he said look, a few years ago the heterosexual market was drying up, and getting into homos—that's exactly how he put it—getting into homos was a strategic move. He had to support his family. He had to pay for my college, he said."

The difference between paying for Sally's college and the money Sid made was so extreme as to make his comment insulting. Sally knew this, of course: despair had crept into her voice. "Oh, Sally," I said.

She shrugged her shoulders helplessly. "It's what he does. It's how he thinks. I have to accept that there's a moral vacuum in him. I found those magazines on a Sunday afternoon, and I remember sitting on my bed, thinking my God, what can I do? You remember that bed Flavio and I had, with the wrought-iron headboard? I thought I should impale myself on that, let Daddy and Ben keep phoning and phoning and then come over and find me. I thought that would be a fitting solution. Impaled on my marital bed."

We sat in silence for a few moments, our food untouched. "I wish you'd told me," I said.

"I couldn't. I was mortified. The root of that being 'mort,' meaning death, like rigor mortis."

I smiled in spite of myself. "You're *proud* of your adjectives!"

"Maybe." We smiled at each other, and for a moment we were our old selves, the best of friends.

———

"WE COULD SEE A MOVIE," Sally suggested later.

I went through the paper, looking for a movie we'd agree on. I didn't want some stupid comedy, and Sally would agree to nothing with a hint of violence.

"How about *Tess*?" I asked.

A shadow crossed Sally's face. "Does anybody die in that?"

I thought of the magazine in my suitcase. Sally knew about the girlie magazines, she knew about the guy magazines, but she clearly didn't know about the magazines like the one I had.

"IT'S A VARIED GROUP," Sid said. "There's a Hasid works out of Brooklyn, and a bunch of Chinese, and Italians and Greeks and hillbillies and a couple Scandinavians. You know, they're people. They have families and mortgages and hemorrhoids and all that stuff. They're not monsters." He reached for his snifter, looked across at me as he sipped. "It's not so bad, Clare. You'll get used to it."

Sally was up in her former bedroom sorting through old books; Esther was in the kitchen. Their absence was calculated, I suspected, so that Sid and I could be alone.

We were in the family room, the wood-paneled room reminiscent of the dimly lit restaurants Sid favored, this room where we'd sat together so many times before. I knew he expected me to smile, to concede, to say "Oh, don't worry." And I almost wanted to, the spell of this room and my memories was so strong.

But I couldn't. "Did Sally tell you how I found out?" I told him about the drawerful of dirty magazines in the residents' call room, tried to ignore his eyes twinkling in approval. I told him how I'd actually enjoyed them, until, until...

"'Sexual torture,' that's what you call it?'" He smiled indulgently, brought his snifter to his lips and inhaled. "Those pictures, Clare," he said, settling himself in his leather chair, "you've got to understand something. They're not real."

"What do you mean, they're not real? She was lying there naked, trussed up, there were two men over her with a branding iron, and in the next picture—"

Sid frowned. "You must have gotten ahold of one of those S and M magazines. Was it *Bondage*? *Sweet Pain*? They're kind of a specialty thing."

"*Sweet Pain,* yes. And I knew it was yours because I saw the name Crown Communications at the bottom of the contents page. It was like—"

"Listen, that stuff is fake. They stage it. S-and-M is very theatrical."

"It was like a knife to my heart."

He bent his head and stifled a smile. "You're sounding a little theatrical yourself."

I was unable to speak.

Sid shrugged, met my eyes again. "Listen, people like that stuff! I agree, it's nasty, it's not what I'm into personally, but people buy it. It's not a big market, but it's—"

I found my voice. I set my snifter on the floor beside me. "Buy it! Sid, the market's not the point. The point is the violence to this woman. To this woman, okay? To this particular woman being brutalized in your magazine and to every woman everywhere in any sort of contact with the kind of sick male who looks at that stuff and enjoys it. Are you crazy, Sid? Is this something you want to promote?"

"Oh, she may not be happy at the moment, but in the end she's ecstatic. That's what these people like, Clare, that's how they get their kicks. Did that woman in the magazine, did she have scars on her arms like she'd been shooting up drugs? These women'll do anything. See, they're masochists."

He was patronizing me: Big Daddy explains the evil world. "Oh God," I said. "Don't make me sick."

Sid threw his hands out, a helpless gesture. "Hey! The pay's not bad. And listen, let me tell you, some of these people don't even want to be paid, they're exhibitionists, you'd be amazed."

"I brought it out with me," I said, "to show Sally."

He glanced up at me quickly. "To show Sally?" Then quietly: "You don't want to show Sally."

I had him. He was on my hook. My voice was maybe more triumphant than it should have been. "Yes, I brought it out to show Sally."

Sid didn't speak for a moment. His eyes moved back and forth, a calculating gesture, and I remembered how when I'd first met him, he reminded me of Rumpelstiltskin. "I don't think you want to show Sally," he repeated, and I wondered, fleetingly, if he meant this as a threat.

"Gratitude is a slippery thing," Sid said into the air, his voice uncharacteristically soft, making me strain to hear it. "Slippery." He stood and walked to the bookshelf, where the decanter of brandy sat on its silver tray. "More?" he asked, waving the decanter in the air, and when I shook my head, he poured two fingers for himself. He didn't speak again until he sat down. "I hope you remember all your trips out here, now that you're a rich doctor and can pay your own way."

I felt my face flush. How many trips had he paid for? Two or three, over the years. And there had been, I supposed, the restaurant bills, the gas and mileage, the movie tickets. I hadn't realized he was keeping track.

"Sally told me you figured something about your father, that he might have embezzled some money?"

It shocked me that Sally had told her father this. But then she told her father everything. "Probably," I said, making my voice light. "He worked for doctors, remember? And he was underpaid, and he needed money for my college and for my first trip out here. But none of that matters now, because he's dead."

"Lost him down the aisle at a Kmart." Sid smiled, resuming his seat in his big chair. "Isn't that what Ben said?"

"He was a good man," I said, blinking. "He loved me."

"I love my daughter too."

We sat in silence a moment.

"Please don't show her." His eyes met mine. He must have seen a flicker of doubt there, a movement toward compassion. "It's nothing I'm proud of, it's nothing she needs to see."

"She thinks they're just blue magazines," I said. "Like, I don't know, some playmate lying in a haystack. The only thing that upsets her is that you cater to homosexuals when you don't like them. She has no idea."

"Please. I'd do anything for her. She's the light of my life. You know how close we are."

I should have said: get rid of those magazines. Sell off your empire, shut down your presses, fire your staff. But I couldn't think that clearly, and all I wanted to do was accommodate him and get out. The light shining from the living room beckoned like a path to daylight. "I'll think about it," I mumbled, standing up.

"You think about it," Sid repeated from his chair. As I hurried to the door, I kicked over my snifter on the floor, and like a fool, I bent to pick it up.

"I'm at your mercy," Sid said, watching me as I knelt and cleaned.

"WHAT ABOUT THE BIGGER, better bombs problem?" Sally asked. "That was a good point, don't you think?"

Oh, Sally. "My mother thinks no source of big money is untainted."

"Oh," Sally said knowingly, "your mother."

I'm at your mercy, Sid had said.

"But when you think about it," Sally went on, "no one actually gets hurt by what he does."

"What about the people in his magazines, don't they get hurt? A woman lying there with her legs spread out, isn't she devalued? And why does she do it? To pay her rent, feed some kids, buy some drugs? To please her man?"

"Actually, it's interesting," Sally said. "Some women pose for the magazines so they can earn more money as exotic dancers. It's part of their résumé."

"People say anything to make it seem okay, right? But it's not okay. Think about it. You're debasing the whole act of sex. You're taking love and affection out of sex and making it nothing but performance. You're making everyone a voyeur, and then when they've watched a man and a woman and a man and man and a woman and a woman, what will they want next? Two people having sex gets pretty boring. Next they'll want a threesome, and then they'll add whipped cream or something, and then a belt, and when that doesn't do it anymore, they'll want some sexual torture."

Sally shook her head. "Isn't that like saying if you take a puff of marijuana you'll go on to heroin?"

She wanted "dis-illusionment"—shouldn't she be dis-illusioned? I went to my room, reached into the bottom of the suitcase, went back out to Sally. "Look," I said, laying the magazine on the table where we'd eaten our elegant dinner. "I found this in the residents' call room."

I didn't have to show her. She didn't have to know. And I've wondered since why I did it, exactly, what percentage was anger at Sid, what percentage anger at Sally, what percentage my own agony about all I'd suddenly seen.

Sally eyed the magazine warily from across the room, the magazine with its very odd cover, the woman's neck and the rope. "Oh," she said, her voice pitched unusually high, "that stuff is the extreme fringe."

"You should look at it," I said.

"Why?"

"Because it's your father's."

She took a quick breath, then approached it slowly, timidly, picking up only the lower edge of the front page, as if to open it farther might let out some evil genie.

"Open it," I urged her. "Just read the table of contents."

She stared at me. "It's okay," I assured her, "there aren't any pictures on that page."

She closed her eyes, holding the edge of the page.

"Sally. You're a grown-up. You should know."

She nodded, threw the magazine open. I watched her eyes dart through the table of contents and down to the small print at the bottom of the page. Her face seemed to deliquesce, her jaw opening and her eyelids and cheeks sagging. She dropped the page, her left arm shot out and swept the magazine off the table; it slapped against the sliding glass window and fell to the floor. "No!" she was screaming. "Daddy, no!"

IT WAS, FOR ME, not a bad time. Especially when Sally moved from her condo to her bouillon cube of a house, a place that always reminded me of our old house in Oberlin. In Oberlin she'd been separated from her family by two thousand miles, but now she was separated by much more. Both times we had each other.

In August 1985, two weeks after my visit to Sally, I started a practice of general internal medicine in a small town, Lisbonville, not far from Akron, where I'd trained. The Lisbonville hospital owned and managed my practice, hoping I would staunch the steady flow of people going from Lisbonville to the hospitals in Akron. My practice started slowly—I remember standing at the window of my office gazing out at the parking lot for arriving patients—but then a Dr. Faud died suddenly (burst aneurysm) and the hospital sent his patients to me.

Dr. Faud's patients were a mess. Over half of them were on Valium, which was about the only medicine they could be counted on to take reliably, and the other ones were on heart pills, water pills, diet pills, blood thinners, and a bewildering array of "bowel relaxers." Often neither I nor the patient could figure out—even with Dr. Faud's scribbled notes at hand—why they were taking a given medicine. Their diagnoses were vague in the extreme: nerves, colitis, recurrent arthritis, organic heart disease. When I asked the patients to put on exam gowns, they were shocked: Dr. Faud had always examined them with their clothes on.

In the first months, I found breast lumps, prostate nodules, goiters, lupus, a bevy of anemias, and three curable and two terminal cancers. I strode into each exam room with a mission: I was going to find disease. But after the first flurry of discoveries, uneasiness set in, both for Dr. Faud's former patients and for me. With Dr. Faud, they had thought they were healthy, or at least healthy enough, but with me, they got the truth. Or was it the truth? Was that heart murmur I'd heard really cause for concern? Was it necessary to lower this person's cholesterol? If the arthritis was rheumatoid and not, as Dr. Faud had dubbed it, elderly joints, did that knowledge make a difference? People talked to me about Dr. Faud with a wistfulness that embarrassed them. "He was sure a cheerful fellow—'course he never checked me over like you do." In the memorial photo on the hospital bulletin board, Dr. Faud was the shape and consistency of a jelly doughnut. "Twinkletoes," a patient called him. "He fought the battle of the bulge just like me." Her eyes swept down my body and its unforgiving thinness.

"I have no idea why they miss him," I told Sally. "He was a terrible doctor."

Sally gave me the same answer Ted did. "Maybe he cheered them up." When Sally said it, I laughed; when Ted said it, I scowled.

We didn't talk about her family. We talked about her work, or my work, or the new furniture she was buying, or my mother. We rarely talked about my marriage. There might be a certain hardness in our conversations, a meanness we'd reveal only to each other, but this was something we enjoyed together, nothing that threatened our bond. *No tickee, no washee*, Sally had taken to saying. *Never trust a man who strokes his chin. She who suffers fools suffers foolishly.* In my new job, I had four weeks off a year and money for plane fare. I went to Los Angeles five times in one six-month span. "Why don't you move here?" Sally kept asking. "Think of the good times we'd have." I would have, but I was married, and I was serving out my three years in Lisbonville.

My office practice might be flat, but my hospital practice was booming. The family docs hated to come to the hospital and care for their suddenly sick patients, their therapeutic failure patients, their dying patients. I didn't mind these patients at all. If they got better, I was pleased; if they didn't, I didn't take it personally. I developed my own set of axioms, ones I repeated to Sally. *You don't treat an eighty-year-old with hypotension like a twenty-year-old with hypotension. Sometimes the best you can ask for isn't much. Where there's urine there's life. If a patient wants to die, why not let him go?*

"Sure," Sid had said when Sally went to him with the magazine, "that's one of mine. You believe those special effects?" His tone was confident, casual; the only thing that gave him away was a gnawed cuticle he tried to hide by curling his finger into his palm.

"DIRTY MAGAZINES?" Ted had said. "He makes his living off of dirty magazines?" He laughed. "I wonder how he lists his occupation on his passport."

SALLY AND I had lunch in a pretty garden restaurant, seated outside under hanging plants. She was wearing sunglasses, and while normally she'd remove them as we ate, this time she wore them throughout the whole meal.

We went to new restaurants, bigger restaurants with smaller, more crowded tables, where men with slicked-back hair and long and slender women in dresses with tulip-shaped skirts approached our table to say hello to Sally. "Expert witness," she'd whisper as they left, or "client" or "trainer of my client." She could tell at a glance if a woman had had a face-lift, although she admitted that with the very best ones, you couldn't be sure. She had a new line of steady cases, women suing over bad cosmetic surgery results, and while this wasn't what I thought of as women's advocacy law, I understood why Sally enjoyed it. She was exploring an uncharted territory of aggrievement. She dealt with actresses, models, exotic dancers, the wives of wealthy men. An eyebrow pulled up too far on one side, a dip and bulge in the tummy—to Sally's clients, these new flaws were worse than their old ones.

"Thousands of dollars for an elective procedure," Sally said, "thousands of buckos for tuckos." She never used to talk like this; this was something I might say. Traditionally, Sally told me, plastic surgery awards were based on pain and suffering, while she was trying for compensation based purely on the value of someone's appearance. She was cutting-edge, really. A lawyer from Houston had called her for advice. Like it or not, Sally said, looks were a commodity in this culture. A nice face and body might be a woman's only asset.

"Pretty damn sad," I said.

"It is sad! I tell my clients that it's sad. Sometimes that helps." She glanced around us at a woman passing our table. "No face-lift," we said in unison, breaking into giggles.

She fixed me more meals at her home—that is, at her condo, and later, at her house. Chicken cacciatore, tabouli, steaks with a mustardy wine sauce. Sally was becoming quite a cook. "Why don't you try it?" she said. "You open a cookbook and read. It isn't challenging."

"I need an audience," I said. "All Ted likes is Mother's Meat Loaf."

Sally's new house was in West Hollywood, on a street off a street off Sunset, in an area filled with gays and a certain type of movie person—set designers and editors and lighting people—who respected a director or two but didn't think much of stars. I thought the area was surprisingly bohemian for Sally, but she liked it because it reminded her of Oberlin, which was accurate, I suppose, although the thing that reminded me most of Oberlin was Sally's house itself, although its market value was ten times greater. Eerily enough, there were also yippy dogs next door, although Sally seemed much fonder of their owner, a Japanese man who had a chain of appliance stores, than she had been of poor Mr. Morgan.

Sally's house was my haven. To me, it was perfect. Ted's and my house had never seemed homey to me; I didn't like my kitchen cabinets or the curtains I'd picked. In Sally's house I could open a cupboard, get out a glass, pour some orange juice, and sit down with the newspaper at the kitchen table, never once meeting with anything that annoyed my eye. I loved the bright rugs and the soft chairs and the well-laid tables. I loved the neat, clean rooms. I loved Sally.

TED HAD A TREMOR. His right hand shook when he lifted a fork or a spoon to his mouth. His hand shook a bit at other times, but most noticeably when he was eating. I thought the tremor was cute when we were dating; I wondered if I made him nervous (although he didn't seem nervous), and then I realized it wasn't nerves, it was Ted, and it pleased me that I'd noticed, because it really wasn't obtrusive, and maybe Ted didn't even know he had it. It was a secret part of him I'd noticed. I was proud to have noticed it, to know.

It came to drive me crazy. There were spills. One night, at dinner with some friends, I told him not to order cabernet. "Isn't that one of the red kinds?" he asked me. "I thought you were supposed to order red wine with beef."

"I'm trying to keep you from embarrassing yourself," I whispered urgently, holding an imaginary glass in my hand and shaking it. Ted's face fell. Later he got melancholy, then angry, and finally after trials of medication, biofeedback, and even acupuncture, he took to sitting at my right, where his tremor would be less visible to me. He blamed himself for my not wanting to go out, he signed us up for a wine-tasting course thinking that would please me, he offered to rent some dirty videos if that was something I thought I'd enjoy. Nothing he did, of course, appeased me. At one point I called him "sniveling."

In every act of willful destruction, there's bound to be a moment when you're in the kitchen, drinking a glass of water, and you suddenly think, my God, what am I *doing*? But then Ted would pick up his fork and scatter rice across the placemat, or drip soup from his spoon back to his bowl, and I was off again.

TED'S PARENTS CAME to visit, and I got home late because of a meeting at the hospital. Ted was a GI fellow then and working almost as hard as I was. He and his parents were eating a meal his mother had cooked.

"How'd it go, honey?" Ted asked. As he lifted his forkful of mixed vegetables to his mouth, he dropped a piece of carrot.

"It was fine. They asked me to be chair next year."

Phil grunted. "Chair of a committee?"

"Imagine that," Lizzie said in astonishment. "Are you on any committees at your hospital, Ted?"

"Nope."

"I can't believe they haven't asked you to be on a committee!" she noted hotly. "You'd be wonderful on a committee! You'd be a wonderful chair. Do you remember being on the bowling team in high school? Remember when you made Eagle Scout?" I thought they'd offer me dinner, but they didn't, and not wanting to fetch my own plate and silverware, I spun out of their orbit and headed for the basement, where I folded laundry meticulously. They were still talking about Ted and the Wonders of Ted and the Sad Underappreciation of Ted when I came up the steps with a stack of folded clothes. "I bet Clare doesn't fold your undershirts like I do," Lizzie said.

"What do you think, Ted?" I asked. "Do I fold your undershirts okay?" I knew this was a crucial moment, that I was forcing Ted, with both parties present, to choose between his mother and me.

Ted had a piece of meat loaf on his fork, and as he brought it to his mouth, there was a wobble and he had to poke out his lips. The hairs on the back of my neck stood on end. Ted maneuvered the meat loaf safely into his mouth, then chewed it with excruciating deliberation. He turned to me and smiled. "You do a wonderful job," he said.

"I have to put away these clothes," I said in a high-pitched voice. I felt as if I were shaking uncontrollably myself. I tried, but I wasn't a natural at folding, not at all. And it seemed like a dreadful responsibility that Ted had chosen me over his mother.

I didn't want him anymore. I went upstairs and put the clothes away. As I started back downstairs, my mother-in-law's insistent voice wafted up the stairwell. "No," I said out loud. I went back to our bedroom and curled up on the bed. When Ted came up a couple of hours later, I didn't even open my eyes. I'd thought of several exit lines, and the one that came to my lips came almost randomly. "I mean this partly as a compliment," I said, "but you're too good for me."

THE FIRST DIVORCE is okay, it can happen to anyone—too young, too romantic, unrealistic—but the second divorce is different. The second divorce is a stigma. I stood in the little garden outside the courthouse, next to a broken fountain, chips of paint peeling off its basin, and thought, well, I'm a two-time divorcée.

Two times divorced means that another marriage could mean three times divorced, and that's impossible. Three times divorced goes beyond stigma into shame or, worse, comedy. So marriage was out for me now. I realized I'd spent a lot of my lifetime looking for a man, and now my searching days were over. A relief, really. A door closed. One less thing to worry about. Oh, I could live with someone. I could be a soul mate (me?), a lover, a squeeze, even a mother, but never again would I ever be a wife. I was free! I was almost giddy, standing in that crummy courtyard. I walked down the street to the Sugar Bowl and ordered a hot fudge sundae.

"LISTEN TO THIS," I used to say when some paradox of human behavior came up: "My best friend hates violent movies, she reads 'The Movie Guide for Puzzled Parents' so she'll know what she can stand to see, and you know what her favorite movie is? *The Godfather.*"

I'd told Sally for years she should see it, just for cultural reference. I mean, hadn't she even heard about the horse's head in the guy's bed, or "make him an offer he can't refuse," or the Godfather's weird voice? "You don't want to be a Woman with No Cultural References," I said, knowing the implication would irk Sally. She finally ended up watching the movie on tape, on a Saturday night, in her house where she could hide in the kitchen during the violent parts, and she was so impressed that she watched the whole thing again that night, and one more time the next day. "Good Lord," I said on the phone, "a Godfatherthon!" By the third time through, she could almost watch the whole scene in the restaurant where Michael Corleone, the Godfather's son, shoots the police chief in the throat, a scene she wanted to see every second of, she said, so she could study Michael's face when he did the deed.

"It's so profound!" she told me. "You see that, more than anything, his father doesn't want Michael in the business, and then he gets drawn into it to protect his father."

"That's true," I said. Somehow the way she put this made me nervous. "And the business ruins Michael," I pointed out. "You have to see *Godfather II* to understand how much." The tug of fear: Sally wasn't speaking to her father then; I could only wonder what she was thinking. "You've got to see *Godfather II*," I repeated.

"Can I stand it?" she asked.

"Piece of cake," I said. "If you can get through the first one the second one's nothing." That wasn't totally true, of course, but I wanted to be sure she saw it. This wasn't my proudest moment with Sally—I was trying to control her perceptions, the same way, perhaps, her father had controlled them before.

AFTER MY DIVORCE, I moved to a town house, a place I ended up staying in almost ten years. I never much liked living there. I had the place redone at one point by a designer from Decorator Depot (a designer, it turned out, who had never known Roger) in a style which at first seemed California and modern, reminiscent of Sally's house, but later seemed no more personal than a hotel lobby. After a while, I didn't go into my living room at all but went straight to the kitchen to heat up my TV dinner then headed upstairs to the bedroom and my magazines and medical journals and TV. I tried to read books, but between my short attention span and the fatigue that hit me between ten and eleven, finishing a book was beyond me.

THE ANSWERING MACHINE clicked on, and Esther's voice, tentative, searching, scratched the silence in the room. "Sally? Sally, would you please call me? This is Mommy." There were several seconds of confused silence before Esther hung up her phone.

Sally, at the kitchen table, lifted her hand to her forehead. "All she does is call me, I can't stand it."

"Did this just start?"

"The last month or so. I don't know what's gotten into her."

"Do you talk to her?"

"How can I not talk to her? She's pathetic. She misses me, she wants me to come over for dinner, she's worried about Ben, Ben needs a haircut, Ben's surly, Ben's hanging out with a funny crowd again. He has a whole new set of roommates now—all the other guys moved out. And then she always slips in how Daddy misses me."

Sally still called him Daddy. "What do you say to her?"

"I say, Mother, if I could come over there without destroying every shred of my integrity, I would. But the way things are, after finding out how you and Daddy lied to me for all those years, I'm sorry, but I can't."

"What does she say then?"

"Oh, I don't know. She cries. She says she understands. They have a weird marriage, she and Daddy. I don't think she's strong enough to get out of it. But she's hardly ever home when he is. She gets in her car and drives. Just drives. She drove up to San Luis Obispo last night and didn't get out of the car."

A disturbing thing, Sally talking to her mother. I didn't know if I should worry. All those years the phone calls had been to *him*.

I HANDED THE NEWSPAPER clipping back to Sally. "Your mother sent you this?"

"I'm sure he told her to."

It was a long article from a business section about Sidney Rose, complete with a photo of his beaming face. It referred to Crown Communications as "one of the largest publishers of adult books and magazines in the United States, and a dominant player in the adult video market."

"Did he really drop those magazines?" I asked.

"In the last year," the article said, "persuaded by his daughter, Sidney Rose has dropped two magazines because of their sexually violent content."

"That's what Mom says. I asked her about it." A pause. "I think he sold them off, actually. I can't tell you they're out of print."

"He must have mentioned you to the guy who'd interviewed him." "Mom" she'd said. Not "my mother."

"I noticed that too." Sally bit her lip. "I asked Mom. I guess things really were bad a few years ago, right after I started Oberlin."

"A near-victim of a seventies über-phenomenon, the sexual revolution, Sidney Rose credits his company's survival to the targeting of homosexual and bisexual males…"

I thought of the Roses' house, Patricia with her color TV, the closets with built-in lights, the constantly tended landscaping. "Things never looked bad. Did you realize?"

"Never. His father made him keep his shoes polished, remember? So he wouldn't look poor. Daddy did sell the Pollock. Not for much, by today's market. And I guess he borrowed. A lot, Mom says. She says she didn't ask him about it. But everything's fine now. They're loaded." This last sentence was uttered with a sarcasm that, even though I should have expected it, always surprised me in Sally.

"How's Ben?"

"He's working. Daddy got him a job at a video store, of all places. Some friend of a friend."

"They stock your dad's movies?"

"Clare. What do you think? There's a huge market. People who are ashamed to be seen at a porn flick."

"It makes sense."

"Everything he does makes sense. He's interested in politics now, Mom says. Going to fund-raising dinners. Guess which party?"

Reagan was in the White House. "Democrat?"

"Republican. Free-trade, libertarian Republicans, not the religious right. But he contributed to Reagan."

I shook my head. "Strange bedfellows."

Sally leaned forward urgently. "His life is strange bedfellows. Think about it."

There was always this intensity when she talked about her father, as if he were still the dominant force in her life, even though she swore she'd cut him out of it.

Later, we stopped at Ben's video store to drop off groceries. Sally pulled eggs, spaghetti sauce, canned fruit, and soup out of the bag to show him. From the supermarket deli she'd also bought some moo shu pork. Ben's eyes, heavily lidded, barely seemed to register the items. His curls were clumped and matted. When Sally was done, Ben gazed into the empty bag. "You get any beer?"

"Is that food, Ben? I'm feeding you. Tell me, is that food?"

Ben wore a droplet turquoise earring and was dressed completely in black. He pushed a dark curl impatiently behind his ear. "Take it to my place, man, I'm not off here for four hours. I don't want that moo shu getting moldy."

Sally sighed and lifted the groceries from the counter.

"Knock first," Ben said. "They'll pull their pants up." A sly grin. "I don't think anyone's there, anyway." He seemed to notice me for the first time. "Clare-ster," he said.

I said hello.

"Hey, Toby," Ben said across a counter, "come here and get a load of some excellent wrists."

It took me a moment to realize what he was talking about.

"Here." Ben waggled a finger at me. "Stick them up on the counter. Oh, come on, show them to Uncle Toby. Tobe's like me, he loves body parts."

"Really, Ben," Sally objected.

"Right up on the counter." Ben turned to Toby, a young guy with a wispy goatee. "She's shy. Aren't they gorgeous? Best wrists I've ever seen."

"Man, this is a compliment," Toby raved. "Ben hardly ever asks anyone to show me anything."

"*Clare's Knee*," Ben said. "That's a Frenchy film, right? Who is that, Malle? Buñuel? How're your knees, Clare?"

I was glad I was wearing long pants. "Average."

"And wrists aren't even, like, private," Toby noted.

Sally grabbed my wrist and pulled me away. "Clare's wrists are private," she said.

FOR MONTHS AND MONTHS, I didn't see Aunt Ruby. Freddie, her husband, had cirrhosis of the liver and an enormous swollen belly. It turned out Freddie was a secret drinker. He stashed vodka in the bottles of rubbing alcohol he kept at his dermatology office. He was retired now, weak, intermittently confused. He spent most of his time in bed.

"Aunt Ruby says if she were a drinking woman she'd hit the bottle too, but of course she's not a drinking woman." Sally paused. "She's an eating woman."

"Has she gained—?"

"Oh, fifty pounds. She can't wear any of her clothes. All she wears is muumuus. It's quite a scene. She fixes him these huge meals she puts on a bamboo bed tray, and then she sits on the edge of his bed and says, 'Freddie, Freddie baby, you've got to eat.' She'll even try to feed him with her fingers. And he lies there and closes his eyes and squinches up his mouth until she starts crying and the food gets cold and she eats it all herself."

"How frugal."

"They kind of hate each other," Sally confided cozily.

"How about Daphne?"

"Still in Bolivia with her Copper King." Daphne had married into a Chilean mining family, one in which all the women, Sally said, dressed as flamboyantly as Daphne.

"Should we go visit Aunt Ruby? I haven't seen her for ages."

"I don't want to see her," Sally said. "I don't want any more reporting about me to Daddy."

THERE WAS NOTHING in Ben's fridge except a jar of barbecue sauce, a dried-up chunk of cheese without a wrapper, a container of tofu, and ten or twelve cans of beer. All the blinds were pulled. While Sally unloaded the groceries, I wandered into the bedroom and was repulsed by the smell of semen. There were no covers on the huge bed, and I didn't dare look at the sheets. I went to the window and pulled up the blind, slid open the window. This place needed to air out. An extravagantly flowered branch bumped against the screen.

To live like *this,* I thought, turning back to the kitchen, in the midst of so much beauty.

Sally put the cans of beer from the fridge into her grocery bag and carried them out to the backseat of her car.

We were quiet driving home. "Daddy says they call themselves the Lost Boys," Sally said at last.

"That's appropriate." I thought for a moment. "It's such a gorgeous landscape, you know, and he has everything, but still..." I hesitated, belatedly struck by what she'd said. "Are you talking to your father now?"

Sally tightened her grip on the steering wheel. "Only about Ben. Only by phone."

I could see the sadness in it, sure, Sally and her father "estranged" when they'd been so close, but I felt frantic too, thinking I could lose her back to him. "Just so he doesn't seduce you," I said.

Sally shot me a skeptical look. "Ben?"

"No, no." I tried not to sound agitated. "Your father."

"He is my father," Sally said after a moment, "and whatever else he did, he was always a great father to me."

"Yes, but, but, here you are doing women's law, women's law of all things, when—"

"Maybe my career's an atonement!" Sally burst out.

I shut up.

THAT CHRISTMAS EVERYONE—my brothers with their wives and children, my mother, me—met at Frank's house. We had a wonderful time: a snowball fight, late nights talking in the kitchen, group breakfasts in our pajamas, Baxter doing his imitations of our aunts and uncles; so much so, I wondered what I'd been doing all these years, why I'd put such anguished effort into a crazy California family when my own family was much more fun. More normal too. What was wrong with normal? You could see why guys like my dad, who fought the War in Europe or the War in the Pacific, came home and married and bought little houses and hoped for children and an unremarkable American life. I found that I hoped for a life like that too.

But how dare I? I was a double divorcée, consumed by work, childless, infertile. My brothers quoted TV characters I'd never heard of, and even my mother laughed when I thought Joe Montana was a professional wrestler. "How'd you get so weird?" Eric asked, his arms stretched out on the back of the sofa, his new wife and their sons—Tahini, Ginkgo, and Eric's son Cody—arrayed around him. "You must have gotten those kooky genes of Mom's."

I went to bed that night in my apportioned corner, a cot tucked between a closet and a chest of drawers in Frank's oldest daughter's room, beneath a poster of Michael Jackson, the most famous lonely person on the planet.

"YOU'RE PICKING UP PACKAGES for Ben now?" I asked incredulously over the phone. "Taking them from point A to point B? What do you think they are? Jams and jellies?"

"Clare. It's not my business what it is. He asked me to pick it up, I said I'd be happy to, and I don't feel it's my place to ask." I could imagine her looking back at me, chin tilted up in her defiant way.

You trusted Flavio too, I thought. You trusted your father. Trust can be a big mistake. "Did it cross your mind it could be drugs?"

"Oh, I doubt it. I don't think Ben would put me in that position. My thought was it was a sex toy or something."

That wasn't totally implausible, but it seemed less likely than contraband. Or someone's severed body part, I thought suddenly: the crowd Ben ran with seemed vague and harmless ("Let's get high and go to Chuck E. Cheese!"), but anyone with money could surely be someone's prey. It crossed my mind that Sally could even be the target. She had money; she had, as a lawyer, a certain exalted position—wasn't that a setup for blackmail? "Oh Sally," I said, surprising myself with my fervor, "I wish you wouldn't do it. Or wait till I get back out there, let me go and pick it up. Nobody could hurt me."

"You can't cut me off from my parents and then expect me to lose contact with my brother!" Sally shrieked.

THERE WERE BASKETS with white yarmulkes set out at the funeral home, and the casket—per Jewish custom, Sally said—was closed, which disappointed me so much I couldn't make sense of it until later, when I realized I'd hoped to see her not for "closure" but to see in her dead countenance, the set of her jaw, maybe, or the squaring of her shoulders, some hint of who she really was.

Sally was not undone. Sally was spookily Sally, resolute, brave, a little impatient. I was waiting for guilt, but she surprised me. As I stood beside her, she scanned the room and nodded at a tall blond woman wearing a bun and a sleek fitted suit, who responded with a face practically melting with sympathy. "That's Sara Tweedles," Sally said. "Have you heard of her?" I shook my head no. "The Countess of Come," Sally whispered.

There were more congregants than I'd expected, many of them glamorously dressed: one woman who hugged Sally had an asymmetrical haircut and a small hat capped with black feathers; her female companion wore shoes with an undersea design pieced in bits of colored suede. The men were sloppier, friendlier; some of them were gathered in clumps, laughing and talking. "I don't know any of these people," Sally said. "Industry people. Not friends of my mom's."

I HAD JUST PURCHASED an answering machine, and I got home after nine from the hospital and flicked it on for my first message. There was a whir and a click, then Sally's voice. "Clare?" she said, and then a peculiar pause. "Clare?" she repeated. "This is me. Call me whenever you get in. Whenever, I don't care. Today, call me today. Right now, as soon as you hear this." There was more silence, as if she were hoping I'd pick up the phone, then a limp click as she hung up.

I thought Ben had overdosed. I thought Sid had shown up at Sally's house demanding that Sally take him back as a father. I thought Uncle Freddie had died. It never crossed my mind that the trouble was Sally's mother, that she'd been killed late the night before—February 5, 1986—in a one-car accident in Topanga Canyon, bashing her car into the stone gatepost of an empty house that had recently been put up for sale.

BEN WAS SLUMPED in a chair with his legs open, his head a circle of unruly curls. Sid was leaning against the closed casket, his back trembling through a tweedy black and gray jacket. Aunt Ruby stood beside him, stroking his back with the flat of her hand. I angled myself to get a glimpse of Sid's face. He did, indeed, look stricken. What had been between them, Sid and Esther? Had he, despite his protestations, loved her after all?

"Daddy?" Sally said softly, touching his sleeve.

Sally's cousin Daphne, just in from South America, dabbed her nose with an embroidered handkerchief. "There're sure a lot of people. You think all these people knew Aunt Esther? I didn't think hardly anybody knew Aunt Esther." She was wearing a garish engagement and wedding ring set and a short black dress knotted across her breasts, a triangle of flesh exposed beneath it.

Uncle Freddy was too sick to come.

I explained who Sally thought the guests were. "Sally was surprised too, she didn't realize Sid was so"—Sally had hesitated, searching for the phrase—"big in his field."

"Look at that," Daphne said in wonderment. "The Countess of Come. I almost didn't recognize her with her clothes on."

We both laughed.

"You haven't seen the Black Stallion here, have you?" Daphne craned her head.

"I wouldn't know him."

"Bow tie. He'd be wearing a bow tie."

I shook my head no.

"Aunt Esther sure was a good cook. Best cook in the family. You don't think she was drinking, was she?"

I said no. I'd asked the same thing of Sally, and Sally had said her mother never drank before she drove. Sally had her own ideas about the accident, but I didn't tell Daphne this.

"I feel terrible for Uncle Sid," Daphne said. "Mommy and I were at his house last night, and he's a mess. You know that Irish woman Aunt Esther used to write to? He called her over there. It was like three A.M. in Ireland. I guess she started crying. Told him she'd come to the funeral if there was any way she could. She told Uncle Sid it was like losing a sister."

So there were people who loved her. I felt relieved.

"At least Uncle Sid thinks that's what she said, some of those accents you can hardly understand." Daphne sighed. "I wish I could stick around here longer and help everybody, but I've got to get back home. Eduardo can't run a house. He's terrible with the help, no sensitivity at all." Daphne lifted her right leg to scratch at her left ankle with her high heel.

"I rented a big car," I said. "I thought Sally would come with me, but she's going with her dad. Do you want a ride to the cemetery?"

Daphne glanced up to the casket, where Sid, Aunt Ruby, and Sally were now huddled together. "Oh sure." Daphne rummaged in her tiny black bag. "Happy to." She grabbed a small plastic box out of her purse and waved it triumphantly. "Breath mints! I knew I brought them. Doesn't it make you feel there's something right in the world when you know there are breath mints?" For the first time in my life, I understood why Sally liked Daphne.

I DIDN'T KNOW ABOUT the Jewish custom of the family shoveling clumps of dirt into the grave. Sid shoveled first.

Oh, the sound of the dirt hitting wood. I can still hear it years later. I think it's the saddest sound I've ever heard.

WHEN IT WAS GETTING dark and almost everyone was gone, Sally found me sitting out on the patio near the espaliered tree. It was a chilly night. I was thinking—seeing the lights of Los Angeles twinkling below me, listening to the chirps of birds settling in for the evening—how it was true what people said, life went on. Even now I was plotting a new life for myself, without this place, without Sally.

Sally looked beat, her eyes blank and hollow, wayward curls sticking up from her crown. "It's strange to be here," she said. "I haven't been in this house for months."

"Did you and your father talk much?"

"We talked. He's demolished. How could he not be? He agrees with me, he thinks it was suicide too. Apparently she'd just made up a will, left everything to Ben."

"Ben!"

"Daddy says she wanted to look after him. He says last week she said to him, out of the blue, that she didn't think Ben would ever be capable of supporting himself. 'So we'll have to look after him,' she said. Daddy didn't think much of it at the time, but when the police came by, it hit him. She had a lot of her own money. Family stock."

"Did she leave you . . . ?"

"Some jewelry." Sally, never one to wear jewelry, smiled ruefully. "And Ben doesn't get any money directly until he's thirty-five, so in the meantime I'm the trust officer."

"You mean you'll control—"

"Right. His funds."

"What does Ben say?"

"Honestly? He doesn't seem to care."

From the house there was still conversation and the occasional clink of a fork or glass.

"How impossible," I said.

"She thought I could handle it," Sally said. "It's a logical position for a lawyer."

"Oh, I'm sure it is, but..." I wavered. Sally would be looking after Ben's affairs? Controlling Ben's money? Esther hadn't done her daughter any favors. The trees stirred in a breeze, a dog barked, and from below us came a thin wail barely recognizable as a siren.

"Clare, I've got to tell you, I'm making up with Daddy. Life's too short to fight. And it's a commandment: Honor your father and mother. And who else do I have?"

I didn't say anything. A tense-looking woman clutching the hands of two sullen young girls swept past us toward the driveway. Sally and I exchanged glances. "Face-lift," we both said at once.

"IT'S GOOD TO SEE YOU," Sid told me. "Thank you for coming out for Sally."

I answered, not totally lying, that it was good to see him too: he's just a person, I thought, a person who makes mistakes like anyone else. When everyone was gone and Sid had gone to bed, while Sally and I were sitting in the living room reviewing the day, Ben walked in. He complained in a slurred way about a musician friend who had cornered him at the reception to ask if Sid ever needed music for his movies.

"Movie music?" Sally said sharply. "Why in the world was he asking about that now?"

"Fucking opportunist," Ben said. He pushed past both of us and out the glass door.

He was standing on the patio where I'd stood, euphoric, years before; where Sally and I had sat just hours ago.

Ben shut the glass door behind him and leaned against it. "Fucking opportunist!" he screamed into the air. His hair was tangled and matted, the back right pocket of his shorts almost torn off. Hairy legs and then black high-top Keds.

"No loathing like self-loathing," Sally muttered. For an instant I wasn't sure I'd heard her right. Then it hit me that she knew as well as I did how hard her life with Ben would be.

ROGER WHISBY'S FAMILY didn't give him a funeral. They had him buried in a plot far from the family's, under a flat marker listing only his name. The obituary stated that memorial contributions could be sent to his parents. I wish any of this surprised me. He died on September 30, 1986, at thirty-eight. I gave birth to my daughter less than three months later.

Roger drove himself, early that autumn, to a hospital thirty miles from his home so he could die under my care. His legs were seeping and his belly bloated from his failing kidneys. "I'm a sight," he said. "Sorry."

"You name the baby for me," he said later, patting my belly on one of his last coherent days. He'd awakened at five that morning and had the night nurses wash his hair, thinking today might be the day his mother would visit. His father was a total loss, Roger said, but he had some faith, now that he'd written her, in his mother.

"Don't get your hopes up," I said. In retrospect I'm almost, but not quite, sorry I said that: if I hadn't, he might have distrusted me.

"You'll remember me," Roger announced implacably. "I'm counting on it."

I called Roger's parents' house that day, their name and number listed on his hospital admitting sheet as next of kin. A woman with a meek voice answered. "Hello," I said. "You don't know me, but my name is Clare Mann, and I'm Roger Whisby's physician. I'm calling to give you some information about him. Are you his mother?"

There was a second's hesitation. "Yes," the woman answered. I noticed a sudden whine in her voice, as if she suspected I was about to ask for a contribution to some unassailable cause she had no intention of supporting.

"Your son's very ill," I said. "He has kidney failure and incipient liver failure and he can't breathe and I don't think he'll make it out of the hospital. Normally I don't call family members if the patient doesn't request it, but he would really love to see you and…"

I finished my spiel breathlessly and listened. The baby inside me gave a ruthless kick.

Silence.

"Mrs. Whisby?" I said. "Mrs. Whisby?" I rattled the disconnect button of the phone, checked the phone cord, picked up the phone and looked under it before it dawned on me that Roger's mother had hung up.

I slammed the receiver into the phone, making enough noise that the charge nurse, thinking there'd been an accident, came running down the hall. "Are you okay?" she asked. "Are you going into labor?"

What kind of monster was Mrs. Whisby? What kind of mother could throw away her own child?

"**LISTEN TO THIS,**" Sally said. "He says he's not gay anymore."

"Not gay anymore! What are you talking about?"

"He's got a girlfriend, a manicurist. She's the backup manicurist for Madonna's publicist, and her dream is that someday Madonna will notice her publicist's nails. Her name's Candy. Ben's moved back in with Daddy, and Candy stays with him most nights."

"You're kidding," I said dully.

"I know, I can't believe it either. She paints Ben's nails. And his toenails."

"What does your dad say?"

"He says whatever Ben's doing is okay, so long as it keeps him off men."

WAS MY PREGNANCY an accident?

Are there ever accidents? That's a better question. As far as my conscious mind went, yes, my pregnancy was an accident. I doubted I could get pregnant, after all my unsuccessful attempts with Ted, assuming that my pelvic infection and miscarriage had scarred me for life. After our divorce, I was always busy and tired, and no, it didn't cross my mind I could be pregnant. (It was actually a ward clerk who told me I was, and I didn't believe her until I sat down and realized I'd missed three periods.) But in terms of what my body wanted—here's where it gets interesting—I think it wanted me to be pregnant. I needed a fresh start.

The father was a one-night stand. Actually, the father was one of three one-night stands: an ER nurse I'd known at University; an old friend of Baxter's who looked me up in Akron; and Ted, who had left his fellowship position after our split, was finishing his training in Baltimore. I should have been on the pill, certainly, but I got pregnant after AIDS appeared, when there was a lot of stress on barriers, and I kept thinking I should get fitted for a diaphragm, but then I'd get busy and put it off. And no, I didn't make my partners wear condoms. I'm aware this is crazy. I have a sort of masochism where sex is involved. Not Sid's magazines' kind of masochism; mine is straightforward human masochism. Deep down, I like the possibility that sex will make me suffer. It was a huge surprise, when my daughter was born, to realize that sex could bring me such joy.

"HE'S FUCKED UP," I told my mother.

She was shocked by my language, but by then I was eight and a half months pregnant and wore my bulk like a shield. I could say anything to her then.

I waddled to the sink and got a glass of water. "There's no other way to put it. He's beyond confused. He's beyond neurotic. He uses drugs, he doesn't have a job, he barely finished high school, he's living back at his father's house with a girlfriend, and now, to top it off, he doesn't know if he's gay or straight."

"How can he not know," my mother said. "He must know. He's just not telling you. He's embarrassed to be a homosexual."

"He's not embarrassed by anything."

"Then he's trying to please his father," my mother said. I wondered if she'd mind my doing crazy things if she thought I did them to please her.

I DON'T THINK the ideal birth experience involves being coached by your mother, but she offered, and how could I turn her down? The exact delivery date was too unpredictable for Sally to come. My mother stayed with me two weeks and three days waiting for the baby, and then she stayed two more weeks to help me with the baby, rushing to pick her up from her crib before I could get there. In truth, my daughter was happiest in my arms. Eventually, my mother and I reached a point of mutual exhaustion, and I stood at the door of my town house madly waving the baby's tiny arm at her, hoping to hurry her off. After that, the baby and I were fine, as the birth itself had been fine, although it was a revelation to me that labor really hurt (I thought there had been some cultural exaggeration), and in the process of labor, my usual coolness in front of my mother broke down. I screamed at her that she always got me upset, and why did she have to be like that? You're exhausted, you're exhausted, she soothed, and I realized that coaching a daughter through childbirth was hard on a mother too. When she tried to feed me ice, the chips fell off her shaking spoon. That made me think of Ted's tremor and the useless end of my marriage, and despite my best efforts, I started crying. My mother gaped, and I realized she'd never, since I was maybe four years old, seen me cry. For some reason, this made me cry more.

My mother was visibly relieved when my baby was a girl, because—as she'd mentioned many times, both before and during my labor—a girl wouldn't need a male role model.

I named her Aurelia Roger Mann. I sent out birth announcements with no mention of a father. I was thrilled.

Sally was the first person besides me, the obstetrician, and the ward clerk who knew I was pregnant. I phoned her. By the time I called, the evening after my doctor's visit, I was over the biggest part of my shock and was excited.

We were at an awkward place in our friendship, and I hoped the news would lure her back to me.

"So," I said, "are you ready to be an auntie?"

She was confused. I kept her dangling for a moment, then spilled it out.

"Who's the father?" she said.

"Sally! Do you think it matters? It doesn't matter."

"Are you going to raise it by yourself? Aren't you even going to contact the father?"

"Sally! The father is superfluous. I promise you, the father didn't plunge in there hoping for fatherhood. This is my baby."

A pause. "Every child needs a father."

She was back with hers. They went out to dinner, talked about Sally's office furniture, browsed together at bookstores. "You've bought into that whole father mythology," I said in what I hoped was a cheerfully complaining way. "Bought into": true California-ese.

"It's a true mythology," Sally answered in a serious tone. "It echoes because it's true. Everybody wants to be in touch with their origins." Then an afterthought: "Do you *know* the father?"

"I know the possibilities. Maybe it'll look like one of them. At least they're all white." I meant this as a joke, but Sally didn't respond.

"How many possibilities are we talking about?"

"Three."

After a moment Sally said quietly: "Oh, Clare. I guess your needs were overwhelming again, right?"

We both laughed, she less heartily than I. "Does your mother know?" she asked.

"I haven't told her yet. You're the first nonmedical person to know."

"Thank you," Sally said in an odd, flat tone. Then she brightened a bit. "Well, a baby is what you wanted, right?"

PEOPLE ASK ME how I ended up in AIDS, and I can tell them exactly. "I didn't want the ambiguity," I say. "When you do AIDS, you know your patients are sick."

It was during my last year in Lisbonville, on a Thursday afternoon when I was eager to get home to Aury, that I realized what I needed.

"I had about all I can take," a Mrs. Hopps, not my favorite patient, said when I walked into the exam room. What did she mean? Was she hurting somewhere, feeling sick? Had she missed her disability check last month? (A frequent complaint.)

"I had about all I can take, is all," she answered, and glared at me from her station on the exam table.

I got no more help from her than that. She denied all specific complaints and answered my questions with angry impatience. "I'm just not right," she repeated. And then, maddeningly: "You're the doctor."

I examined her. Nothing. Everything I could think to check was normal.

"So what are you going to do with me?" she demanded as I sank onto my stool.

I sat there, pen in hand. I couldn't stand it. Mrs. Hopps was driving me crazy. She could be dying. She could be depressed, she could be manipulative, she could be totally normal and having an off day. Dear God, I thought, give me some real disease.

I answered her with the usual doctors' stall: "We'll do some tests." They were normal, of course, but people can have normal tests and die the next day. Another ambiguity.

Shortly after, I heard about the doctor-with-an-interest-in-AIDS job at University. They wanted a physician both to see people with AIDS in a clinic and to supervise their hospital care. The doctor who had previously done these things had quit. He was a young rheumatologist who had hired on with the expectation of injecting joints with steroids and managing patients with lupus, but when AIDS hit and the cretins in the infectious disease department punted management of the disease to rheumatology (because AIDS was a problem of resistance, not virulence, and who could be sure it was infectious; why deal with those patients if you didn't have to?) the burden of the AIDS-stricken had fallen to him, the most junior rheum physician. Nobody blamed him explicitly for leaving, and infectious disease didn't jump in to say the next AIDS doc must be an infectious disease person. In retrospect this was crazy, but at the time that was how it was. And I had been reading, I was interested. In fact, during my six weeks of maternity leave, on our way to California, Aury and I spent two days at an AIDS conference in Chicago, where I was not only one of the few women attendees but the only breast-feeding mother.

When I heard about the possible opening at University, I phoned one of my former professors.

"They're looking for someone," he confirmed.

"Do you think they'd consider a general internist with a special interest?"

"Why not? There's nobody beating down the door. Infectious disease docs who want to do AIDS stay on the coasts, and any ID person who comes to the Midwest is trying to avoid it."

"Interesting."

"Call Dunswater, the new medicine chief, he's the one you need to talk to. You have a good reputation here; you could have a chance."

So now I do AIDS. There is no doubt, not one jot, that each of my patients has the disease. It's impossible to get into my practice without a positive blood test for HIV. By the early nineties, I wasn't even seeing partners or possibles. Other doctors could see them. My criterion was so strict, my practice in its way so exclusive, that when people were referred to me, they felt as if they'd won a prize. I kid you not. People with AIDS came to me from as far away as Toledo. I don't know if I'm the best AIDS doctor around, but I have my advocates. Patients like me because I'm thorough, I move quickly, I'm writing orders for tests and medicines while they're still reciting symptoms. I'm very up-to-date; I read everything. I can look someone in the eye and discuss their death. I can tell relatives to mind their own business. For my chosen patients, I'm a protector, a doctor who's in some way fierce.

I HADN'T REALIZED Sally had such a thing for babies. "May I hold her?" she said the second Aury and I were off the plane.

She held her, rocked her, cooed to her our whole trip. Several people took Sally for Aury's mother, which shouldn't have bothered me but did. I began to nurse Aury more frequently in public, to prove I was the mom.

"They really called you an *elderly* primip?" Sally asked. An elderly primipara is a woman over thirty having her first baby. We were thirty-one.

CANDY MET AN ELECTRICIAN who'd done work for Lionel Richie and she left Ben, but when I went to visit Sally, he had a new girlfriend, a girl he'd met in line for an Iggy Pop concert. Her name was Helga and she looked like a Helga, although she was from San Diego. Her father was a doctor, and he rented her a house in the Hollywood Hills, where she lived with three female housemates. Ben stayed at that house a lot, so Sally and I took his groceries there.

It had struck me that Ben should be capable of shopping for food himself, but I didn't say this to Sally. The stuff she bought him was touching: good healthy food like milk and yogurt, a few steaks because, as she said, men like steaks ("men"—was Ben a man?), top-of-the-line frozen entrees for convenience, and, just for a treat, candy bars and chips and salsa.

"Hey, Ben's sister," one of the housemates said as she answered the door, apparently forgetting Sally's name. She called into the house behind her, "Foodmobile!"

All four housemates were home, peculiar in the middle of a weekday. Two were sunning topless by the pool, the girl who answered the door was walking around munching on a Pop-Tart, and Helga was lying on a sofa watching TV. She was wearing a man's shirt (not Ben's; he was far too thin for this shirt) and no apparent pants, and one foot was propped up on the back of the sofa. I clutched Aury to my shoulder, a little ball of warmth.

"Sal," Helga said, not moving, "Ben's at work." The house stank of smoke and something else distasteful, even though the glass doors were open.

"I didn't think he worked Thursdays." Ben was still employed at the video store.

"I don't know, someone called off or something. I had to get up early and drive him." Helga swung her leg off the back of the sofa and sat up, reached for a cigarette in a pack on the table. Sally turned away and walked to the kitchen, her heels clicking disapprovingly. "My house, Salster," Helga mumbled, rolling her eyes in Sally's direction, then sat up and hunched over her cigarette, the shirt bunched between her legs. She looked at me: "You guys get Doritos?"

"I think so." I clutched little sleeping Aury tighter. The girl who'd answered the door hadn't even noticed the baby, nor had Helga. I wanted to leave Helga's presence, to follow Sally to the kitchen, but the kitchen was dark and probably even smellier than the rest of the house, and here there was at least fresh air and a touch of breeze. I thought about these things now that I had a baby.

"God, I hope they're real Doritos and not the fucking store brand," Helga said. "I hate those store brands, they taste like absolute shit."

You ingrate, I thought. I couldn't think of a single thing to say out loud.

"What kind of baby's that?" Helga said suddenly.

"A sweet baby," I said. Helga gave me a blank look. "She's a little girl, if that's what you mean. She's five weeks old. Her name's Aurelia. It means 'golden.'" I held my hand behind Aury's head to tilt her back and show her to Helga, but she wasn't looking anymore.

"I wouldn't mind having a baby girl," Helga said. A chill ran through me at the thought: Helga and Ben having a child. What a doomed creature that would be. "She'll be hell on you when she gets to be a teenager, though," Helga noted, nodding sagely.

"You'd know about that," I said.

Helga threw me a quick appraising glance. I smiled blandly. Satisfied, Helga leaned back on the sofa, brought an ankle up on her knee, and started rubbing her toes. I glanced out to the pool area, thinking I'd step out there, but the topless girls' breasts jutted out so aggressively I didn't dare.

The girl with the Pop-Tart appeared. "He said he'd call, that shit-for-brains said he'd call!"

"Get over it, cupcake," Helga said. "You can't think you're the only one."

Cupcake: I knew Sally hated that expression. I wondered if she might have heard. I could hear her laying into Helga, listing things one two three, telling Helga exactly what she thought of her scuzzy life.

The Pop-Tart girl made a disgusted sound and disappeared again.

Helga yawned. "She's crazy for Axel. Everyone's crazy for Axel."

"Who's Axel crazy for?"

Helga smirked. "Himself."

Where does Ben meet these people? I thought. And why am I meeting them? I wasn't a prude, but these were people I didn't have to meet. I remembered something Baxter used to say about needing a shower after talking to certain people. I stroked Aury's back, ran my finger down the bones of her tiny spine.

Sally came back, clutching a handful of empty grocery bags. "Do you save these bags, Helga? Where should I put them?"

Helga waved her hand. "Just get rid of them, I don't know. Take them out to the garbage or something." There was a bong sitting on the coffee table, and Helga's eyes lit up as she reached for it. "Hey, gals, you know what this is?" Helga said. "This is a sixties sort of thing. You remember it?"

"We were in grade school in the sixties," Sally said. I felt excited, thinking she would say more, a purge of invective and anger, but she didn't say another word. Instead, she put her free hand on my back and pushed me toward the door.

WE WERE SITTING in a coffee shop, Aury sleeping in her car seat beside me. A funny fluorescent light shone down on Sally's face. "A morass," Sally said.

"It was better when he was gay," I said.

Sally looked surprised, then nodded. "It was. The guys weren't so . . . predatory." She paused. "I think Helga is a call girl."

"Really?" I was shocked, although I knew I shouldn't be.

"What else can she make money on? And she has money."

"Maybe her dad sends her—"

"He pays her rent, but that's it. She told me."

"Maybe she sells drugs."

"No," Sally said, definitely enough that I didn't question her.

"Maybe she acts in your dad's—"

"Not unless she uses another name. I asked him." She hesitated, ferociously stirring her tea. "Of course they all use other names. But he couldn't think of anybody matching her description. She has a lock and chain tattooed on her rear. Ben told me."

"I guess that would show up."

Sally smiled wearily.

"I sort of hoped you were going to light into her," I said.

"Into Helga?"

"Uh-huh. She's such a scum."

"You're not going to believe this, but I don't totally hate her."

I looked up in surprise.

"She has some zip to her. She helps Ben out. Ben had some medical problems, and she got them taken care of."

"Medical problems?"

"He had a reaction to some substance he was taking. Put his right shoulder through a window. Anyway, she got him to the emergency room immediately. Thirty-four stitches."

"Incredible."

"He was lucky. The plastic surgeon said the cut was near an artery. Helga took him to her dad's office to get the stitches out."

Helga's father was a pediatrician. I tried to imagine Ben, spooky hairy-legged Ben, sitting in the waiting room. Thinking how he'd scare the mothers was almost hilarious.

"And she got him off of whatever he was taking."

"Really?" This surprised me. Sulkily aggressive Helga did not seem like the woman who'd get someone off of anything. "How'd she do that?"

"It may be simple substitution, actually. But he's better."

EXCEPT FOR HIS JOB at the video store, Ben never got out, because Sally had taken away his car. When he said he wanted to go to Nordstrom's to buy some underwear and socks, we left Aury with Sally's housekeeper and picked him up and took him. He sat in the backseat of Sally's white Volvo like a wraith. There was no conversation. We'd been driving ten minutes when Ben said he had to use the bathroom. His actual request was coarser than that, something like "I've got to shit."

There were a couple of gas stations nearby, and I thought Sally would stop at one of them, but instead she said, brightly, "You know what? We're near Aunt Ruby's. Let's go there."

I had no idea why she'd want to go to Aunt Ruby's and show her aunt how terrible Ben looked. "There's a gas station," I pointed out.

Sally wrinkled her nose. "Too dirty."

We drove maybe another ten minutes to Aunt Ruby's, as Ben started to get frantic in the backseat. We parked the car in the circular drive, in front of the jewel box of a house, and headed for the front door.

The doorbell rang in a series of tones, and then Aunt Ruby peered out at us from behind an ornately barred screen door. "Sally!" she said in surprise. "Clare! What a treat." Her eyes, darting inquiringly to Ben, seemed smaller to me than they used to, and I realized that the face around them was simply fatter. She was indeed wearing a muumuu, blue with silver threads.

I saw Aunt Ruby's dismay the moment she recognized her nephew. "Is that little Ben?" she asked. "Ben, what's happened to you? I haven't seen you since your mother's . . . You must have lost twenty pounds."

"We're here to visit, but first Ben needs to use the bathroom," Sally said. "We were right nearby and thought we'd stop in."

"Now?" Aunt Ruby said, looking at Ben. "You need to use the bathroom *now?*"

I was thinking about the strangeness of Sally's asking for permission for her grown brother to use the bathroom, when I realized that Aunt Ruby didn't want to let us in. "But Freddie's so sick," she was saying, "his liver disease has compromised his immune system. I'm sorry, darlings, but I can't have him exposed to people who . . . surely you understand."

"Fine," Sally said, making a motion with her hands like she'd hit a chord on a keyboard, "we won't disturb you or Freddie at all. Clare and I can wait out here while Ben uses your bathroom."

Aunt Ruby's little glittering eyes grew rounder. "Freddie's very sick," she said. "Cirrhosis, you know," she said confidingly to me. "An awful disease."

"Oh, shit," Ben moaned, slumping against the wall. "I don't believe this shit, I—"

Aunt Ruby backed away from the door. "Is he all right?" she whispered loudly.

"He needs to go to the bathroom, Aunt Ruby. Just let him in your house." Sally's voice was getting desperate. I remembered Ruby and Freddie's house. There was a guest bathroom just off the foyer. Ten feet from where we stood, there was a toilet.

The three of us stood looking at her in silence.

"Fuck it," Ben mumbled, turning away. "I'll just go in my fucking pants."

We were almost off the porch when Aunt Ruby rushed out the door. "I know what we can do," she was saying. "Any port in a storm!" She gripped Ben's elbow and hustled him through a gate at the side of the house and into the backyard, leaving Sally and me gaping.

"She does look like a ship in full sail," I said.

But Sally didn't laugh. She threw me a searing glance. "You know what she's doing?" Sally asked ferociously. "She's taking him to the gardener's bathroom!"

I laughed uncomfortably. I thought of the AIDS patient blinded by a virus, back in my residency days, whose mother had refused to wash his sheets. "Have you ever tried doing a load of wash when you can't see?" he'd demanded, craning his head this way and that, as if he were trying to meet anybody's gaze.

"Bitch," Sally said.

"She must have some kind of phobia," I said. "Remember how she was always wiping off her tables? And now with Freddie sick, she's decompensated."

"What?" Sally demanded, turning toward me. "Are you saying she's mentally ill? Is that supposed to excuse her?"

"No, but—"

"Ben's her nephew. I'm her niece. We're *family*."

I thought better of saying something soothing. I spread my hands in a helpless gesture.

"Unforgivable," Sally said.

SALLY WAS AS BUSY as ever at work, and looking after Ben required lots of driving.

"Don't tell me you're still carrying packages around for him," I said over the phone.

A pause, then a hesitant answer. "Not exactly."

"Not exactly! What does that mean?"

"Clare, I've struggled with it, and I have to say he's happier now than I've seen him in years. He's not ecstatic, he's not bubbling, but he's normal. There are moments you'd think he was an average young man working at a video store. He likes his job, he has friends there, and his boss thinks he's functioning fine. He never misses a day. And Helga, for whatever reason, looks after him. She's an earth mother, in a way. I used to take food to the apartment he shared with those guys, and when I came back a week later, all the stuff I'd brought would be rotting in the fridge. But now everything's eaten. He gets out some, he goes walking, he swims in the pool, he watches TV. It's a relief to see him. He's been to every drug rehab facility in southern California, and what have they done for him? Now he's reasonably happy. He's peaceful. I'll do what I have to do to keep him that way."

I understood something. "What's the substitute?"

"What do you mean?"

"You said Helga had given him a substitute drug and now he's better. What is it?"

A hesitation. "It's heroin. It's a peaceful drug, Clare," she said into my silence. "You don't hear about people getting high on heroin and going out to shoot up a convenience store. Heroin addicts aren't killers."

"So, are you helping him get it?"

"You know Mom's will. I'm the executrix, I control Ben's money. So indirectly, I control his buying habits. That's another good thing: I can limit his consumption."

"What about methadone? He could get in a treatment program."

"Methadone is maintenance. I've talked about it with Ben. He doesn't want maintenance. With heroin, you get the rush."

"He wants the rush," I said flatly.

"He hasn't had a lot of joy in his life, Clare."

I couldn't believe what I was hearing. "But Sally, he'll keep needing more and more. And remember what I do for a living now? How did a quarter of my patients get their disease? Drug abuse. It's incredibly unsafe."

"He has a doctor, and he's been tested for AIDS several times. And I have a source for new needles for him, so he never shoots up with a used needle. And he's not having sex with males anymore. Or even with Helga, she says. Overall, I think his risk for AIDS is as low as it could be, under the circumstances."

My ears perked up. "How do you get him needles?" I asked.

"One of the plastic surgeons I've used as an expert witness. He thinks I'm a diabetic. He gave me a prescription for insulin syringes."

Fraud, I thought. Delivering heroin. And she's a lawyer.

"Have you stopped to think that what you're doing is illegal?" I asked.

"Clare, I don't want to be a judge anymore. I'm just a lawyer doing what I have to do to look after my family. Nobody's going to care. And even if by some wild fluke I got implicated in something and dis-

barred, it wouldn't be the end of the world. I'm not wedded to practicing law."

"Sally," I said, trying to sound humorous, "your brother does not
need this much help."

"Clare, if I could get him on chronic intravenous morphine I'd do
it, because he deserves some peace."

"You think he's that—" I hesitated, not sure what word to use.
Where was one of Sally's defining adjectives when I needed it?

"He's miserable, that's what I know. He's tormented by Mom's
death. I'm so angry at her. If she'd ever really thought about Ben, she
wouldn't have..."

I was silent.

"He's my only brother," Sally said. "There are only the three of us
left."

Sally, Sid, and Ben. "How about Aunt Ruby?" I said, but Sally cut
me off with a disgusted sound. She had not been kidding about unforgivable.

"Another problem, Sally, is the drugs aren't pure. They put in
sugar, novocaine, tooth powder, all sorts of things."

Sally sighed. "Don't think I haven't thought of that. I know Ben's
supplier, and he's reputable. He checks what he gets, and he's a
chemist, actually, a Chinese guy who used to teach at USC. He maintains a certain quality control."

You're loony! I should have said. You're absolutely bonkers! If I'd
said it at that moment, things might have turned out differently. Sally
might have listened to me, Ben might still be alive. But I didn't have
the guts to say it. I didn't want Sally to cast me out, to erase me from
her life the way she'd erased Aunt Ruby. I said something limp instead,
like I couldn't believe what she was doing.

"I can't believe it myself half the time. But Ben's my brother, and
I'm trying to be practical. And I don't actually buy the drug. I give Ben
the money, and he buys it."

"A fine distinction," I mumbled.

"It is a distinction," Sally agreed eagerly. "He doesn't have to use the money for drugs. Every time he buys heroin, it's his choice. He can use the money for anything. I think that's important. It gives him free will."

"I don't think a heroin addict is overflowing with free will."

"He's a user, Clare," Sally corrected me. "I wouldn't call him an addict."

Then: I could have said it then. You're insane! You're talking like a crazy person! You're asking for trouble!

But I said nothing, nothing at all.

I POPPED IN EARLY at Aury's day care. Aury was in her crib on her back, eyes wide open, being entertained by a circle of girls. "Where's Aury's daddy?" a girl with bulging eyes asked me.

"Her daddy?" I repeated, mouth gone dry. "Aury doesn't really—"

"Don't you know anything?" another of Aury's little tenders burst out. "Aury doesn't have a daddy. Miss Jackie said Aury doesn't have a daddy."

"What?" screamed the girl with bulging eyes, looking at me.

"IT'S A CRAZY PROBLEM, Cliff. I don't even know how to explain it." Dr. Cliff Dunswater was the head of medicine, the man who'd hired me.

"Try me."

"Well, my old college roommate, she's my closest friend, and she's a lawyer in Los Angeles, she used to want to be a judge; anyway, she has a younger brother who..." On and on I went, with the whole story. It was wrong of me to tell him, but he looked at me so raptly.

He rode a bike and ran and did marathons, but there was something soft about him, some almost feminine quality. His name didn't suit him. Clifford was more apt, but he hated it. He wasn't a big man. He would smile a beseeching smile, and the skin around his eyes would crinkle, and he'd lie there and stare into my eyes.

Married, of course. Two kids and a third on the way. Wife fifteen years younger, so she was five years younger than me. She was finicky and neurotic, one of those vegetarians who have to balance their proteins. Midway through each session, he'd start feeling terrible. At the end, he'd sit on the edge of the bed and stroke my arm and talk, trying to tear himself away. Why in the world did he find me irresistible? I puzzled over it all the time. If I'd asked, I'm sure he would have told me, but I didn't want to ask.

"I hate to see you suffering over your friend," he said. "You're too loyal, you know that?"

It was one of those strange periods of time when the future seemed impossibly unclear. In Akron, Cliff came over most Tuesdays and Thursdays, the evenings he was free. In California, Sally was taking her groceries and supplies to Ben at Helga's house on the hill. I imagined her getting arrested, whom she'd call, probably first another lawyer or her father. Cliff was as concerned as I was, taking in my agony, my sighs, my sudden looking away—as if I were putting on a show. As if he were suffering vicariously, the suffering diluted by distance to no more than a pleasant twang.

"Heroin?" Cliff said. "I thought that was more of a street drug. TB'ers can be heroin addicts."

As if we were in a holding pattern, circling in the air. It is not a lie to say events unfold, because they do.

At work, I was extremely efficient. I did good things. I did a complete history and physical on each patient I saw for the first time, including those who had been followed at the clinic for years. My rheumatologist predecessor had been getting lax, and even an illiterate drug addict can spot a lazy doctor. After I took over, the no-show rate at HIV clinic dropped from 55 to 7 percent. By the time I left, about the only patients missing appointments were dead.

THE PHONE RANG LATE one night. May 1987. I knew when I heard Sid's voice that this was the moment I'd been waiting for, that things were going to change.

"Clare? Sid. How are you?"

"Fine." My tone was uncertain. Clearly there was something he wanted. "You?"

"I'm a wreck, to tell you God's honest truth. You're probably wondering why I called."

A man who got to the point. "Yes..."

"I'm worried about my daughter."

"Sally?" What a stupid question.

"Listen, I know you don't like me, I know you think I'm below you, but I thought you'd agree to talk to me for the good of Sally."

Below you. I'd been prepared to forgive him, even like him, until the obvious hostility of those words. "Okay," I said, haughtily. If he wanted to be below me, fine.

He seemed to be thrown for a second by my cool answer, or maybe by my agreeing so readily to talk with him. "You're not on a portable phone, are you?"

The paranoia! "No."

Sid cleared his throat. "It's not her directly, it's what she's doing for her brother. You know he's had this drug problem, he's been in and out of rehab, he..." Sid stopped. "You know all that."

"Sure."

"And he's not cured. You know that, right?"

"Sally told me he's using heroin."

A pause. "Okay. You know that. And you know Sally controls his day-to-day income, she's the executrix, she holds the purse strings. And normally, she has good judgment, I mean she's a lawyer, she's savvy, but now—"

"Is he requiring more and more heroin?"

"Requiring it, yeah, I guess that's what they do, addicts, they require it."

"So Sally's giving him more and more money, is that it? You're worried she'll exhaust the fund?" I was pleased with myself for thinking of this, for showing Sid my financial acumen.

"No. She's using more of the fund, no question, but that's not my problem. My problem is she's, she's—"

I felt a surge of impatience. "Is it the needles? I knew she was getting him needles."

"She's buying heroin, Clare. For Ben. She buys it for him herself."

Now it was my turn to be shocked. I tried to imagine Sally buying drugs, pulling up to a street corner in her sedate clothes and white Volvo. "Sally? She buys drugs?"

"Almost every other day."

"You're kidding. She told me she gave Ben the money to buy it. *She* buys it? Where?"

"A place in the Valley, she told me. She drives out and gets it and takes it to Ben. Like I said, almost every other day. She has a thousand rationalizations, you wouldn't believe. And this is Sally! You know Sally." Sid started to sound teary. "She's my good child, Clare. She's my little girl. She's always been the light of my life."

"How do you know she's doing this, Sid?" I thought of the listening device in Ben's old room. "Did she tell you this herself?"

Sid snorted. "She can't keep a secret from me. I saw her drive right by here, right down Mulholland, like she was on a mission. She never passes this place by, not lately, she'll always stop in. So I called up. Sally, I'm here by myself now, I said, don't I matter to you anymore? Oh, Daddy, she says. She was taking some supplies to Ben. What do you mean, supplies? I said. Like toothpaste? Dish soap? And she got rattled, I knew something was up. I pressed her. And she told me everything." Sid moaned. "How do you think I feel, my good child ruining her life for her no-good brother?"

"Her life's not ruined, Sid. It's chaotic, sure, it's unusual, but it's not ruined. I mean, if she got caught, it might be ruined—"

"Of course it would be ruined!" Sid was almost hysterical. "And if she gets caught, that's the best of it! What's keeping someone from killing her for the drugs she's carrying? You don't know what kind of neighborhoods she goes in! What's keeping someone from finding out who she is and blackmailing her? She wanted to be a judge, remember?

She had a big future! She used to dream about being on the Supreme Court."

"She doesn't want to be a judge anymore. She told me." I made an effort to think practically. "Can't you get Ben back in rehab?"

"I tried, I took him down to a place in Redondo Beach two weeks ago, and the next morning he escaped, and right after that I saw Sally driving past headed to that Brunhilde's house where he stays. A rehab place can't lock him up, you know. He's over twenty-one. He's got to agree to be treated. Sally says the drugs give him joy in his life. Is that crazy? So what about joy in my life? She was always the joy in my life, until she got mad—you know all about that—but lately we've been happy. I hate to say it, but her mother's death made us closer."

"Could you get a drug counselor to talk with her?"

"If I get a counselor to talk with her, they're going to know about her, and I don't want anyone to know about her. She's a lawyer, for crying out loud. She has her career to protect."

I agreed that was a point.

"Why don't you come out here, Clare? That's why I called you. Why don't you come out and talk some sense into her?"

I'M A BASIC DOCTOR. I'm not a brilliant researcher, I'm a normal everyday doc for people with a given disease. I ask them simple questions. Are you coughing? Are you wearing your condoms regularly? Do you have any anal discharge? There is nothing glamorous in my job. Maybe it was more glamorous early on, when I started at University, when the blood test for HIV had just been approved, when inhaled pentamidine to prevent pneumocystis pneumonia had just come out, when there was only one drug—AZT—to treat the virus. The general public, then, found AIDS more frightening; people were shocked that a person like me (who looked normal! who had a baby daughter!) should want to work with people with the disease. When Sally introduced me to her clients, they looked at me with something approaching awe. I'm not what you think, I'd tell them in my mind. I'm not a saint, I'm not brilliant, I'm not a hero at all.

"IS THIS TRUE, SALLY? Are you really buying—"

"Excuse me, Clare, but are you on a portable phone?"

"Your father asked me that too."

"You're sure you're not on a portable phone?"

"No, I said I wasn't. Don't be paranoid. Sally, your dad said you were—"

"Now you're listening to *him*? Did he call *you*? Clare, things are complicated, I'll explain them more when I see you."

"But I'm worried about you, Sally, I—"

"I'll explain things when I see you." And she hung up.

HERE'S WHERE SHE GOT the heroin: from a Chinese takeout in Encino. They sold normal Chinese food to normal people, but to special customers like Sally they tucked wax-paper packets encased in foil into the cartons of food. Ordering the drugs went by a sort of code. There were even different grades of heroin, the highest being "Happy Family." Heroin quantity was measured in bags; Ben used five a day. The nephew in the family that ran the restaurant, the chemist, had been a high school friend of Helga's older sister.

Initially, I wasn't going to go. I was a mother now, I had responsibilities, and going meant the risk of arrest, embarrassment, physical harm. But Sally said it was all very slickly done. I didn't have to go, of course, but if I wanted, she'd be happy to have me. I might find it interesting.

When else in my life, I thought, am I going to have an opportunity to go buy heroin? I thought of my new patients for whom picking up drugs was as normal as buying fast food. Why not, I thought. See what they go through.

And she had asked me.

I left Aury crawling around Sally's backyard with Sally's housekeeper, Teresa, trailing her. We closed Sally's front door. We took Sally's sober car, the white Volvo.

There was nothing exciting about Encino. The stop-and-go traffic, strip malls, fireplace shops and beauty parlors and grocery stores. If it weren't for the sunshine and the numerology parlors, we could have been in Ohio.

The Chinese takeout was in a strip mall with a dry cleaner on one side and a pet shop on the other. The takeout was fronted with windows covered with signs and posters; inside, a few ice-cream-parlor chairs were lined up against the wall, and an illuminated menu sign hung over the metal counter. The shocking thing was how ordinary the place looked, how it smelled of Chinese food. In the middle of the afternoon, we were the only customers. "You have friend," the elderly Chinese woman behind the counter said to Sally. She smiled, but her voice was not friendly.

"My sister," Sally said quickly, and I realized I was an object of suspicion. "Visiting from Ohio."

We looked nothing alike, but I wasn't sure the woman would notice. She hesitated and peered at me a moment. "Your sister look at menu," the woman said, whipping out a plastic-covered menu and pointing me toward one of the chairs. In this way, my gaze was diverted from the actual transaction, which Sally said involved slipping extra bills underneath the money for the food. The woman then disappeared into the kitchen, emerged with four small Chinese-food cartons, and put them in a white paper bag.

By then I was standing behind Sally. "You want number four?" the woman asked me. "Number four very good."

"No, thank you." I felt awkward and stiff, as if I were in a play. I tried to hand the menu back to the woman, but she nodded at me to lay it on the counter.

"She'll share with me," Sally said. "Thank you, Libby, thank you very much."

The Chinese woman gave a tight smile and dropped a hand under the counter as if reaching for something. Duck sauce, I thought, and I hesitated, thinking how hard Libby was trying to make this transaction look normal, but when I turned halfway back to take the sauce, she gave me a look so piercing I hurried out the door.

"Damn," Sally said as we drove away. "She must have thought you were a policewoman. Did you notice? I think she was reaching for a gun. Damn, I really like her. I like their whole operation. I always feel safe when I go in there. I thought buying heroin would be sordid, but dealing with them has been"—she waved her hand, and for once, I thought her way with adjectives would fail her—"unremarkable."

A gun! I felt a little weak. "You don't think she would have shot me?"

"Oh, heavens no. She'd never shoot. She was just making a point. They have a business to protect, and they're right here in the wilds of suburbia. They'd have to be fools to resort to violence. The woman behind the counter is an aunt, I believe. Damn. I hope they keep selling to me."

When we crossed the ridge and descended into Beverly Hills, my mood lifted. We drove within a half mile of Sid's house on Mulholland, and somehow the proximity made me feel safe. No one could catch us now. "Here we are driving down Benedict Canyon with ten bags of heroin," I said, and started giggling. Sally giggled too.

"Here we are turning onto Wilshire with ten bags of heroin stashed in cartons of Chinese food," she said. "Here we are, a doctor and a lawyer, pillars of society, turning onto Wilshire with ten bags of heroin stashed in cartons of Chinese food. Wait a minute, I'm going to drive down here." She turned down Cienega to Rodeo Drive, which was out of the way but hilarious. "Here we are driving down Rodeo Drive with ten bags of heroin. Robin Leach, where are you now?"

We became hysterical with laughter. "Beverly Hills's finest!" Sally said, picking up the Chinese food carton by its wire hanger and dangling it.

"Yum yum yum," I said, "I love Chinese." We stopped at a light next to a Ferrari. "Do you love Chinese?" I said to the driver through my open window. He looked at Sally and me hopefully, and we collapsed into fresh paroxysms of laughter as we sped off.

"This is the most fun I've had on any heroin delivery," I said as we pulled into Helga's drive. "Really, Sally, we should do it again."

"And have old Madame Chiang Kai-shek peering at you? She'd better not tell me not to buy there. Every other day," Sally said. "I'm more reliable than the mailman."

"Mailperson," I corrected her. "This is the eighties."

Sally drew herself up in mock offense. "No," she said, "I'm a mailwoman."

The front door swung open before we could reach it. There was someone there, blank and skeletal and hairless, leaning on the doorframe, engulfed in an orange T-shirt and shorts. I thought at first it was another of Helga's female roommates. I almost said to Sally, sarcastically, Now *there's* a woman for you.

It was Ben.

"Ben, what did you do, you . . ." I faltered; there was no way to ask him anything without letting on how bad he looked. He'd lost his job at the video store—accused of stealing, Sally said, although why should he steal? Sally took care of all his needs—and now spent all day in the house. One of Sally's campaigns was to get him out and walking; a little exercise would do him good. "You shaved your head," I noted limply.

He looked right past me to Sally. "You got it?" he said.

I saw lots of addicts in my new job. One of them had told me that the only thing important to an addict was the high. Nothing else mattered—not family, not friends, not honor or health or safety. "They be seeing you, they be talking to you, and they be thinking: How I get this doctor to give me some *stuff*? Or say it's my sister that's the addict, my sister be thinking: How I use this weasel brother of mine to get me some *stuff*?"

"Yes, Ben, I have it," Sally said.

He held out his hand. "Lay it on me."

"Ben, wait at least until we get inside." She pushed her way past him into the door. "You don't want anyone seeing you from the street."

"I don't care."

"You may not care, but I care, and if you want me to keep on procuring for you, you'll need to put up with my quirks."

"Malarkey," Ben said.

The word startled me. He was correct, of course: Sally would "procure" for him forever. Did Ben really have a sense of humor? I eyed him with fresh appreciation, and when he looked back, we exchanged a smile.

Absurd to think I thought he was all right, considering how he dug in the rice container with his fingers, spilling rice all over the foyer floor, how he grabbed for Sally's purse for the fresh needles, how he scampered away toward the bedroom without even a thank-you. But I did. I thought maybe he wasn't an addict like other addicts. I thought Ben appreciated Sally, I thought she was giving him—just as she said—a shot at joy. Maybe her buying heroin for Ben was precisely what she thought it was, an act of love. All this was on the basis of a single word—malarkey. I realized later why that word had consoled me: my father used it. It took me back to my childhood, to sitting in the backseat of the car, to the clean pure world where hope was possible.

"Are we going to see your dad at all?" I asked Sally as we drove home.

She shot me a surprised look. "Do you want to see him?"

"Not really." I was thinking about his charge to me, his demand that I come out here and talk some sense into Sally. I could imagine him talking to me, getting bigger and bigger and closer to my face, saying, "Well? Well?"

I had to admit, there was symmetry to it. Sally tolerated her father's publishing pornography, but not pornography with violence against women; Sid tolerated a son addicted to drugs, but not a daughter who delivered those drugs to her brother. With both of them, there was a malfunction of their moral barometer, an inability to calibrate certain decisions. At some point, after all, wrong is wrong. Isn't it?

I thought about this as I flew home, Aury on my lap. It was a long ride. If I held Aury on my shoulder, she squirmed, if I held her on my lap facing out she cried, if I held her sitting looking at me she grabbed my earrings and laughed. I couldn't understand why she was so keyed up.

"Aury, please, Aury. I'm very tired."

I wasn't very comfortable holding her. I wasn't a natural, like Sally would be, a child slung on her hip, bouncing happily through zoos, supermarkets, airports. I'd imagined I would be like that, my daughter and I contentedly together, complete unto ourselves, the envy of anyone who saw us. But no one envied us. I wore a frazzled look; Aury's big diaper bag knocked people's arms and caught on doorknobs.

When I'd phoned Margaret after Aury's birth, she said wasn't I lucky, I'd created my own friend—a nice idea, but it wasn't like that. My mother had told me I was a problem baby, which I found surprising considering her experience, but as she pointed out the babies before me were boys, "and they're different, they're programmed to love their mothers."

"What are you saying?" I objected. "Aren't girls programmed to love their mothers too?"

"I rest my case," my mother said.

"But you wanted me to have a girl! You were excited because you thought a girl wouldn't need a father figure!"

"Of course she needs a father figure. Every child does. You're the one who wants to dispense with the father."

I held the phone away from me and looked at it, realizing there was no way to respond to this coolly.

"I do hope you'll reconsider letting the father know," my mother said. "It would be a benefit to all three of you."

"So sayeth the great swami," I said, slamming down the phone.

"IT'S AMAZING," Cliff said, laughing. "My wife won't eat processed flour, and your best friend's shooting up heroin."

I was shocked. "Cliff! What are you talking about? Sally would never use drugs. She just buys heroin for Ben."

He was still giggly, titillated. "You don't think she sets aside a few bags for her personal use?"

"Cliff," I said. "Get off me."

"Oh come on, sweetie"—he was going limp now, I could feel it—"don't be mad. You can't think a thirty-something woman who's putting out major bucks for drugs isn't going to use them."

"Major bucks?" I pushed him off me. "Major bucks? You really think she's worried about major bucks?"

Cliff looked hurt. He propped himself up on an elbow and stroked the side of my face. "Oh come on, lover, if she's buying heroin three, four, times a week, she's putting out thousands of dollars."

I hated that "putting out." "She's from an extremely wealthy family. What's major bucks to you would be minor to her."

Cliff smiled. "That may be true. What's the money from?"

"Pornography. And anyway, Ben's money is in a trust fund from his mother. It's not Sally's money, she's the executrix."

"Pornography?" Cliff repeated, his mouth open. I could see he'd missed everything I'd said after that word. He ran his hand down my body, obviously excited. "What kind of pornography?"

"Get off me." I squirmed. "You disgust me."

"Hot pornography? Dripping pornography? Is your friend in the pictures? Do you two do it together?"

I've given a lot of thought as to whether what happened next could technically be called rape. I never would have made that charge publicly, because after all, I was already in bed with the guy, but I think that's what it was. "I'm going to disgust you," he said, pinning me down, "I'm going to disgust you all over." Stop it, I kept saying, stop it, and I fought him some, but that excited him more. After a while, I just lay there. He was in every orifice. When he was done, he collapsed on his back and closed his eyes, saying God, that was fantastic, God, you are a sex machine.

I fell asleep. When I woke up, Cliff was gone, a note I refused to read left on the bedside table. I tore it into twenty pieces, put on a nightgown, walked into Aury's room, and sat in the rocker beside her crib. She was lying on her back with one arm stretched out over her head, a position so trusting and confident it filled me with a kind of awe, and as I sat there, her easy breathing calmed me. She was a good baby. I'd done something right. I could hardly believe how tarnished I felt, partly because of Cliff but even more because I'd made my stories of Sally into cheap entertainment.

I wrote Cliff a letter. I told him we had to stop seeing each other; since I was a mother now, I was thinking about the morality of seeing a married man, and I hadn't liked our last encounter. Cliff took it fairly meekly; he knew he'd gone over the line. I still saw him almost every day. We worked together for over eight years. As a department chair, he did all my performance reviews and approved my raises and bonuses. At one point, he backed me up in getting special nurses for my patients. "I owe you one," I said then, and he raised his eyebrows slightly and kept writing. I had to smile. Even after all we've been through, I like the guy. He improved markedly after his third daughter was born, when his wife came down with breast cancer. She was treated at our medical center, so everyone got to see Dr. Dunswater in husbandly action, and he did astonishingly well. His wife did too. People do change, I thought, transfixed; and then I wondered if our affair had simply brought out the worst in him. His older two daughters are now adolescents, and Cliff and I occasionally have coffee together and commiserate.

"God, how can you complain!" he'll say. "Your daughter's an angel!"

"That's the problem," I retort.

He could take this as suggestive, but generously, he doesn't. "She's doing it to get your goat," he points out. "They're geniuses like that."

I snort and roll my eyes. Cliff, having spared me an obvious comment, now thinks he has me softened up. "Listen," he says, "that old friend of yours, the one who used to buy heroin supposedly for her brother, whatever happened to . . . ?"

I shrug and glance away. "That was ages ago, Cliff."

"What? Eight years? It wasn't a lifetime." Then he seems to remember his wife, the chemo, his daughters with their bouts of rebellion. "Jeez, it seems like a lifetime, doesn't it?"

"DID YOU TALK TO HER?" Sid bellowed over the phone, his voice almost hurting my ear. "Did you explain to her what she's doing to her future? I'm going crazy here. Did you make her see she's acting like a madwoman?"

"It's a terrible situation for her, Sid. Here she is responsible for a person who's not responsible for himself, and all she wants is for him to have a little peace and—"

"But did you talk to her?" he interrupted. "What about her career? What about her reputation? What about her morals, for God's sake?"

"I can't say it's ideal, Sid, but I understand it. I understand exactly what she's doing."

"Let me get this straight," Sid said. "You think what she's doing is normal?"

"No, not normal, but...understandable."

"You didn't talk to her." His voice was muffled.

"No. I'm sorry."

"What am I going to do?" His voice was barely audible, the sentence less a question than an exhalation.

I bit the inside of my cheek. "You could take him away, Sid. You could get him into a facility somewhere where Sally wouldn't have access to him."

"He won't agree to a facility."

"Do you know any judges? Is there any way you could get a court order?"

"*He's* not the person out there buying."

I pressed my eyes closed with my hand. An impossible situation. "You need a deserted island somewhere," I said, imagining Ben being dropped on one.

"That's it, I'm taking him out of the picture." Sid's tone was full of sudden resolution. "You're absolutely right. I've been thinking about this a long time, but talking to you makes it clear. I'm taking him to Mexico."

"Mexico!"

"One of my buddies has a house down there on the west coast. I'll take Ben down there and dry him out."

"I don't think you can just take a heroin addict and 'dry him out,' Sid. Can't you get Ben to a detox facility? Or a hospital?"

"There's a doctor down there, Clare. I've been talking about this with my friend. Don't you think Mexico has doctors? My friend has a friend who's a doctor in this little town where his house is, and this doctor said he could get Ben on methadone and wean him down. I've got to get him away from this whole environment. I've got to get him away from Sally."

"Sid, I'm not an expert on drug addiction, but someone who's been shooting up thirty-five, forty bags of heroin a week is—"

"Let me handle my own children, Clare, okay? You've been great to talk to me, don't get me wrong, but I don't see you being very helpful. I hope someday that little girl of yours doesn't break your heart."

"I'm sure she won't." I wasn't sure of this at all.

"All I can say is, thank God I have Sally."

The length of time I knew that Sally delivered heroin to Ben wasn't long, only a few months. But sometimes knowledge makes a month seem like a year.

Aury was six months old. She reached each of her milestones—smiling, rolling over, crawling, sitting up—just slightly ahead of schedule. Her progress was spectacularly steady. Most parents say the first year of their baby's life goes by in a flash. Aury's first year lasted forever.

ONE DAY WHEN I drove home from the hospital, there was a cop directing traffic around a lump in the center of the road. After a moment's hesitation, I stopped.

"I'm a doctor," I told the cop. "Anything I can do?"

The cop snorted. "I doubt it." He nodded at the lump, a body covered with a blanket. "Want to see him?"

"No, that's all right." I walked back to my car quickly.

After I got home that day, Aury, in a pink gingham sun hat that tied under the chin, was sitting in her stroller and watching me water the sunflowers in the tiny backyard of our town house. The phone rang and it was Sally. Ben was gone.

"What do you mean, gone?" A phrase swam into mind: What, he vanished down the aisle at a Kmart?

"He's dead, he's drowned!" Sally was hysterical. "In Mexico. He left the house Daddy rented and walked to the top of a sea cliff and jumped off!"

Another suicide. "Clare! Clare!" he'd said years ago. "Watch me do a cannonball!" His little feet rattling the diving board. His head on my knees, his arms wrapping my legs, his hair under my hand as wiry as a terrier's. I glanced out the window at Aury strapped in her stroller, trying to grab her toes so she could suck them. Innocence gone smash,

I thought. I saw Ben do the cannonball again, the waves surging around him.

IT JOLTED ME to see her walking toward me down the concourse. She looked so ordinary, dressed in a polo shirt and jean shorts, her mouth half open and sagging, her stomach a little bulgy. "Sally!" I called from behind Aury's stroller, and Sally looked around in confusion, not seeing me right away. "Sally!" I called again, but softer, walking into her line of vision, trying not to make her feel foolish—because it was clear to me, for the first time, that she was capable of feeling foolish.

I'd never known that. I'd thought whatever she did was done with absolute confidence, loony confidence, which was what made her buying heroin for her brother bizarrely threatening and even funny. But here she was, a blister on her toe, legs incompletely shaved, bending to cluck over Aury before she had the nerve to face me.

I grabbed her and hugged and hugged her.

One excuse for my behavior during this whole period was that I was shell-shocked from dealing with AIDS. I hadn't developed the requisite hardness. The rashes, the tongues coated with fungus, the eyeballs blossoming with virus all disconcerted me. I had changed my career, convinced it would be interesting, that I would be useful. It was interesting, I was useful, but the tragedies were realer than I expected. I had weird dreams. In one I was the doctor for Neil Armstrong, who had nothing but a simple cold, and I couldn't save even him.

I had a male patient then, an actor who'd come home to Ohio to die. "Oh, really?" I said, "which James Coburn movie?" I rented it on video. It wasn't a big part, but there he was on my TV, casting a quick glance over his shoulder, bringing a cigarette to his lips, turning to regard a girl. In the movie he was gorgeous. Now purple Kaposi's lesions sprouted all over him like psychotic mushrooms, his belly was hollowed as a bowl, and his cheekbones, which you could see had been an excellent feature, now were grotesque in their protrusion. I couldn't help but think that he'd been doomed by his good looks. His AIDS had been transmitted casually and sexually; in his day, he said, everybody wanted to sleep with him. In a way, Sally was lucky, because in the end Ben died quickly, and she didn't have to watch him wither away. Not that Ben had HIV (he didn't, amazingly enough; Sally's fresh-needle program worked), but the natural course of a heroin addict was decay. And Sally had tried to subvert that.

I guessed the death was a suicide, at least that's how the local Mexican doctor—who was also the coroner and who had, admittedly, his own interest in the affair—characterized it. North of the town there were sea cliffs, and early one Thursday morning, Ben had climbed to the top of the highest cliff and jumped off. His father, walking on the shore, looking for the son missing from his bedroom, saw him falling. He recognized Ben's orange T-shirt. The sea was too noisy for Sid to hear the thud as Ben hit the rocks, but Ben's body bounced twice, maybe three times, and as Sid ran toward him, the waves rushed in; Ben, swept into them, disappeared. Because the body never was found, there was no autopsy, no toxicology report; Ben had been in Mexico with his father almost five weeks then, the Mexican doctor tapering his narcotics, and by the time of his death, Ben was supposedly on a stable dose of methadone.

"I don't know," Sally said. "Maybe. I do know he was desperate. We'll never know."

We were talking about the possibility that Ben had taken drugs before his fall.

"I never should have let Daddy take him down to Mexico."

"But he wanted to go," I objected. "You told me that. You thought you were giving him everything to make him happy, and all of a sudden he wanted to quit."

"He wanted Daddy to accept him. He didn't really want to quit the drugs. He agreed to go so Daddy would accept him. The way I see it, I sent Ben down to Mexico to die."

I was learning, with my patients, not to rush right in with questions, but to let a person's thoughts unfurl.

"I might as well have taken a gun and shot him."

"Sally. That's nonsense."

"It's not. I knew when Daddy took Ben down there that he was trying to get him away from me. There was the rehab angle, yes, but that wasn't Daddy's prime motive. His prime motive was to get Ben away from me. Daddy gave up on Ben years ago. Right after I found out about Ben and Flavio. I remember Daddy standing in the doorway of Flavio's and my old apartment. 'I've given up on him, Sally,' he said. 'Your mother won't, but I have.' It was awful. Like Ben died right then and there for him. So when Mom died, I felt an extra responsibilty. Because she always looked after Ben, and Daddy looked after me."

I thought of Sid's frantic phone calls, his worry about Sally's being found out. I tried to remember if he'd expressed any concern about Ben, or if Sally was his only focus. "He was frightened someone would find out about your trips to the Chinese place. Your safety, your career, your future—"

"God, my future. Who cares about my future? I'm representing women with screwed-up face-lifts, basically. How rewarding is that? After Mom died, I tried to think what she would do for Ben. You know how she handled the marijuana. Keep him in a controlled environment, she said. If I'd kept taking Ben what he needed, he'd be alive today."

"Well, maybe today, Sally, but tomorrow? Or next month? Your father was working with a doctor. He was keeping Ben on maintenance—"

"Maintenance! Think about that word: he was maintaining him. That methadone stare. Like their eyes are *pinned*. Would you want to spend your life maintained?"

I said nothing, waiting.

"He called me. From Mexico. Ben called Monday night and said he was going crazy. 'I've got to get out of here.' Well, easier said than done. Daddy kept the car keys and the money. I asked Ben about taking a bus, but he never learned Spanish. I don't know how, growing up with Patricia and the gardeners, but he didn't. And his confidence was shot. A normal person could take a bus without speaking the language. But Ben..." She hesitated. "I said Ben, give me three days. I'll start down there Friday morning. I'll bring you what you need and we'll deal with Daddy later. It took a little doing, but I did it. They didn't trust me totally, I hadn't been buying for weeks and it was a big order—I had to order twenty Happy Families—but they gave it to me, finally, and I got my partners to cover my cases for a week, and I loaded up the Volvo and I was just at my office tying up loose ends when all of a sudden Dr. Ramirez—that's the doctor down there, the do-it-all detox doc—is on the phone to tell me about Ben."

"Wait a minute," I said, trying to understand, "you planned to drive down to Mexico with heroin for Ben? Is that what you were planning to do?"

Sally nodded impatiently. "I was only going down. Where they're looking for stuff is coming up. And I had cash for"—she rubbed her fingers together—"you know, *la mordida*. Bribes."

"That's incredible."

"It's credible! I was almost there, Clare. I almost saved him. I had a whole suitcase—drugs, syringes, alcohol pads. When Dr. Ramirez called, I thought something had happened to my father. 'I am sorry to say this, but there's been a death in your family.' I thought, Daddy's had a heart attack! But then Dr. Ramirez said, 'Your brother fell from a cliff.' I couldn't believe it. I thought Ben, Ben, why Ben? He's innocent, why not me? Why not Daddy or me?"

It took me a moment to get my bearings. "What are you talking about, Sally? You think it would have been better for you to die than Ben? Ben wasn't innocent, he was a drug addict."

"He had a disease. A disease!"

"You told me he was HIV-negative—"

"Not AIDS! He had an addiction disorder! First he was addicted to sex, then he got addicted to drugs. He never chose to do the things he did."

"Oh, come on, Sally." I heard that sort of thinking about drug abuse all the time, but more from family members than from the abusers themselves.

"You tell me it's not true."

"It's not exactly true. There's a tendency for some people to get drug-addicted, yes, but no one nabs them walking down the street and sticks a needle in their vein."

Sally shot me a quick and bitter glance. "You make it sound so easy."

INEVITABLE, SID SAID.

Look at his flaws, Sid said.

Disrespect of his body.

Disrespect for his family.

Self-absorption.

Greed.

"Greed?" I objected. "He never was greedy. He didn't want material things. He wanted a good high, he wanted love, he wanted to know who he was. Sid, for years he didn't know if he was gay or not. Can you imagine?"

"He was gay," Sid said flatly. "I don't care if he lived with that Teuton or not. And three days before he died, he asked Sally for drugs. He called her up and told her to bring him heroin. Just flat-out told her, like she owed him or something. And she was going to do it!"

"I know," I said. "Sally told me." A thought struck me: "How did *you* know?"

"I heard him on the phone. I eavesdropped. Listen, I had to eavesdrop! He was always calling people asking them for things. He called that girlfriend of his and asked her for drugs too, but she wouldn't bring them."

Lack of respect for others.

Lying.

Ingratitude.

"Helga didn't love him like Sally did," I said.

"You call potentially destroying your life for someone love? I call it insanity. Wait a minute, that's not true: you can potentially destroy your life for someone grateful, for someone who deserves it—like for your child, say—that could be okay." A hardness set into Sid's face. "But to destroy your life for a drug addict—no. That's unacceptable."

SALLY BLINKED BACK TEARS. "I can't believe it, I'm so disappointed in him. It's as if he thinks Ben deserved to die. I could stand someone else thinking that, but Daddy..."

Back then, what was Sally's joy? She was so concerned about Ben's joy, but what was hers? If I'd been more perceptive, I would have asked her; as it was, the question didn't cross my mind. I could have told her my own joy: leaving an exam room and hearing someone say to his companion: "She's nice, isn't she? She treats you like a real person."

"It's the day-to-day stuff that really wears you down," Sally said years later, biting her thumbnail. She was caring for her father then, besides her, the one remaining Rose. The remark hit me in the chest: she was right. At some point, I hadn't faced that with her, I hadn't asked her: Is there anything you'd like to do today? How well are you sleeping? What's your favorite thing to eat? So when she reconfigured her life without Ben, without her mother, she didn't leave much space in it for me.

IT WAS A SMALL FUNERAL. Helga came, but I, stuck in Ohio with my patients, didn't arrive till four weeks later. In his office off the parking lot, in a room fillled with pictures of trees and rivers, the son of the funeral director who'd done Esther's funeral tried to console Sally. She had her suspicions of him already; she'd noticed his eyes following her at her mother's funeral. When he saw her again, his voice quivered, as if he couldn't believe the luck that death had brought his way. "You should have heard him, Clare! He doesn't have to rend his shirt, but this he's-looking-at-you-from-the-trees-and-flowers stuff is a travesty. This was a young man. This was a tragedy. 'His spirit is joining the great life source.' Excuse me? My brother *dies,* and he still has no dignity? I'm supposed to be consoled to think he's coming back as an evening primrose?"

"Oh Sally," I said. I'd never felt such compassion for her. I felt as if my chest were breaking, all the love I felt gushing out and over her. I hoped she knew I felt this way. I hoped she could feel my love.

A MONTH LATER, Sally came to Ohio to visit me. I thought she needed to see me, but when she arrived, I realized she had needed to leave home.

We were seated in a restaurant, and behind us, people were meeting each other. "Frank," someone said.

"Nancy!" Frank answered. "How's summer school?"

"I can't stand it anymore," Sally said. "I can't stand all the stupid superficial things people say to each other."

"It's life, Sally," I said. "It's people exchanging pleasantries."

"You don't care about me at all, do you?" Sally said.

A strain of heartlessness had settled into her. She no longer had sympathy for anybody else's woes. Minor travails—traffic jams, an extra ten pounds, disagreements with in-laws—she greeted with irritation, as if such silly things only proved how worthless the complainer was. She weighed more major traumas—asthma attacks or wayward children or sick friends—against her own and found them wanting. How could a kid getting drunk one Saturday night compare to a dead brother and a mother dead at forty-nine? A man in the supermarket checkout line told us about his sister with multiple sclerosis, who wore diapers and was confined to a wheelchair. "At least she's alive," Sally said. With Teresa, her housekeeper, who was despondent over her own mother's illness, Sally was unforgiving. "I can't understand her. It's like she expects her mother to live forever. Her mother's eighty-nine! Does Teresa think she should never die?"

I wondered then what Sally thought of me. I'd think of my father's death, his embezzling, my divorces, my pelvic infection and miscarriage, and wonder if Sally thought they were worthy of any respect. Then I'd get angry, thinking of course I'd suffered. Every day I suffered. One of my patients, a sportscaster, had histoplasmosis in the sack around his heart. I didn't give him two weeks. Another of my patients, a prostitute, had a sinus infection that had eroded her facial bones and was pushing out her eyeball. Did Sally think I went through my days untroubled?

It was during this visit that Mark Petrello made his difference in my life. Sally and I ran into him at the hospital cafeteria. He was as wired and skinny as ever, piling his tray with potato chips, pop, two slices of pie.

"Mark," I said. "This is Sally. Remember my friend Sally?"

Mark rubbed his hands on the hips of his scrubs and looked surprised. "The famous Sally," he said. "All those phone calls. You visiting from L.A.?"

Sally said yes. "Nice to meet you finally," she said; I was relieved she was polite.

"Yeah," said Mark. "Me too."

"Care to sit with us?" I asked.

Mark made an apologetic face. "Can't. I got two codes coming in by squad. I just got this to . . ." and he waved at the food on his tray.

"Same old Mark," I said.

He moved ahead of us in line, paid, took the food from his tray, and trotted halfway across the cafeteria before he turned around and headed back to us, his snack foods bunched like bouquets at the end of his sinewy arms. "Hey, Sally!" he said when he was ten feet away. "Just wanted to tell you: Clare was my best girl. By far." He was on wife number three by that time, with innumerable girlfriends in between.

"She's a lot more than that," Sally retorted, but Mark was already scampering away, and I barely registered Sally's comment, riding as I was on a wave of pleasure—of pride, really—over what Mark had said. I was his best girl. Of everyone, of all Mark's women, I'd been his best girl.

But by the middle of lunch, without Sally saying another word, my view of my life had changed. What drove me to do things? I picked Oberlin as a college, thinking it would still have demonstrations; I had Aury because I liked to picture myself carting around a baby; I chose to work in AIDS not out of scientific curiosity or altruism but simply so I'd know all my patients were sick. When you came right down to it, my major life decisions—even my marriages—had been based on whim. But when Mark Petrello's measly compliment sank in, something inside me rebelled. If the best I was was Mark's best girl, how could I not want to be more?

We finished lunch without mentioning him at all. "You know, this is a disease," Sally said, touching her cheeks with her hand. "This redness. One of the plastic surgeons I work with told me. It's called rosacea."

Of course. But rosacea was a trivial thing, something I'd never dream of worrying about in my patients. "It's not a disease," I said quickly. "It's a malady. A disorder." I struggled to find another word. "A distinction."

"He gave me medicine for it."

"Are you using it?"

Sally frowned. "I'd look better if my cheeks weren't like a clown's, don't you think?"

Oh, Sally, I thought. My apple-cheeked girl.

I WENT BACK to California in November. The stock market had crashed, and Frank, who'd been buying stocks on margin, was in trouble. Baxter, too, had woes: a "friend," it turned out, had been sharing the cabin and set it on fire when he moved out. Baxter, busy rebuilding before the winter, told my mother he had no plans to press charges. He said he didn't blame the arsonist.

"It's hard losing a parent any time," I hazarded to Sally, trying to arouse a little sympathy for her maid, Teresa.

"You don't know," Sally said. "Your father was different. He was young, he died before his time. That's what's hard. I can't see mourning a mother who dies at eighty-nine. Where's Teresa's perspective?"

"You sound like a doctor," I said.

She didn't seem to hear me, or maybe she took it as another of the thinly veiled insults I was making—I admit it—more frequently those days. I don't know, she irritated me. She wasn't the only person in the world with a difficult life.

I feared for Teresa's job—Teresa, who was always so kind to Aury. I was especially nice to her that week, making my own bed, carefully rehanging my towels after each use, carrying my clothes to the laundry room rather them leaving them in the hamper. It was there that I found Teresa weeping, curled up against the washer in a pile of sheets.

I tried to convey my sympathy, but language was a problem. She didn't look consoled. She cried more. We parted in confusion. The noise she made followed me down the hall, through the walls and vents, and I can describe it only as keening. It clung as fiercely as lint. By the time I reached Sally in the backyard I knew exactly how my friend felt. "Maybe you should fire her," I said.

ON A CLOUDY SUNDAY afternoon, we went to visit Sally's father.

He was in the same house off Mulholland, behind the same gate, surrounded by the same vegetation and trees. All the plants looked as I'd remembered them, and the espaliered tree beside the pool seemed not to have grown at all. Sally and I talked as we went in: it had been almost two years since I'd been here for the reception after Esther's funeral, and ten months before that, I'd been here with Ted.

Now the front door, Sally said, was rarely used, so we entered through the garage. Once this garage had held four cars—Sally's little Kharmann Ghia, Ben's green Gremlin, Esther's Cadillac with the white leather seats, and an earlier incarnation of Sid's Mercedes. Now there was only Sid's car.

That near-empty garage hit me with what Sally had lost. The floor was carefully swept, tools hanging neatly from pegs on a wooden railing. The gardener would have done this, I was sure. Against the far wall, a plastic bin filled with games had been shoved under a cabinet. Twister was on top, and underneath, Green Ghost and Monopoly; a glimpse of a basketball was visible through the bin's webbing.

"Daddy!" Sally called as she pushed open the door to the kitchen.

This house had been so tantalizing to me, so extreme and glamorous and unattainable. But now it had lost its luster. It was only a rich person's house, a house made exceptional by the money poured into it. Nothing was new. The microwave had an analog clock. The peach dining room table looked dated and sad. The house could have been a museum, a painstakingly preserved piece of the seventies.

"Clare. You're back."

He didn't remember, I realized, that I was coming. He looked awful. His shoulders were hunched and his face was gray, and as he descended the long staircase from the second floor, the staircase I'd stood on the first time we met, he leaned against the railing as if a knee or ankle hurt him. A break in the clouds sent light streaming through the wall of windows and made all of us squint.

He hit the bottom of the stairs and winced. I gestured at his legs: "Hurt yourself?"

"Old war injury," he answered, which was surely a joke, and Sally and I obligingly smiled. "Actually, I fell off a ladder," he said. "I was trying to clean some stuff out of Ben's closet."

"Oh, Daddy," Sally said, her voice breaking, "you're not already going through Ben's...?"

"It's a room, not a shrine! Have you been in there lately? It's a mess."

Sally's face clouded. "Are you throwing anything away?"

"Sure," Sid said. "Believe me, there's not a lot worth keeping. I just tossed out a bunch of underwear."

"Why don't you let me go through things? It must be too painful for you."

I glanced at Sally: too painful for Sid? It would be far more painful for her. But maybe she wanted the chance to preserve—or inspect—Ben's things.

"It's not painful. Listen, as far as I'm concerned, I lost my son ten times before he actually died. The actual death crap was a formality, as far as I'm concerned."

Sally blinked quickly. "Ben had a lot of pain in his life, Daddy. He was always looking for joy."

"Joy." Sid gave a bitter shrug. "Whatever."

We left not long after that, shutting the door to the garage, hurrying past the bin of games and the navy Mercedes, past the pool, past the espalier which Carlos still, after all these years, tended like a child, past the tubs of flowers hanging from below the windows. "God,"

Sally said as she got in the car, her right hand shaking so much she had to steady her wrist with the other hand to get the key in the ignition, "it's like I don't know my own father anymore."

BACK IN OHIO, I woke up suddenly in the middle of the night, thinking of Sally. I called her, since it was only midnight in California. She was awake.

"Sally, I worry about you. I don't want another person in your family gone."

"I worry about me, too," she whispered.

She sniffed. "Can you stay on the phone?"

"Sure."

"You don't have to talk. Maybe I can fall asleep if I just hear your breathing. God, if I could only sleep. Clare? You can fall asleep too. That wouldn't hurt my feelings."

"Okay. I'll put the phone right beside me on the pillow."

And I did.

I DIDN'T LIKE HIM, never liked him, and years later I liked him even less. But if I'm honest (and I try to be, as Sally does) I have to admit that Peter saved Sally's life. I had a supporting role, but he was the one who saved her life.

A new man. A newcomer, Peter James Newcomer.

"Newcomer? That's his name?"

"Newcomer."

"How appropriate." I realized I didn't want a newcomer. "He doesn't look like Flavio, does he?"

"No. I am capable of learning from experience."

I could almost hear her smile on the phone. "Sally," I said, astonished, "you sound almost normal."

She laughed. Laughed! "Almost normal?"

"What does he do?"

"Do? He knows people. You'll see." She had met him in the basement of a Methodist church, when the AA session before her grief recovery group had run late. Was Peter in AA? She sidestepped the question. "Serendipitous," Sally said. "That's how I meet all my men." "All her men" meant Timbo and Flavio, not a huge number. Now she was meeting a man at a twelve-step program. How California. How modern. Peter Newcomer.

I MET THE NEWCOMER a couple months later. Sally was right, he looked nothing like Flavio. He had thinning brown hair pulled back in a ponytail, an inverted tepee of a goatee, hands that waved when he talked, and intense gray eyes. I distrusted his eyes; Sally thought they were his best feature. So what did he do, exactly? I understood that the previous summer he'd gone with a client to the Harmonic Convergence at Chaco Canyon. And how was it? He shrugged. "Fine. Why not? Peace love groovy."

He'd been trained as a social worker, U.C. Berkeley. Early on he'd been into community organization. "So are you working as a social worker?" I asked.

"I have a client base," he said.

"What does that mean? Is it like I'm a doctor, so I have a patient base?"

"I suspect you're thinking about this too conventionally."

"Wait a minute," I said. "I'm lost."

"Don't you have patients whose lives you know you could improve? Don't you have patients you'd like to take to the grocery store, help buy a new wardrobe, sit beside when they talk to their in-laws? Aren't there people you know you could do a lot for if you had the time and the access? Well, I have the time and the access."

I was stymied for a moment. "How do you get paid?" I finally blurted.

"Oh, I get paid. Not in a conventional, sixty-bucks-an-hour way. I get paid what people think I'm worth. Yesterday one of my clients, a record executive, gave me twenty thousand dollars. Now, taken as an hourly rate, that's excessive. But I gave him the confidence to make a multimillion-dollar deal. Looking at it as a percentage rate, you could say—and I will, I assure you, the next time I see him—I was underpaid."

I tried to imagine Peter, His Manginess, in the company of a record executive. But then I remembered the father of Ben's friend, long before, burrowed in his chair in Malibu. Record executives probably looked something like Peter. "Do you have an office?"

Peter opened his hands in an expansive gesture. "I stayed with clients in Provence last summer. My office is the world."

"That's very odd."

He smiled. "Clare. You've got to release your mental boundaries. Be a global free thinker."

"That's pretty hard for me," I said, "being from Ohio."

He took me seriously. "Don't worry," he said consolingly. "I'm from North Dakota."

I looked desperately from him to Sally, trying to find a chink between them. But Sally looked calm, adoring. Her bare feet sat in his lap. I felt sick. Where are you, Sally? Where's the woman who drove our Oberlin neighbor behind the house with fear? Who had the defense lawyer blubbering over her poster? Who drove every other day to Encino to buy her brother drugs? Sally, where's your gumption?

But she was just as sure about Peter as she'd been about any of those things. And I was just as unable to ask her why.

Was he expecting Sally to pop up with a big gift? Would he call her up the next day, say: "You know, I'm really worth more"?

"I don't know why it surprises me," I said to my mom on the phone, "she's never had good taste in men."

SALLY LEFT US ALONE in a restaurant while she used the restroom.

A setup, I thought. I've sat like this before with Sally's men. I appreciated her giving me the chance to talk to them alone but wondered why she felt she had to.

"Sally's a great g—" Peter started, then quickly corrected himself: "Woman."

"I'm glad you think so," I said curtly.

"She really loves and respects you. Says those nights with you on the phone kept her going, through some very rough times."

I looked at him in surprise, not expecting his appreciation. "They *were* rough times."

But he was already moving on. "I haven't met her dad yet. It's interesting, I'm nervous about meeting him, and I've met lots of dads." Peter grimaced confidingly. "Sally's different from my other lovers. She's deeper, she's natural, it's like she gets her strength from the deep motherwell, if you know what I mean. Everything about her is feminine, but not weak-feminine, strong-feminine. You think that's her Jewish heritage? She's like the original woman. She's Eve. While all the other girls I've met out here are—"

He was ten thousand times worse than Flavio.

Peter hesitated, shot me a quick glance, smiled a colluding grin. "I can say this, you're a doctor." I braced myself. "It's just so great to feel breasts without implants. Man"—he hunched over the table, his fingers spread—"I tell you, it's like touching God."

COULD SHE LOVE HIM? Who was I to say she shouldn't? Maybe he was perfect for her; maybe being perfect didn't matter, and all that mattered was Sally's having another of her definite feelings: a woman who loves not wisely but well. The pornographer father, the onanist, the bisexual, the drug-addict brother. While I, with all the (relatively normal) people around me—my mother, brothers, two husbands, even my own child—was a miser of love, pinched and crabbed and dry.

I thought of Sally at her mother's funeral, wrapping her arms around her father, making him safe. Her strong soft arms.

Where was my excessiveness? My suitcases filled with heroin? What could I do, what grand and foolish gesture had I ever made for love?

AURY GREW. At her one-year checkup, she weighed twenty-nine pounds. She was putting words together: Eat now. Me up. Mommy go. The pediatrician was delighted at her speech. "You've got a bright girl there," he said, smiling a secret smile. "Bright girls can be quite an adventure." I remembered that his daughter had gone to Washington to receive some science award when she was in high school. I asked about her. She'd quit college, the pediatrician said, and was on a Greenpeace boat in the North Sea tormenting whalers. This didn't seem to displease him.

"HOW'S AURY?" I said from California. This trip she stayed home with my mom, who had become her usual sitter, driving forty minutes daily to my town house. I paid her; I would rather pay my mother than Wee Ones Happy Haven. My mother was financially strained these days, since her school system had forced her, at age sixty-seven, to retire. Whatever savings she'd built up after my father's death had disappeared, probably (although she never said this) on Eric and his two families and the drive-in-restaurant-slash-money-pit he held on to for three desperate years.

My mother answered, "I've finally met a child more stubborn than you were. She screams 'No go bed!' when I try to nap her, and she'd rather starve than eat a lima bean. And just try to keep her away from the stairs! There's Aurelia's way and the wrong way. You know about that."

"Me? Moi?" I answered. We laughed. My mother and I laughed together.

I'm not so horrible, I thought as I hung up the phone. I'm not unlovable.

"CLIENTS, HA! It's like he's a guru to them."

"He's been through a lot," Sally said.

"What? His marriages?"

"Well, that, yes, but he had a horrible childhood. His mother was chronically depressed, and his father used to drink and beat him up. He used to take Peter's head and bang it on the wall and say, 'Look how hardheaded you are.'"

A gasp inside me, I swear. But I said, "There's a lot of child abuse in the world. I hear about it all the time from my patients."

"It amazes me Peter's turned out so well. He's loving. He wants children. He says that years ago, he might not have been able to trust himself with them, but now that he's pulled himself out of himself, he really wants them. He thinks it would complete one of his life's tasks to raise children successfully."

"Huh."

"Clare, I know you don't like the wording, but he's talking about real things. You know that."

I shrugged, conceded. "Is he quality?" I asked.

Sally sighed. "I think he threatens you, Clare."

"Come on, Sally, now you're talking like him! He doesn't threaten me. He reminds me of that guy back at Oberlin who sat on your bed and mooned over you. Remember him? The bicyclist. I saved you from him! There you were lying in that bed, blanket up under your chin, looking at him like Little Red Riding Hood. Remember? That was the start of our friendship. Peter reminds me of that guy."

"Lars Little."

"Actually, are you sure Peter's not the same guy, just grown up fourteen years?"

"His name was Lars Little. He was in the Oberlin magazine last issue. He was killed in a biking accident."

"You're kidding. Peter doesn't bike, does he?"

Silence.

Silence.

Silence.

"I defend you so much," Sally said.

"What do you mean?"

"All the time, to everybody, to Peter, to my dad, to Teresa, to my mother when she was alive. I'm always defending you. She's hostile, they say. She wants you all to herself, they say. Even Ben said that. She doesn't hug her daughter. She was supposed to talk some sense into you, but she folded. All that stuff. And I'm always, always defending you. That's why it hurts so much when you attack me."

I could barely speak. "I'm not attacking you."

"Of course you're attacking me. My judgment, my insight, my whole way of living. Don't you think it hurts my feelings?"

She was looking me in the eye, firmly, steadily, and I had to look away so I didn't cry. "I just don't want you hurting yourself, Sally. I don't want you to—"

"I want to be part of a unit, Clare. This is my chance to be part of a unit. Peter's a good man. He can love me."

SHE IS SUCH A fount of practical knowledge. She had my stock holdings diversified in two days. I didn't even think about that sort of thing!"

"So what do you teach her?" My questions were tentative, cautious. I felt I was being listened to and watched, even the moments when Sally wasn't there.

"Oh, I teach her about life. About uncertainties, pain, instability. Embracing the gray."

"Embracing the gray?"

"There's a lot of gray to the world. I'm helping Sally to appreciate that."

Another time I would have smirked. Now I felt too beaten.

"You should embrace the gray too," Peter suggested.

I frowned, then spoke softly. "You know what my job is, don't you? I think that's pretty gray-embracing."

"Gay-embracing?" Peter smiled at his joke. "Sally told me something interesting. She said you couldn't stand not knowing if someone was really sick. But now you know all your patients are sick. Seems like you cut out the gray, didn't you?"

He was not stupid.

"That's true," I said.

For a moment His Manginess looked surprised. Then he attacked again: "Have you ever wondered if Sally's father's business had anything to do with your choice of a specialty?"

"How so?"

"You know Sid's audience."

I was starting to get angry. "Not personally. Are you part of his audience? I'm not into porn myself."

"Gay men!" Peter said, exasperated. "Your past and future patients. Gay men! Come on, Clare. If you take any sort of sexual history from your patients—and you do, don't you?—you know porn's a big player in gay men's lives. In a lot of people's lives. Sally says you hate it, that you convinced her for a while her father was an evil man. But listen, my good doctor, I told her porn is wonderful. It's direct, it's messy, it's life-embracing. It makes you horny! What's a more basic human feeling than horny?" Peter winked. "I'm trying to get Sally to watch some hot flicks with me."

Suddenly I knew who Peter reminded me of: Sid. The same self-confidence, the same big statements about "life," the same bland assurance in speaking about Sally, as if she were a quaint yet priceless possession.

"Sally says in college you were a regular hot tomato," Peter went on. "You had 'needs.'"

My face colored. I looked back at Peter's grinning face and perky shirt, and the first thing I thought at him was: You know too much. How could Sally tell him those things? Didn't she respect my privacy? Then I remembered Cliff Dunswater and the stories I'd told him about Sally and Ben: how the follies of the people closest to you can be used as a kind of currency to buy your own allure.

"I BOUGHT THAT flavored cream you like," Sally said, lifting her tea ball from the steaming cup. "You want a full cup?"

That trip to California, in the late winter, was a treat: Peter was accompanying a client on his yearly retreat to an ashram, so Sally and I were alone. The ashram visit was a triumph for Peter; the previous year, his client had taken a mistress.

I sat in a big plaid chair, a more muted plaid chair than the one at our house in Oberlin, but still. It was raining. "Of course," I said.

"He's a little afraid of you, Peter is," Sally said, approaching with my coffee. "You know me too well."

I smiled. "I know what you think of Anaïs Nin."

"And Martin Luther."

"And white noise."

"And barking dogs."

The coziness of lamps set on low tables, the echoing timbre of our words, reminded me once again of our old house. "You know me too well, too," I said.

"I know about your Sabbath."

"The demonstration I went to."

"I know about your needs!"

We looked at each other and laughed. In that instant, I had no fear that I would lose her. We had—we would always have—our past. We'd grown up together, in a way.

"You knew Ben," Sally said quietly. "You knew my mother."

I BROUGHT AURY to the wedding. She and I and Sid and Peter's younger brother, who sold penny stocks out of a brokerage in Fargo but wouldn't at all mind relocating to L.A, were the only guests. The brother had several stock suggestions for me—cash or check or credit card, whatever—each of which he offered with a nudge.

"I don't want stocks," I said. "My brother is hurting from stocks."

"What's with this guy?" Sid sidled up to me. "Continental Kitty Litter? Ibis Rare Mineral?" Sid had some of his old vigor back. He wore a navy jacket with gold-toned buttons.

The wedding was in May in Santa Monica, at a hotel on a balcony overlooking the sea. A chuppah had been fashioned out of a white wire

arch entwined with ivy, and a rabbi officiated, because Peter had converted from humanistic agnosticism to Judaism, a move Sally—to my
surprise as much as Peter's—had insisted on. "Fastest conversion on
record," Sid muttered in my ear. "Poof! You're a Jew. Sally had to call
eight rabbis. Think this one got a contribution for his troubles?"

Peter wore a woven cotton pullover with an open neck and carried
a calla lily, both of which made me hate him more. He had lopped off
his ponytail, and the hair at his nape was ragged. Sally wore a blue silk
suit with matching shoes and looked like a lady banker or a doctor's
wife; of the two of them, she looked infinitely more mature. The
guests stood behind them. My eyes were fixed on the ocean because
Sally had told me that sometimes from this point you could spot dol-
phins. The sea breezes did a real number on Peter's wispy hair.

At the end of the ceremony, Sally and Peter exchanged a kiss. Beside me, Sid winced and looked away. Peter's brother took several pictures of the kiss, and later had them pose doing it again. They hadn't
hired a photographer, because Peter's brother had a very fancy camera.

How can she stand it? I thought. How can she kiss those lips? They
were soft and blubbery, horse lips.

"You do much photography?" I said to Peter's brother at the
restaurant afterward. Lobster ravioli, champagne. Maybe I was tipsy.
Sid was on my right beyond Aury, Peter's brother on my left at the circular table. Aury was sitting on phone books on a chair, after making
herself rigid and screaming, "No baby!" when I tried to put her in a
high chair. "Sid can use photographers."

"Oh, really?" Peter's brother said, cocking an eyebrow. I suspected
he wasn't the sort to let a business opportunity go. "You need photographers, Sid? What kind of work are you looking for? I'm not a professional, but I do all sorts of things in Fargo. I've done weddings,
advertisements, model shoots. I have a portfolio if—"

Peter was eyeing me warily across the table. "It's wonderful, Clare,
that you made the effort to come out for our wedding," he said. "We'll
never forget it."

"Thank you." I knew he was being sarcastic: I always came out.

Sid waved his hand dismissively at Peter's brother. "I've got my own crew. Thanks, but I'm not looking."

Peter's brother stared at his plate for a moment, then perked up. "I can't believe you two are going to San Diego for a honeymoon. Isn't that just military guys and old people? Why not at least go down to Mexico? It's sexier."

Sally met my eyes across the table. Her brother had been dead less than a year.

"God, Mexico," Sid said. "Mexico's a black hole. You couldn't pay me enough to go back there."

"It wasn't *Mexico,*" Sally said, leaning toward her father. "It was me I blame for Ben."

Peter turned to his brother in explanation. "Ben was Sally's brother who committed—"

"Wait a minute," Sid interrupted. "Let's blame Ben for Ben. That's accurate. That's realistic."

Sally looked desperately toward Peter. He brought an arm protectively around her chair. "We're working on that, Sid," he said. "We're getting Sally past guilt. We're reframing the real."

Sid raised his eyebrows and pressed the fingers of his right hand to his upper abdomen. "That's pretty," he said. He turned his face to the side and belched. What if Ben were here? I thought. Would he already have disappeared into the bathroom? Sally's life was truly simpler since he was gone.

What a terrible thing to think about a dead person.

It seemed to strike us all at once that we were inappropriately silent, and Peter's brother lifted his glass with a toast to the bride and groom.

Outside the restaurant, as our dinner broke up and the sun sank into the ocean, Peter finally took notice of Aury. "How old are you, Aury?" he asked. "Are you two?"

Aury stared at him unsmilingly.

"She's eighteen months," I said. "But she thinks she's eighteen."

"Do you have a very old soul?" Peter asked, crouching in front of her. "Did a very old soul fly into your body when you were born? I bet it did."

Aury frowned and looked extremely skeptical.

"Right there." Peter pointed at her chest. "Right inside there is a very old soul."

Aury brushed his finger away and looked up at me. "No wike man!" she announced.

"Shhh," I said, loudly. Out of the mouths of babes. "Be nice to Uncle Peter. He's married to Aunt Sally now. You can call him Unkie."

"Uckie," Aury said. I glanced around me to see if this had delighted anyone else, but all I saw was Sid, looking pale, sick, standing beside a fountain with one hand gripping the railing.

"Are you feeling okay?" I asked him. "You look a little pale."

"I don't know, something came over me, I—"

Oh God no, not another death for Sally. Not on her wedding day.

"Are you having chest pain? Are you short of breath?"

He wiped his brow with his sleeve. "I think it's something I ate."

"Are you feeling faint, like you're going to pass out?" My thoughts raced. An arrythmia? A blood clot? Sudden cardiac death? I was reaching for his wrist, his pulse.

"I've got to lie down."

"That's okay, lie down here on the sidewalk. Peter, can you help get him down? I'm feeling your pulse, your pulse is fine. Lie your head down. I'm going to undo your tie here, that's okay, I'm feeling your pulse."

Sally above us . . . hand on her mouth . . . horror . . . the other hand reaching out to her father.

"I've got to, I've got to—"

His neck twisted away, veins sticking out

> *My God this is it*
> *What grand and foolish gesture could I do for*

Fist on chest, bam   Cardiac thump

Love

I swept my finger through his mouth. No foreign objects.

"What are you *doing*? What—?"

I clamped my mouth on his lips. I pushed air in. I had to save him. Hot, wet vomit in my mouth.

"Clare, I'm breathing, for cripe's sake." Vomit. "Clare, get off me! I'm not dying, for cripe's sake." Pushing himself up, shaking his head. "Clare, listen to me. I'm fine, okay? I'm fine. I just had to puke. It was that lobster ravioli, I always puke with lobster. I should have known better than to eat it. My mother wouldn't have eaten it. What, you think I was dying? You trying to do CPR on me, was that it?"

His vomit in my mouth. Tasting familiar, normal, like my own vomit. Her soft arms around me.

"Clare," Sally was saying, laughing and crying, "oh, Clare, that was so *sweet*."

THEY SEEMED HAPPILY MARRIED. After only a few months, they sold Sally's house in West Hollywood and moved up to a house in Pacific Palisades. The comments Sally made about the house they had left ("Too cramped"; "That bathrom was an antique!"; "Not exactly a family neighborhood") rolled around my brain like stones in a tumbler, never getting polished smooth. Sally knew how much I loved that house. I didn't care if I ever visited her new house—her and Peter's new house—with its view of the ocean. Sally said her father was jealous. I was sure the bank had loaned them money based on Sally's earnings.

They ended up a cozy trio. Peter and Sid actually hit it off. Peter was going to write some articles for one of Sid's magazines, and pen a defense of porn he hoped to publish somewhere upscale, like *Harper's*. Sid thought Peter should codify his services and bill on an hourly rate for "consulting." This love-offering stuff was okay in theory, but it made real businesspeople uncomfortable, and real businesspeople, Sid pointed out—not what Sid called the "flaky fringers"—were the people Peter should aim for. He could put out a series of motivational tapes. He could do seminars.

———

"SAY GOOD-BYE TO YOUR mommy," my mother coaxed.

"Mommy go. Bye-bye, Mommy!" I wished it made her more un-happy. I wished there was some sense of her being troubled at my leaving.

"God, I wish my kids were like that," Lois, my clinic head nurse, said. "They go crazy when I leave. They're screamin' and cryin' and hangin' on me. I can't even comb my hair."

"So *that's* the problem," Mr. Ervin, CD4 count of 12, survivor of disseminated legionella and cryptococcal meningitis, said brightly from his chair in the hall.

"I thought you were a nice man," Lois said, swatting Mr. Ervin's bony head with a rolled-up piece of paper.

"Me? Never been nice," Mr. Ervin said. "Uh-uh. Not one minute."

SALLY GOT PREGNANT. She would be, we agreed, a *very* el-derly primip: thirty-four. She cut back on her private-practice hours and did more pro bono work with the Women's Project of Los Ange-les County, a legal advocacy group. Peter put out a motivational au-diotape: *Making the Best of Your Best.* He was very pleased with Sally's public-service work; through it, she was coming to the attention of wives of film producers and directors who he thought could throw her law firm some business. "It's amazing," Sally told me, giggling, "he's got an angle for everything. I just sit back and watch."

I sighed. I asked her what kind of compensation she was getting for loss of beauty these days; had she had any interesting cases lately? But Sally didn't want to talk about her work; she wanted to talk about be-ing pregnant. Had my breasts tingled? Did I sweat more? Did my vagi-nal secretions increase? I realized I wasn't used to talking about bodily things with Sally. I wasn't sure I liked it. On the other hand, I was grateful she was making trivial conversation. She was back in the world of the living, and if I was honest, I had only Peter to thank.

About this time, I started taking Aury to the parent-child swim ex-perience at our suburban rec center, because I'd never learned to swim and I regretted it. By the second lesson, Aury was floating; in the third, she did a backstroke, which is really, as the teacher pointed out a trifle disparagingly, a variant of floating. Most of the other toddlers were still clinging to their parents' necks. "Your girl's been in the water a lot, hasn't she?" the teacher said. "Oh no," I said, "never." The closest we'd been to water sports was turning on the sprinkler in our patch of backyard. It was weird. I could barely stand to get my face wet, and suddenly my two-year-old daughter was swimming. I wondered if this was some genetic trait she'd gotten from her mystery father. But I refused to think about him. I wondered what other surprises my daughter held in store for me.

ALL OF A SUDDEN it wasn't so easy to go off to California: my patients were sicker, more dependent, I worried about them more. The coverage available in my absence wasn't good. One of my covering infectious disease colleagues missed the diagnosis of a pneumocystis pneumonia, *the* basic diagnosis in AIDS, and the patient ended up on a respirator and then dead. He might have died anyway, but a pneumonia diagnosed Monday fares better than one found Thursday.

When I was at Sally's second wedding, an HIV-positive woman who wanted children found out she was pregnant and, in a state of panic, had an abortion. Had I been there, I could have told her to take AZT and keep the baby. Also during that absence, a drug abuser I'd been dosing with methadone ran out of his supply and shot up his partner's suppositories, which turned out to be an antinausea drug and not, as he'd hoped, Dilaudid. No harm was done, but still.

And three new patients waited an extra week to be seen. It's okay to wait a week with hypertension, but my patients needed more. My patients needed me.

SO I TOLD SALLY "I'll get there. It's been unbelievably busy."

"I'm sorry. I know I'm snappy. Peter says it's hormones. He's a great one for avoiding personal responsibility. Everything is either your immune system or hormones." Sally dropped her voice confidentially: "Forgiving but vague."

When Sally had been married to Flavio, she had disappeared—all those trips, the postcards from South America and the Orient—and now she'd disappeared again, this time into a life so determinedly suburban and "normal" that it seemed like a rebuke to me, a single mother with a fatherless child. From the fortress of her four-bedroom house in Pacific Palisades, she hired decorators, took Lamaze classes, worried about her landscaping, and talked about the preservation of shoreline. I had no idea how to reach her. It seemed that I was, like my patients, stuck in strange eddies at the shore, wallowing in tree limbs, reeds, and branches, while Sally rode the central current of American life.

"Peter's making a video next. Daddy offered to let him use his equipment."

"You mean let Peter film—?"

"In his studio. He's got a regular studio, you know. Cameramen, cinematographers, grips, the works. It's fortunate, because that way Peter can get a professional product."

I knew what she was talking about, of course: the famous studio in the Valley, where Daddy Rose made his pornographic films. Sally had never been there. She had only an inkling where it was; its location was as clothed in secrecy as a mistresses' apartment. But now her attitude was different. I imagined her parking in the lot beside a low cinder-block building painted an inoffensive tan. I saw her sitting on a stool in a cavernous room, holding up cue cards for her husband, the beds and harnesses and dildoes tossed in a pile out of view of the camera. "Are you going to go up there when Peter films it?"

"Not while I'm pregnant. Although I wouldn't be pregnant, would I, if it weren't for sex? Of course, they always use condoms." Sally's laugh was tinged with sarcasm, giving me a second of hope, but when she continued, her tone was serious. "Peter and I had dinner last week with Lee Smith, have you heard of her? She's a literary critic-at-large for *Rolling Stone*, Peter knows her from way back, and she said she thought the label of pornography was a class thing. Cultivated people read erotica, not porn. It's the hoi polloi that look at dirty magazines."

"That's interesting," I said politely. I was pretty tired of the subject.

"Who's not interested in sex?" she said. "Who would be here if not for sex? People talk about it very freely to a pregnant woman, did you notice that?"

No, I had not noticed that. People didn't talk freely to me, Dr. Mann of Lisbonville, Ohio, great with child and silence and clearly unattached. People talked to me as if they were frightened of the things I might blurt out.

"WHY NOT THIS SPRING?" she said during another conversation.

"I'll probably wait till the baby's born now."

"It's been almost a year, Clare. You haven't been here since my wedding."

"I'm tired of traveling. You haven't been to Ohio very often."

I think I was trying to goad her. I imagined what she might say: "Are you punishing me somehow? Do you feel like I betrayed you by getting married?" Or "Don't you like me anymore?" Or "Remember when we used to share a half gallon of ice cream back in college? What's happened to us since then?" I wanted something definite, confrontational, something to prove to me she cared. But:

"Yeah," she said softly, her voice filled with regret.

"Is Peter still playing Beethoven to your belly?"

"Mozart. Beethoven's a little too mature for Peter. Yes. And Peter talks to it. Want to talk to it? Since you won't see it in person for a while. I can hold the phone on my tummy for you."

Oh, my, I thought.

"Talk to the baby," Sally said. "Tell it you're its only auntie. Here."

The sound went muffled, and I realized she'd moved the phone.

"Hi, little baby," I said. "This is your aunt Clare speaking. How do you like it in there? Are you looking forward to being born? Your mother and I used to . . ." After a bit, I started to enjoy it.

Suddenly I heard air through the phone, and Sally's voice returned. "Peter just walked in. I don't want him to think we're crazy."

"How can he think we're crazy when he plays Beethoven to your belly?"

"Mozart. That's a point. Okay." She put the phone back, and I talked to the baby some more.

"We're not crazy, Peter," I heard her say in the distance.

I WENT BACK TO HAPPYVILLE to spend my mother's birth-day at her apartment (I let infectious disease cover for me that time), and when I was at the supermarket picking up candles, who should I run into but Dr. Danforth.

He knew me right away. "Why Clare Ann," he said, "you're all grown up." Aury was sitting in the grocery cart, looking clear-eyed and calm, as she always did with adults. "This must be your little girl."

"Aury," I said, and before Dr. Danforth could look blank, I rushed in to spell it. "She's two and a half." We chatted a bit; he was retired, his wife had had a kidney removed for cancer. "I'm an internist now," I told him, pleased to watch his eyes crinkle upon hearing this news (he'd always had a nice smile). "I specialize in AIDS."

That surprised him enough that he moved quickly to another question. "Is your husband in medicine?"

"I'm not married."

"Oh," he said, puzzling, "not married." Aury tilted up her chin and studied his face; Dr. Danforth reached out and abstractedly patted her hair.

"Your father embezzled from us, you know," Dr. Danforth said, as if this were all he could think of to say. "Did you know that?"

"I suspected it."

"I've thought about it for years. We didn't pay him enough. I was always sorry to see him go." He aimed his words at Aury. "We never found another manager as good as your grandfather."

Aury tugged on my sleeve inquisitively.

"He's Dr. Danforth, Aury." I looked back at him. "My dad embezzled for me. He embezzled for my college tuition and to pay my plane fare for a trip to California."

Dr. Danforth smiled apologetically. "We never pressed charges. You went to Oberlin, didn't you? Expensive school." He paused. "He was a good man, Clare Ann."

"Thank you."

We parted awkwardly. Give my best to your mother, to your wife. So good to see you after all these . . . you look well.

I MIGHT AS WELL have been a nun. It wasn't a conscious decision; I just stopped looking for partners. After a while, I sort of desexed myself. I'm not the first person that's happened to; it certainly happens with some of my patients. Aury was getting to the age of awareness, and I didn't want to expose her to men coming and going from our home. And, frankly, most of my patients had been infected through sex—subconsciously, that probably affected me. Then there was the matter of Sid's brutal magazine. I think it's accurate to say it hurt me. Without a partner, all I could do was masturbate, which is what people buy those magazines for, so whenever I thought of masturbation, I remembered those awful pictures.

Sex was not a life-enhancing activity in my book.

"IT'S ASTONISHING how something so small can change your life. He's only eight pounds. He weighs less than a bag of flour. But he's an entire miniature person. He's all there! You know that, after Aury."

"What's he doing now?"

"Oh, you know. He loves to nurse. He likes to look at me. His eyes are wobbly, and his neck is wobbly, I have to steady his head in my hand, and then he looks right up at me."

I could see it. I felt a sharp pang, half wanting another child.

"Who does he look like?"

"He has my mother's eyes. And his head is square, like mine. And he has this little round tummy that reminds me of Peter."

Incredible that she should find Peter's round stomach appealing. "I bet he's really cute." The baby's name was Ezra, after Esther; it was too early, Sally said, to name a child after Ben.

"He looks like a little old man. Do you want to talk to him? I'll put the phone to his ear."

SALLY AND PETER had a bris for Ezra, eight days after his birth, but I missed it. Only Sally's father and a a few of their neighbors came.

"What about Aunt Ruby?" I asked.

"I didn't invite Aunt Ruby."

"You don't have that many relatives," I hazarded.

"We don't need Aunt Ruby."

I went out three months later, leaving Aury with my mother.

Ezra was a wonderful, larky baby. He had a thick head of dark hair, a huge smile, and dimples; it was possible to look at him and forget that Peter had played any role in his creation. When I spoke to him, he craned his neck and his arms and legs whirligigged.

"He knows you!" Sally said. "See, he knows you!"

"He's certainly animated." I couldn't pick him up fast enough.

"You see those kids in the mall and they're too well behaved, they stand there like zombies. Too much television."

"I don't think you'll have to worry about that with Ezra." He was flirting with me, turning his chin away and looking up at me on a slant. Was Aury a zombie? As long as she was treated like a grown-up, she was certainly well behaved.

"Do you miss your work at all?"

"I talk to the office every day. I went in last week and took a depo. I have a trial in six weeks, but it'll settle."

I cooed at Ezra between questions, gave him big openmouthed smiles, and made my mouth into an "O." No, Aury was not a zombie; she was definite. She had a will. "What about your welfare women? Are you missing any trials with them?"

"Trials?" Sally sounded surprised. "I've never done a trial with them."

"I thought you were doing more work with them. I thought you'd cut back your office hours and were doing more for the legal clinic."

"I do a ton for the legal clinic, but it's all phone work. The lawyers there call me up and I give them my opinions. I don't actually see their clients."

"Really? I . . ." But I wasn't sure what I'd thought, or why I'd thought it. I'd pictured Sally getting out of her Volvo in her stylish clothes and striding into a lobby filled with battered women. So tell me, Mrs. Morales, on what date did your husband break your right arm? Mrs. Jones, were you aware your boyfriend had other children he'd abused?

"It wouldn't be efficient for me to see clients. The lawyers and the legal aides see them. They get their stories, and then if the lawyers have questions, they call me. I'm a consultant." Sally grinned at my obvious surprise. "I'm an eminence gris. See?" She grabbed a hank of her hair and waved it at me; there were, to be sure, strands of gray.

I had no idea she was that respected. She was only thirty-four. Maybe she would make judge. "Did Peter ever make that video at your father's studio?" I asked. Where that question came from, I'll never know.

"Oh sure. It's good. I'll let you watch it."

"Did you go to the studio with him?"

"No. Peter went up at eight on a Saturday morning and came home at ten that night."

"Did he say what the studio was like?"

Sally shrugged. "A normal studio. Like a TV newsroom. I think Peter was disappointed. He did say there was a poster of an erect penis on the door to the men's room. And assorted beds."

We looked at each other and laughed.

"That reminds me," Sally said, "Daddy wants you to have breakfast with him while you're here."

"Breakfast?"

"The new meeting meal. Haven't you heard of a power breakfast? He wants to take you out. He asked specifically. I know you don't care for him, but he's been peculiar lately. I hope you'll go."

"How do you mean, peculiar?"

Sally hesitated. "He's not his definite self. I ask him what he's been up to, and he can't say. I thought he was trying to do more video business, but he seems to be working less, not more. I thought he might have a girlfriend, but he never mentions anybody. He spends a lot of time just driving around, but he often drives near here and doesn't visit. And that's odd, especially now that I'm home on leave. I thought he'd be ecstatic about Ezra, especially with Ben gone, but he's really remote with him. He never offers to hold him."

"Is he depressed?"

"When Daddy gets depressed, I expect activity, not lassitude."

Lassitude, ah. I got a jolt of joy, a small electric shock, as I always did hearing one of Sally's precise words. I wondered if there was anything I did that evoked such a response in her.

"Did I tell you he's put his house on the market? It's true. I don't know if it'll sell, it seems like he's asking a fortune, but it's a prime piece of real estate."

"Where would he move?"

"He's got his eye on a place in Malibu, up in the hills, not far from here. He wants that ocean view, remember? All of a sudden he has to have it. It's the only thing he gets excited about anymore. Ocean ocean ocean."

I missed my patients. In California I couldn't stop worrying about them. They all died. AZT was a nice medicine, it helped, but then it started reminding me of Bactrim, the nice medicine for urinary tract infections that wasn't totally benign, the drug I'd complained about to Mark Petrello years before. With AZT, some people's blood counts dropped, or they got headaches or threw up, and then there were people it didn't seem to do a thing for, good or bad, who continued their steady downhill slide.

Sally came closer, opened out her arms. "May I have him back now? Are you sated?"

Ezra's little body strained to her voice. I passed him back.

IN MY NIGHTMARE, Aury's sixteen, tall and beautiful.

"I took a vow of abstinence till marriage," she announces. I think of Aury's precise handwriting, the perfectly aligned shoes on the floor of her closet.

My mind scurries. "You did? Where?" I think of her polite friends, their sober voices on the phone: "Hello, Mrs. Mann, is Aury home?" Her friends would always call me Mrs. Mann.

"At Cathleen's church. You know I've been going to Cathleen's church."

"Not that abstinence is bad," I say, talking almost to myself. "I'm abstinent. I haven't always been abstinent, of course. Obviously. Where would you be if I had been?"

"Did you have any respect for my father?" Aury asks, her eyes filled with pain. "Or was he just a lay?"

"Oh, Aury."

"I thought so." Her eyes pin me with angry despair. "What was his name?"

For some reason, I start laughing. "I'm not sure."

"Mommy, what was his name at least? Don't I deserve to know his name?"

"Honey, I'm really not sure. There were..." I spread my hands helplessly.

Her perfect mouth falls open, her deep eyes fill. She starts to breathe very fast. "You mean it could have been more than one? More than two? You mean you don't even know?"

Well, a nightmare. But how will Aury handle the knowledge that her parentage wasn't clear? She wasn't yet three years old, but she was already such a particular little girl. She combed her dolls' hair daily with a special comb. She pressed her lips together and crossed her arms when I tried to coax her into the cowgirl jacket Sally bought her. Who's my daddy? she'd say one day, inevitably—or rather, because her speech was becoming as precise as the rest of her: Who is my father? There's always the myth of the father. It had been a lie to think the father wasn't important, and it astonished me to realize that I—princess daughter to my own father, with a best friend forever meshed with her father—once believed that my daughter's father wouldn't matter. In reality, he was no more than a sperm donor, but Aury wouldn't understand that. What child would ever want to?

SID PICKED ME UP in his Mercedes from Sally and Peter's house in Pacific Palisades and drove inland on Sunset to the Beverly Hills Hilton. It wasn't in honesty all that posh a hotel, which made me wonder if this whole breakfast was an elaborate slap in the face. I felt uncomfortable in his car, like a prisoner, and sat with my knees together and pointed toward the passenger door.

His face was lined and sagging, and while the front part of his hair had always been thinning, he had had a burst of hair loss. Now his forehead shone, as if greased. "Sally tell you I'm moving?"

"She did say your house was on the market, did you sell it?"

"The Mulholland house is still on the market, but I've bought a place in Malibu up in the hills. It's smaller. Got a view of the sea."

Just like Sally said: ocean ocean ocean. "A smaller place. That makes sense with only one of you—" I hesitated, realizing what I was saying, and stopped before the word "left."

"Eli," Sid said. "The surviving patriarch." It took me a second to realize that this must be a Bible reference. But who was Eli?

"He lived on a hill. Eli was the high priest who told Sarah she'd have a child. His sons took over the priesthood, but they drank, they let him down. Thank God for my daughter."

"And for Ezra," I prompted. I could still smell Ezra on my blouse.

"Oh, Ezra," Sid said. "Right."

We fell into silence except for desultory remarks about weather and scenery until we reached the hotel dining room, which was below the lobby and opened on one side to a patio. We sat in a booth with high-backed seats.

Good Lord, I thought, I hope nobody thinks I'm his girlfriend. I flattened my back against the seat.

Moguls surely did not come here. Second-tier players, maybe. In the booth behind us, the people were talking industry, margins and talent and a "killer promo." People came and went, extravagantly greeted and released.

"This is Merv Griffin's hotel," Sid said. "He bought it."

"Really?" I said, inspecting the menu.

"Sid," someone said, "Sid Rose"—and then a tall man about Sid's age wearing jeans and a polo shirt was leering beside us.

"I thought I'd say hello, I don't want to interrupt you and your . . ." He stopped.

"Friend of my daughter's," Sid said.

"Aren't all the best ones," the man said, giving me a wink. "You two have fun! See you courtside, Sid." He looked my way again, eyes twitching. "Pleasure meeting you."

"He thinks you're my mistress," Sid said in satisfaction when he left. "Or maybe he thinks you're a hooker, that's even better." His shoulders, behind his menu, shook with suppressed laughter. I had laid down my menu and was sitting very properly, my ankles crossed and my hands in my lap. Sid put his menu aside and looked straight at me. "You know I'm using tons of condoms in my videos," he said. "Gay videos, straight videos, bi videos, all of them. I wanted you to know that, especially now that you're doing the work you're doing. I'm doing everything I can to be socially responsible. You know"—he waved his hand—"the ejaculations, we have to show them. But any time there's an insertion, I guarantee, there's a condom on that penis."

"Is that so?" I said. "Admirable."

"It's not great for business, either. Nobody likes to be reminded of that...plague. But in my earnest opinion, and it's not just mine, believe me, the adult entertainment industry helps prevent the spread of AIDS. It gives people an outlet. Especially now, with the video market. People can sit at home alone and have a sensual life."

"Maybe the birth rate will fall."

Sid appraised me for a moment, then decided I was serious. "That's great too," he said. "I'd love to lower the teen pregancy rate, the abortion rate, all that stuff."

I nodded. "You should run for president."

A thin wash of suspicion crossed Sid's face.

The waitress came and we ordered. Sid leaned back and stretched out his arms along the back of the booth. I sensed that whatever he'd brought me here for was about to be revealed. I started biting the inside of my right cheek. "I've been thinking about you and Sally. You have a lot of influence on my daughter, you know that?"

"We're best friends."

"I know that. She doesn't have other friends, really. She never did. I was her friend, and then she went off to Oberlin and needed someone there."

The implication was mildly insulting. "We were lucky to be roommates."

"You didn't think so at first, did you? Lord, I remember all those phone calls Sally made home when she was a freshman. She would *cry*. I almost flew out to Ohio to rescue her myself, but Esther said calm down, Sid, a girl's got to have a life of her own."

I was startled to hear Sid talk as if he'd known there were too many phone calls. I was startled to hear Esther mentioned as someone who'd offered sensible advice. Maybe I'd underestimated them both.

"Remember that first boyfriend of hers, died jerking off in his car?"

"Timbo."

"Timbo, that's right. Funny name. I got a guy works for me they call Jumbo. They met in line at the college bookstore, remember? She was buying two of all her textbooks—remember how she always sent a book to me? I got a college education with her, I really did." Sid smiled wistfully, and to my surprise, I felt a surge of affection. Sally, a married woman with a child, had to a large extent vanished from his life. "Listen, I told Sally after she knew about my magazines, I told her: Sally, kiddo, that guy of yours I could have saved. Timbo could have been reading a magazine sitting in his bathroom, safe as toast."

I smiled. You could see where Sally got her talent for description. I relaxed in my seat. "Anyway," Sid went on, "my point is, you and Sally have been through a lot together, you being roommates, that boyfriend of hers dying, that little house you two shared in Oberlin with the dogs next door, your dad dying, that no-good fruit husband of Sally's, et cetera and so on. You two have been through a lot."

I nodded.

Sid leaned forward and put his elbows on the table. His voice softened. "And she looks up to you. Really. Remember those six months she wouldn't talk to me? That was you."

I felt my shoulders tense. "That wasn't me," I said. "That was you. When Sally found out about some of the stuff you put out, she felt betrayed."

"I was protecting her," Sid interrupted, his voice rising. "Period. End of story."

"But at some point, you must have realized she'd find out."

"About my business?" Sid looked around helplessly. "I hoped she'd never find out. Okay?"

"Sid, do you hear what you're saying? You're essentially saying what you do is something you should be ashamed of."

"I'm not ashamed," Sid said. "Not one iota. But it's an adult business, and Sally was a little girl."

I frowned and did some quick calculations. "She found out what you did just after she finished law school. Sid, she was twenty-five! You probably have actresses in your movies half that age."

"I'm not into kiddie porn," Sid said firmly. "And Sally was my little girl. She still is, in my mind. She'll always be. You wait and see when your daughter gets older." He drummed his fingers on the table and tossed a glance across the room. "Or maybe it's a daddy thing, I don't know. That's what Esther said." His gaze abruptly shifted back toward me. "Sally tells me you're living like a nun."

Where had that come from? I shifted in my seat, feeling suddenly and uncomfortably prim. "I'm not dating, if that's what you mean."

"You a lesbo?"

"No!"

"Just asking." Sid smiled. "I'm going to ask you something else now, something I really want you to try to remember." He paused, hunching over the table, and I bit the inside of my cheek again. "You remember when I phoned you up in Ohio over two years ago? Back in May, eighty-seven. When I told you Sally was taking drugs to her brother and I begged you to make her stop?"

I swallowed. "Yes."

"You remember that?" His voice had gone wheedling and soft. "You remember it? I called you twice, didn't I? I begged you, didn't I?"

What was he driving at? I thought of Sally at her depositions, touching on the truth and then circling away, approaching and retreating, slipping in an arrow when it was least expected. Her father's daughter. "You asked me to talk with her, sure," I said. "I remember that. I don't recall thinking you were begging."

He leaned even farther into the table. "You didn't? You really didn't? Because I was begging you, sweetheart, I was—"

"Sid, you rascal!" a woman's voice said. I almost jumped.

Two attractive people, impeccably dressed, were standing by our table. The woman was blond with a sweeping hairdo, and the man looked like a model for Armani. The woman eyed me and smiled, her gaze sweeping down my entire body. She held out a manicured hand. "Marilyn Thornberry," she said.

I introduced myself. Sid explained that I was a doctor from Ohio, an old friend of Sally's. "You'll like this, Marilyn," he said, "she's specializing in AIDS."

Even the Armani-clad male perked up at this. "Isn't that wonderful," Marilyn said. "We certainly need dedicated doctors like you. I'm sure you're very big on education, that's so important. I just love what

Sid's doing in the condom line. And the dental dams! Safe sex is a sort of mission for me. It's like I tell Fred"—she glanced over her shoulder at her companion—"a condom's nothing more than another piece of equipment!"

A porn star. We were talking to a porn star. I noticed a peculiar glint in her mouth and wondered if her tongue was pierced. "Do you work with Sid?" I asked.

"Oh, all I can. He's wonderful, he really is. All the best people work for Sid. Even the soundmen are professional."

"That must be reassuring," I said, thinking of Sally's adjectives.

"Oh, it is. It's like I tell Fred, the only crew we're missing is wardrobe!" She laughed a bit too heartily, as if this were a line she'd rehearsed. There was without question a gold stud in her tongue. She winked at me. "Props, lots of props. You ought to come down to the studio. I'll show you around."

"That's very generous of you," I said. "Thanks." What was Sid doing to me, I thought, why had he brought me here to parade all his seamy friends in front of me?

After the waitress took our order and Fred and Marilyn left—Marilyn looking back over her shoulder and waving prettily with her fingers—Sid asked me again if I remembered how he'd begged me.

"I'm sorry about that," I said, thinking of Sally and me heading off in her white Volvo to the Chinese place in Encino. It was true, I'd never tried to stop her. I shifted in my seat. "I don't think I behaved well during that period."

"You didn't behave well," Sid repeated flatly. I nodded, looking down.

"And you were a mother!" he burst out, his anger suddenly incandescent. "A new mother! I was another parent begging for the sake of his child, and you ignored me."

"Sid, I'm sorry."

"Sorry's not enough. Sorry's"—Sid waved his hand—"sorry's nothing."

He was right. And maybe if I'd stopped Sally from buying heroin,

Ben would be alive today. But Sally, in a real way, was better off with-out him. And what did Sid want of me now?

"I've always been a good friend to Sally," I said hotly. "I've always loved her."

"That true?" Sid exhaled loudly and looked away into the room. "Funny way of showing it." His eyes wandered from table to table. "I'll tell you," he said, "your not talking to her about Ben sure left a hell of a mess for me." He straightened up, blinked, and leaned forward over the table, looking me straight in the eye. "I killed him," he said slowly.

"What?" I thought I'd misheard him.

"Ben. My son. I killed him."

I sat for a moment, trying to sort out the implications. "That's ridiculous. You can't be responsible for every self-destructive decision your child makes."

"Listen to me, I'm telling you something. I killed him. Directly, myself, it was"—he held up his hand in front of me—"my hand."

"In Mexico?" I said, stupidly.

Sid nodded.

"Did you get really angry at him? Did you hit him and not real-ize—"

"Of course I got angry! I'm calling Sally, he said, she'll get me out of this hellhole. She'll bring me some junk. She always brings me junk, he said. Just like that, whiny just like that. I don't like your tone, I said. What business is that of yours? he said. You'll call your sister over my dead body, I said. Fine, he said, I'll try not to trip.

"And he called her! After all that, he called her.

"We had him totally drug-free down there, he was detoxed all the way, and then he calls up Sally and asks her to bring him heroin. He gets her back into it! I'm dying, he tells her, I'm a prisoner, they're not feeding me, I can't go to the bathroom by myself. . . . All that crap. He was fine. He was living like a prince in a palace. He had videos, he had a pool, we even had a cook down there, an American cook that could make him hamburgers.

"And the worst thing was, Sally fell for it. She was going to come!

She was going to risk everything she had and carry him a suitcase full of heroin. It was sitting in the trunk of her Volvo in her driveway in West Hollywood. Fifty bags or sacks or whatever they call it. For Ben she'd ruin her life. She'd get in that car and ruin her life."

Of course, Sid knew Sally was coming. He'd tapped the phone. I found my voice, accusatory, angry: "Why did you listen in on them? Why couldn't you give Ben his privacy? Why did you have to interfere?"

"How could I *not* interfere?" Although his words were exploding within me, I realized he was speaking in no more than a whisper. "You don't think they'd catch her? Some sweet-young-thing American lawyer crossing into Mexico with a suitcase full of drugs? Think about it. Think what they'd do to her. In Los Angeles they'd ruin her career, she'd end up disbarred, bad enough, but in Mexico...Listen, she'd be dead in a second, or taken hostage and they'd be calling me for ransom, or thrown in some jail and raped ten times a night by all the guards. You know what those Mexican police are like. That's an old joke—is it worse to meet a cop or a criminal in a dark alley down there? I know those people. I used to sell down there. You wouldn't believe what they buy. The sort of stuff you went apeshit over. The sort of stuff you showed Sally back when, back when..." He couldn't seem to finish.

The torture magazines. The magazines from the med center's dirty drawer.

"I was doing everything I could think of to save him. But finally it was him or her. That was my choice. Him or her."

I saw the final scene dimly in my mind, Sid screaming at Ben, hitting him, Ben drawing up his scrawny arms.

"You think it was easy?" Sid whispered. "I'm the one who woke him up early, said come on, Ben, I'm showing you something, and walked him out of town and up that hill. It was awful. Where we going, Pops? he said. You know how he talked. He didn't even sound curious, that was just something to say. Just keep going, I said, I want to show you something. He went up like a lamb. I think he even thought I had something stashed for him, some drug I'd decided he could take, buried under a pine tree or something. He got short of breath walking up the hill. I could make it up the hill easier than he could, isn't that strange? But he went right up. There, I said, isn't that a beautiful view. Not bad, he said." Sid's voice choked. "He was my sacrifice. I was like Abraham up there, I kept waiting for God to save him. But God—"

"What, you slit his throat?"

"I'm not a barbarian! I shot him."

"Jesus."

"Back of the head, very clean. I had the pistol in my pocket. It didn't hurt him."

"This is some sick joke, I know it is, you're, you're…"

Sid spread out his hands in a querulous gesture. "I had to do it, okay? I had no choice. And he didn't have a life, anyway. If he'd had a life, God would have saved him. I asked God to save him. I said, God, if Ben should stay alive, give me a sign."

I realized my mouth was open, so I shut it.

"Pretty day," Sid went on. "Pretty day, not many clouds, a little breeze off the ocean. It's the western coast of Mexico, same coast as here. Quiet, peaceful, no one around."

"What kind of sign were you looking for?"

A burst of laughter rolled from the booth behind us. "You dog, Jake," a boisterous voice said. "You dog!"

"That!" Sid said, pointing in the direction of the laughter. "I don't know, anything. Clap of thunder, plane overhead, somebody walking up a path. A chipmunk, I would have taken a chipmunk! We were standing beside this spindly little tree, high up, right on the edge, looking right over the ocean. I was waiting for a sign. But there was nothing. Not a thing. So I did it."

"What did you do with his body?"

"He didn't weigh much, you know. Not eating, drugs, wasting away. I picked him up and kissed his forehead and tossed him out over the cliff. I thought someone would find him, you know, and then maybe they'd suspect me, at least come ask me about it. But no one found him. He must've just gotten washed out by the tide. I ended up telling the doctor down there that I'd seen him jump."

"This is true?"

"Look, I did it for Sally. It's like business, okay? Sometimes you have to divest something to keep the company solvent. And Sally's better off now, right? You think she'd be married with a kid now if Ben was still alive? I mean, it was a terrible price, but she's definitely better off."

"You're evil," I breathed, not even realizing I was thinking it.

"Yeah, maybe." Sid frowned, conceded. "But basically, I'm a realist. Not many people can stand to look reality straight in the face."

He always said he could do the deed.

I thought of the woman in the magazine, her twisted face, the flesh beneath the branding iron. One man holding her down, the other above her. Look, Sid said, I'm a realist. I'm giving people what they want. There's a market! Can't a fellow target for a market?

"What about the Ten Commandments?"

His response was quick: "Honor thy father and thy mother."

I shook my head. I knew why he had done what he did. I understood his rationalizations.

"Why are you telling me this?" I said. "Do you expect me just to listen to you and say okay? Don't you think I'll get right back to Sally's and call the police?"

"It was in Mexico. And there's no proof. You think if someone asked me I'd admit it?

"And this is why I wanted to tell you, because you were involved, because you're the one who knew what Sally was doing. Your best friend! And you didn't even try to stop her. Why didn't you say, Sally, you're acting crazy? Why didn't you say, Sally, by everything you hold near and dear, swear to me you'll stop this? But you didn't ask her to stop at all. You drove with her to that rat-hole Chinese place in Encino. Left your baby daughter with Sally's maid, who can't speak English! How a mother can leave her baby daughter with a Mexican maid to go buy heroin is beyond me."

"I didn't want to lose her," I said, but I couldn't speak, the words came out in a broken whisper.

"What?"

I pressed my lips together, swallowed, blinked my eyes. "I didn't want to lose her," I repeated, the words like an infant's bleat. I felt as if I'd plucked my soul out of my chest and was handing it, small and quivering, across the table to Sid.

He didn't seem to recognize it. "Insanity," he spat. "You were participating in insanity."

I felt a spurt of anger. "No more insane than shooting your own son."

"It wasn't easy!" Sid's voice rose briefly, then he whispered again. We were, after all, in a public restaurant. "It wasn't easy, and it wasn't what I wanted. But when I found out Sally was coming down with that suitcase, I knew exactly what I had to do. I told you, I'm a realist. You know what I think of it, ultimately? I think I bought Sally her future.

"He wasn't quality," Sid said. "He would have died anyway. An overdose, an argument over money. Could have caught AIDS like those sad sacks you work with. At least this was quick. And we were right by the sea, we were looking over the sea. He didn't know what was happening."

"Why are you telling me this?"

"I told you," Sid said with impatience, "because it's your fault too! Oh, I know what you're thinking; 'Me? Me? I'm an AIDS doctor, I work with the poor, I did mouth-to-mouth on that disgusting Sid Rose. I'm a perfect person. I'm Ohio's own Mother Teresa.'"

"I don't think that."

"You don't? Oh come on, baby. Every time I turn around, Sally's telling me how virtuous you are. You don't charge people, you go to their houses, you sit up late with them till they die. You can hardly make it out here anymore to see your best friend, your patients keep you so busy. But listen to me, Florence Nightingale, I asked you to make Sally stop taking drugs to her brother. You were the one who could have stopped her, the only one—she's not a girl with friends, she's private, like me—and instead, you're driving with her through Beverly Hills tittering away, la-de-da and little waves like the queen makes, that's what you were doing. You rode with her to get Ben drugs, you got out of the car and stood with her at the counter."

"How do you know?"

"You think I didn't have a private detective?"

"I don't believe this."

"Then you were the one who said take Ben down to Mexico. Remember that? Get him away, you said, get him out of Sally's hair. Your suggestion! Get rid of him, you said. So that's what I did. You should thank me. You didn't lose her after all, did you? Because I saved her."

Sid sat up straighter, looked down at the table. "It's not that I don't miss him," he said, his voice suddenly thick. "On the dirt on the hillside I found, I found..." He faltered, reached in a pants pocket, and tossed a tiny zippered plastic bag, the size used to store a ring or earrings, on the table. "Here," he said. "My memento."

I picked up the bag automatically, glanced uncertainly at its contents. It looked like a fleck of swiss cheese.

"It's a tooth," Sid said. "It's part of one of Ben's teeth."

I dropped the bag on the table. He had shot his own son in the back of the head and blown out his teeth.

Sid picked up the bag and gazed at it. "It's a comfort to me," he said. "I know it's crazy, but it's physical evidence I had a son. I take it everywhere."

"Here's your Mexican omelet," the waitress interrupted, shifting Sid's plate up her arm and sliding mine to the table.

"Thanks," I said automatically.

"How can you eat all that fat?" Sid slipped the tiny bag back into his pocket. He had a slice of melon and a muffin. "You're a doctor!"

Eggs, cheese, sausage. A dribble of salsa. He was right. "I don't know," I said. I couldn't believe he was talking about food, and as seamlessly as if we'd been talking about the weather. I pushed the plate away. "I can't eat."

"I think that's why I had that problem at Sally's wedding. Remember? I ate that lobster ravioli, and my internist says lobster's higher in cholesterol than eggs." Sid leaned forward. "Did you really think I was dying?"

"Yes."

"And you wanted to save me, huh?" Sid grinned and wiped his mouth with his peach napkin. "I'm flattered."

"You're Sally's dad," I said. I felt as if I couldn't breathe, the tables and chairs and banquettes were splintering in front of me, the chair legs and tables at ungodly angles, the water glasses glinting in shards.

"I love her," Sid said, his voice cracking. "She's a wonderful daughter. Ever since she was a little girl, we've had this bond, Sally and me. What I did, that Ben thing, I did it for her. But she can never know, because she misses her brother—I don't blame her, he was her only brother—and if she knew why I took care of him, she'd blame herself. And I won't have her blaming herself. Never. She's been through enough. But you, you had to know. You see, Clare? I'm teaching you something: things have consequences. You had a chance to set Sally right. Why didn't you? I can't figure that one out. You're her best friend. Did you think it was glamorous, driving around Beverly Hills with that little box of heroin? You don't think that stuff was killing Ben? You're a doctor. Why didn't you say, Sally, this stuff is poison to your brother? Couldn't you tell that just to look at him? Sally admires you, she thinks you're some kind of a saint, working with those people you work with, and it looks to me like you think you're a saint, and I want to tell you, you're not a saint at all. You know what you are?" He leaned forward.

"What?" I breathed. I couldn't think.

"An accomplice."

"No." I recoiled.

"Yup. An accomplice." Sid sat up with satisfaction, his job done. "Now eat your omelet."

I stared.

"My treat! Eat your omelet."

And, believe it or not, I did.

SID DROPPED ME OFF at Sally and Peter's. A typical prosperous California house, wide lawn, curved sidewalk, a huge and ornate front door. Sid drove away, not waiting for me to go inside.

Sally came down the inside stairs all gleaming, eager.

"How was it?"

Ezra curled on her shoulder, his wide neck and fringe of hair.

"Okay."

"Did he tell you anything? Did he open up to you?"

"Not really." I hesitated. "No, not really. He talked about Ben some."

"I don't think I understood how bad losing Ben was for him until I had Ezra. You go through your life expecting your parents will die, but your *child*..."

"You lost your brother," I pointed out.

She smiled at me sadly. "That's true. He was always lost, and now he's"—she stroked Ezra's back—"really lost."

"Sally, I don't know how you've survived it."

"I had my black spell, remember? When everything seemed trivial. And then I met Peter, and now, with Ezra, I've been lucky. And I always had this underlying optimism. Even when it drove me crazy that people asked me how my day was, I had a certain optimism. I don't know why. It was just there."

I shook my head. "You were lucky."

"Maybe I was raised right," Sally said. "I was raised to expect good things would happen to me. It's the reverse of paranoia: I think people are out to do me good. Daddy got me thinking like that." She walked to the living room and sat down in an armchair, lifting her shirt to give Ezra her breast.

I opened my mouth but nothing came out.

"Glom on, Ezra," Sally said to her son, shoving the nipple in his mouth. "Come on, honey, glom on."

"We went to the restaurant at the Beverly Hills Hilton," I said at last. "I had a Mexican omelet. It wasn't bad."

Three

Three

IT WAS DIFFERENT NOW. Years before I'd been on fire, streaming across the country like a bullet, dying to tell Sally the truth about her father. Now I was inert, immobile, surprised yet unsurprised. Brushing my teeth in Sally's guest bathroom, I felt I was being corroded from the inside, that at some point I'd collapse into a pile on the floor, a totem pole attacked by termites. When I'd first seen Sid's magazines, when I'd first realized how he made his fabulous living, I'd burned with a rage that, even as it scorched me, scorched him; now I was being eaten away, coldly eaten, the way I was sure Sid wanted.

"Eat your omelet."

"Yes, Sid. Of course, Sid."

"Eat it all. I bought it for you. Eat it."

What had Sally said? No loathing like self-loathing? And by what perversity did knowing Sid's secret make me loathe myself?

"DID HE SAY ANYTHING ELSE?"

"No, not really."

I'm not a barbarian.

"Did his memory seem okay?"

"His memory? Yeah, his memory seemed fine. Very good, in fact."

He wasn't quality.

"I'm relieved. I worry about his memory. He forgot Ezra's middle name."

"What is Ezra's middle name? I forgot too."

I was waiting for a sign, any sign.

"Isaac."

Ezra was nursing again, eyes closed, hands in intense fists on each side of his head. "Whatever happened to Helga?" I said suddenly. The girl Ben had lived with, the doctor's daughter who owned the hillside house.

"I have no idea," Sally said, her voice trembling slightly. She hugged Ezra closer to her. "None."

If she hadn't been through so much. If she didn't have a dead first boyfriend and a dead mother as well as a dead brother. If she didn't make chicken cacciatore and artichoke quiche especially for me each time I visited. If she didn't say, recounting how she left the table one night while her father blubbered mournfully about Esther, "I refuse to wallow." If she didn't have a dream of growing asparagus in the patch of garden outside her solarium. If she didn't have a husband who'd forget about the real Sally, Sid, and Ben and talk instead about the Mythic Father–Son battle or Sally as the Torchbearer of Truth. Then it would be easy: truth will out!

But I couldn't tell her. No. I wasn't that kind of person. I could handle it. I was quality. And if she didn't notice my sleeplessness, my not eating, the way I sat and stared when I should be listening—well, she was a new mother, devoted to her infant, and these were things I worked to hide.

At the airport, she threw her arms around me. "Come back soon, Clare. You're like my sister. Ezra won't be nursing every twenty minutes next time, we'll have more flexibility."

"He's a nice baby, Sally. I'm happy for you."

"He is a nice baby, isn't he? He looks so much like Peter. Bring Aury next time, it's been too long since I've seen her."

"I will."

"And come back soon."

Of course I will, I thought. How could I not?

After passing through the metal detector, I turned around one last time. She was blowing me a kiss, as she had for years whenever I left. "Bye! Bye! Daddy says good-bye too!" I knew she meant Peter, not Sid—since Ezra was born, she sometimes called Peter Daddy—but still, the comment jarred me.

"GUESS WHO I RAN into at the airport after you left," Sally said on the phone. "You won't believe."

Mentally I ran through the usual suspects. "Margaret?"

It took Sally a moment to register who Margaret was. "No, not Margaret! Flavio."

"Flavio?" I had just been thinking about him. I had seen a male model in an underwear ad, and I'd thought, I wonder what happened to Sally's gorgeous and amoral ex?

"Guess what; he was with a woman."

"Really?"

"A very androgynous-looking woman. The Louise Brooks look, short dark haircut. She does something in fashion."

"They were . . . an item?"

"Seemed to be. Remember, I told you he was bisexual!" Sally seemed pleased. "They were sharing a carry-on. I didn't even ask where they were off to. They were just passing through. Thank God I had Ezra with me. Gave us all something to talk about."

"Is he still so handsome?"

"Are you kidding? Even more so. It's depressing that someone dissipated can look that good. He had some crinkles around his eyes that were really, well. . . . I can hardly believe it, but it's been seven years since I last saw him."

"Did you tell him about Ben?" I thought of Ben and Flavio in the pool house.

Sally hesitated. "I couldn't. He was just passing through, he didn't have any time, I...it would have made things too complicated. I might have started crying, and what a fiasco that would have been. I suppose I could have told him about my mother, but even that—"

"I'm sure he'll never hear, you two don't have anyone in common."

"He said his father wanted to get in touch with Daddy, something about a new product line from the Orient. Remember what Flavio's father did?"

"Probably some new sex toys."

Sally sighed. "Probably. I'm sick of thinking about these things. I wish Daddy would retire."

"What, and leave the company to you?"

She laughed, but underneath the mirth, I heard a wariness that caught me off guard. Was his leaving her the company possible? Was this something they'd discussed?

I HAD A NEW PATIENT, Mr. Wahl, who'd just been diagnosed. He didn't yet have symptoms. The guy who had given Mr. Wahl HIV was a flight attendant who'd found out he was infected and set out to infect as many others as he could. Several months after Mr. Wahl had sex with him, Mr. Wahl received a letter, a letter that basically said ha-ha.

"How do you live with that?" I blurted. "How do you stand thinking about what he did?"

Mr. Wahl brushed the air with his hand. "It's not that I forgave him," he said, "it's more like I was tired of having him dominate my life."

I sat there a moment, pen frozen in midair. "That's smart."

"Survival," Mr. Wahl said.

WHY DIDN'T SID CALL her up from Mexico, bark, "Sally, don't come down here!" She would have listened. He could have scared her. He could have told Sally months before to stop buying her brother drugs. He had power over her; Sally would listen to her father more than she'd listen to me. Why, instead of shooting his own son, didn't Sid ask Sally to change?

I STOPPED EATING. I knew this was crazy, but I stopped. I ate yogurt at breakfast, yogurt at lunch, and if I remembered, a Lean Cuisine for dinner. I did feed Aury. "You're not eating, Mommy?" she would say. "You take your vitamin?" I felt like an alcoholic mom, sticking my daughter in a caretaking role. Eventually, when my patients starting worrying ("You don't got what I got, do you?" "Dr. Mann! You're not doing a Karen Carpenter on us, are you?"), I forced myself to drink three Ensures a day on top of my yogurts, and from there I gradually returned to the land of food. Sally never realized. She didn't see me at my nadir, and when I next went to visit her, she thought, in her California way, that my weight was just right. She herself was dieting between babies.

AS IT HAPPENED, Mr. Wahl's brother was a lawyer.

"I have a legal question," I said to him one day. Mr. Wahl had sickened quickly; we were standing outside his hospital room.

"Sure," he said. "Anything."

"If a crime happens in another country, and there's no direct witness," I said carefully, "can that crime be prosecuted?"

He made a hopeless face, and I could see what an impossible question it was. "What country are we talking about?"

"Mexico."

"What kind of crime?"

I hesitated. "A death, an accidental death."

He waited.

"A boating accident, actually. The father of a friend of mine—he took his son out boating and didn't know how to operate the boat. His son got hit by a mast or something, and he fell in the sea and drowned."

The lawyer winced. "Tragic."

"But there was carelessness involved. I mean, the father really didn't know how to use the boat, he took his son out knowing he didn't know, so even though it was an accident, the father should have some responsibility."

"Look," the lawyer said, touching the air with his index finger, "it's not sounding like a criminal matter. There may have been negligence, true, and I don't know Mexican law, but—"

"They're American citizens."

The lawyer nodded. "In the death of a person's own son by misadventure, I doubt anyone, anywhere, is going to prosecute. I'm sure the father's already suffered enough."

I stared. "Maybe."

"Oh, I'm sure he has." The lawyer frowned. He was searching my face now. "Are you a friend of the mother's?"

"The mother is deceased. I'm a friend of the sister's."

"I see. Does she blame her father?"

"No. I do. I'm the one who blames the father."

The lawyer bit his lip, stepped back a bit. "When Timmy got sick"—Tim, his sick brother—"I can't tell you what I went through. This was my little brother. We used to play walnut wars together. He used to get inside the dryer and I'd turn it on. We had such a happy family, I never dreamed..." The lawyer stopped, took a deep breath. "When he told us how he got it, how he'd gotten that letter—Dr. Mann, I bought a gun. But Timmy said, don't go crazy. You've got to accept what's real. That's what my little brother said."

I nodded.

"It's a family matter, Dr. Mann. Families go through these things, and if you're not part of the family, you can't judge."

"I can't judge," I repeated dully.

"It's not my business, of course, but extrapolating from what I've been through." He muttered as he walked away, "A boating accident. You never know, do you? You never know how the blow is going to come."

"I HEARD FROM SOMEONE in our residency program that Ted got married and has a daughter," I told Sally over the phone.

"Really? A daughter with his wife?"

"Of course."

"Are you ever going to contact him?"

"Sally! Why should I?"

ONE OF MY PATIENTS had died about a year before—I'd gotten him into hospice, which was a huge deal, because back then hospice wanted only people with cancer—and one day his sister called and said that his family wanted to make a panel in his honor for the AIDS quilt. "That's great," I said. "So we want you to tell us what to put on the quilt," the sister said. "Well," I said, you make something that honors his life. If he liked music, you do an instrument or musical notes: if he liked flowers, you put on flowers; that sort of thing." "We didn't really know him," the sister said. "You saw him all the time. What should we put on the quilt?"

For some people, I realized, being their doctor wasn't enough. Maybe I really had to love them. Because there was nobody else to do it.

EZRA'S INITIALS WERE were E.I.N., which meant—as I discovered when I next went out to California—that Sally could hold him in the air above her and sing "E-I-E-I-O!" with an accent on the "O" and a little toss. Ezra would collapse in delight. Sally also had several personalized songs she sang to him, and when she worked in the kitchen or the garden, she popped him into a canvas-covered frame that sat on her back. She was a natural at motherhood, really. She never used a stroller. I thought back to my early days with Aury and how I felt as if I were playing a part. I still felt that way.

Ezra was leaning forward now, tilting his head so he could peer around Sally's neck and catch her eye, and Sally, sensing his motion, twisted her face to meet him, and there they were smiling at each other. Together they made a sort of circle. Ezra giggled and reached for his mother's nose. The moment was astonishingly intimate; I had to look away.

"You see people carrying them around, and they look adorable. They're lots cuter than puppies. You'd probably meet more guys like that than walking an Akita."

"I've got to get out of L.A.," Sally said, staring into the display case of food. "This is no place for children."

Peter wasn't useful. His video didn't sell well, despite his rounds of self-improvement bookstores. I'd seen it, and I thought the problem was too much earnestness. His client base was eroding. A producer friend of his had suffered a real tragedy—his daughter had drowned in the family pool—and I suspected that Peter lost credibility there. "I kept telling him, what is death, you know? What is it? You've got to keep on living, because what is death?"

Now Peter spent much of his time playing golf with two aging rock stars, who pricked my interest only until I met them. They both had coarse laughs and talked about nothing but money and stocks. "Oh, a doctor," one of them said, sidling up to me, tilting his head in a calculated way, "what do you think of Genentech?"

"Do you believe in chronic fatigue syndrome?" demanded the other.

When Ezra's diaper was dirty, Peter delivered him to Sally. This startled me, because I'd often wished, when Aury was a baby, for a partner to help with diapers. "We made a deal," Sally said, "I'll look after the kids."

I shot her an inquiring look.

"He's not really child-oriented," Sally said, wiping Ezra's bottom. "Oh, he is, in the abstract, but sitting down and playing with them, or changing a diaper, that's another thing. Look, you're a single mother, a true single mother. I figure I can do it as a partial single mother."

I blushed.

"You're an inspiration to me," Sally said.

I'd never thought I was a good mother at all. I'd certainly never thought Sally might see me as one. Later, I felt all tingly lying in bed thinking about it. An inspiration. An inspiration!

YOU ADAPT. An impossible idea becomes imaginable, thinkable, logical. Three easy steps. This must be how sin starts. Sid was right, Ben might have died of AIDS. Sally might have been arrested, her cache of drugs found, her life ruined. You couldn't say Sid did the right thing, but what he did had a logic. His motives weren't purely evil. He didn't kill for fun. He didn't kill wantonly. In the old days, a child was a possession, to do with what the parent wanted. In the most extreme way, Sid declared himself Ben's possessor. And really, if there was a God, God could have intervened. It didn't sound like Sid was waiting for much. A breeze, an animal skittering across the path, a cloud over the sun. Sid would have taken any one of those for a sign, a sign to spare Ben's life. You'd think, if there was a God, that God could have done that much.

WE WAITED IN LINE at a chicken place, Ezra in a pack on Sally's back. Two young women were waiting behind us. "Isn't he cute?" one of them said, and then, "Oh, I'm sorry, I didn't think."

"It's all right," the other one said forlornly.

"It really is bad for your body," the first one said. "The breasts, like, go."

"And your abs."

"You did the right thing."

Sally and I eyed each other. Ezra reached up with his hand and patted his mother's hair.

"It could've been so cute. Could've had those eyes."

"Could've had those hairy hands, too."

ANOTHER PREGNANCY AND A new baby, Barbara this time, named after Ben. Barbara was an exotic name in California; Brittany or Bethany or Brianna would be more common. "She's beautiful," Sally said over the phone. "She has tiny ears." It struck me then that Ezra's ears protruded, a feature I'd never noticed.

"She's not going to be Barbie, you know that," Sally warned in a friendly tone. "Not even Barb."

Sally wanted me to come out for the naming, but to do that would be to risk seeing Sid. I had managed to avoid him in the year since our breakfast. He was in his new house in Malibu with a beautiful view of the sea, Sally said, in a house that was clinging (Sally's word) to the side of a hill. All the furniture in Sid's house was new: he'd had some hotshot interior designer fly in from New Jersey.

"Does he like Barbara?" I asked.

"He thinks she's a riot," Sally said. "When he sees her in her pump-kin seat, he drops things on her." I glanced at Aury, sitting at the table beside me, coloring neatly in a My Little Pony coloring book.

"I want to talk to Aunt Sally," Aury whispered.

"At least he's cheerful," I said into the phone, smiling at Aury. "How's your work?"

"Oh, same old thing. I just got a set of twins who had face-lifts so they'd look distinct, but they ended up looking more alike."

"Same surgeon?"

"Yup."

"What *were* they thinking?"

Aury placed a pink crayon in her box and removed an an apple-green one. She looked back up at me, her brown eyes wide, her hair falling back from her forehead. "Are you going to let me talk to Aunt Sally?"

I wondered how Aury would be with a sibling, in what subterranean ways she'd express her jealousy. She was almost too tractable. "Why don't you clean up your room, sweetie?" I'd ask, and five minutes later it was perfect, books in piles, shoes paired on the closet floor, stuffed animals marched across the bed. Of course, the room hadn't been messy to start. She was three and half, but so serious and tall that people guessed she was in kindergarten. I handed her the phone.

I wondered what was in store for her. An eating disorder? Migraines? A psychotic obsessive disorder like one that had hit a woman resident I knew, who after a family bout of strep made a pile in the backyard of all her children's clothes and torched them? At one point Aury threw away (I found them in the trash barrel in the garage) a new pair of pink shoes because they weren't the right pink, they didn't match her favorite pink sweater, and I'm afraid I got hysterical. I made her put them on and wear them, wear them—with her pink sweater, with her green top, with her royal blue lace-trimmed pants, with anything and everything, matching or not—thinking that somehow this would cure her, would spare her the years of perfectionist misery I could see she had coming, the disappointing marriages, the bosses who took advantage of her, the housekeeping she could never get done.

On top of that, she had a tremor. Not a bad one, but clearly noticeable when she was drawing. How did she end up so fussy?

A NEW DOCTOR ARRIVED in the division of infectious diseases. I met him at a faculty meeting. His name was Theodore Quiver. "You do the HIV clinic, right?" he said. "I don't understand why we don't run that clinic. Every other major med center in the country has an HIV clinic run by infectious disease. Nothing personal."

I left the meeting wondering if I should worry. It was hard to imagine anyone else wanting my patients. There's really no redemptive power in illness. A dying young drug addict is still a young addict, and addicts care about nothing—I repeat, nothing—more than their next high. That's what I tell the volunteers who come to the AIDS ward: listen, you don't have to like everyone with AIDS. A lot of them, frankly, are creeps. But they deserved basic human decency and respect, which is really all you need to offer.

Sister Mary Klein (motto: "All things work together for good through the Lord") didn't like to hear this. "Ooh, listen to her..." she said, brushing past the outskirts of my group, fluttering her hands. "I've seen Dr. Mann sit on a dying man's bed holding his hand. I've seen her hold an emesis basin." She leaned into the group and winked. "Her bark is worse than her bite." The weird thing was, she thought she'd given me a compliment. She thought I secretly liked her telling people about my softer moments, but I knew much better than to tell people about Sister's occasional hardness. Would she want people to know she'd called Herbert Melrose, leaking parasitic stool on his sheets, a "big lazy poop factory"? Or that she'd snapped to the thrashing prostitute whose nurses were having problems inserting her IV: "You manage to stay still for your johns, don't you?" These cracks might have been what I liked best about Sister Mary Klein, but I doubt they're what she liked best in herself. Ditto the image of me holding the emesis basin, cringing with each poorly aimed squirt of vomit. It's true, it's real, I did it, but it's not something I wanted to be known for. I wanted to be known as tough.

IN OCTOBER OF '90 I could avoid him no longer, and when I went to visit Sally in Los Angeles, I was driven to Sid's new house.

The smell, there was a smell—a green smell, a cooking smell. The breeze came off the water, which we were, truly, high enough to see: it was no exaggeration to say the house was clinging.

It was a small stained-wood one-story house, smaller than my town house in Akron, and although the house was for only one person, this surprised me. A year before, Sid's female interior decorator had come with a legal pad to Sally and Peter's house, peppering them with questions to help her capture "the real Sid Rose." Now Sally and Peter and I waited for Sid on a patio held up by stilts and cantilevered over the hillside. We were surrounded by pots of vegetation, patio furniture, a hanging sundial with a lascivious-looking sun, its tongue sticking out to cast the shadow. Barbara was perched on Sally's shoulder, and every thirty seconds or so, Sally popped up to run after Ezra, to keep him from the railing or out of the plants or off the chairs. "Could you maybe take him over, please?" she asked Peter in irritation. He uncoiled himself slowly from the chair to pick up Ezra and walk him back out to the drive. I'd left Aury at home in Ohio with my mother because Aury didn't want to miss preschool. "I wish he'd just let us in," Sally said. "But it's like some stage set, he has to get everything ready. I'm sure he wants to impress you."

I shrugged.

"It's not like a home, not in my opinion. Wait till you see it. It's decorated within an inch of its life, there's nothing in it from our old house except some pictures, and on top of that, it's falling down the hill."

I lifted my eyebrows inquiringly.

"The hillside sinks toward the sea about half an inch a year, which doesn't sound like much, but..." Sally shook her head, and her hair bounced. Her hair was looser now, less styled, back to its old wedge shape. With two kids, Sally said, a haircut was a luxury.

"Oh, it does. A foot in twenty-four years."

"Exactly. He's had some bracings put in and several engineers out here; I don't know what he's going to do next. It's not unique, everyone on these hills has this problem."

"And I'm sure the property's expensive around here."

"Exhorbitant."

So Sid was living in a house sliding down the hill into the sea. How appropriate.

When he emerged, he seemed smaller than I remembered, less substantial. It was as if the house were an elaborate carapace and he, inside it, was shriveling away. Maybe I thought this because he didn't scare me. He appeared on the patio silently, wearing a polo shirt, chinos, and sandals made from recycled tires. It was the sandals that threw me. On a man his age—he was in his sixties now—they looked goofy, the sandals of a man desperate to be young and hip. Quintessential California.

He looked at me and said a peculiar thing. "Clare. I thought I'd gotten rid of you."

"Daddy!" Sally laughed, and he raised his hand as if to silence her. "Where's Ezra?" he asked her.

"Out back with Peter."

"Oh. How's little..." Sid stopped, stared at the baby on Sally's shoulder.

"Barbara's fine."

"Good. Come on in, Clare, I'll show you the house."

Nothing was quite accurate. Everything was real enough, the facts were in their way inarguable, but nothing was right. "From the old house." Sid waved at a basketball hoop hung high on the kitchen wall, and while I did remember it from the house off Mulholland, I didn't remember ever seeing any of the Roses shoot baskets. In the living room, a large chest of drawers—a Biedermeyer, Sid informed me—sat in front of a curving window looking out on the sea; beside it, a folding wooden screen was hung with maybe fifteen photos. The photographs were happy and glamorous—Esther standing in front of the espalier near the pool, Esther in the kitchen, glancing up from a pot. I recognized the kitchen photo: I had taken it on one of my first trips to Los Angeles, in the first flush of my excitement with the Roses. Where had Sid gotten it? Sally must have passed it on. Esther looked shockingly young to me, not far from my own age now, and not passive, as I remembered her, but pixie-ish, mischievous. Her lips were set in a half smile, ready to bubble into a laugh. She was adorable.

Then I remembered she'd been looking at me. She must have liked me, I realized, and this brought up another slight inaccuracy: the implication of the photograph was that it had been taken by Sid. Esther may never have looked so happily at her husband.

"Where's your kid?" Sid asked me.

A glassed cabinet filled with Judaica hung in a hallway. I recognized this only because Sally had told me about: the decorator thought that since Sid had been raised in a religious home, he'd appreciate religious objects.

"You find a new husband yet?"

His bedcover was a Mexican quilt.

"You still working with those sick fags?"

His questions were pure aggression. My answers didn't interest him, he turned away each time before I'd finished. You prick, I thought as I trailed him around the house. You bastard. He'd lost weight, and with it, any padding in his bottom. The seat of his pants was loose. I've seen enough old-men patients that I could imagine his limp and wobbling buttocks.

"So you used a decorator," I said. "Did you have one for your other house?"

He didn't look at me. "Not there," he said. "Esther had taste. I don't have taste. I told you, Esther's dad was an art dealer. Look at this." He had stopped in the TV room in front of a small painting, an industrial scene. A water tower, rocks, a conveyor belt. "Look at that," he said. "You think that's me?" I peered at the painting closer, baffled by his comment. "There." He pointed. "The glittering slag heap of my life."

I was dumbstruck.

He cocked an eyebrow and looked at me aslant, then turned away. "It's not good, but at least it's interesting."

"You still reading that Bible stuff?" I asked.

He turned around, then, to look at me full-face, and the expression in his eyes was unreadable. I thought of what I knew about him, what he was capable of, what he'd done. He was probably silent only a second, but the time stretched in an agony of suspense. His eyes burrowed into me. "No," he said.

The house was quite small, all the rooms opening out from the central living area, so it was easy for Sally—on the sofa nursing Barbara, Ezra beside her playing with her car keys—to overhear us as we approached. "I'm interested in other things now," Sid said, walking in front of me, and Sally, from her sofa, called out: "What's that, Daddy? Do you have a girlfriend?"

"I could," Sid answered. "Why not? I'm a man." He turned his head in my direction and smiled. "People thought you were my girlfriend. Remember?"

SALLY HAD TO ANSWER a call on her cellular phone as soon as we got in her new Acura. Hers was the first cell phone I ever dialed myself, her car the first I'd seen with the cell phone installed. Sally wore a beeper, too, like a doctor. Barbara was two months old, and Sally was back at work. "What kind of emergencies can a lawyer get?" I'd asked her. "A lot of them are reassurance and accessibility," Sally answered. The call tonight was from a breast-reduction plaintiff whose breasts hurt. Sally sat listening, cooed to her for a while, suggested Tylenol and heat.

It seemed to me she took inordinate interest in the call. I could tell the woman on the other end was an idiot. Finally, Sally hung up. She was driving, with Peter in the passenger seat and me in the back between the children's car seats. Sally twisted around to glance at me. "He forgot Barbara's name."

"What?"

"Daddy. He forgot her name. Didn't you notice? I find that ominous."

I tried to think of an excuse. "She's a pretty fresh baby. It's a new name for him, names can take a while."

"It's Barbara." Sally exaggerated the "B" sound. "Named after Ben. Do you think he remembers Ben?"

My mind flashed to the Beidermeyer chest, the focal point of the living room, hulking like an altar in front of the window that faced the

sea. I felt like Abraham up there, Sid had said. Like Abraham sacrific-
ing Isaac. I didn't say anything.

"I'm worried he's getting Alzheimer's," Sally said.

I hate that term. I hate people saying "Alzheimer's" when what they
mean is dementia. Alzheimer's is a specific diagnosis of a certain type
of brain degeneration. For accurate diagnosis of Alzheimer's, you need
a brain biopsy. Not everybody who has dementia has Alzheimer's, and
not everybody who forgets things has dementia. Medications, fatigue,
depression, all those things can affect memory. AIDS has its own dementia. I said all this to Sally, sounding harsh even to myself.

I could see the fury in the set of Sally's head. "I figure he has lots of
reasons to forget," Peter said, turning to me. "If he wants to forget, let
him forget. Maybe forgetting will get him some peace."

Sally turned on her husband. "It's not getting me peace!" she
yelled. We almost hit an orange barrel blocking off a road repair.

"Jesus and Buddha," Peter said, "can't you just drive?" Ezra, the
happy baby, the baby who never cried, started wailing in his car seat.

"I don't know how he can run a business," Sally said. "I've been
talking to Virginia about it."

"Virginia?" It was the first I'd heard the name.

"Virginia Luby. She's been with Daddy for years. She used to be his
secretary, but now I think she does everything. Ezra, Ezra-honey."
Sally reached back and stroked his foot. "Mommy loves you." Ezra
gulped, stared; his crying stopped for a moment.

"I don't know what he has, but he's not right," Sally said, with-
drawing her hand. "I don't know if it's Alzheimer's or de-men-tia"—
she drew out the word, mocking me—"but I hate it, I hate it."

"Maybe he's got AIDS," Peter said. "Listen, some of these old guys
used to play around. Maybe he used to get it on with the Countess of
Come." I was shocked and thrilled to hear Peter talk this cavalierly
about Sally's father. Peter seemed different this trip, looser, angrier. It
occurred to me that he might consider himself beleaguered.

"Why don't you and Clare get him tested?" Sally shrieked. I'd once
gotten so mad at the ticket agent at an airport, on a long-ago trip to

visit Sally, that for a moment I literally could not see. I hoped, since Sally was driving, that this wasn't happening to her.

Barbara awakened with a scream, and Ezra started crying again too. The two babies wailed in throbbing synchrony, Ezra mournful and betrayed, Barbara desperate. Her tiny fists clenched, she turned red.

"And he wouldn't catch AIDS from Sara," Sally said loudly over the noise of the babies. "She's married with three daughters, she's very responsible, and I'm sure she's been tested. Not that she'd sleep with Daddy anyway."

There was something disturbing about the proprietary way Sally spoke of Sara Tweedles, the Countess of Come. I remembered her, tall and elegantly dressed, from Esther's funeral. Did Sally consider Sara a friend?

"Can't you quiet them down, Clare?" Sally asked irritably. "You're sitting right between them."

I hunched over and searched the car floor for a pacifier. I found one and stuck it in Barbara's mouth. She furrowed her brow a second, then stopped crying. Peter glanced back at me between the babies, a gleeful and conspiratorial glance. "There should be another pacifier back there," he said.

I found the second binkie on the seat beside Barbara's car seat, and popped it in Ezra's mouth. He sobbed for a few moments around it, then settled down. It wasn't until we got to a red light that I learned the cause of Peter's delight: Ezra was sucking on Barbara's pacifier and vice versa. Sally looked back, sighed heavily, stopped the car, and got out to make things right, wiping each pacifier with germicide. "There," she said as took her place behind the wheel and slammed the door. "Somebody's got to be competent."

"TODAY'S BEN'S BIRTHDAY," Sally said.

It was a beautiful day overlooking the sea, a day of breezes and buttery sunshine. I love you, Ben, I thought; I belatedly love you. That wasn't quite true, but I had to think it. We were sitting on the roof of Sally's garage in deck chairs we'd dragged through the second-story windows. "He was lucky he had you," I said. "Who else would drive to Encino every day and buy him Happy Families?"

"Every other day," Sally corrected me. We sat in silence for a while. "I can't believe he did it," Sally said. "I've wondered a thousand times, if I'd gotten down there in time, could I have stopped him?"

My mind was in Mexico, as it was often was, following Ben and Sid up that hill. Sally's words called me back to her and the trunk of her Volvo with its cache of drugs and needles, the rolled-up hundred-dollar bills for bribes. "Sally, if you'd gone down there, you could have been killed," I said. "What if someone had realized what you had?"

Sally didn't say anything for a moment. Her face twitched. "I don't know," she said at last.

"Would you want Barbara to do something like that?"

Sally pinched the base of her nose, closed her eyes. "No."

"What did you do with all the stuff you'd gotten together?" I said, to say something, but as she answered—she flushed the drugs down the toilet, left the needles in a Dumpster—I barely heard her.

"Clare?" Sally said. "Are you all right?"

"Sure," I said, shaking my head quickly. "Fine."

"Oh, Clare, I watch you, and sometimes you look haunted. It's your job, isn't it? I admire your doing it, but how do you stand all that death?"

"My job's not that bad."

"How can it not be bad? I worry about you. I have it easy here, really, the kids and Peter and my stupid cases, but there you are in Ohio with all those..."—her voice broke—"those lost causes." Like Ben, I knew she was thinking.

"You couldn't have saved him, Sally. It was too late."

She was quiet for a good minute. "You're probably right," she finally said. "But I wonder."

We sat in silence on the roof overlooking the sea. "Haunted," she had said. Yet there was another adjective you could apply to me: proud. A fearsome pride, that I could know something terrible and refuse, out of love, to share it.

And maybe guilty. Because I saw that I had been, in a passive way, just what Sid had said—an accomplice in Ben's death.

"Mommy!" we heard from inside the house. "Maaaa-mee." It was Ezra. Sally rose to the cry eagerly, but when I heard it, my heart sank. We had so little time alone.

"LOOK AT THIS."

I did. A Polaroid, a woman's naked torso with her arms above her head.

"You don't see the problem?"

I inspected the breasts. They looked like ordinary Los Angeles breasts to me, round and perky. "No."

"The left nipple's a little higher than the right."

"You're kidding." I brought the photo right up to my nose. "If you say so."

"She's heartbroken. She says she never would have gotten implants if she'd known. Says she can't go braless anymore."

"Can't you not take the case?"

"I've got to take it." She sighed. "It's one of my paralegals."

We exchanged a glance. "I'm tired of the young," she said. "I'll get her a couple thousand." Sally ran her hand through her hair. "I can't believe the practice of women's law has come to this."

I thought of Sally's first small office and her first client from the hairdresser downstairs, the breathless article about her practice in the *L.A. Times,* my fantasy of her suing her own father on behalf of a porn actress client. "You had such high hopes."

"I did."

"You still doing that consulting stuff for legal aid?"

"Oh, a little. But with the kids, I have only so much time, and this is the practice I created. And the legal aid stuff is thankless too, honestly. The last thing they called about was helping this woman with five children get back her kids. Well, I read the case report, and I don't want her to get her kids back."

"What did you tell them?"

"I told them look, she doesn't deserve her kids. And the lawyer there said I was looking at it from a biased white Anglo middle-class perspective."

"I don't know how you stand it."

"No," Sally answered to my surprise, "I don't either."

"THE PLAY GROUP'S HERE today," Sally announced one morning. "I should get home from the office by two, and the moms and kids start arriving at three. I told Kasey and Robin and Sara you'd be here in case I'm late."

"Those are the mothers?"

"Uh-huh. Kasey and Robin have four boys, and Sara has three girls. Clare, you should get Aurelia out here. Why don't you bring her next time? It's not a sin to miss a few days of preschool."

"Aury hates to miss preschool." This was true, but I wasn't really thinking about Aury. Sara was coming over, Sally had said, Sara and her three girls. "The Sara who's coming, is she by any chance Sara the Countess of Come?"

"Oh." Sally waved her hand dismissively. "She's ordinary. You'll see."

"SARA AND I ARE going to a sushi bar," Kasey said, tossing her hair from her face, her one-year-old wiggling furiously under her arm. "You and Sally want to come? They have a baby-sitting room. It's great. The kids sit in there and watch videos."

Sara arrived at the door beside Kasey, her brood lined up behind her. "The hostess keeps an eye on the kids," Sara explained in her high, breathy voice. A porn queen and her daughters: it gave a whole new meaning to the term "play group."

I imagined Sara's and Kasey's children quiet, inert, anesthetized by videos as grown-ups sushi'ed around them. "How nice," I said, unsure what else to say.

"It's good business," Sara said airily. "Keeps us yuppies happy." By now, Sally had joined us. "Good-bye, Sally dear," Sara said, kissing Sally on both cheeks. A flurry of perfume and thank-yous and the whole group was out the door.

"Sara called herself a yuppie," I noted after the door closed. "That's the first time I've heard a porn star categorized as a yuppie."

Sally conceded this. "But Sara's lifestyle is yuppie-ish. Her husband's an accountant. She's nice, don't you think?" And then, not waiting for my answer: "I like her."

WHEN I GOT HOME, Aury had a new friend. My mother had been staying in our town house with Aury, as she always did when I went away, and during my five days in Los Angeles, a divorced woman and her daughter had moved into the town house next door. The mother's name was Sheila, and Aury's friend was Brittany.

I hated the mother. Vapid, stupid, big-haired. She subsequently turned up with a string of boyfriends, several of whom liked to hit her against the wall. Brittany was always with us at those times, playing My Little Pony or Twister with Aury on the living room floor, the thumps on the wall as much background noise as the ubiquitous Disney video. This is sordid, I'd think, this is terrible, and I'd take the girls to Dairy Queen.

Brittany was a thin, worried little girl who always had a cold. You would think, with her lousy family background, that she would have clung to my daughter, but Aury clung to her. I can't count the weekend mornings I read to Aury in bed until it was late enough for her to go next door and knock for Brittany. Every place we went, the grocery store, the gas station, the library, Aury wanted Brittany to go. It was maddening, because there was absolutely nothing remarkable about that child. Her hair was stringy, she didn't laugh, her favorite word was "gross." Aury was a thousand times smarter.

"Why do you like Brittany so much?" I'd ask her. "Is there a reason?" She's my best friend, Aury would say.

"Does Brittany have to go with us everywhere?" I'd ask. "Can't we just go out on a little date, you and me?" Brittany would miss me, Aury answered. They both liked Cocoa Puffs with chocolate milk for breakfast; they both liked purple; they would end up at the same elementary school with the same teacher.

"Why are you so enmeshed with that girl?" I said once in exasperation. I liked the word "enmeshed." It reminded me of Sally's adjectives.

"Mother!" Aury said.

SALLY HAD TO TAKE a deposition in, of all places, Cleveland, so after she was done, she drove her rental car to Akron to spend the night. It was the first time since she'd met Mark Petrello that I'd seen her on my turf, the first time since the birth of Ezra I'd seen her without a child, the first time since her wedding that she'd seen Aury. I was ridiculously excited. She'd be gone from Barbara less than thirty-six hours and, capping weeks of careful planning and pumping, had left twenty-six bags of breast milk in her refrigerator at home. She negotiated highways and parking lots and hospital tunnels to appear at the door to my office at exactly, as we'd planned, half past five.

"Wow," I said, "you get around. How'd the depo go?" It was another botched implant case.

"I nailed him." She'd interviewed the defendant's expert witness. "I'm sure it'll settle."

I stood up and we hugged, and while I finished dictating my day's progress notes, Sally wandered out to the hall and struck up a conversation with one of my nurses.

"It was a great job," the nurse was saying as I left my office. "I got to see everything. I got to see organs being harvested."

Out of the corner of my eye, I saw Sally start.

"But that was okay because it was, you know, giving life." The nurse, new the clinic, turned to include me in her audience. The clinic nurses liked to impress me; after all, I was their boss. "It was a kid, too. Auto accident, crushed chest. About two or three years old. Oh, and he was a gorgeous child. Thick blond hair, blue eyes."

Sally left. I saw her walk down the hall into the restroom, shut the door.

"Excuse me," I said to the nurse. "You can tell me about this later." I nodded to the restroom. "She has small kids."

I have a kid, I thought. But with me it was different.

I knocked on the restroom door. "It's safe, you can come out now."

"Just a minute."

"Are you okay?"

"I guess so."

"I'm sorry."

"It's not your fault. It's like noise pollution, all of a sudden you hear something and..."

"I know. It *is* noise pollution." I thought then of Sid's magazine, sitting in the drawerful of dirty magazines. Vision pollution. "Like all those little things that hit you."

"Man feeds son to pigs."

"Eyactly."

She came out, blinking her eyes. "Without my kids, I wouldn't survive."

"Oh, you would." My response was automatic.

"I wouldn't want to."

Not that I could imagine losing Aury. But in my business, parents lost their children.

We went out to dinner. By the time we got home that night, my mother had fallen asleep in a chair, and Aury was in bed. Sally and I stayed up talking until two. She saw Aury the next morning briefly over breakfast, but she had a flight to catch, and before I left for work, she drove away.

WHEN SALLY SPOTTED ME at the airport, her eyes widened. "You look great." she said. "You look like a different person."

"I had a makeover by my patients. Jose, a hairdresser, and Frank, who owns a clothing store called Serendipity, and Kevin, a set designer. They all came to my house, and we ate cookies, and they went through my wardrobe and worked on me. It was great. It was the most fun I've ever had in one afternoon. Aury sat on Kevin's lap and supervised."

"You look like you belong here. You look L.A." Sally seemed surprised at this notion. We hurried down the concourse to the baggage claim. "What exactly did you do to your hair?"

"Well, it's cut, obviously, but then Jose dyed it darker and then streaked it. Extreme, huh? But it was getting mousy."

"You look L.A.," Sally repeated in wonderment.

"Amaying," I said, hurt. I thought I'd looked L.A. for years.

"Eyactly!" Sally cried.

I knew she was soft-soaping me, trying to make up for my obvious disappointment at seeing her pregnant again.

I couldn't believe it. It was almost more than I could stand, that she and Peter had thrust themselves together again. "Talk about amaying," I said, waving a hand at her belly, "how do you get pregnant that fast when you're nursing? You're not supposed to ovulate when you're nursing. Nursing is supposed to be natural birth control."

"I know. That's what my OB says too. He can't figure it out."

I shivered at the thought of Peter having super-vigorous sperm.

"I think it's pure will," Sally said. "I want children so badly I will them into conception."

Had she forgotten? I thought about how desperate Ted and I had been to have children, how our marriage foundered on the lack of them. I thought of reminding Sally, but then I hesitated. After all, I did have Aury.

BY LATE 1991, Sid was officially diagnosed with Alzheimer's. Sally was thirty-six with four children—Ezra, Barbara, and the twins, Joshua and Gabriel—under three years old. She kept up a full-time law practice but managed to do much of her paperwork at home, late at night after the kids were in bed. She cooked, she entertained, she drove Ezra to Gymboree.

"What else can I do," she said. "What bigger act of faith is there than bringing a new child into the world? And motherhood is an amazing job because you can use everything—your intelligence, compassion, imagination, endurance, strength—everything, every resource you have. It's incredibly challenging."

"Gosh," I said, "and all I do is drive Aury to swim class." I reminded myself that Sally was a lawyer. Persuasion was her stock in trade. "But you can use those things in any intense relationship," I said. I thought, fleetingly, how I had no intense relationships. "I use them with my patients."

"Well, work," Sally conceded, making a slight face. She was nursing with both breasts, one baby tucked like a football under her right arm, the other laid across her belly. "But with your children, you discover talents you didn't know you had. You can make such a difference: point their way in the world, give them memories that'll inform their lives years later"—she was caught up in her argument, leaning forward—"like my dad did."

I'd had poison ivy climbing up the back wall in my backyard, and a neighbor told me—so logical! why hadn't I thought of it!—to simply cut off its stem at the root. Sure enough, the vine withered away. Like Ben, I'd thought, cut off at the root. What took Sid so long to think of it?

"Whatever my father's faults," Sally said, "you can't say he's not a wonderful father."

I didn't say anything.

Sally looked at me with a frown, then, sighing, rearranged the babies.

THERE WERE SOME SIGNS: Sally went to pick him up for a dinner to celebrate her and Peter's anniversary, and Sid was on his patio in his swim trunks, puzzled by her presence. At his birthday, Sid tore into his gifts and seemed perfectly happy, but after the party, Sally found him puzzling over the boxes, unable to fit the tops onto the bottoms. Later, the attendant in Sid's gym told Sally that some days her father came in two or three times a day, while other days he didn't come in at all; but Sid told Sally he exercised every morning like clockwork. One night Sid said his mother was a good woman, and Sally had the distinct impression that her father believed his mother—who had died before Sally was born—was alive.

"I know it's Alzheimer's." Sally's voice curled through the receiver and into my ear. "You can't know someone for thirty-six years without knowing something's wrong."

Maybe what he did is driving him crazy, I thought. Interesting that his mind was going. Justice.

Sally, who refused to wallow, was sounding wallowy. "I hate to see him like that. And he knows, I know he knows, that's the worst part, he was looking at those boxes like what's wrong with me?"

"It's hard to watch," I said quickly. I hated people with

Alzheimer's, I hated their families, all those brimming eyes and meaningful looks behind the victim's back. We get old, we deteriorate, we die. The heart, the liver, the kidneys go. That's accepted. Why should the brain be sacrosanct?

"Oh, Clare, it's awful to watch. I think: Is this the end of the daddy I knew? Is he dying by inches?"

I thought of Sid that distant morning at the Beverly Hills Hilton, snapping at me to eat my omelet, pulling out his tiny plastic bag. Had he been losing his mind then? A newborn dementia, possibly. Disinhibition, they called it.

And maybe Ben's murder was the act that opened Sid's mind to deterioration. Come on in, Sid's mind said, destroy me too.

The body doesn't lie.

Of course this is a personal, not a medical, opinion.

"If it's Alzheimer's, it'll get easier for him," I pointed out. "After a while he won't realize there's anything wrong."

A pause. "Yeah," Sally said softly. Then more directly, more the Sally I knew: "I'm going with him to the doctor."

"Good," I said. "Ask that doctor. Make him tell you the truth."

They didn't give him a biopsy; his diagnosis was confirmed by a PET scan at UCLA. This was kind of exciting: as I told Sally, there were only a few centers in the country with a PET scanner, and she was lucky to know for sure. My words didn't console her. "Alzheimer's!" she said. "I don't even know if he's eating. I went through his refrigerator and found cream cheese that was six months old."

"Are you going to start taking *him* groceries now?" I asked.

She didn't catch my implication at all. "I may have to," she said. "Every time I go over there, he's sitting in the living room in his sandals and shorts with no shirt on, staring out the window. And anything I talk about, he'll stop me and say, 'You know what you need?' 'What, Daddy?' I say back. And he taps his finger on his head and says, 'You need a plan.' Every time I go over there! I had a bad time at the office today, Daddy. Peter found a leak in our roof, Daddy. Barbara said Mama today, Daddy. Whatever I say, it's the same answer: 'You know what you need?' Tap, tap. 'You need a plan.' When I'm driving over to his house, I start to sweat. It's all I can do to make my car turn up his drive. You know what I did the other day? I started north on One, but then I drove up Sunset and went up Topanga Canyon and crossed Mulholland and drove down into the Valley. I drove seventy minutes through the Valley, putting off arriving at his house."

I squeaked in incredulity. "You drove in the Valley?" Sally hadn't driven in the Valley since her days of Chinese food.

"The Valley," Sally said. Her voice on the phone was suddenly light, pleased as always at our private jokes. We were best friends. We knew each other better than anyone. "Can you believe it?" She laughed. "It makes me crazy enough I'm driving in the Valley."

It was only after we hung up that I realized something more. She'd driven up Topanga Canyon, past the stone gate where her mother died.

"YOU KNOW WHAT WE NEED?" Sally told her father. "We need a plan." A vacation, she called it. A holiday. She and her father made a deal: he'd stay with her and Peter until he was stronger. She moved some of Sid's things into a bedroom and hired a male companion to stay with him during the day. The companion was a young man named Troy, and Sid didn't like him. *Fegala!* he called Troy—fag! in Yiddish—probably accurate, and one day Sid locked himself in his room and wouldn't come out. The next day Sally briskly had the lock removed—"What can I do? What if he fell and he'd locked himself in there?"—and when I visited in September, Troy was still there, wearing white pants and a white shirt with short sleeves and a high collar like an attendent in a mental hospital, carrying Sid's medicines on a little metal tray. His outfit was preposterous, a costume, and then I thought with a vengeful frisson of Ben and his gay friends and how Sid hated them. From the back, Troy looked a little like Ben, the same flat rear and dark curls.

AURY KEPT GROWING. She continued to play with Brittany almost every day after kindergarten, reading aloud (Aury was reading by five) when Brittany got restless with videos. I'd come home sometimes to find them heaped together on the floor, asleep, sharing Aury's favorite blanket and a pillow, a book splayed open on the floor, my mother reading a newspaper at the kitchen table. "I didn't want to bother them," my mother would whisper. I would wake up Brittany and walk her next door to her mother, then sit on the sofa with Aury and hear about her day.

Aury lost one tooth, then another. I called up the Tooth Fairy Hotline while Aury was in the room, requested a gift rather than money under the pillow. "What does the Tooth Fairy do with all the teeth she collects?" Aury worried. I talked about the great Tooth Pit in Iowa, how corn grew beautifully over a layer of fertilizing teeth. Aury nodded sagely. "That's because teeth have roots," she said.

ON MY NEXT VISIT to L.A., I was sitting at the kitchen table after dinner with a cold cup of coffee, the children upstairs with Sally and Peter, when a shadow fell across the table. A strangler, I thought suddenly, irrefutably, and swung around, my arms raised to push the invader away.

It was Sid. He was smiling, his face as blank as a jack-o'lantern.

"You scared me," I said. Sid's smile broadened. He sat down at the table beside me, close enough that I had to push my chair away. "Troy looks a little like Ben from the back, have you noticed?" I asked, aware that in saying these words I was trying to scare him back.

Sid's smile faded and his eyes rolled lazily in my direction. "Ben?" he said.

The ceiling fan clanged over and over. Around and around it went, uselessly stirring the air.

"You erased him," I said, a hopeless awe filling my voice. Sid's breathing, my breathing. We were alive, both of us were alive. But only one of us remembered. "You erased him," I repeated.

"No," Sid said.

I must have looked hopeful then, I must have turned to him with something like avidity. Repentance, confession, fear of God, fear of death—any of that. Instead:

"You know what you need?" he asked.

I waited for him to go on. When he didn't, I prompted, "What, Sid?"

He tapped the side of his head with a finger. "You need a plan."

"You know about plans," I said. "So, did you plan to lose your mind?"

Sid looked at me a trifle less blankly. There might have been a thought there, a shadow moving behind his vacant eyes. He turned away from me and looked at his reflection in the glass door to the patio. He frowned, leaned over the table, sat back up. He stole another glance at his reflection, looked at me for an instant, then slid his eyes back to the mirror Sid. Who is that? I knew he was thinking. Is that someone I should know?

"LISTEN TO THIS," I said to my mother, reading from the local gay and lesbian newsletter. "'My brothers and sisters: we live in a country where the government spends millions of dollars—millions!—every *year* for toilet paper to wipe our dirty asses, yet refuses to spend one dime for the clean needles that would save a recreational drug user's life. Is this justice? Is this proper? My brothers and sisters: we must change this country around!' Cleve Burton. What do you think?"

My mother sniffed. "A bit excessive for my taste." It was 1992, and she'd moved in with me and Aury. She could no longer afford her apartment, all her savings having mysteriously disappeared, probably (although she never admitted this) on my brother Eric's latest venture, an emu farm (emus! Eric had never even owned a parakeet) that had succumbed to avian infighting and an invidious molting disease. In exchange for room and board, my mother now looked after Aury and the town house, although because she was concerned about the immorality, not to mention the power issues, of unpaid labor, I gave her an hourly rate for evenings after six and any weekend time she spent alone with Aury. People to whom I mentioned this arrangement seemed shocked that my mother expected payment at all, but it seemed normal enough to me, knowing my mother. My weekly payments created a perennial clean slate between us.

"I get a kick out of Cleve," I said. "He writes a column every week. Supposedly he stations himself in park restrooms on weekend nights and passes out condoms. He's a black guy. Actually"—I grinned—"he reminds me of you."

"Of me!"

"In your rowdier days."

"I'm not saying I don't respect his social consciousness," my mother admitted, "but the lifestyle issues!" Lust for her was always suspect. Still, her interest was a tiny bit piqued. "Have you met him?"

"Never, and he's a local figure. I don't even know what he looks like."

"Let's hope he doesn't end up as your patient," my mother said primly.

MY NEXT TRIP TO L.A., Sally looked exhausted—worse than after Flavio left her, worse than after Ben died. "He knows me, and he usually knows the kids, and he knows Peter if Peter's with me, but it's like he's a baby again, we just float in and out of his vision and he doesn't have a clue why we're here, or what we're doing, or what kind of effort we're making for him. Last week he missed the toilet, and when I met him coming out of the bathroom into the hall, he looked at me and said, 'You'll need to clean that up.' Just like that, like my cleaning up his urine was the most normal thing in the world. He can't go to the office anymore."

He still had his office in the Valley, and a cadre of people, led by the mysterious Virginia, who apparently kept his business going. I didn't ask.

"And some days he's almost lucid; some days..." Sally sighed; she was blinking back tears. "He can say terrible things. Memories, or—" She stopped, sniffed, wiped her nose on the back of her sleeve. "He thanks me sometimes. He thanked me last week, as a matter of fact. I can't even tell you, Clare. These sweet and terrible days."

It surprised me that Sid's disease was progressing so quickly, but sometimes Alzheimer's did. The medicines they'd tried had done nothing for him. "What does his doctor say?"

"Not much. He says it's progressive, and I need to think whether he'd want to be resuscitated if his heart or breathing stopped. What do you think, Clare?"

"If his heart stops, I'd let him go."

"But Clare, his heart is strong. And he never gets sick, not even a cold. He could live like this for years."

"If a dementia's really progressing, people may stop getting out of bed, stop eating. If you don't put in a feeding tube, they sort of fade away."

"Starve to death."

"Well. They have no interest in eating."

"I can't let him starve to death, Clare. I can't do that."

I nodded. She probably couldn't.

"You remember how he used to study with me? He always wanted to learn. That's how I met Timbo. Remember? He thought I was a twin."

A moment of silence in honor of Timbo.

"And now I have twins."

Onan spilled his seed in the desert. Another great biblical moment. Another scene for Sid's movie opus.

What happened to Cain after he slew Abel? I looked it up. God was mad and made Cain a ceaseless wanderer on earth. Eve had another son, Seth, so all mankind wasn't condemned to be descended from a murderer.

Another scene in Sid's apocryphal movie.

And how brutally unjust, really, that Sid should get a disease that let him forget, that cast its long shadow on Sally, whose only crime was being his daughter.

"I COULD RETIRE." Sally had just turned thirty-seven. Her husband barely worked. She had four kids.

"You could afford to?" I blurted. The twins were upright now, peeping over the seats of kitchen chairs. Ezra, wearing a paper crown and a cape, was drawing monsters. He was three years old and seemed to have artistic talent; his monsters were recognizable as monsters. Barbara lay on the floor with her feet propped on the wall, inspecting her glittery shoes. Staggering, to retire at thirty-seven. Had Sally's law firm been that successful?

"Not without what I get from Daddy." Sally gave me a rueful smile. "Lots of green in those blue movies."

"Right-o, sister." I smiled back. Blue movies. There was something quaint and innocent about that term, something almost endearing. A lie, like any euphemism. But Sally could live with it, and who was I to deny her the smallest sliver of comfort? Her mother and brother were dead, her father disappearing.

"I just don't want to do law anymore," Sally said. "I don't know, I've lost my killer instinct."

"Wook at this one," Ezra said zestfully, holding up his picture. "Wook at his big teeth."

I saw Sid, arm outstretched, approaching Ben. A green hillside, wind, sea, rock. I flicked a Cheerio, which skittered across the table and hit one of the kitchen chairs. "Not such a bad thing to lose."

Sally drove her hand into her hair. "No," she said. "I think not." She looked around the table cluttered with bowls and placemats. A twin—Joshua, I thought—had dropped back to his kness and was now under the table trying to suck on my toes. "You think I could stand being retired?"

I drove in every morning and put my plastic card in the meter to open the gate to the parking lot, crossed the pedestrian bridge to the clinic, walked up two flights of stairs and through a metal door. There the pasty-faced, the cachexic, the splotchy all awaited me. Could I stand being retired? Probably not.

Soon after, another new patient arrived in my clinic, Larry Cotton, a school psychologist with a chiseled face and soulful eyes who wore plaid flannel shirts and was referred by a Dr. Nicholaides. He'd just been released from the hospital after a bout with pneumocystis. His HIV serology was positive; the Western blot, the confirmatory test, was positive too.

"A friend of mine told me about you," Mr. Cotton said. "He'd read about you somewhere."

Probably gay, I thought. A male friend.

But Larry Cotton denied any risk factors for HIV. According to him, he was a monogamous heterosexual who lived with a girlfriend. He'd never even smoked marijuana.

I don't really care how people get AIDS. Other than to learn what behaviors I should warn people about, the mode of transmission doesn't interest me at all. There is a weird tendency for gays, and not drug abusers, to get Kaposi's sarcoma. Some people blame this on a concern with appearance, since Kaposi's can be disfiguring, and gays care a thousand times more than drug addicts what they look like. HIV has this amazing propensity to hit people where it hurts. The weight lifters get muscle wasting, the brainy people get dementia, the fastidious get diarrhea.

"No surgery lately? No dental procedures?"

He'd gotten it somehow, but I wasn't going to press him. "Your girlfriend should get tested," I pointed out. "She should go to the health department for that. And I have a set of guidelines for safe sex." I handed Mr. Cotton a booklet I'd written up, an explicit and (I thought) rather humorous guide to safe sex in the nineties. One of my first and longest-gone patients had done illustrations for the manual (the "Kannot Sutra," he called it), and the text had been vetted by the University Internal Review Board, who approved it with the caveat that only I could hand it out, as personal advice not sanctioned by the

University, and that I must keep all unused copies locked up in my office. Mr. Cotton glanced at it with little interest, then rolled it up and stuck it in his pocket.

"What's his story?" LaTonya, the clinic's brightest nurse, asked me as he walked down the hall.

"Beats me," I said. "From what he tells me, he's the Virgin Larry."

ONE NIGHT SALLY NEEDED some Q-tips to clean out her dad's ears, another night Mylanta, another night an antifungal cream. One time she asked for Vaseline and rubber gloves.

"I'll run out," Peter would announce eagerly, standing up. All four kids would be in bed, after their protracted bedtime ritual, with Peter and me sitting around with the TV on, talking about the amazing durability of Saddam Hussein.

"Oh no," I'd say. "You sit. I'll run out." I often used Sally's car. "Have some time with Sally."

Yes, Peter and I parried over who'd get to leave: it was that bad. Weekends, when Sally slept late, Peter spent hours with the kids. Late in the day, after going to his time-share office in Malibu, he played squash. Every time I saw him now, he was just arriving or just getting ready to go. He was in a transition time, he said. What do you mean? I asked. His father-in-law wouldn't be living with them forever, Peter said. After he was gone, they'd have a normal life. Crazy optimist, I remember thinking.

"Rubber gloves and Vaseline? What's the problem tonight, Sally?" Peter asked.

"Fecal impaction," I said, recognizing the supplies. "Can't the night nurse do it?"

Sally looked at Peter, her red cheeks flaring. "He's my father," she said tonelessly. "He won't live forever, and I have to think I've done everything I could." And she bounded away from me and Peter and up the stairs to her father's room.

I LEFT L.A. on a Sunday in March 1992, and the very next night, Sid, being fed his supper, choked and aspirated on a piece of Sally's excellent chicken cacciatore, a leftover from my visit. Troy the companion and Peter struggled with the Heimlich maneuver while Sally phoned 911.

Sally called me at eleven her time, forgetting in her grief that it was two A.M. for me.

It took me a moment to grasp the situation. "He's on a respirator?" I said, that fact alone jolting me into awareness. Usually I dozed through late calls, even when I was talking.

"He has pneumonia. I can't just let him die."

He'd been losing his memory for at least two years; his mental status was marginal at best. The odds of his getting off the respirator and returning to a coherent existence were slim to none. "Didn't he have a living will? Did you ever decide on resuscitation?"

"I can't just let him die," Sally repeated. "Even if he's a vegetable, he's alive. He's a person. There's a value to life itself, you know. Only God can know the place and time. I can still take him home. We'll have to hire someone extra, but I can be there all day."

"But you'll have to run your office too, you'll—" I hesitated, thinking this wasn't the time for practicalities. Sally reminded me of some of the partners or parents of my patients, rushing in, at the moment of diagnosis, with all sorts of exalted plans. We'll build a new wing on the house, sell our business, quit work, and stay at home. Sooner or later, daily life sifts in. The plans are less a framework for the future than a flimsy wall tossed up to block it out.

"Listen, Daddy's doctor just got here, is it okay if I have him call you? You'll understand everything and then you can tell me."

I wasn't really hearing her, I was thinking of Sid on the respirator, the tube taped into his mouth, the catheter in his penis, the nurse drawing up syringes of Valium for sedation, restraints around his ankles and wrists. Whatever happened to "pneumonia, the old man's friend"?

MR. COTTON, the Virgin Larry, went into the hospital. I spoke to his mother in the hall. "He's better, but he's not out of the woods yet. He still needs the oxygen, and his CD4 count is low."

"That's from the chemotherapy," Mr. Cotton's mother said.

A strange way to put it, but I supposed AZT was a form of chemo. Sometimes nonmedical people try to sound knowledgeable and end up not making sense. I was trying to be kind to Mrs. Cotton.

"But he's looking better," his mother said eagerly. "His color is better." She closed her eyes. "It's a terrible disease, isn't it? Every day I pray for a cure."

I agreed and hurried off.

I had at that time, apart from Mr. Cotton, a bunch of particularly unloved patients, including a man with Elvis hair who gripped my hand and twisted it whenever I left him, and what I thought over and over as Sid sickened and rallied, rallied and sickened, was how lucky he was to have Sally, who loved him, who sat beside his bed and challenged the nurses, who held cups of water to his lips and rubbed lotion on his arms and hands. Why did Sid get this, how did he deserve this?

The next time Mr. Cotton was in the hospital, he agreed to have a feeding tube inserted into his stomach, a procedure that would entail some help at home. I left several messages on the answering machine for the girlfriend, but she didn't call back.

"Sometimes the cure is worse than the disease," his mother said cryptically. No one seemed to visit but his mother.

"His accountant's in there with him again," the head nurse muttered one day as I headed for Mr. Cotton's room.

The accountant was a slight, pleasant-looking black man in a suit, wearing shoes so perfect I wondered if they were scuffed even on their bottoms. Papers that looked like tax forms were spread out on the bedside table. "Hello," he said politely.

It wasn't one of Mr. Cotton's better days. He drifted off in the middle of my questions. "He agreed to a feeding tube yesterday," I told the accountant, "but maybe you could help me. I really should speak with his girlfriend."

"Girlfriend!" the accountant said sharply. "I've been invisible, but I've never had my sex changed."

Mr. Cotton roused, gave a weak, apologetic smile.

"It's a secret to his family," the accountant went on, "but you're his doctor, I thought you'd—"

Mr. Cotton was shaking his head weakly, admonishing his friend not to say more. The accountant picked up Mr. Cotton's hand and stroked it. "I only come here under cover of business," the accountant said. "I'm the helpful neighbor next door." He stroked Mr. Cotton's bearded cheek. "Don't you worry, Larry. I'll take care of you."

THROUGH IT ALL, I talked once a week or so with Dr. Farouk, the Rose family internist. Sally told me he looked like Cesar Romero. At first he spoke to me in an avuncular manner that teed me off—the doctors in Akron are afraid of me—but as time went by, he loosened up and became, in a strange stiff way, flirtatious.

"Hi, it's me," I'd say when he got on the phone, "sorry."

"I am always happy to hear from my eminent colleague," Dr. Farouk would answer, or some such drivel, and then he'd tell me, elegantly and concisely, what was going on.

The family was difficult and full of tragedies. Sally was the strong child; Ben had had "too-much disease." At first I thought Dr. Farouk was referring to multiple illnesses, then I realized he meant something more philosophical. "It is a common disease in my practice," Dr. Farouk said, "too-much disease. The American disease." He pronounced the word dis-ease. "The parents were too lenient." The mother was off in a world of her own. Dr. Farouk did not believe it was the happiest marriage. The father had perhaps sought "comfort outside."

Dr. Farouk would make an awed, despairing sound, half rattle in the throat, half sigh, a sound I came to recognize and even anticipate, as Sid kept going week after week: "Now your friend, he is off the respirator, but his kidneys have shut down"—the awed sound—"and Sally tells me yes, she wants a nephrologist."

—"These last two days he has developed intractable diarrhea"—the sound again—"and we will have to stop the tube feeding."

—"It is surely a stroke, and maybe"—the sound—"I told this to your friend, maybe this is a blessing."

—"Sally, she continues to want him alive. He is her only family, you know."

—"I told her, Sally, I have known you twenty years. You must get home and get some rest. You have your husband and children to think of. He can open his eyes for you, he can breathe, yes, but that is not really being alive. This bedside vigil, it will end, but it may not end soon."

—"I told her we will not do dialysis again."

—"Sally just left, the nurse went in to check his vital signs and he was not breathing. They tried the CPR. He had ST elevation on his EKG, anterior leads, so clearly it was a myocardial infarction."

"Finally," I said.

"Yes, finally." He made the sound again. "But, Dr. Mann, your friend, she wanted the respirator, and he is still alive."

"He's alive?"

"He is stabilizing. He is not at all alert, but he is peeing."

Peeing. A doctor knows that if a patient is putting out urine, he or she may survive.

"SALLY?" I said into the phone. "Sally?"

Her voice sounded faraway and hollow, as if she were standing in a cavern. "He doesn't respond at all, Clare. Dr. Farouk persuaded me to let them take out the breathing tube, and when they did, I thought that would be it, but now he's breathing on his own. He doesn't open his eyes at all now, he doesn't squeeze my hand, he's just...breathing."

"Sally," I said. "I'm sorry. I'm very, very sorry." He was her father; she was my best friend. And my memories of him were not all bad.

"Dr. Farouk says he could last like this a long time. He thinks I should look for a nursing home."

"Oh, Sally."

She had his power of attorney. It was all legal. When Sid had choked, Sally hadn't missed a menstrual period; when he was moved by ambulance from the hospital to a fancy nursing home, she was three months pregnant with her fifth child. She was also the guardian of his business, of the magazines, the mailing lists, the contracts, the licensing agreements, of everything, even his studio.

FOUR CHILDREN THREE and under.

Pregnant.

Lead partner in a law office with twenty-three employees.

An unwanted inheritance.

A husband without steady interests or income.

A dead brother.

A dead mother.

A breathing father.

No faith.

"I thought you hated faith," I said.

"I hate psychology," Sally said. "How could someone hate faith? I'd love to have faith. Come on, Clare, do you think I'm a barbarian?"

HIS ROOM LOOKED OUT on a butterfly garden, and he rested on a technological marvel of a bed: a plastic top stretched over a metal box frame, and underneath the plastic a layer of sand puffed and blown by electric jets. All this to prevent bedsores. The aides in this facility were unusually attractive, and all the female staff wore white dresses and white nylons.

He looked the same but blanker, his mouth and eyes open, his tongue fissured and dry as leather. "Hi, Daddy!" Sally said, kissing him on his cheek. She held his hand and told him about our day.

VIRGINIA LUBY, SID'S LONGTIME assistant, was a woman of close to sixty wearing a yellow button-down shirt, a plaid skirt, stockings, and beige sandals with soft soles. She appeared to wear no makeup, but her hair was carefully curled. She reminded me of the church ladies who had done the reception for my wedding to Ted. She sat on a swivel chair in Sally's extra upstairs bedroom—Sid's former room—which had been transformed into a sort of porn command center, complete with computers, modems, phone lines, and a table-top movie projection device that accommodated editing. Sally kept the door to this room closed; she had had the lock restored. On the computer screen in front of Virginia Luby was a close-up of a lipsticked mouth and an erect penis. "Nice to meet you, Ms. Luby," I said.

"So you're Clare." She shook my hand heartily. "Call me Virginia. I've heard about you for years. How are you, Sally? How's your dad?"

"It's a better room," Sally said. He'd been moved; the neighbor next door to his old room was a screamer. "He looks out on the butterfly garden."

"That's good." Virginia made a little pout. "Nice scenery never hurt anyone." She waved at the computer screen. "I'm just going through Sean's latest."

"Anything good?"

"Oh, the usual." Virginia looked at me and smiled. "Sean's a specialist in males."

"How in the world did you get into this line of work?" I blurted. I'd been inspecting her hair: I would place a bet that she used rollers.

"Same reason Sally's father did." Virginia indicated Sally with her thumb. "Take care of the kids. It's a good business. Lends itself to organization. Sid was quite a guy that way."

"Virginia, don't say was," Sally objected. "Daddy's not dead. He still *is*."

"I keep forgetting, honey," Virginia said. "But you're right, he still is."

We were quiet for a while, Sally studying circulation figures on another computer, me picking up and reading a *Newsweek*, Virginia scrolling through photos.

"Wow," Virginia said, "look at the dingdong on this one." She turned the computer screen toward us; Sally and I glanced at each other and smiled. "Not that I'd want a thing like that poking around in me," Virginia added.

She turned to the computer screen again. "Amazing," she said. "How the heck does he find these people?" She held out her hand quickly, palm to us. "Don't tell me."

THERE WERE A THOUSAND things Sally had to do, business meetings, lawyers' meetings, accountants' and tax people's meetings, but the thing she dreaded, the one thing, was simply going to his Malibu house and sorting through his things.

"I'll do it," I said.

If I could just throw away the clear dross, the toiletries and the junk in drawers and the magazines, pack up any cans for the food bank, go through his clothes and separate out what could be turned into rags and what could be donated to Goodwill. "He has some outfits from the seventies." Sally rolled her eyes. "Those shirts with wide collars and belts with big buckles—they can go in the trash. But don't touch the furniture, and leave anything personal for me to go through when I can stand it."

I was surprised and touched me that she trusted me after the bad things I'd said about Sid in the past, the way I'd helped estrange her from him years before.

God knows what I'll find here, I thought as I drove up the hill. A muggy summer day. I remembered Sid's garage in the house off Mulholland, the kids' toys piled up, the parking spaces empty of cars, the pool net hanging on the wall.

The rosemary bushes were overgrown, and a rolled-up newspaper had petrified beside the door. I let myself in and turned off the alarm. As soon as the beeping stopped, the silence was sepulchral. No clock, no refrigerator running, no air conditioner. Peter had unplugged almost everything when Sid moved to their house in Pacific Palisades. Every week or so, a neighbor nosed around the outside. No one had been inside for months.

The first thing I did was open some windows. I glanced around the living room, the long sofa and the heavy chest fronting the curved picture window. Next to the chest sat the floor-to-ceiling folding screen covered with framed photographs. The only pictures of Ben were a portrait when he was perhaps three and Sally ten—young Ben sitting on Sally's lap—and a snapshot of him grinning beside their old Mulholland pool. That second picture was probably twenty years old. Atop the big chest lay some shells and a wooden box, ornately carved with a screen in the top, about the size of a deck of playing cards. Beyond the bric-a-brac, down the hill, I saw a jumble of obscenely expensive houses and the implacable sea. I turned away.

I did his bedroom closet first, then the kitchen. There was surprisingly little stuff. The outfits from the seventies weren't there. I realized Sid must have pared down his possessions in the move from the house off Mulholland, and the overcrowded feeling here was simply because it was small. I was piling Sid's few pots and pans and wooden spoons into a packing crate to take to the disaster response shelter, wondering if I'd find anything disgusting in his bedroom chest of drawers, when Aunt Ruby walked in.

I hadn't seen her for years, since Esther's funeral. It wasn't clear which one of us was more astonished. She remembered me right away, which touched me, and in a glance, she took in what I was doing.

"You're alone," she said.

"Sally couldn't handle it yet."

"I was driving past—I drive past all the time, checking on things—and I saw the kitchen window open. You hear about these squatters." Aunt Ruby lifted her right hand from behind her skirt—she was wearing a very large dress, not quite a muumuu—and held up an enormous knife.

"I'm glad you recognized me!" I said, and Aunt Ruby laughed. She waddled over to one of the kitchen chairs, laid her knife on the kitchen table, and sat down, peering around her at the crates and boxes I'd filled. "Anything interesting?"

"He didn't have much stuff here, really," I said. "He'd stripped down."

"Well," Aunt Ruby said, lifting her sleeve to rub her eye, "he wasn't himself after Ben died." I remembered Sally telling me about Uncle Freddie's disease, how anxiety had made Aunt Ruby an eating woman. She'd might have gained another fifty pounds since she'd hustled Ben through the side gate to the gardeners' bathroom. She'd been big before, but now she was enormous. She looked like you could stick her with a pin and deflate her.

"Is Sally managing everything?" Aunt Ruby had left the door ajar, and the scent of rosemary wafted through the room.

"You mean Crown?"

Aunt Ruby nodded. "I figured no one needed me. I've been by to see him; it's a clean enough facility. I was surprised Sally didn't take him back to her house."

"He's too total-care. She couldn't find the help."

"So how is she handling being a pornography queen?"

I shrugged. "She views it as temporary. She's hoping to sell stuff off."

"Oh, I'm sure. It's much too tawdry a business for young Sally." Aunt Ruby emphasized the word "tawdry" in a mocking way.

"You think it isn't tawdry?"

"Of course it's tawdry, but Sally grew up on it. *Tit World* put the meat on Sally's table."

"So to speak," I muttered, but Aunt Ruby didn't hear me. She put her chin on her hand and gazed at me.

"I'm not speaking against Sally, I love Sally," Aunt Ruby said, "but I hate it that she's running away."

I started back on my packing. "She's not running away. She's planning to sell a business she doesn't want a part of."

"Did Sid tell you about his scholarship program? He had a scholarship program for his employees. What's going to happen to that?"

I glanced incredulously at Aunt Ruby. "And he loved AIDS education," Aunt Ruby said. "Every movie since 1985, the men are wearing condoms. I know that's important to you."

I taped shut a box of canned goods, not sure what to say.

"If she didn't want his business, she should have told him. He knew he was losing his memory, he knew he was as good as dying. He would have sold it off if she'd asked him. But no, she let him keep things going, thinking his daughter would take over. Like Christie Hefner, sort of. He dreamed about that."

"Maybe she just didn't want to make him unhappy. She did everything she could for him, always, especially after he got sick and she moved him in with her. You should see the things she did for him." I shivered, thinking of the disimpaction.

"I called there all the time to come over and see him. Did she tell you? She always put me off."

"I thought you'd visited him a couple of times."

"Oh, a couple. I would have visited much more if I'd felt welcome."

I wandered from the kitchen into the living room and cast my eyes out over the ocean. "How's your husband?" I said.

Aunt Ruby's disembodied voice wafted from the kitchen. "He's holding his own. He gets a shot now, interferon, have you heard of it? Boosts his immune system to fight off the hepatitis virus. Horrible side effects. He hardly eats."

"He got hepatitis from a virus? I thought—"

"What? Didn't Sally tell you? Sure, we thought it was alcohol, but there's this new virus they've found, hepatitis C, and it turns out Freddie..."

She went on. My eyes swept through the knickknacks on top of the chest and lighted on the carved wooden box. It had a hinge, I noticed. For no good reason, I picked up the box and opened it.

"And it's a terrible disease, hepatitis. I had no idea. I thought it was something only degenerates got."

A tiny plastic bag inside the box. I slipped my nail under to dislodge it, and the bag fluttered to the floor.

"He thinks he must have picked it up from a patient. That's how doctors get it, you know. It's a needle-stick disease. Or with all the skin biopsies he did, and they used to do them very casually, not always wearing gloves. And he did deal with alternative-lifestyle patients."

I bent over to pick up the bag. A tiny plastic bag, the kind you slip earrings into.

"It's a good thing we have a great sex life, or I'd be worried. About where he got it, I mean. But his hepatologist says in almost half the cases the source isn't..."

Ben's tooth.

I froze, leaning over the floor, my hand out to pick up that tiny bag. The same bag Sid had slipped out of his pocket to illustrate the truth about Ben's death.

"That's true," I said to Aunt Ruby, my voice sounding wavery and odd.

I could hear her rising in the kitchen, her heavy standing and plodding to the kitchen door.

I slipped the bag into the pocket of my jeans.

"It's kind of you to come help Sally," Aunt Ruby said, looking at me.

"She's my best friend."

Aunt Ruby sighed. "I worry about her, I really do. How old is she? Thirty-eight?"

"Almost."

Aunt Ruby gave an irritated wave of her hand. "My brother spoiled her, that's the problem. He made everything so easy for her that she never had to think about life. It's like they say, he fed her steak every day but never showed her how he killed the cow. He didn't do her any favors. Pitiful girl—finds out when she's well into her twenties that her father puts out dirty magazines. You know how she found out, don't you? I let it slip when we were having a conversation. Of course, I never in the world dreamed she didn't—I mean, the girl was a lawyer! He was a fool like that, my brother. I loved him, but he was a fool for his children."

I shrugged. "Worse things to be a fool for."

Aunt Ruby gave a short laugh. "Yeah, sure. But your children you have the rest of your life." She stopped, apparently remembering Ben. "At least you hope so." Her tone changed, and she narrowed her eyes and peered at me. "Did he have AIDS?"

I wasn't sure who she was talking about.

"You're an AIDS doctor, right?" Aunt Ruby asked. I nodded. "You can tell me, I'm up on the ways of the world, didn't Ben have AIDS?"

I thought of the blood tests for HIV that Sally had gotten on Ben every few months, the clean-needle stash she'd accumulated, the heroin she procured for him, all the effort that had gone into keeping Ben AIDS-free. "No, he didn't."

She didn't believe me. "You can tell me, I won't tell anyone, I won't go crazy like Sally would. It's for my own peace of mind. I figure Ben found out he had AIDS, and Sid took him to Mexico for some of those crazy treatments, and then he kept getting worse and killed himself. That's how I figure it."

"It didn't happen like that." The words popped out of me. I slipped my hand in my pocket and felt for the plastic bag.

Aunt Ruby eyed me with fresh suspicion. "Then what did happen?"

I started to stammer.

"I figure Sid called you up when he found out about Ben's AIDS. How could he not call you up? You're an expert! A family friend!" Aunt Ruby moved closer to me, her voice growling now, insistent. "I know Sid wouldn't tell Sally that Ben had AIDS. Sid told me after he got back from Mexico that he'd done everything to protect her."

"He did. Everything."

"So what happened? Ben just die one of those sad AIDS-y deaths down there? Or did he kill himself? That's what I think."

Maybe only I could remember him properly, because only I knew how he'd died.

"I can't see him using a gun." Aunt Ruby stepped back and gazed, frowning, into the air, as if worrying an old question. "There was something feminine about Ben, and I can't see him shooting himself at all. Pills, maybe. Slit wrist, maybe. I know Sid said he threw himself off a cliff, but I'm not sure about that, either. I asked Sid point-blank about it, and he didn't answer. I think Sid didn't want to bring the body home. He got Ben buried down there so there wouldn't be any questions at the border."

I couldn't stand it. This hopeless guessing, this misinformation. Before I even realized, I was blurting it. "I'll tell you what happened. Ben didn't have AIDS. He never got AIDS, because Sally used to get him his heroin and clean needles so he wouldn't have to share. Sid took Ben to Mexico to clean him out, but Ben couldn't stand it and called Sally, and Sally was going to drive to Mexico with heroin for Ben, but Sid found out—tapped the phones, you know, he always bugged Ben's room—and then to make sure Sally didn't leave L.A., Sid took Ben outside of that little town in Mexico and shot him dead."

I felt a little sick at my last words, guilty that I'd ended with a flourish. I never dreamed I'd tell this story. I glanced toward the window, then back at Aunt Ruby, with the sensation of my eyeballs rolling around in my head like a frightened horse's. She was stock-still, mouth agape, and there was absolute silence until she started laughing.

"That's hysterical!" She was beside herself, wheezing and braying. She threw her head back, she bent over and slapped her thigh. "Sid told you that?" At last she had to stop and take a breath. "That's the wildest story I ever heard."

"It's not a story, Aunt Ruby. It's true. Sid told me."

"Killed Ben. Sid killed Ben." Ruby was shaking her head and chuckling. "I'll tell you, he must have stayed up late thinking up that one. And you believed him? I can't believe you swallowed a story like that. What's that word for people who'll believe anything? Gullible. Gullible's Travels."

My eyes filled with shameful tears. "It wasn't a story. Ben didn't have AIDS. It's exactly what happened. Sid told me."

"Oh, horsefeathers. Did he tell you with a twinkle in his eye? You bothered him, Clare. You always did. Sally thought too much of you. Remember when she wouldn't speak to him? That was you. Don't think Sid didn't know that."

"He took me to the Beverly Hills Hilton. He made me eat breakfast, and he told me." I was crying now.

"Oh, Clare, Clare." Aunt Ruby wrapped an arm around my shoulders. "He was an old bugger, you know? That's what he was." She sounded tearful now. "I sure miss him." Her head lifted, a light came to her eyes. "When was this, exactly? When did he spin you this tale?"

I told her when: after Sally was married, just after she'd had Ezra.

"See? I rest my case. Sid was jealous of you, Clare. He wanted to get rid of you. Who did he ever have but Sally? And you got in his way. Oh, not just you. That silly Peter got in the way, Ezra got in the way. But you were the one Sid thought he could get rid of."

Clare, he'd said on the deck of this very house, *I thought I'd gotten rid of you.*

Aunt Ruby stepped back for a moment and stared at me. I fingered Ben's tooth in my pocket. "That AIDS is a tragedy, a tragedy," she said sighing.

I nodded.

"Do you feel better now?" Aunt Ruby asked gently. "Oh, Clare. It's sweet you believed him, it really is. And I'm sure if he'd been more with-it mentally he would have set you right. But you know, right after he told you, he started losing his mind."

I nodded. That was true. She could be right.

"You should tell Sally about Ben's disease," Aunt Ruby said. "You should. She's the only person in that little family left, and she deserves to know the truth. It'll help her understand things. It'll help her grow up."

I had never before thought of Sally as incomplete, not as adult as she could be. I quickly shook my head to knock the thought away.

"Sid killing Ben." Aunt Ruby was shaking her head and smiling again. "Oh, Claresy. Sid could no more kill his children than I could break through this ceiling and float up to the moon."

Her feet were swollen, her thighs as big as turkey breasts. The image of her floating away was so unlikely that I started to laugh.

"Little Claresy," she said, putting an arm around my shoulders. "Ohio Claresy. How'd you ever get mixed up with us crazy Roses?"

I closed my eyes and leaned against Aunt Ruby's massive shoulder, feeling for a moment so buoyant that I myself could have floated to the moon.

"WHY DON'T WE GO on out to the patio?" Virginia suggested. "It's not that hot out. Come on, Clare. Sit and chat with Sally and me after my hard day at the office."

Sally brought out plates and glasses of iced tea and chopped vegetables with dip. "Just a few minutes, honeybear," she called to someone. "The grown-ups need to talk. Teresa will find your LEGO man."

Virginia told me about her three children, her two daughters living near her and her son who worked in Sid's warehouse, about her ex-husband who'd run off and gotten hit by a train, about the bingo games she organized for her parish (she was a church lady!). She told me about her grandsons, one with ADD, one with a multiracial father, one with a genetic disorder that made him slow but musical. After a bit, she reminisced about her early days with Sid. At the beginning, she was his only employee, and she chaperoned while he took photos of the girls. "You couldn't show much," she said. "We covered up their pubic hair. A nipple was a shocker. We got really high-grade models, nice girls." The years went by and they got the free spirits, girls not as likely to employ good grooming. By the late sixties anything went; Virginia would have quit but her husband was gone and dead. Things got slow in the seventies, as I'd heard years before, until the gay market opened up.

"The gay market opened up?" Sally repeated, her spoon clanking the inside of her glass. "I thought Daddy went after it."

Virginia laughed in a nervous way. "Well, you don't create a market, you recognize it. It was hard for Sid at first. He didn't really, you know, like gays."

"I know."

"He didn't even want to review the photos, and he always reviewed them, that was part of his quality control. He'd have me look at them."

Sally murmured and shook her head; I had no idea what she was thinking.

"Didn't matter to me," Virginia said. "Although I have to say, at first I'd get surprised. Those gay guys, they're creative." She laughed. "But Sid got used to it. You can get used to anything.

"Boy, I miss him. We used to call him the philosopher porn king. Didn't he have a mind? That's why I can't stand the thought of him lying there drooling. I'm not going to see him, I'm sorry. I want to remember him like he was."

"You're lucky you can," Sally said.

"Like he *was* was," Virginia said, ignoring Sally's comment. "These last few years have been bad enough." Virginia turned to me. "You knew Esther, right?" I nodded. "Esther and I used to drive to this drugstore in Los Feliz and get strawberry sundaes." Virginia sucked on her cigarette, then blew out two long streams of smoke through her nose. I hadn't seen that effect since high school; I wondered if Virginia did it to annoy Sally. "I loved that woman. Such a lady."

Sally said nothing.

"You have some of that, you know," Virginia said to Sally. Virginia sat up straighter, lifted her chin, turned her head in Sally's direction, held her cigarette far from her with her arm and wrist extended. A pose.

"My mother never smoked," Sally said. She stood and reached for Virginia's crumpled napkin, then headed inside for the kitchen.

"I shouldn't do this in front of you." Virginia sagged into her chair again, looking at her cigarette. "You being a doctor."

"I used to smoke. It was hard to quit."

Virginia was stressed. She could handle the editorial side, but their

customer-service people were having problems with inventory management. "And then Buck's out of commission," she said.

Buck. I'd never heard of Buck. "What's his specialty?"

"Category management." I looked blank. "Shelf space," Virginia
explained. "Displays."

"Is he sick?"

Virginia laughed. "Income tax, the putz. He'll be out in eight
months, though."

It took us several minutes to realize that Sally wasn't returning, and
then we heard her laughter through the window of the den. "Playing
with the kids," I murmured.

Virginia said her good-byes from the kichen. "Back to the salt
mines tomorrow," she called to Sally. "See you here."

"You tell her I can't do everything," she muttered to me at the
door.

"THERE'S A LITTLE strangeness there," announced Timothy Quiver, the new head of infectious diseases who'd covered for me during my trip to California. Mr. Cotton's mother was standing outside his room, hypervigilant as a prairie dog, watching people who moved past her down the hall. "She thinks her son has cancer."

"Cancer?"

"The whole family believes that, sounds like your patient drilled it into them in his better days." Dr. Quiver grinned. "I didn't disabuse them of anything. Be interesting if he has to go to hospice, right?"

I was walking toward the mother just as the accountant approached her. "I'm afraid he won't be able to see you today," the mother was saying. "He's very weak, he needs his rest, and he's certainly not in any shape to be bothered by financial matters." I glanced quickly at the accountant's face to see how he took this.

"I'm sorry," the accountant said. "He's weaker, is he? I'm sorry." He raised his voice ever so slightly, just enough to be sure I caught his words. "Cancer is a terrible disease, isn't it?"

I looked at him in sudden recognition: another person who could keep a secret.

"Oh, terrible, terrible." The old woman, slipping from her vigilance for a second, closed her eyes. When they opened, I was in her line of vision, and her eyelids fluttered like a movie heroine's. "Dr. Mann! Dr. Mann is back!"

"CLARE?" SALLY HAD CALLED out one evening. "Come upstairs." It was after ten; the kids were all in bed, but when we entered the office, Sally closed the door. "Thanks for going through Daddy's things. I can't tell you how I appreciate that."

She opened a drawer in the credenza and brought out a folder of pictures. "Maybe you can help me with this too."

Boys. Young men, really, trussed and bound and cowering in positions of submission.

"Oh, yuck, Sally."

"I know. But you can help me! A new photographer sent me these pictures, and these"—she waved a second folder—"are from our staff photographer. Virginia doesn't know which ones to use, so she's punting them to me."

"I don't know, use them both." I turned toward the closed door. "Use them in different issues."

"Clare. I'm kind of the boss. I have to give an opinion. It's like she's testing me."

"Why don't you show them to Peter?"

She stared at me, and I could read her mind: After Flavio, I'm going to show homoerotic photos to my husband? "I'm in an awkward position, Clare. Please. I thought you might have some insight."

"Okay, okay." I looked through the photos and picked one set. "Here," I said, handing the packet to Sally. And suddenly—standing in that room with the computers and the closed door, down the hall from Sally's four sleeping children—our lives just seemed impossible, so far from our college days that an outsider could never track the connection, would never dream the two women in this room had started out as ill-matched roommates in a quad.

In retrospect, this whole period was for Sally an extended scream. I didn't see that at the time. I thought I was the one screaming.

"HOW ABOUT THIS ONE?" I asked my mother. "'Am I, a gay male African-American, any less a person than our president-elect Bill Clinton? Is my good friend Julius, who lives under a bridge and goes through garbage to find food and also items he can sell to earn cash for the heroin that sustains him, any less a person than Bill Clinton? These are the questions we must answer for ourselves. If we are not less, should we let ourselves be so treated?' Old radical Cleve again."

My mother knitted her brow. "It *is* nice to hear someone angry. I'm tired of people being tired."

"Me too," I said, sitting up straighter. I was going to see Sally next month, a long weekend to greet Linnea (Linnea! Peter had picked the name), her new baby girl.

I KEPT BEN'S TOOTH in its little bag, tucked it in a cloisonné pillbox my brother Frank had bought me once for Christmas. I slipped the pillbox in a satin jewelry bag, which I kept in the back right corner of my underwear drawer. For months I didn't really think about it. I should have, I suppose. Out of respect for the dead.

LARRY COTTON DIED, his mother at his side. I never told anyone not to tell her his diagnosis, but there was a silent collusion, and the nurses—all the nurses, on all shifts—never used the words AIDS or HIV.

His mother asked me to the visitation. The line snaked out the funeral home door into the bare trees. Mr. Cotton had died in the prime of life. There were neighbors, teachers, old and current students, family friends. His mother introduced me to his high school girlfriend.

"Stay with me," Mrs. Cotton whispered, clutching my arm. "I may need a doctor."

Mr. Cotton's only sibling, a sister who kept twisting the strap of her purse, stood on my other side. She was a secretary, divorced and childless, at a private school for girls. "You were his doctor?" she said in a low voice. I nodded. "So you're a cancer specialist?"

"I'm not a specialist, I'm a general internist," I said, and she looked at me with pity and revulsion, as if I were less than she had thought.

Larry's accountant friend, looking spent, approached us in the line. "I was your brother's accountant," he said to the sister. "Larry spoke of you often." He glanced at me furtively, then seemed to gather strength: "He was a great friend to me."

The sister stared past the accountant at something across the room. "Oh," she said, "one of Larry's *friends.*" The accountant held out his hand, but she ignored it. I wondered which scared her more, his blackness or the fear he might be gay.

"You certainly were his friend, I don't know how he could have done his will without you," Larry's mother broke in. "Samantha, shake hands with Larry's nice accountant. What's your name? I'm afraid I've—"

The accountant, dropping his hand, mumbled a name. I tried to catch his eye, but he looked away, and his hiding from me—who knew everything—hit me as something sad.

"What's that again?" Mrs. Cotton asked, tapping her hearing aid. "I'm rather hard of hearing."

"Cleve Burton," the accountant said more loudly.

Cleve Burton. I knew that name. "Cleve Burton?" I said. "You're Cleve Burton? You're not the Cleve Burton who writes—?"

But he was moving past us. "I love to write," Cleve Burton whispered, touching the back of my forearm with his manicured hand. And he was gone.

"I VISIT EVERY DAY," Sally said. "I missed the day I had her"—Sally gestured at her new baby, nestled in a sling that hung across her chest—"but the next day I took her to meet Grandpa.

Didn't you meet Grandpa, little sweetums?" Linnea's tiny hand was gripping Sally's finger.

"Any responsiveness at all?"

Sally shook her head. "But I talk to him. Sometimes I hold his wrist to see if his pulse speeds up when he hears me, and you know, maybe it does." Linnea was tiny, only six pounds at two weeks, and if you didn't know there was a baby hiding in the sling, you might think Sally was a home-improvement salesperson carrying a sack of nails.

I stood up and walked over to the stovetop, lifted the lid on the pot. "What's this glop?"

"Tofu sauce." Peter had requested less meat in their diet.

"Is this what the guru eats?" The guru was my new name for Peter, who enjoyed his role as a media co-mogul and regaled me with a thousand reasons why Crown Communications was important to the world. He talked at times as if he ran it, which I knew wasn't at all true.

"New recipe," Sally said. "I don't know."

I turned away and paced to the paned windows overlooking the backyard. The shrubs and flowers were beautifully groomed, even in November; Sally and Peter had hired a gardener with their blue money.

"I've been thinking about something," Sally said. "It's not enough to say you're sorry. You have to make peace with the person you hurt. That's from the Kol Nidre service. Yom Kippur." She looked at me and added an explanation. "Yom Kippur. The Jewish Day of Atonement. Last month. I mean, I don't think there's anyone I've hurt directly who I need to atone to, but it's an interesting concept, don't you think? That atonement should be active."

I wasn't used to hearing about Jewish holidays from her. I didn't remember her observing any Jewish holidays back in college, except maybe a Passover dinner or two. "Are you getting religion all of a sudden?"

"Who knows?" Sally said.

I WENT OUT AGAIN after Christmas. It was only eight months after the L.A. riots, after the police were found not guilty of beating Rodney King, and I was thinking how I liked the upbeat signs in the airport—LET'S REBUILD L.A. TOGETHER!—and why didn't Sally pay attention to those signs, why did we always stay in the prosperous suburbs and never go, say, downtown?

She wanted to go to some mall, to a Disney store of all places—how consumerist—and of course I went along.

An ad on TV had started me worrying about college costs for Aury. How would I ever do it? For a doctor I didn't make much, and I was supporting my mother too. "I have almost no investments," I told Sally. "I have a pension fund at work that's invested in Akron Gas and Electric or something."

"It's probably in a mutual fund," Sally said. "Pensions don't usually invest in a single stock."

"Whatever. But I've been thinking, I need help. I mean, this is the nineties, even Frank's talking about stocks again, everybody's investing. Do you remember when those patients of mine got together and did my makeover? That was a great moment."

"It worked."

"Sure it did. Expert advice is helpful. So I've been thinking about my money, and I think I need expert advice."

"I can go over some things we're invested in," Sally said. "I'm certainly no expert, but..." The kids were lapping around her like waves against a boat; I found it hard to concentrate.

"I was thinking of an accountant," I said. "Don't you think I could use an accountant?"

EARLY IN THE MORNING, Sally stood in the kitchen with a robe on and a towel around her wet hair. "I need my list," she said. "Where's my list?"

Peter slapped a sheet of paper on the counter in front of her, her daily schedule, which Peter typed out each night on the computer. Really, the man tried. I had realized he was an overgrown boy: he wanted to please her.

I read the list over Sally's shoulder:

8:00: Ezra to preschool (permission slip Marine Museum field trip)
10:00: conference call with Celina and Jorge (Mexican Hot Tamales)
10:30: Malpezio depo
noon: preschool pickup; lunch with kids, Clare, and Sara
2:30: twins checkup Dr. Weisbrot
4:00: meet Ezra, Barbara, and Peter Discovery Zone
5:30: Bruno
7:30: Ezra's parent-teacher conference
Etc.: Derek's twins portfolio, call Kiki re: leather maid outfit, Rosa b-day present, broker re: Disney, Peter's shirts, letter re: Ursuline

"Wow," I said. "That's a day."

"That's not a day, it's my life," Sally said, annoyed. "I'm sure your life's just as hectic." She removed the towel and started combing out her hair with her fingers.

A small voice rose from the door. "Mommy, can I have some glue and the M&M's?"

Sally made a face, but her tone didn't show it. "Sure, Ezra. Here they are. What are you making? Another pirate ship?"

"When do you go to your office?" I said, reading over her schedule. I was disappointed to see Sara joining us for lunch.

"Every time not listed, I'm in my office."

"Who's Bruno?"

A small sob sounded through the baby monitor. "Uh-oh," Sally said. "Linnea's awake. Personal trainer," she added, answering my question.

"Mommy, where's my cereal?" Barbara demanded.

"Up," Joshua said beseechingly, his arms around Sally's leg.

"Where's Teresa? Is she sleeping late again? I don't believe this. She goes to bed hours before I do." Sally scooped up Joshua and opened the door to the basement level where Teresa lived. "Teresa! *Levántate! Por favor!*"

Linnea, her sobs ignored, started to wail.

"I'll bring her to you," Peter said.

"Oh, God, let me at least get my hair combed out before she gets here."

"Stop it, Barbara! Stop it!" A thud and a scream. "Mommy, Barbara's eating my M&M's!"

"Ezra, don't hit Barbara. Violence solves nothing. Nothing, do you hear? Barbara, those M&M's aren't for eating. They're for art."

Suddenly Sally was staring at me while her fingers explored her hair. "Which side do I part my hair on?"

"What?"

"Which side? I can't remember."

I couldn't remember either. "It's pretty much in the middle."

"Yes, but it's more to one side."

Peter rushed in with Linnea, her face almost purple with rage. Sally set Joshua on the floor, tossed herself in a kitchen chair, pulled open her robe, and stuck Linnea on her breast. "Peter, which side do I part my hair on?"

"Too much on your brain," I said to Sally.

"It's a wonder I'm not a raving lunatic," Sally said.

"Mommy, what's a—"

"Do you have that form for Dr. Weisbrot?" Sally asked Peter.

"Why not look at your driver's license?" Peter suggested.

The phone rang and Peter answered it.

Gabriel, who was pulling himself onto a kitchen chair, fell and knocked his head on the table.

"Can you FedEx out that Urseline letter this morning?" Peter shouted over Gabriel's screams.

"It's on the list, Peter."

"A little to the left," I said, finally locating the license in Sally's wallet.

"Okay. Come here, Gabey." With her free hand, Sally stroked and inspected his head. "Ouch! Linnea, don't bite me. This is ridiculous," she said, looking at me. "This is more than one person can stand."

I WAS WATCHING a stream of videos on the monitor over Virginia's shoulder. Rumps, breasts, penises, the old in and out, in umpteen variations. Of course, the door was closed. "Important thing is to keep things moving," Virginia said. "Can't have people lying there like logs."

"Don't you get tired of it?"

Virginia shrugged. "I can't even say they look like people to me anymore. I think of them like those little dolls you can bend all around, and they're stuck together in all these crazy ways. The only time I get confused is with some of the orgies."

I laughed. "What are the models like, do you meet them?"

Virginia considered. "The actors? They're a mixed bag. I don't deal with them."

"I've met Sara Tweedles," I said. "At Sally's play group."

Virginia's face lit up, her eyes still on the screen. "Sara? She's different, she's a crackerjack. Work, work, work, you don't often run into a work ethic like hers. And she's so clean. She's the top of our line."

"Sally says she's starting law school."

"Really? Good for her." I noticed a sudden hardness in the set of Virginia's jaw. She didn't look at me. "Bad for us, though," she said, punching a button that made the screen go blank. "I got those grandkids."

"YOU DON'T NEED ME." Cleve Burton shuffled some papers. "I'm an accountant. What you need is a financial planner."

"Really?" Even I could hear how crestfallen I sounded.

"Well, yes. I do cut-and-dried things, taxes, pro formas. I'm not a visionary."

"Not in this part of your life," I muttered. And then I burst out with a speech that surprised me, how I didn't have anyone else to go to; how my mother, who I'd thought was a good investor, lost her money; how none of my brothers had any money sense—Frank having lost his thousands on margin calls, Baxter with his odd jobs barely making his pickup payments, not to mention Eric and his bankruptcies. How my best friend was in the adult entertainment business with plenty of money but God knows what she invested in, and I wanted to be socially responsible, at least minimally. How I was a single mom with a bright young daughter who'd probably want to go to an expensive college like I did and I didn't have anything saved, not a penny, even though I made a lot of money by normal—if not by doctor—standards. "But I don't know how to start investing!" I finished. " And then I thought of you, and it seemed exactly right because I know you're, I know you're—"

He looked up at me, bluish circles in the dark skin under his eyes. "Gay," I swore he was thinking, and this pained me.

"Trustworthy," I finished. "You're incredibly trustworthy. You're like this hero to me."

I don't know how I, Clare Ann Mann of Akron, Ohio, ended up talking California-ese. I do it more than Sally, a California native. "Like this hero to me"—I winced at my own words. But my way of saying it was typical for me; imprecise, distanced, mildly ironic. Skirting the emotion rather than embracing it.

"You're my hero," I said.

He looked up at me and blinked, clearly startled, mistrusting. I could see him searching my face for a clue to my intentions, and I looked back as steadily as I could. Trust me, I felt myself pleading.

"Why your hero?" he asked.

"Everything you've done for the gay community. The alarms you've sounded. The free-needle program you started. The outrageousness of your column. Your anger! And then you were kind to Mr. Cotton. And not just to him, to his mother, his sister, all of them. And even though I'm sure it cost you, you never let it show."

The accountant's eyes slipped from my face and focused somewhere in the middle distance. "It did cost me," he said.

"I could tell. But you never wavered."

"I did waver."

"Not when it mattered."

"No." We sat in silence a moment, me watching Cleve Burton, Cleve Burton looking away. When his eyes met mine, he made the obvious statement: "I loved him."

I nodded.

"We were very . . . anachronistic. The love that dared not speak its name. That was something he felt strongly about, with his job at the school, with his family and the way they—" Cleve Burton waved his hand. "It's not an issue for me, everyone in this office knows, everyone in this city knows, but Larry was extremely private. I believe that's the right word. I don't think he was ashamed. He felt deeply that there were some things other people didn't need to know. And for me, telling people about us was never an issue. I did what he wanted to the end." Cleve Burton gave a quiet smile. "And beyond."

I wondered then, as I often had, about Mr. Cotton's will, if Cleve Burton had gotten any remembrance. Cleve held out his wrist. "Larry's watch."

When I'm "on," when I'm right there with my patients, I do have a kind of telepathy. I've noticed that. Cleve seemed to have no regrets, and as I thought this, he spoke again.

"You do what you think is kindest. That's what you do for love. Willingly, I guess. Happily."

"You could teach me a lesson about that." I thought of Ben's tooth. Why did I keep it?

Cleve smiled. "Look, my good doctor, I'm not a certified financial planner, but I could probably help you with your stocks. Personally, as much as I hate drug companies, I have to admire Merck. Rubbermaid's a nice stock too, and there's a little company called Filenet, have you heard?"

BARBARA KNOCKED ON MY bedroom door and brought a book to show me, a picture book about cats. It was January, and she was wearing her favorite outfit, an iridescent swimsuit with high-cut legs and crisscross straps in the back. You could tell someday she'd be a knockout. All of Sally and Peter's children were beautiful, with tousled gold-brown hair and glowing round faces. They were the sort of children older couples stepped aside for and watched, smiling, as they passed. Barbara sat Indian-style on the floor and showed me the Manx cat, the tortoiseshell cat, and her favorite, the Persian. "Look at this booful kitty," she said, stroking the fur in the picture. A lovely girl, named for her dead uncle. Nearly three years old. The pornographer's daughter.

I didn't want to take Aury out there. I didn't want her in a house with an upstairs door that was always shut, where she might drink tea at a play group with the polite daughters of Sara, the Countess of Come.

"I've made a decision," Sally said on my last night there, when the kids and Peter were all at last in bed. "I'm selling out."

My heart leapt. It's a funny sensation, and I've always been skeptical of that description, but there it was: my heart leapt. I was stretched out on the Oriental rug in the family room next to the kitchen, and Sally was collapsed on the sofa.

"Really, Sally? That's wonderful. I know you'll never regret it."

"I know I won't. I talked to all the partners today, and it's no problem."

"Partners? I didn't know you had partners."

We looked at each other, confused. "Oh," I said. "You're selling out your law firm."

Sally gave me a rueful look. "Clare. You know I don't have a decent buyer for Crown."

"I was hoping..."

"It's noise, Clare. Crown is noise." I lifted my head inquiringly. "Daddy and I were sitting out there"—Sally pointed toward the kitchen and the kitchen table—"and it was maybe his best day, I mean the day he seemed to remember, and he said that what can break your heart is the shape of someone's life. And he said Ben's life was like this"—she made a swooping downward gesture—"and my life should be this"—predictably, a gesture up—"and his life was more bumpy"—a sine wave—"but it ended here"—she dropped her hand to the floor. "But you, he said, meaning me, you lift me up." She lifted her hand a couple inches above the floor. "Only that high," Sally said, looking at me. "All I did, and I only lifted him that high."

"I'm sorry."

She nodded, stared off into space, as if piecing together something. "Oh, and noise. He said that night that life was basically two things, secrets and noise, and the secrets were all that mattered, because the rest was—"

"Noise," I finished.

"Exactly."

She didn't say "eyactly," I didn't say "amaying."

"So Crown is noise," Sally said. She raised her eyebrows assertively. "It is."

I felt my eyes fill with tears. I'm losing you, Sally, I thought. I come all the way to California to lose you. "Not noise to me," I said in a small voice.

AS TED TELLS IT, he was dropping off the eldest of his three daughters at a hotel baby-sitting room before a medical conference in March 1993 when he was startled to see another young girl who resembled her. In fact, the similarities between the two girls—one six, one almost five—were so great that one of the sitters asked Ted if they were twins. Ted asked the six-year-old her name and was surprised to find she shared a last name with his ex-wife, also a doctor. Is your mother Clare Mann? he asked the young girl. Yes, the girl said, and she and her mother lived in Akron, Ohio. Ted quickly realized I must be a conference attendee too. It took him several more minutes to realize, on an elevator heading to the venue, that the young girl he'd just spoken to was his daughter.

We'd split up at least partly over not getting pregnant. We'd slept together once after the divorce, and Ted had heard I'd eventually had a baby on my own, but he never, given our infertile years together, thought to wonder if my baby might be his. I'd thought it. I believed it was actually likely, but letting Ted know was nothing I cared to pursue. He was married. He had a new life, his own children.

I was in the hotel conference room seated at a chair behind a long table, surrounded by two hundred doctors; the lights were off, slides were on, and the speaker was droning on about osteoporosis. I was falling asleep, thinking, Lord, nothing in AIDS is this boring, when there was a tap on my back. I thought I must have started to snore. "Thank you," I said automatically, sitting up and half waving behind me.

There was another tap. A little irked, I swiveled around. It was dim, and I couldn't make him out right away. He was leaning over the table behind me, between two older doctors who were eyeing him with annoyance. "Ted," I said.

I knew immediately. "I have to talk with you," he whispered urgently. I nodded and gathered up my papers and followed him out mutely, past the rows and rows of chairs and tables and all the doctors who glanced up without the slightest interest, assuming I'd been paged.

"Why didn't you tell me?" Ted burst out when we got to light.

We were standing in an atrium, an outsize flower arrangement erupting from the table beside us, a green and peach carpet under our feet. I remember that carpet so clearly, and a strange flower that looked almost like a pink pineapple, with hairy brown bands separating each petal.

"Tell you what?"

He told me.

I wanted to touch that flower. I was trying to figure out if the hairy bands were stiff or soft. "So?" I said.

"She looks like my daughter, Clare. Your daughter, Aurelia, looks like me."

He'd gotten grayer and paunchier, yet the whole effect of him was sleeker than I remembered. I realized he was dressing better. He wore pressed trousers and a jacket, an outfit he might have worn to a wedding, not to a conference, in the years we were together. He still had that tremor in his right hand; he seemed to see my glance and dropped his hand to clutch the side of the table.

"Don't tell me you haven't noticed," he said.

I couldn't speak.

"Are you married?" I shook my head no. "Are you seeing some-one?" No again. "Are you raising her all by yourself?"

I found my voice. "My mother helps," I said. "She lives with us." My eyes met his, challenging.

"You hated your mother!" Ted seemed on the cusp of either laugh-ter or tears, I couldn't tell which.

"She's not so bad," I said quickly. "We've accommodated."

Ted pressed his lips together. His question, when it came, was less a demand than a plea: "Is she mine?"

Oh, the confusion. The green and peach carpet and the flowers; the air and the chandelier; and Ted's hand, with its graying hairs, gripping the table. If his voice had been less soft, if he'd sounded angry, if he hadn't been so kind. But he was kind. He reminded me, as he always did, of my father.

"Probably," I said. "You'd have to get genetic testing to be sure, but..." I waved my hand at Ted's hand. "She has your tremor."

We walked together to the baby-sitting area to pick up our chil-dren. "How did you end up at a primary care conference?" I asked. "You're a gastroenterologist."

"We're getting so much managed care that we're starting to worry about losing referrals. My gastroenterology group thought someone should come here to scope out the primary care scene. Find out how primary care doctors think. How about you?"

"I'm getting updated. Pressure from above. I think the hospital wants me to see some primary care patients on top of people with AIDS. I'm resisting it, though."

"You can't resist forever, not these days."

We sounded so normal. We sounded like old acquaintances chat-ting in a businesslike way. Who would have guessed at the web be-tween us.

Aury was the only child left in the baby-sitting area. Ted and I chased the sitter away. "Aurelia," Ted said. She was sitting at a table drawing—a table she'd shared (although I didn't know this) with her three half sisters until their mother came to pick them up. Aury glanced inquiringly at me. I suppose I looked stricken, my face red and my fists clenched, and for this reason, Aury told me later, she thought Ted was a policeman and I'd been arrested and was going to be taken away.

Ted reached his big shaking hand over the table to pat Aury's hair. "I have three other little girls," he said, and Aury thought if he wasn't a policeman, he must be a child snatcher come to snatch her.

"Aurelia," I said, addressing her in a quavery voice, "this is your father."

She thought I was teasing. "I don't have a father," Aury said quickly.

It broke my heart. "Yes, you do," I said. "You have a father, and this is him."

"You mean this is he," Aury said.

Where did she learn grammar? I laughed in astonishment, a whooping and out-of-control sound. Ted started laughing too. "Yes," I said, "this is he."

Ted left Aury and me at the day care, tracked his family to a fancy toy store, and that evening told Mary, his wife. The next day we adults planned a lunch, right there in St. Louis, our four girls left together—this time as sisters—in the hotel baby-sitting room.

"You know the male determines the sex," I said to Mary, to say something.

"Pardon?"

"The father. The father determines the sex of the child. He puts in the X or the Y chromosome. And a girl, you know, a girl's XX while a boy's XY. So I guess Ted's really shooting X's. With four daughters, I mean."

"It's okay," Ted said, shifting his glass of water on the table, "I warned Mary about your sense of humor."

"At least he's not shooting blanks!" I regretted this the instant I said it.

"No," Mary said, "certainly not." She was tall, elegant, composed, immaculately dressed. In California I felt stylish; here I felt outlandish, overdone. A patient who had seen me in my current outfit—a scoop-necked blouse with bright stripes, bead earrings, and black pants—had asked if I was going to a fiesta.

"To be honest," I said, thinking I must be truthful, "I'm almost sorry for Ted's sake that I didn't have a boy. But being a single mother the way I have been, it's good I had a girl, because I haven't had to deal with the male role model issue. At least that's what my mother tells me."

"Yes," Mary said. I had the sensation of a door clicking shut. "Ted tells me you're a doctor for people with AIDS?"

I nodded.

"How admirable. That must be quite stressful."

"Oh, I love it. The people are great, and I like people with a real disease."

Ted touched Mary's hand. "Clare was always the hardest-driving resident in our group. She needs a challenge."

"It's neat, working with people who are sick," I said. "They don't sweat the small stuff. People can adapt to almost anything. What do you do, Mary?"

"Mary has a business she runs out of the home," Ted said. "And our daughters keep her hopping."

"Really?" I asked. "You have a business in your home? Computers or something?"

"Actually, I design and publish macramé patterns."

"How interesting!" I couldn't think of a thing to say about macramé. I barely remembered what it was. "You know," I finally managed, "a lot of my patients are in the arts."

"So I'd imagine," Mary said, casting an eye over my clothes.

—"I'M NOT THAT FAR AWAY. We're in eastern Pennsylvania, and you two live just west of Pennsylvania."

—"Of course I'll acknowledge her. Of course she's mine."

—"I'll help support her; do you need help? At least a fund for college."

—"I want to see her, I want to be with her."

—"I want her to know her sisters."

—"I don't in any way want this to make your or Aurelia's life worse. I want this to make your life better."

"HOW'S SALLY?" TED ASKED.

I opened my mouth and closed it. How could I explain the deaths, the disarray? Ted and I were alone, which relieved me, but still I worried about what I'd say. "She's okay, I guess, but she's had some rough years. Her mother was killed in a car crash and then her brother, Ben—you know he always had a drug problem—he died, and then her father ended up with Alzheimer's, and now he's in a persistent vegetative state. They did a PET scan on him," I added uselessly.

"Clare, that's tragic," Ted sounded shocked. He shook his head. "Poor Sally."

"So now she's running her father's pornography business."

"Sally a pornographer?" Ted shook his head. "How bizarre. Well, at least it's an honest business. It's not Murder, Inc., or something."

"As a woman, I find it very hard to see Sally running that business." Ted shrugged. "I'm sure she isn't happy about it either."

"She even retired from her law firm."

"Really? I thought she was married to that firm."

"Not now. Now she's married to a man named Peter Newcomer. They have five children."

"Five!"

"Sally just had another baby, a girl. Linnea."

"And her husband?"

"He doesn't work. He's California." With a pang of guilt, I remembered Peter's carefully typed-out schedules. "He tries, he really does."

"How did Sally's brother die, did he overdose?"

I hesitated. "Probably suicide."

Ted shook his head in silence. "I'm sure you've been a big help to her," he said after a moment. "You two were always joined at the hip."

"We're two thousand miles apart."

"Still."

"I see her pretty often. I go out there. It's weird, with all she's been through, but we don't talk about anything of substance. We just sort of...chatter."

"You know each other so well, you don't need substance."

Is that true? I wondered. But Ted said it with such certainty, as if I'd never think to disagree.

"ARE YOU SITTING DOWN?" I said. "I'm at this conference in St. Louis with Aury, and I ran into Aury's father."

"You mean Ted?" Sally said.

She'd known for years, she said. Aury looked like Ted. But she'd never asked me about it because I'd never mentioned it to her.

"And besides," Sally went on, "she has Ted's tremor."

WE PARTED ON A Friday after a big communal breakfast. Ted and Mary's girls, resplendent in dresses and hair bows Mary had made herself, clustered like gaudy stars around my daughter. "You call us on the phone, Aurelia, okay?" the oldest said, arms around my daughter's waist. "You come see us."

"You can play with Malibu Barbie and everything," a younger voice chimed in.

Aury nodded solemnly and looked at me. "Sure, you'll visit," I said.

The little girls wanted to kiss Aury on the cheek, but she wrinkled her face up and stuck her chin down in her chest.

"Aury, Aury," I said. "Let your sisters kiss you! You'll hurt their feelings." I glanced at Mary to see how she was taking this, but from her perfect hair to her buckled pumps, she was politely, firmly opaque.

The daughter of two alcoholics, Ted had told me. As a little girl, she had raised her own little sisters.

"It's okay, Aury," Ted interrupted. "You don't have to let them slobber all over you." He crouched down in front of my daughter. "They're kissers," he said. "Can you stand it?"

Aury studied him with her big brown eyes, her tight brow relaxing. She had Ted's droop at the edge of her eyes. "I like you," she said. "You're my nice daddy."

I had never—until I saw Ted, until he asked me—planned for Aury to know, or for him to know. I had done my best not to know myself. And now both of them knew, as well as Ted's "real" family, and they were making plans together. Already, three days after becoming aware of each other, my daughter and her father had a relationship independent of me. A week ago, I was worrying over whether to bring Aury's winter coat to the conference. Now that memory bespoke such stunning triviality that the winter coat itself (which I had brought, and she hadn't used) seemed to be bursting in the air above us, its down feathers drifting over us like snow or wedding rice, or the confetti that rains down on a cavalcade of heroes.

THERE WAS SOMETHING WRONG with Ben's tooth. It wasn't a normal tooth. Aury's teeth, when I retrieved them from under her pillow, had tiny tubes running into them where the blood vessels and nerves had coursed, but Ben's tooth had no tube at all. It wasn't intact; it was a fragment of a tooth, and why it was a fragment was either a mystery or a proof.

I would take out the tooth —untying the satin jewelry bag, unsnapping the pillbox, unzipping the plastic bag—and lay it on my palm. I held it up to the light, rubbed it between my fingers, even touched it to my tongue to check its texture. One sharp edge and no tube. Something had happened. Maybe exactly what Sid told me.

I should tell her. I should give her the possibilities. I should break through her moral oblivion.

I'm tired of the young.

I supposed she could get a tooth forensically and genetically tested, if she wanted to take it that far.

TED AND I STOOD in line at a Burger King in western Pennsylvania, exchanging Aury, the girls in a gaggle behind us comparing Barbie clothes. "Ted, you're rational," I said. "Can I ask your advice? If you knew an awful secret about someone that a friend of yours loved, would you tell your friend? Aury'll have a fish sandwich and fries and a milk. She finds the kids' toys insulting."

"What's the point?"

"The point is because it's true, because this person is an adult and deserves to know, even if it's painful. Because otherwise they may think of the world, I don't know, in a wrong sort of way."

"Go ahead, girls, you sit down. Daddy'll order for you. Clare, are you trying to tell me something?"

"Well, not in a wrong sort of way, exactly. An inaccurate way."

"What are you talking about? Just come out and tell me."

"I worry about this all the time."

"Just tell me." Desperation in his voice. "Tell me. Don't keep me in the dark about anything else. Did you have an abortion back when we were married? Did you have a miscarriage? Did you have an affair with someone? Clare, I can handle it. Look at me! I can handle anything. Please tell me. Please, Clare, don't torment me any more."

"It's Sally," I said quietly. "I'm talking about me and Sally."

"Oh," Ted said, embarrassed, both of us understanding what his outburst had revealed. The guy still loved me. Still. After all these years.

"HOW OFTEN WILL AURY visit them?" Sally asked over the phone.

"A weekend every month or two. Ted wants it to be when he's free. He's incredibly busy, he has lots of weekend calls, plus he goes off and speaks at seminars. He's an expert on the esophagus. He calls it his ten inches of fame."

"Is meeting him awkward?"

"A little. I'm grateful his wife doesn't come."

"What a bizarre situation," Sally said, and I was pleased, somehow, that Sally thought the word "bizarre" fit a situation of mine. "What about his mother?"

"Oh! She moved. When Ted went off to Baltimore, she and her husband realized they should let Ted be independent and they moved to Texas. Ted sees them maybe four times a year. It sounds like a normal relationship now."

"She made the ultimate sacrifice," Sally said, and her voice had a wistful quality. "She let him go."

JOSHUA TODDLED UP to Sally in their kitchen, holding a cloth diaper which he, with some fanfare, draped over his head. "Is Joshua hiding?" Sally asked. Joshua's diaper nodded. "Where's Joshua?" Sally asked. And to me: "Have you seen Joshua?" She walked a few steps away. "Joshua! Joshua!"

Joshua whipped off the diaper and stood beaming at his mother. "Oh, lovie," Sally said, stroking his cheek with her hand. She glanced at me. "I love these kids more than life itself. I can't believe how much I love them."

"All of them?" I heard myself yelp. Because that had been Sid's flaw: he'd loved his daughter more.

Sally looked at me in astonishment, then—to my horror—understanding flooded her face. "Oh, you don't love them any less when you have more. I forget that you only have one. But trust me, if Aury had a sister, you wouldn't love Aury less."

"No," I said, flustered, feeling unaccountably guilty. "I'm sure I wouldn't."

"YOU TALK TO THE BANK?" Virginia asked. We were in the upstairs room. I had brought a gift from Ohio, a box of chocolates, and Sally was lifting the lid.

"Not yet. I wanted to talk with the Compunox people first." Sally glanced at me. "Virginia thinks we should expand onto the World Wide Web."

"It's not all my idea. Buck thinks so too."

"Is Buck out?" I asked.

Sally nodded, biting into a chocolate. "Did Daddy have to go to the bank when you expanded into videos?" Sally asked. "Was that capital-intensive at all?" She turned to me. "This could actually be fairly cheap. But we'll need a partner with computer know-how."

"How about Peter?"

Sally gave a tight smile. "Way beyond him. Don't quote me."

What would it be like, I wondered, to sleep with a man you didn't respect? I felt a surge of pity for Peter.

"Your dad get over that urinary tract infection?" Virginia asked.

"He's much better. No fever. You should visit him, Virginia. It's a nice facility."

"The aides all wear dresses," I put in.

Virginia gave a little shiver. "It's like I said, I don't need to see him drooling."

"It's like I said," Sally noted, "you're lucky you don't have to." When she picked up a sheaf of papers, I noticed her hands shaking. "You only worked with him for thirty-five years, Virginia."

There was a knock on the door. "Mommy?" said Ezra's voice. "Linnea's not breathing." Sally tore out into the hall, slamming the door behind her. Virginia and I looked at each other. Both of us were sure Linnea was fine. Ezra had a low threshold for alarms.

"It didn't happen overnight, you know," Virginia said. "He hasn't been right for years." Her voice dropped; she seemed to be studying the side of my head. "I could tell you things about Sid and his family that would curl your hair."

I smiled at her and shrugged, as if that were just the sort of ridiculous inflammatory thing Virginia would say. "Care for an Ohio buckeye?" I asked, holding out the box of chocolates.

"SHE SEEMS," TED SAID, "I don't know, a lot deeper than my girls. Little Stephanie was talking about some kid at school who wears a hearing aid, and Aury said, 'Stephanie, everybody has their own problems. Everybody is different, and there's nothing wrong with that.'" We were standing outside the Route 10 rest area just east of the Ohio-Pennsylvania border, while Aury, whom we were passing from one car to the other, used the bathroom. After our mutual revelation, we didn't meet at the Burger King again—that would have been too intimate.

"When you work in AIDS, you tend to stress the tolerance angle."

"It wasn't tolerance, it was empathy. How do you teach a kid empathy? Come up to Cleveland and meet me for lunch next month," Ted urged. "I'm speaking at a seminar there."

"Your ten inches?"

He seemed to blush, and then I blushed too.

"We need to make plans for August," Ted said.

"August?"

"Mary and I would like to take Aury with us to our place in Colorado. For a week, maybe, not long. If you'll let us."

I drove to Cleveland the next month, June, and ended up sitting in the dining room—a very spiffy dining room, with cloth tablecloths and big windows and a city view—at the Ritz-Carlton Hotel, as Ted, post-speech, told me the details of his Colorado time-share.

"So you want to time-share Aury at your time-share," I said, relieved that he and Mary didn't have a whole Colorado house, which would have been unacceptable extravagance, really, on top of his cream-colored shirt and elegant olive jacket and buffed brown shoes with tassels. ("Hey," Ted had said when I commented on his outfit, "speakers have a standard to uphold.")

Ted grinned. "Exactly. We'll time-share her. She and her sisters get along really well. Does she talk to you about them at all?"

"Of course. She likes visiting you. She gets home and goes up to her room and sleeps for three hours. I think you guys are a bit overwhelming."

"It's 'you girls.' I certainly don't overwhelm her. She ignores me."

I rolled my eyes. "Me too."

"I read somewhere that the strongest predictor of a child's intelligence was the intelligence of the mother," Ted said.

"But I don't do that much with her. Really, I don't." I felt almost desperate, wanting Ted to understand. I wasn't much of a mother. At some point, I was sure, Aury would slip and let her father know how few hours she saw me each day, how much time she spent with my mother or at school or with Brittany from next door, how often I slipped away to California. "Aurelia just kind of . . . made herself. She's a self-made girl."

"Oh, Clare," Ted said, shaking his head, "you can never take a compliment." He looked at me across the table with exasperation, a sliver of cream shirt peeking from his sleeve. I remembered Ted when he wore flannel shirts with frayed cuffs and underwear left over from high school. There'd been worn spots in the seats of his briefs.

"I love compliments," I said, honestly. "I'm a glutton for compliments."

"You're amazing."

I made a puzzled face and glanced around us, as if he must be talking to someone else. "Moi?"

Ted grinned again. "Wait a minute, too direct. Wrong tack." He cleared his throat and spoke in an television anchorman's voice. "Your hair's different, Clare. Are you dyeing it?" He was leaning backward now, the glass of wine trembling slightly in his hand.

"I dye it darker and I streak it. I had a makeover, years ago, from some of my patients." I reached for my glass of wine and tried to pick it up calmly, but I was shaking myself. "Dead, all of them. But the makeover lives on."

"Clare, how do you stand it?"

A moment or two passed, and still Ted watched me. "Your tremor's less," I blurted.

"Inderal." A drug you could take for a tremor.

He wanted to say, then, "I love you." I could sense it, I knew it was on his mind. And I would have said it back if he had said it first, so it was our collusion at the end of the meal when he rested his shaking hand on the small of my back and guided me to his room.

"SHE'S STEALING," Sally said. "It's not even very subtle. I mean, it's clever but not brilliant."

The bank man had picked it up. "Are you shipping to Juarez now?" he'd asked Sally, because he went down there sometimes for fun, and he'd seen a bunch of Crown magazines in a shop.

"We don't ship to Juarez, do we?" Sally asked Virginia.

Oh no, Virginia said. Not for years. Maybe resale, she suggested. A garage sale for magazines. Those Mexicans can be thrifty.

But no, the bank man said, these magazines looked fresh. He was picky that way; he wouldn't buy anything used.

"Magazines in Spanish?" I asked, and Sally gave me a incredulous look.

"See, she takes the magazines that don't sell—I mean her son takes them, he's in the warehouse—and she sells them to her outlets. In the meantime, she's credited the legitimate stores for returning their un-sold copies. It's like she's stealing from us twice: she's crediting stores for merchandise we never got back and she's taking that merchandise and selling it herself."

I shook my head, trying to understand it. "It is clever," I said.

"It's not brilliant. I figured it out myself, after the bank guy men-tioned it. I've talked to about thirty stores. The son's involved, of course, and Buck may be involved too."

"It's what my father did," I said. "He embezzled." Bigger shrimp. An extra fifty dollars for clothes. I had never even thought about the mechanics of it. How had he managed it? What tiny mistake had tipped the doctors off?

Sally smiled sadly. "Oh, Clare. Your father was a mini-embezzler. Not like her."

"How much are we talking about?"

"Real money."

"Why?" I asked.

"Why? I don't care why. She's stealing, Clare," Sally's voice rose. "Stealing is wrong. We have to be very careful with her. We can't let her get an inkling that we know."

OH, HE HAD CHANGED.

Of course, maybe I'd changed too.

"After all these years," Ted said, stroking my shoulder. "All these years and it's better than it ever was."

The hair on his chest bristled against my cheek. He had a wonderful new smell, a piney smell, and it didn't matter that it was surely a cologne his wife had chosen.

"VIRGINIA!" I closed the door behind me. "How are you? How are the grandkids?"

Everyone was fine. She and her daughters and grandkids were planning a cruise to Alaska. She'd been saving up for years. The only one who couldn't go was her son, because he was on probation (she didn't say what for) and couldn't leave the state, but that was okay because he was the one who got seasick.

I sat down in a chair beside her. "How's business?"

"Same old, same old."

"You don't mind driving down here every day?"

"How could I? I want to help Sally out. I know what it's like being a working mother."

"Nice of you." I looked at her guilty profile.

WHAT CAN I SAY? We loved each other. We loved each other happily and well.

We left Ted's room that evening and drove out to dinner in the Flats, an area of restaurants and nightclubs by the Cuyahoga River, and ate in a big loud seafood restaurant. We weren't loud. We sat at our table and smiled at each other—loving smiles, sheepish smiles, I-can't-believe-we-did-that smiles. When I reached for the salt, Ted reached across the table, and I left my hand on the salt shaker as his fingers explored mine. His tremor was gone.

"YEAH, IT'S STILL OKAY," I told Sally. "We chat some. We're polite."

Sally shook her head. "Milk? Your flavored cream?" I visited Los Angeles that summer while Aury was in Colorado, leaving Ohio a day early so my mother would take Aury to the airport to meet Ted and Mary and their daughters.

"No thanks, I'm drinking black now."

Cheerios, crushed and intact, scattered across the floor, the refrigerator door open, the twins in shirts and diapers walking on tiptoe carrying full cups of milk, baby Linnea seated on the floor chewing a sky-blue Ferragamo pump, a message on the answering machine from a La Vonda about having the photos once they'd found the right harnesses, the sucking alarm sound from Peter's computer, a noise he'd created himself: in Ohio, I missed this familiar chaos.

"You should bring Aury next time," Sally said, handing me my mug of black coffee. "I miss Aury."

"Maybe I'll bring her."

"I talked to the prosecutor's office," she said. "Monday. You'll be here."

THE PLANNING WAS ELABORATE. Virginia had been secretly indicted by a grand jury (Sally's legal connections helped her make the case), and the local police agreed to arrest her at Sally's home between nine-thirty and eleven A.M. on Monday. The police needed the early morning for speeders and the later morning for lunch; Virginia's own home was in a different jurisdiction.

Virginia arrived for work Monday through Friday by eight-thirty, so having her at Sally's was no problem. She'd be in the upstairs office with the door closed, overlooking the backyard and the glass roof of the solarium; the police would park in the driveway; the doorbell would ring, which Sally would get up and answer, and the police (who'd be polite, who understood this was an older woman and white-collar crime) would come up the stairs and arrest Virginia. Sally didn't think she'd fight; underneath it all, Virginia had morals, and Sally imagined she'd be like a child caught in some misdeed, distressed but secretly relieved.

The kids were going out with Peter and Teresa and wouldn't be back till noon. It was quite a feat to get them all dressed and out by nine A.M., but Peter and Teresa did it. Virginia arrived on time and entered, as she always did, through the back door into the kitchen, a Styrofoam cup of coffee in one hand and her sack lunch in the other. As she put her lunch in the fridge, she had to make her way through the kids: Linnea in a car seat, the twins pushing at each other and making unintelligible noises, Barbara in a dress, crown, and sparkly shoes, and Ezra barking worried commands at them all. "They clearing out?" Virginia asked, looking relieved.

"Toy train festival," Sally explained (this was true), and Virginia nodded and headed for the front foyer and the stairs.

The three of us trooped up to the room with the closed door. I read some magazines, Virginia logged on to her computer and keyed things in, and Sally kept herself busy reviewing a ridiculous cartoon strip in which women's waists were barely bigger than their necks and men's penises hung down past their knees. I was glad not to be looking over Virginia's shoulder: since Ted was back, the sight of naked people did not leave me unmoved.

At nine Sally went to the kitchen and made a pot of coffee, bringing me and Virginia two big mugs. "I wonder how Monica Seles is doing," Virginia said. "I miss her. Can you imagine? Stabbed in the back. Sheesh."

At ten Sally asked Virginia if there was something else she could review. "I'm done with this strip," she said. "It's just juvenile."

"People like it," Virginia said. "I mean, men people."

"That's interesting you say that," I said. "Isn't your market pretty exclusively male?"

"Not anymore," Virginia said, and she launched into an explanation of the lesbian market, the lusty hetero market, and the women who wanted magazines like romance novels with pictures.

At eleven Sally cracked the door open—"to get some air"—but really, I knew, to be sure she heard the doorbell.

By eleven-thirty Sally was sweating. There were streaks on the fabric under her arms. "I'm getting hungry," Virginia said. "I don't know about you, but I'm getting through these *Balls Almighty* numbers, and then I'm going to eat."

"Me too," Sally said quickly. "Let me run down and start heating some soup."

"Soup in the summer?" Virginia said.

"In an air-conditioned house, it doesn't matter." Sally disappeared downstairs.

At about noon Virginia yawned and stood up. "That's a wrap, kid," she said, and headed downstairs. She always ate her lunch at the house, either in the kitchen or outside at the patio table. It was staggering to think that a woman who functioned on such intimate terms with her employer was capable of stealing her money.

Virginia's lunch was a peanut butter and jelly sandwich (one of the pieces of bread was the heel), carrot sticks, an apple, and a soda from Sally's fridge. She laid out her lunch on the big kitchen table and ate it with deliberation. I began to feel sorry for her. It seemed cruel that a person eating such a modest lunch was about to be arrested. Sally wasn't sure that Buck—whom she would certainly call—would be able to make bail. "Nice and quiet here today," Virginia said. "Bet the munchkins like those trains."

"Any word?" I whispered to Sally.

"The dispatcher says they're coming."

Sally had heated up the soup but wasn't eating, and when I asked for some, she plunked the pot in front of me and waved at the bowls and ladle.

A car door slammed, then another, then—after an excruciating pause—a third, which meant that Peter and Teresa were in the garage unloading the van. Sally went out the door to the garage, waving desperately at Peter, but it was too late: the kids were at the door.

"What the—" Peter said, noticing Virginia.

"We're eating lunch!" Sally said, her voice pitched high. "Just a normal Monday."

Virginia was picking up her things. "I'll move outside, leave you guys room."

"No!" Sally said, and I wondered how she'd try to make this command sound normal. "It's too hot out. How were the trains, Ezra?"

"Barbara got to ride three times," Ezra complained.

The doorbell rang. Peter and Sally exchanged a quick glance, and Peter went to the front door.

The policemen did not look like those in Ohio: the female was Hispanic and the male was Asian. "You're Virginia Luby?" the Hispanic policewoman said. "We have a warrant for your arrest for grand larceny. We're here to take you to the station."

"What is this?" Virginia said, twisting in her chair to look at all the adult faces. To me she seemed to say: "You knew?" She ended up fixing her eyes on Teresa, and seemed to be sending a warning.

"I'm not going," she finally said.

"You can finish your lunch," the policeman said in a reasonable way. He pulled out a chair and sat across from her. "We'll just wait."

"Mommy, is that a policeman? Why are there policemen here? Is that woman a policeman too?"

"Let's go upstairs," Peter said. "Come on, Ezra. This is boring stuff. Let's go read *Peter Rabbit.*"

"You telling me this is my last meal?" Virginia said, setting down her sandwich. "You planning to execute me or something?"

"Oh no, no." The policeman smiled.

"What the hell for? You're going to execute me and what the hell for?"

"Mommy, she said a bad word." Barbara this time.

"Will you get them out of here, Peter? Take them upstairs. Just get them out!" Sally said. Teresa was already scampering toward the stairs, carrying Linnea in her car seat.

"You don't think I'm owed something?" Virginia turned on Sally. "Thirty-five years with that man, and you know what? He ruined my life! When I met him, I was a clerk in a drugstore, and he came in and asked me if I wanted to be a secretary. I thought it was a step up. I thought I'd never have to do stocking. I thought I'd do typing or something. I thought I'd answer the phone!" She turned to the policeman. "You know what she does? You know about her family business? Oh I know she looks all nicey-nice, but you know what she does? She's a pornographer! She's got computers upstairs filled with two thousand naked people. Doing everything you can think of. Things you couldn't think of! What do you think of that?"

"Adult entertainment," Sally said in a small voice. "It's adult entertainment."

The policeman glanced at Sally, then dropped his eyes quickly.

"Peter," Sally repeated lowly. "Please get the kids out."

"I went to Catholic schools!" Virginia burst out.

The policewoman seemed to wince, then she, too, looked at Sally.

"Catholic schools with nuns!" Sally had gone to Catholic schools too.

Teresa reappeared behind Peter and tried to grab the twins. One of them ran into the family room, and Teresa followed. Peter scooped up the other one.

"We understand this is a shock to you," the policeman said. "Come with us to the station, and this will all go nice and easy."

Virginia stared at the policeman. "I know things that could curl your hair." Her voice rose. "I didn't take anything I wasn't owed ten times over!"

I thought of her standing in the drugstore, wearing one of those smocks like the drugstore ladies of my childhood used to wear, and I understood that her words had been exactly true: to become a secretary would have been a step up. I thought of my father, his pride in working for doctors, his shabby suits, the doctor's wife who criticized his clothes. What had he ever given his employers but time and respect? And he didn't even earn enough to dress himself properly.

"My father was an embezzler," I said, leaning toward Virginia. "I understand." I knew that saying this betrayed Sally, but out of human decency, I had to let Virginia know.

"Understand?" Virginia hissed at me. "Understand? You'll never understand. You know what Sid Rose did to me? He made me watch things. He made me look at things. I worked for him for years and I lost everything, I was like a—like a robot. I thought everything he said was right. I thought everything he did was okay. You can't pay a person enough for something like that. He took my life!"

Well. But she had colluded: the money had to have been better with Sid. And Sid was fun; he was an interesting person who liked her, who appreciated her work, who let her do more and more. A glance passed between the two policemen, and I understood that their sympathies were shifting: this woman was becoming irrational, a threat. The policeman stood. "Come on now, Mrs. Luby. You understand you're under arrest, anything you say can and will—"

"And not just my life! He took his son's life too! Ben's life. Her brother!" Virginia pointed at Sally.

"Get the cuffs," the policewoman murmured.

"He killed his own son!" Virginia screamed. "He told me! You believe that? What kind of man would kill his own son? That kind of man."

"She's hysterical," Sally said to the officers, and the Hispanic officer responded with a you're-not-kidding look. Then: "Peter! Do I have to do it myself?" Peter was glued to the spot, eyes wide, Ezra and Barbara beside him.

"You can't do this to me!" Virginia was shouting. "I'm almost innocent!" The officers were on either side of her, gripping her by her upper arms.

"Come on, Ez," I said, reaching for his hand. "Come on, Barbara." I thought I could take them out the back door, where they wouldn't have to hear this, but Virginia was kicking at the two officers, and we couldn't get past.

"You're crazy to come out after me. You need to go after Sid Rose. You need to take Sid Rose out of his electric bed and put him in the electric chair!"

The officers lifted her two or three inches off the floor, holding her suspended in the air.

"Oh, my God," Sally said, clamping her hands over her ears. "I can't believe this."

"You open the front door, ma'am, we'll get her right out."

"I'm sorry about this," Sally said. "I appreciate your coming."

"You're as bad as he is!" Virginia shouted. "Little mother, what kind of little mother are you?"

"'Heat not a furnace for your foe so hot that it do singe yourself,'" the policeman said.

"Is that Shakespeare?" Sally asked in astonishment. She held the front door open, the grass a dazzling green, the inground sprinklers spritzing.

"You want Shakespeare?" Virginia shouted, swinging her feet from side to side in the air, aiming at her captors. "'The slings and arrows of outrageous fortune...'"

The cops laughed. She was no match for them. She seemed to be shrinking in their arms. A scent of cut grass wafted from the lawn.

"'A little madness in the spring / is healthy, even for the king,'" the Asian cop quoted.

"Mr. Literature," the woman cop teased. "It's not spring anymore, though."

"I played Laertes in high school," he said, addressing me and Sally.

They were truly a team. Virginia's feet were still working the air. I wondered if they'd charge her with resisting arrest.

"How dare you criticize my wife," Peter said as Virginia was carried through the door. "You'd be working in a shoe store if it weren't for Sally and Sid."

"I've never worked in a shoe store!" Virginia shrieked, twisting her head to look back at Peter.

"You can close the door," the policewoman said. "We're fine."

"Must be a weight lifter." Peter nodded at the woman officer's back.

They carried Virginia wiggling and crying to the police car, pushed her in the backseat, and slammed the door. We watched through the windows on either side of the front door, Ezra and Barbara in front, eyes wide. As soon as Virginia got in the car, she disappeared, slumped down in her seat. The police partners opened their respective front doors and got in without hurrying, conversing over the top of the car.

I felt as if I'd witnessed an astounding thing, a woman in the middle of her lunch who finds herself accused and makes herself, for a brief instant, a tragic figure but then just as quickly becomes—at the hands of both herself and those around her—an object of derision. I wondered if this would be the shape of Virginia's whole life. I felt like crying. No one but me seemed to notice what she had said about Sid and Ben.

"Mommy?" Ezra asked. "Is Mrs. Luby a raving lunatic?"

I ACCOMPANIED SALLY that afternoon on her daily visit to see Sid.

He was actually fatter, from the tube feeding, and he lay flat on his back, his electric bed—which sloshed if you pressed on it—making its humming noise. He wasn't responsive. His mouth was open, and he stared into the air. Still breathing.

I rubbed the bottom of his foot from heel to big toe and his toes fanned, a classic brain-damage sign.

"Hi, Daddy!" Sally said. She stood beside the bed and held his wrist as she told him about Virginia and the police, how that was taken care of and he didn't need to worry. Then she kissed him on his forehead and marched right to the nursing station to tell them that his pulse rate was eighty-four.

"Okay," the nurse said warily.

"That's really fast for him," Sally said. "It's not normal."

"Sally, the normal pulse rate is between sixty and a hundred," I said. "You're allowed some variation."

"He's never over eighty," Sally said. He's always in the sixties or seventies. Would you call Dr. Stevens, please?" Dr. Farouk did not come to nursing homes.

"It's not our policy to call a doctor for a normal pulse," the nurse said.

"Then I'll call him."

"Okay, okay. Let me check the pulse myself, and then I'll call the doctor."

"HE SAYS NOT TO WORRY," Sally told Peter at dinner, raising her eyebrows skeptically.

"Even after you told him your father was always in the sixties and seventies?"

Sally shrugged.

"Mommy?" Ezra said. "Do you really have naked people in your computer?"

Sally laughed. "Ezra! Can you imagine? Why would I have naked people in my computer? That Mrs. Luby is crazy."

Ezra smiled at his mother and nodded, but Barbara had her question: "Mommy, did Mrs. Luby know Uncle Ben?"

"Just a tiny bit, Barbara. A tiny bit."

"Why did she say Grandpa killed him?" Barbara, despite her ornamental clothing, was a tough little girl: I'd seen her fall off a swing and angrily wipe off her bloody knee with a handful of grass before getting back on.

"She's a raving lunatic, Barbara," Peter said. "Raving lunatics say crazy things."

Barbara frowned.

"She didn't mean it the way you think, Bubbles," Sally said. (Bubbles? I glanced at Barbara; she didn't look surprised.) "It was a figure of speech. She didn't mean it like, bop, you hit somebody on the head and it kills them. She meant she sort of blames Grandpa for Uncle Ben's getting sick." Getting sick? I wondered what Sally had told them about Ben. "Because Uncle Ben had drug addiction, you know, and that's a sickness, and maybe Mrs. Luby thought he'd sort of caught that sickness from Grandpa."

"Does Grandpa have drug addiction?" Barbara asked in a surprised voice.

"No, honey," Sally said. "He never did."

Barbara and Ezra looked confused. Their eyes met. No one asked any more questions.

"You won't see Mrs. Luby again," Sally said in a blithe tone. "Don't worry. She's out of our lives." I looked up, almost aghast at how quickly she'd dispensed of her—chop, chop, two quick vertical slaps—the same way she'd dispensed of Anaïs Nin, or Ben's girlfriend Helga, or Aunt Ruby. But that was Sally's way, and who was I, considering what she'd been through, to ask her to change?

"I JUST WENT THROUGH the stuff from Daddy's, and I found a Havdallah box."

"A what?"

"And it wasn't from that Judaica display, either. This was something he cared about. It's a box that you fill with spices, and you sniff it at the end of the ceremony that ends Shabbos. It's a Jewish thing. I didn't even recognize it. Peter figured out what it was. He remembered it from his conversion class."

I was startled to hear that Peter had once taken a class, and that he'd learned anything in it.

"I took it to our rabbi, and he confirmed it. He gave me a copy of the prayer ceremony that goes with it. Isn't it interesting that Daddy kept that box? I mean, he certainly wasn't religious. Even though he grew up that way." Sally's voice over the phone seemed unusually intense, the pitch a note or two higher than usual. "Peter got on the Internet and found the synagogue where Daddy was a bar mitzvah. He sent a message to the rabbi. I can't wait to hear back. People come to California and shed their pasts. It's accepted. It's a California tradition. But you can never shed your past, not really."

His pulse had gone back down. He was fine.

No, you can never shed your past.

"**HOW IS EVERYONE?**" Ted said.

"Fine. They're here with me right now. Mom's making spaghetti for dinner, and Aury and I are playing chess."

"Chess! Is she any good?"

"Very good. She just castled."

"I'm going to do a speech in Indianapolis in October. Want to meet me?"

"Your ten inches again?"

"Twelve inches, for you."

I dipped my head and clenched the phone, stifling a smile. "You rogue."

"And then I'll see you next week when we transfer Aury."

"Good. Looking forward to it. Here she is."

I handed the phone to Aury. My mother was standing at the stovetop looking at me, her wooden spoon frozen in the air.

THE NIGHT AFTER VIRGINIA Luby was arrested, Peter came downstairs and lured Sally and me up to his computer. "You've got to see this." The old boyish excitement: a little gift for us. He left messages for people in France, Idaho, and Sri Lanka, then clicked to a live video monitor of a coffeepot at the end of a hall somewhere in England. "Look how small the world is now, it's tiny!" Peter said, and Sally recalled when she'd been married to Flavio and flown to Argentina for a wedding.

"I realized everywhere was just a few plane rides away," Sally said, "and now everywhere's closer."

Peter got out sheets of messages from Moscow, which he'd downloaded and printed, then sent a message to someone in the Ukraine. He asked me if I had anyone to send e-mail to, and I thought of Ted, but his computer was in his home.

"Oh Peter, you're finally center stage," Sally said from the doorway. Down the hallway, Linnea started to wail.

"Good," Sally said, "now I don't have to wake up to nurse her."
And she was gone, leaving me and Peter to the tiny world.

"I WAS THINKING OF our wedding. Remember that guy with
the pickup?"

"The one who brought the flowers."

"He said he was good luck, remember? He said no wedding he'd
delivered flowers to had ended in a divorce. I guess we cooked that,
huh?"

"Why were you thinking of our wedding, Ted?"

"I don't know. A sentimental moment. I was thinking of your col-
larbones and that necklace you wore...."

"I was an idiot, Ted."

"What do you mean? Are you saying you're sorry we ever—?"

"No, no. Later. I was an idiot to ever hurt you."

"Yeah?"

"Yeah."

"You mean that?"

"Oh, God, do I mean that."

"Okay, make it up to me."

"Right now? Right here? Like this?"

"YOU HAVEN'T GOT JUST yourself to think of," my mother
said. "There's Aury, and need I mention Ted's other children. And his
wife."

"I know." In six months Ted and I had met alone only three times,
at the seminars where he was a lecturer, on nights it was logical for him
to be away.

"You say you know, but do you know? You act as if you don't."

"We have a special bond, Ted and me."

My mother bounced a gaze off me in an exasperated way. "When did you get sentimental? 'Special bond.' You have a special bond with a man who fathered your child, but you never picked up the phone to tell him he had a daughter? What's wrong with you? You think I don't notice your moony look? Tell me, does Ted have a 'special bond' with his wife too? Do you have a 'special bond' with me and Aury? Or are your only 'special bonds' adulterous ones?"

"WHY DON'T YOU BRING Aury over Christmas break?" Sally said. "You know I'd love to see her."

"How's your business? You keeping busy?"

"Busy enough. Has Aury been to Ted's again?"

"Twice. She goes again after Thanksgiving."

"You and Ted still getting along okay?"

"Oh, sure. I like Ted. We're friends."

"I can't believe how mature you're being with all this. I'd be a wreck if I had to pass my kids off to someone else, and you're doing it voluntarily!"

"I don't know. You and I are just different that way. And Ted's her father."

"YOU'RE HOME," my mother said flatly.

What a day. Hospital rounds, clinic hours, a noon meeting with the clinic nurses, credentials committee at six, back to the hospital to see an inpatient whose lover was threatening to sign him out, a stop at hospice on the way home to get my visits in before Christmas, another stop at the twenty-four-hour Everything Store to buy amaryllis bulbs as presents for my nurses. "Whew," I told my mother, "I'm beat." I headed for the refrigerator. "Anything left over?"

"Oh, I didn't much worry about your dinner," my mother said.

Peculiar. Something eating her.

"Where's Aury?" I said. "Did she go to bed already?"

"It's after nine."

"Look," I said, irritated, "I didn't have time to call. Every minute, *every minute* I was busy. And normally I would have called from the car, but the cell phone's broken, you know it's at the shop being re-built. I'm sorry, but I don't think you have any idea what my life's like." It's not normal, I was thinking, to be thirty-eight years old and still have to answer to your mother. Is it my fault she gave Eric her life savings? Am I really my mother's keeper?

"I used to work," my mother said.

"Not like I do."

"Maybe not."

I was opening a can of pop from the fridge when my mother sprang her question. "What day is it, Clare?"

"You're doing the mini–mental status test on me now? You think I'm losing my mental functions? It's Monday, that's what day it is."

"And what's the date today, Clare Ann? Did you write it on any of your charts?"

"The date is December thirteenth."

"December thirteenth."

"Oh my God." Aurelia's birthday. I had forgotten my daughter's birthday.

She was still awake, lying in her narrow bed. It made it worse that she didn't seem angry. "Mommy!" she said, in her high, thin voice. "I'm seven years old now!" I sat on her bed, and she hugged me. "Is your emergency all better?" she said.

The next day, I got off early and took her out for pizza, to Captain Crawdad's to play video games, on a long drive to look at Christmas lights. "This is a fun and rainy birthday," Aury said from the backseat of the car. "I'll tell Daddy we had lots of fun."

I twisted my head to look at her face, dappled with the shadows of raindrops on the window. She was smiling maybe a hint too broadly, her right hand, the hand with the tremor, clutching a plastic bag filled with prizes from Captain Crawdad's. "I love you, Aury," I said.

"You're a wonderful girl. But you don't have to cover for me with Daddy."

"A fun and rainy birthday," Aury repeated, and I understood she'd never tell.

The wipers smeared my windshield more than they cleaned it. I blinked and peered through the streaks. "You're too good for me, Aury," I said.

"LOOK," Sally said over Christmas. I hadn't brought Aury.

I knew it was going to be bad because she'd taken me upstairs into her office, late at night when the kids were sleeping, and unlocked the dreadful door.

A Crown Communications product. A magazine, one of her father's. One of hers. Why was she doing this to me? Was it revenge for the way I'd shocked her years before?

She wasn't opening the magazine to the centerfold, but to a side pictorial. At first I was simply relieved. Sunny, bright photos. No violence. The photos seemed to have been taken at a playground. A girl wearing a Peter Pan shirt and no bottoms leaned over a tire swing, or hung upside down on a monkey bar with her pubis exposed, then peeked around a wooden tower, breasts revealed.

"Did she have some botched plastic surgery?" The nipples looked even to me.

"How old do you think she is, Clare?"

"I don't know, eighteen?" She did look young, come to think of it, and when I thought about it more, the playground setting must have been an intentional attempt to make her look younger.

Sally seemed disconcerted by my response. "She is eighteen, I looked into it, she's definitely eighteen, but—Clare, who does she remind you of? Look at her, who does she remind you of?"

I looked. There was no one I knew who looked like her. I realized her hair was done in pigtails. They did want her looking young.

"Who does she remind you of?" Sally's voice was insistent, almost shaking.

"I don't know." I cast my mind about wildly. "Margaret?" I seemed to recall she had occasionally worn her hair in pigtails.

"Margaret!" Sally almost shrieked. "Does everyone remind you of Margaret? Doesn't she remind you of Aury? Or of Barbara? Doesn't she look like a child? Can't you see what they're doing with her? They're making this young woman into a child, and they're making a child into a sexual object of desire. Doesn't that disturb you?"

I felt like an idiot. I'd missed the whole subtext.

"They're" I realized. Sally had said "they're"—as if the photos had nothing to do with her.

"It certainly disturbs me," Sally said. "I saw this two weeks ago. The photographer had been phoning me about it, he wanted me to see it, it's in his portfolio. Said it was 'tasteful.' I just want you to know I can do tasteful photography, he said. His name's Derek Winslow, he's been working with us for two years. He's sleeping with the girl. She's eighteen according to her driver's license, that's a legal thing, you can't knowingly distribute adult literature with a subject under eighteen. But that's a legal nicety here. Derek clearly wants people thinking she's younger. He must imagine her younger."

What kind of a mother was I? I glanced at the cover of the magazine, which wasn't a name I recognized. "Is this a popular—?"

"This issue sold out. Look." Sally flipped the pages. The playground pictures got more graphic. Another girl, this one wearing only barrettes and patent leather shoes and anklets, appeared. The second girl's pubic hair was pale, her breasts tiny buds. The two girls interacted.

It was interesting, there really was something sexy about these photos. The girls seemed real. The photographer seemed as excited as they were. He must be crazy about her, I thought. And that, of course, was why the pictures were so disturbing.

"Every person in these magazines is someone's child," Sally said.

"Or someone's parent," I said, thinking of Sara the Countess of Come.

"Yes," said Sally distractedly, not seeming to take in my comment. "Who would raise a child to be part of this?" She leafed through a few more pages, segueing into the next feature, two women playing with penis-shaped lollipops. Pedestrian, I thought.

"I'm out of this business," she said. "I'm out. I know you think I've been waffling, but I only wanted a better deal. Daddy was always a businessman, and I wanted to be a businessman too. But this is the final straw."

I was shaking my head. "And not only this, but the violent stuff."

Sally waved her hand dismissively. "Noise. The violence is theatric. I don't worry about the violence."

I knew that was a lie. This was a woman so disturbed by violence that she'd never seen a James Bond movie. She'd convinced herself, I realized, that the violence portrayed in the products was fake. She ignored it on those grounds. But the reality wasn't my point. "Sally, if the violent stuff makes people associate violence with arousal, then maybe in real life people will—"

Sally brought her hands up to her ears. "Clare, I don't need this. Didn't I tell you I'm done? I'm done I'm done I'm done." To my astonishment, she started crying.

I didn't know how to deal with a crying Sally. I stood there like a lummox. Tears were streaming down her cheeks, her face was deformed. What had she been doing? Why had she been deluding herself? What would she tell her children? All she'd been trying to do was honor her father, and look what she'd done to her kids.

"Sally, Sally," I said. I patted her on the back. "Sally, your kids will never even realize." Then I asked gently, "Do you have buyers?"

Sally sniffed. "So-so buyers. I don't care what I get now. I just want out."

"It'll be all right, Sally," I said. "It's wonderful, really. It's over."

She broke into a fresh keen. "It'll never be over, there'll always be that"—I remember the pause so clearly, that sliver of abeyance as I waited for what she'd say—"*meat* on my hands." She threw her arms around me then, and as I held her, I cried too. She was right, there would always be that.

"I FORGOT AURY'S BIRTHDAY," I told Sally later that night, as we sat with our mugs in her deserted kitchen.

"What?"

"I did." I told her the story. "I haven't let my mother say one thing," I finished. "I won't be around her unless Aury's around."

"Your place isn't that big."

"Big enough."

Sally sat for a moment looking into her cup of tea. "You're hiding behind Aury," she said quietly, raising her eyes to meet mine.

We both smiled. "She protects me," I said. There had been so many tears that night. I felt as peaceful as I had in years.

"We all protect you," Sally said.

THERE'S THIS LOONY IDEA—American, Christian—that what you do doesn't ultimately matter, that anything can be forgiven and redeemed. I don't buy it. Nothing disappears, nothing is canceled out. A stain in the wood, meat on the hands, a virus in the cells. These things don't go away. In the end, imperfectly but largely, you reap what you sow. I think in my life that's all I've learned.

"GONE," SALLY SAID. "Totally. Up in smoke. Peter drove by to look. I can't believe I forgot to tell you." She was talking on the phone about Sid's hillside house, bought by an insurance executive after Sid went into the nursing home and destroyed in one of the fires that had beset Malibu back in November. "I bet the owner's not too torn up about it. He'll probably rebuild bigger." So Sid's house had burned, not slid into the sea. I wasn't sure which end would have been more appropriate.

"Have you seen the house off Mulholland lately?"

"Oh, it's the same. The neighbors hate it." The house had been bought from Sid by a French actress, who sold it to a fertility specialist when she gave up on American film. The doctor had replaced the driveway's vegetation with rows of topiaries and decorated the balconies with minarets painted gold and aqua. "Like little colorful penises," Sally said. The espalier, she'd heard, was dying or dead; Carlos had retired.

The espalier dying? Carlos retired? I felt a pang as if I'd heard of a betrayal. But that was silly. The espalier had lived longer than Ben.

"But I hear the doctor may be moving," Sally went on. "Nothing stays static here, that's for sure."

Nor here either, I thought, rolling over in bed. I was naked in

Wilkes-Barre, Pennsylvania, in a Holiday Inn, waiting for Ted to return from his brunch with the drug rep who'd arranged his trip. "How's the weather?"

"Fine. Sixties. Pretty clear."

In Wilkes-Barre, the snow was deep enough that not a blade of grass showed through. Behind the curtain, a small drift had accumulated on the inside windowsill. It was cloudy and the wind was moaning. More snow, lots of snow, was predicted. I'd driven here yesterday, thinking I was crazy to be traveling. It surprised me that any local doctors had shown up the night before for Ted's post-dinner speech, but doctors will do anything for free food. Now it looked as if Ted and I would have a bonus night together, snowed in.

"How's it there?"

"Winter storm warning."

Sally was enough of a southern Californian to believe in the romance of snow. "Oh, Aury must be excited! Have you been sledding yet?"

"No. Maybe this weekend. She's still asleep."

"Is your mom okay?"

"Fine." Another of your assignations? my mother had asked. I should charge you double. Believe me, you do, I'd answered.

It was cowardly of me not to tell Sally, but I couldn't. There was no one on Ted's side who knew, either. In a way, we were the perfect people to conduct an affair. Not everyone can keep a secret.

I WOKE UP at about two in the morning. Ted was awake too. "That light out the window reminds me of those flashing license plate frames. Remember how you used to want one ?"

"Boy, I forgot about those."

"You should get one, now that your mother's in Texas and won't go crazy over it. You should buy one. Maybe I'll get you one for your birthday. What do you think, should I get you one for your birthday?"

"It would certainly be a novelty in the doctors' parking lot."

"It would be great. Rakish. Rakish: Do you like that adjective? I think I'm improving with adjectives. Want me to get it?"

"Are you kidding? Mary would divorce me in two seconds if I put one of those on our van. Two seconds."

"Oh dear," I said, rolling away from him in the dark.

We were snowed in for two bonus nights, until Monday morning, and when we turned on the TV for the weather, what we got instead was news of the Northridge quake.

Earthquake. An earthquake in Los Angeles. I watched the film of the broken highway and the cracked buildings and the map with the little diagrammed epicenter, and my hand was on the phone before Ted even fully grasped what we were seeing.

An automated voice came on the line and said all circuits were busy.

"Look at it," I said. "It's not near her. I know where that highway is. I think we're okay. That's the thing about Los Angeles, it's sprawling. You might as well say an earthquake hit Ohio as to say it hit Los Angeles."

Ted called his wife, then went to the hotel restaurant and brought us back some breakfast, which he seemed determined I should eat. He sat beside me on the bed, hunched in front of the TV, stroking my back. "Clare, Clare. I'm sure she's all right."

There was footage of some of the biggest houses on Mulholland: they looked okay, and I wished Sally had never left her parents'.

In the middle of the morning, the phone rang. Ted and I glanced at each other, not sure who should answer. I had left the hotel number with my mother; Ted had left it with his wife.

Ted picked up the phone. "Sally?" he said. "You're okay?" I scrambled over the bed to get closer. "I was sure you were dead!" To my astonishment, Ted started sobbing.

"Give it to me," I said. "Don't scare her." And then, into the receiver: "Sally?"

"I'm on our cell phone," she said. "I've spent the last few hours finding out about Daddy. He's fine. We're fine. Everyone's fine." She sounded perfectly calm. "You live here, you have to expect this. And it wasn't that bad. Linnea and the twins didn't wake up. Ezra was hysterical, but Barbara loved it."

"Good," I said. "Good."

"Barbara wants another earthquake." I listened for sounds of the children, but the background was deathly quiet.

"Where are you?" I said.

"Outside." And then Sally fell apart. "Clare, what are you doing? I tried to call you at home, and your mother told me you weren't there. I don't even know where you are anymore. Where are you? And what are you doing with Ted?"

I FLEW OUT THREE weekends later. Sally seemed reflective: their house was sound, and nothing but knickknacks had been damaged, including a framed photograph of Sally and her family taken before she went off to college, which had slid off a table and disappeared, hidden for minutes as Sally pillaged the room for it in the predawn light, believing somehow the earth had cracked open and swallowed it. "You know," she said, "like something biblical."

"Jeez, it sounds terrible."

"It was better than I thought, really. The picture was only under a chair."

Houses around them had cracks, but theirs had no cracks at all.

—"I WALKED THOUGH the kitchen door and I saw you and I thought: Do you live here? Aren't you supposed to be living in Ohio? I think Ohio's a figment of your imagination. I think you're always here."

—"What do your patients do when you're gone? Do they manage to survive without you?"

—"What about Aury? You ship her off again with her new dad?"

Peter was amazingly hostile. I couldn't understand it. Here I was in post-earthquake L.A., being brave, showing up. And all Peter's little-boy enthusiasm was gone. He had no snakes or interesting rocks to show me this time.

—"Why didn't you just get a sperm donor, if you didn't want your daughter to have a father? What made you decide to drag a real man into it?"

—"You could have even had an egg donor. You're a doctor. Why be personal? Why stick your own genes in a child?"

I defended myself to Peter: "I come out here frequently but only for short times. Like Friday through Monday on a holiday weekend. I hardly ever miss more than a day of work. And the infectious disease docs cover me when I'm away because they covet my business. And, yes, lately Aury has spent some weekends with her father and half sisters. Don't you think that's good? Aren't you in favor of children interacting with their fathers?"

"I hear you're interacting with the father too," Peter said.

"PETER THINKS I'M A horrible mother," I said. Sally was in the rocker in Linnea's room, rocking her sobbing baby back and forth, back and forth. Sally had thought that by the fifth child, a new baby would be a piece of cake, but Linnea proved differently.

"He believes people should be honest. And look at you, Clare! First you didn't tell Ted you and he had a daughter, then when he finds out by accident, you start an affair with him and don't even tell me."

I was trying to figure out where in that welter of accusation was the crime that most disturbed Sally: it was not telling her, I was sure. But I answered another part. "I didn't know Ted was definitely Aury's father. And we were divorced when I got pregnant."

"I understand that." Sally stroked Linnea's hair, and the baby's cries slowed to gulps. "But you should explain it to Peter." Linnea's eyelids fluttered.

I made a skeptical noise. What did I care about Peter? I hated weird old Peter, shut up with his computer for hours, more intimate with people in Greenland and Vietnam than he would ever be with me. Did he even have clients these days? I doubted it. "It's not worth it," I said impatiently.

"I never dreamed you were sleeping with Ted."

I sighed.

"I can't get over that last time I talked to you before the quake." Sally held Linnea's head against her chest, tracing the baby's ear with her finger. "I mean you were there, you were in some ratty hotel room with Ted, and all along I'm imagining you sitting in your kitchen."

I felt accused, naked, a hundred times more naked than I had felt in that Pennsylvania motel room. "It was a Holiday Inn," I defended myself. "Ted's never ratty."

"And Ted, Ted!" Sally shook her head. "Why in the world are you seeing Ted?"

"I love him."

"Why didn't you stay married to him, then?"

"Sally . . ."

Linnea let out a quick yelp. "Linnea, Linnea," Sally murmured, pressing her fingers gently against Linnea's lips.

"He thinks the best of me. He makes me feel like I'm worth something." I hesitated, thinking how to explain the sex of it. "He makes me feel alive."

Lots of other ways to feel alive! I imagined her saying. Or: You need a *man* to prove you're worth something? Or: And you thought my business was immoral!

"It just surprises me. You were so done with him."

"You can never tell what'll ring your bell," I said. An old quote from Sid. I knew it would make Sally smile, and it did. He was a bugger, but he had a way.

"But what are your expectations?" Sally went on. "He has three daughters by his wife. I worry about you. No quality man is going to leave three children."

"I don't need him to," I said. "I'm happy having him for my few hours. I'm happy being able to think of him and know he cares. That time we were stuck in Wilkes-Barre? Three nights was almost too much."

"Marriage is a lifetime. Day after day after day."

"I don't need a marriage, I need friendship," I said. "Look at us." By this I meant: look how close we are and yet we only see each other a few days every few months.

But she thought I meant something different. "I don't mean to let you down, Clare. Give me some time to adjust."

Linnea gave a final sob and collapsed, suddenly asleep, her head lolling back on Sally's arm. Sally could have been holding a rag doll. She gazed down at her littlest child. "If a chest of drawers fell over, it would kill her."

"IT CAN'T LAST, you know," Sally said to me at the airport. She carried, as usual, a baby in a backpack.

"What do you mean it can't last?" I objected. "It has to last. He's Aury's father. It's, it's"—I struggled for a word—"ongoing."

Sally raised her eyebrows and gave me a look. She'd always been much more of a realist than I was.

I thought of Ben's tooth in its tiny plastic bag. I thought of what Sid told me, of Aunt Ruby's doubts, of Virginia's confirmation. Something had happened. Sally had a right to know the possibilities, a right to be fully adult. Absurd to try to protect her.

But two months later, over the phone, Sally dropped her own bombshell: "We're moving to Idaho."

I thought I'd misheard. "The state of Idaho? As in potatoes?" I scanned my brain. I'd never known anyone from Idaho, or even anyone who'd visited the state. "Isn't that where the white supremacists live?"

"I know it sounds precipitous, but it's not. We've been talking about leaving Los Angeles for ages. And now Daddy's business is sold, and we found an excellent nursing home up there, and Peter can work out of anywhere with his computer, and then the earthquake: I don't think I can stand living here after the earthquake. If a cabinet fell over, it could—"

"I know, I know," I interrupted. "Kill one of the children."

"It's true, Clare. Don't make me sound melodramatic. We bought land in Idaho. With a very primitive house, but one we can stay in until we build."

"Have you ever even been to Idaho?"

"Last weekend. Peter's been e-mailing people up there, we already had leads on the property."

"And you're moving your father up there?"

"It's a very nice nursing home. Private, in a little wooded glen; the staff is wonderful."

"How soon are you moving?"

"Anytime, really. Ezra starts kindergarten in the fall, and I'd like to get him established. As soon as we get packed up. We'll get an ambulance to take Daddy."

An ambulance! The cost must be staggering. I wondered if his electric bed was going. "Can you sell your house?"

"Oh, sure. No cracks."

"Incredible," I said. It was just hitting me that I would not be visiting California, that the cheap flights from Cleveland to Los Angeles would mean nothing to me, that the landscape in which I'd always envisioned Sally and her past and future would be hers no longer. "I can't believe it."

"Idaho's beautiful," Sally said. "You'll love it. We're in the southeast corner."

"Won't you miss the ocean?" I would.

"There are mountains. There are rivers. Did you see the movie *A River Runs Through It?* That was actually filmed in Montana, but the landscape—"

Oh sure, I was thinking, there's a movie Sally could tolerate. A drippy movie. "How do I fly there?" I interrupted. "Do I go through St. Louis?"

"I'm not sure," Sally said. "I'll look it up for you."

"Where do I fly to, Boise?"

"We flew into Salt Lake City; we're pretty close to the Utah state line."

"I'll have to check a map," I said. "You've lost me."

I HAD A NEW PATIENT at two-thirty, and I was in such a hurry that I barreled into the exam room without looking at the name on the chart. There was Cleve Burton, Mr. Angry Man himself.

I don't see partners, I don't see possibles.

"I was hoping it wouldn't come to this," he said drily, catching my eye and looking away.

I opened the chart, leafed to the lab results section. It was true. I sighed. "When did you find out?"

"I took an antibiotic for a sinus infection, and then I got this yeast infection that would not go away. That concerned me. So I went to the health department for the test."

"I'm sorry."

"To quote Hymen Roth talking to Michael Corleone: 'This is the life we've chosen.' I'm not surprised, in a way." We looked at each other. I knew that the choices he was talking about had nothing to do with any harebrain theory of homosexuality as a conscious preference. "*Godfather II*," Cleve said. "Do you know that movie? I watched it last night on video. Great film."

"It's my best friend's favorite movie. That or the original *Godfather*, she can't decide. She loves those movies even though she hates violence. I don't think she's seen every minute of either one. She closes her eyes. She ran into James Caan once at a dry cleaner, and she said, 'Santino!' It just popped out."

"And what did James Caan say?"

"Nothing. He winked." I added an explanation: "My friend used to live in Los Angeles." She was thrilled to be out, she'd told me, now that everyone in the city was obsessed with O.J.

"Oh, she must have seen all kinds of stars."

"She did. She actually used to make movies, or her father did. Not Hollywood-type movies. They made what they called blue movies—a euphemism if I've ever heard one."

Cleve smiled again. "I've seen a couple of those."

"Her father used to target the gay market, actually."

"Really? Any famous titles?"

I tried to remember the few I'd heard. "Let me think. *Bathhouse Fantasy* was one."

"I know *Bathhouse Fantasy*."

"You're kidding. Really?"

"Intimately. It's very good. Excellent production values, and some exceptionally well-endowed actors. There's a real favorite of mine in it, a certain man of color who wears a bow tie."

Oh, my. Mr. Bow Tie certainly got around. "I hope the movie had lots of condoms," I said firmly. "My friend's father was very big on condoms."

"Thousands of condoms," Cleve said. "Condoms on everyone."

"It *is* a bathhouse fantasy."

We both chuckled.

"I'm glad you have a sense of humor," Cleve said, shifting in his chair. "That'll help me. I'm not known for it myself."

I thought of his tirade-laden articles, the picket lines he'd organized outside selected restaurants unfriendly to gays, his "gays and druggies walking hand in hand with their executioners."

"I try," I said.

"I hear you're the best."

We looked at each other again. I shrugged. "Thanks," I said. For some reason, tears came to my eyes.

"IT'S NOT BEAUTIFUL, the cottage I mean. It's cinder-block with a metal roof, but it's responsible, it's nearly fireproof, we'll never be calling in the forest service to rescue us if there's a fire. And we've already got ideas for the house."

"A fire? You're in Idaho, Sally, not L.A."

Sally laughed. "There are lots of fires up here. It's all national forest, and there's been a drought for years. If lightning hits or someone tosses a match, things just go. There's this whole urban-outcasts group up here—urban outcasts with money—and they build these big wooden houses with cedar-shake roofs up one-lane roads, just asking for it, really—tinderboxes—and when the fires hit, they go crazy and want firefighters helicoptered in. It's like you'd say, they don't believe in natural consequences." Sally laughed a bitter laugh. "But who does? Not when it's us. But our new house will be fireproof." She laughed again. "A point of pride, of course."

"You sound happy," I said cautiously.

"The scenery is gorgeous. And the kids can walk down to the river and fish a mile away, and there are all sorts of trails, and the school bus is a converted minivan."

"I'll have to come out and visit you." I didn't really want to.

"Oh, you will! It's idyllic. It's paradise."

Was it? It didn't sound like paradise, with its prideful residents and antagonisms and competing houses. Probably Range Rovers roving down dirt roads, and fax machines clicking away in kitchens-cum-offices. Why should I want to see such people? Why would Sally want to leave Los Angeles for such pretensions? At least in L.A. the pretensions were up front.

"COLORADO AGAIN?" I said, swallowing.

Ted paused, looked over at me: "I thought you might agree to two weeks this year."

We were back at our Burger King. Stephanie, Ted and Mary's oldest daughter, was wearing lacy nylons and little heels. The younger girls were just as fancy. Whatever their mother's idea of style was, wasn't mine. "I want a salad, Daddy," Stephanie said. "No dressing. And iced-tea with a sweetener." Stephanie was a good year younger than Aury. I looked at Ted with alarm, but he didn't seem to notice.

"Aury will have a Whopper meal with milk," I said.

Ted turned to face his fancy daughters. "How come Aury eats and you girls don't?" he teased, turning away before anyone could answer.

"TWO WEEKS! OH, CLARE. Did you feel forced to agree to that long?"

"He *is* her father. And she really enjoyed Colorado last year."

"Why don't you come to Idaho when she's there?" Sally said. "The house won't be done, but you can see the construction." They were building a glorified log cabin, with a two-story living room, dorm rooms for the boys and girls, a master suite with a deck, and a spare bedroom for me.

"I don't know, Sal, I've been so busy."

"You always made it to Los Angeles."

"I know, I know, but it seems like every weekend now there's something, I'm transporting Aury back and forth to Pennsylvania, or she's got a swim meet, or...I don't know. It's really busy. And I'm seeing more patients than ever."

"Even a couple days," Sally said. "It's been months. I miss you. I want you to see Idaho."

"You could come here."

"With almost six children?" The baby was due in four months, although why Sally was having another one after her experience with

Linnea, who still awoke screaming at night, was something I would never understand.

"You wouldn't have to bring your kids, Sally. You could come yourself."

"Come on, Clare. That's not me. I wouldn't be myself going somewhere without my children. I'd feel empty."

7/28/94

Dear Clare,

At last, pictures of our new garden! I'm waiting for the day you can come out and see it yourself, but until then, here are some photos. I enjoyed taking these because I remembered you looking at the photos of our Mulholland garden when we were freshmen. No espalier here, but there's a vegetable garden and the beginnings of a rose bower. Carlos did roses on the patio by Daddy and Mom's bedroom, do you remember?

I tried calling you the other night and talked to your mother and she told me you and she were going to Niagara Falls when Aury's in Colorado. I don't think I've ever heard your mother sound so excited!

Daddy is fine. The aides are lovely to him, and the new doctor seems very caring.

I should tell you that Peter and I are having difficulties. They're not major (I don't think), but with so many children involved, I'm scared. He's withdrawn from me and the kids almost totally and spends the majority of his time either reading all the newspapers about O.J. or "surfing the Net" (gag) or out roaming our property. (Alone, although the kids would love to join him.) He won't talk to me about what's disturbing him, and since I got pregnant, he has no interest in me as a partner. He's not drinking or using drugs, which is fortunate, and there's no gay community up here, so that's not a concern, but he's just turned off on me as if someone hit a switch. The kids are starting to see it. We'd go to a counselor, but there's no one close enough so we could leave the kids home, and no one will sit with all five. We may try (you won't believe this) an Internet counselor. Peter agrees to counseling. He says he doesn't know what's eating

*him, either, but maybe he misses L.A.? Then he says he'd never go back
there. He's invited a few of his old clients to visit us, but so far no one's
come. Sara and her girls visited (did I tell you she's in law school?), and Peter barely spoke to them all weekend. It's hard. I miss you. I wish you'd
come visit, Clare. I don't mean to beg, but I'd love to see you. You make me
feel like a complete and normal person, something I'm not always feeling
lately. Could I buy you a ticket as a belated birthday present? I'll call the
travel agent and everything, just send me the dates. I know you're busy.
Think of what you can see. Beautiful Idaho! Scenic Idaho! Pristine Idaho!
All this and your old roommate too!*

Lots of love,
Sally

"HOW WAS IT, HONEY? Did you really have a good time?"

Aury nodded. "It was great."

"Good. I'm glad." I patted her bony shoulder, made a joke of
pinching her skin under her shirt. "Did they feed you enough?"

"Sort of." Aury grimaced and confided, "All they eat is canned fruit
and chicken!"

"WHAT DO YOU MEAN, not meet again? We're always going to
meet again. We have a child together."

"Clare, you know what I mean. I mean not meet like this. I mean
not meet in hotel rooms. I'm a married man. I have responsibilities to
my wife, to my children, I—"

"Aury's your child!"

"Of course Aury's my child. Clare, what are you saying? I'm talking
about responsibility to Aury too. She's very attached to her sisters now,
and it's not going to do her any good to break up the girls' and my and
Mary's family unit."

"Family unit? Family *unit*?"

"You know what I mean."

"What is this, newspeak? Are you going to tell me next how sleeping with me has *impacted* your life?"

"Clare, please. I don't want to argue about my language. I'm trying to think of the children."

"How nineties of you."

"I'm trying to think of you too."

"Oh, right. Take away my one joy, and you're trying to think of me. I don't ask for much, you know. I see you, what? Every six weeks? Every two months? Am I calling you in between times? Am I writing you letters?"

"That's not the point, Clare. The point is, I'm always mentally in some other place. When I'm with you, I'm thinking about Mary and the girls, and when I'm with them, I'm thinking about you. We're almost forty now, Clare. Don't you get it? We don't have our whole lives left. Statistically, we're over halfway through. And I want to live in the moment, I want to be totally...invested in whatever I'm doing at a given time. It's a philosophical issue for me."

"Invested? Have you thought about how invested we are in each other? Wherever I am, whatever I'm doing, I always think of you. Last week I had a new patient call me a white bitch who enjoyed seeing people like her suffer, and you know what? I didn't fall apart. I listened to her, I talked to her, and when she left, we had an understanding. And I felt proud, because I imagined you there watching me the whole time. I never do stupid things when I think of you watching me. How can you say we won't see each other anymore? You'd be taking away a part of me. The good part of me."

"Clare. You could have a normal life. You could love a man who loves you and could see you every day. Really see you, not just you imagining he sees you. You could get married again! I was wrong to even start this. It's my fault. I lie in bed at night and think, what am I doing? How can I do this to my family?"

"So I'm not your family. I'm the mother of your oldest daughter, but I'm not—"

"You divorced me, Clare, remember? You divorced *me*."

"I'm not going to beg, don't think I'm going to beg."

"I was too nice for you, remember?"

"You walk out that door, this is the end. I'm not going to beg!"

"Then stop begging!"

"ANOTHER GIRL!"

"You got to the hospital on time? I was worried."

"Oh, fine. Piece of cake. Tiny hospital."

"Is she cute? What's her name?"

"Shoshana Miriam."

"Wow, that's a mouthful. How do you spell it?"

Sally spelled it. "The names are Hebrew. They're kind of my names. This is my baby.

"Love you," she said when she hung up. I didn't respond for a second, surprised to hear those words. We used to say them all the time.

"Love you too," I answered.

HE DID SOMETHING to me. He made me fully alive. His body up against me, penis insistent through his clothes, his hands barely touching me, running over my shoulders and down my arms as if he were stroking not me but the nimbus around me, so all the tiny hairs rose to meet him.

Unbuttoning my shirt, undoing my bra, a breast in each hand, barely. My nipples stood up.

I was a bridge arching. I was melting into the mattress. That little push, to meet him.

How could I give that up?

"YOU AND MR. COTTON used condoms, didn't you? After you found out his diagnosis?" It wasn't really my business, but Cleve and I were friends now, and I could ask.

"Not consistently."

I'd heard that story so many times. Still, it wasn't everyone who admitted it.

"And you know what?" Cleve said with a loopy smile. "It was worth it."

My voice was surprisingly sharp. "Worth your life?"

Cleve didn't lose his smile. His eyes were open, but they seemed to be focused on a memory, not on me. "Larry couldn't come wearing a condom. Nothing we tried. So I let him come inside me without one." Cleve's eyes met mine. "It was worth it. Know what I mean?"

I did know. I knew exactly what he meant.

"IT'S LOVELY," I SAID. November in Idaho, and the wind might have rattled the windows, but this was a house built not to rattle.

"It is." Sally shook out the match and placed the fat candle on a dish. "Aromatherapy," she said, taking a seat on the sofa. The sofa was low, with wooden arms like sticks, upholstered in a rust-colored, hempish fabric. Native American rugs were scattered across the blond wooden floor; the lamps were made of tubes of rusted metal. "I never thought I'd live in a glorified log cabin, but"—she waved her hand—"it fits. Peter's the one who's really crazy about it. He designed it, figured out the lighting, where to put the outlets, what size windows. It's his baby."

The kids were in bed, mostly, in their beds in the two big rooms—the boys' room and the girls' room—that opened onto the balcony looking down on the vaulted living room where Sally and I sat. Linnea, the difficult child, was asleep on the floor beside us under a blanket, splayed out with a foot protruding, and Shoshana, the baby with the Hebrew name bigger than she was, curled on Sally's lap. I didn't know where Peter was. Out.

"Peter's been more friendly than he was the last few times I've seen him."

"That was L.A.," Sally said. "He's not jealous of you anymore. It's a relief to him that you're here. Now he doesn't want my attention."

"You are pretty isolated up here"—they were halfway up a mountain—"and with neither of you working, well... What do you talk about after a while?"

"There's a couple down toward town who's been married sixty-one years. They bicker. But any couple who's been together that long, they know how to get what they need from each other. I always dreamed I'd have that long-term thing with somebody. That I'd be part of a unit." She sighed.

"I'm not exactly part of a unit, either."

"What's happening with you and Ted, are you two..."

"It's ending," I said. "I can feel it." And then, quickly, so she wouldn't ask me more: "You're not feeling like your marriage is doomed, are you?"

"It may be." Sally's gaze shifted to Linnea and she dropped her voice dramatically, as if the sleeping child, barely two years old, could possibly understand her: "There's someone else."

Her melodramatic way irritated me. "Oh, come on," I said out loud, casting my eyes toward the arched front windows, "where in the world would you meet another guy up here?"

Sally's eyes pooled with hurt. "Not me. Peter. He's found an abandoned wife. On the other side of the mountain. She lives in one of those cedar-shake houses." One of the firetraps, Sally was saying.

No wonder she was agitated about me and Ted. "Are you sure?"

"Ninety percent. She's married to one of those computer millionaires who flies back and forth to Seattle in his private plane and leaves her here to fend for herself. She's cute. Young." Sally's mouth twisted on the word. "We befriended her, all of us. Peter and I felt sorry for her. She's been here for dinner I don't know how many times. But not anymore." Sally paused and looked at me. "Her name's Laurie. He's become quite a hiker, Peter has."

"Oh, Sally."

"He told me last week she wants children. You know what I thought? *What the hell are you doing talking about children with Laurie, Peter?* He doesn't make a penny anymore. It's all me, what I got from the law firm and Daddy's business." She turned to me with an anxious look: "Do you think I'm getting fat?"

She was a little heavier. I'd seen her, as she cleaned up in the kitchen, eating leftover food with her fingers off her children's plates. "Oh no, Sally," I said, "not at all."

"She's very thin. Fit."

It was almost too painful to see the self-doubt in her face. I rubbed my hands together to warm them and watched the candle flicker on the low table in front of us. Linnea stirred, cried out, stuck her other foot out of the blanket.

"Dreams," Sally said, bending over to tuck the blanket around Linnea. "At least she doesn't wake up anymore. You know what I realized? Linnea doesn't like being held. She's better if I just tighten the blanket." Sally pulled Shoshana closer to her, looked over her shoulder toward the kitchen, then turned her gaze to mine. "Clare? You should let Ted go. It's wrong what you're doing."

I dropped my eyes from hers back to the candle, felt my face burn. "I know, Sally."

"It's wrong. There's a reason the Seventh Commandment forbids adultery. Fornication is one thing, but adultery! In adultery, there's betrayal."

"Don't forget that Mark Petrello ran around on me," I said. Lavender, I remembered. He came home smelling like lavender.

"But you and Mark Petrello didn't have children!" Sally burst out, passionately enough that Shoshana stirred on her lap, flexed a tiny arm, and waved a fist in the air, as if she were seconding what her mother was saying.

"Would it really make a difference if Peter moved out on you?" I said. "You're the one who does everything with the children."

"But he's their father," Sally said quietly. "And besides, Laurie's husband will never put up with it. She's his possession."

"What's he going to do, hire a hit man?"

Sally gave a quiver, brought her hand up to shield the baby's ears. "I just want Peter back home," she said in a prayerful voice. At that very moment Peter came in, stamping his feet in the mudroom off the kitchen.

"Racoon-a-rama at Laurie's," Peter called. "Even got in the kitchen. I had to chase one out with a yardstick." He moved through the kitchen shedding clothes: a jacket to a hook on the wall, a sweater to the back of the chair, his boots to a mat in the corner. He had shaved his goatee; his wispy hair was groomed now, slicked back from his forehead. "God, it's like a palace over there. Way too much house for two people. Usually one people. Laurie feeds the raccoons, that's the problem. She's got to quit. I told her that. Can't be a soft touch!" He moved from the kitchen into the glow and fragrance of the candle, and I noticed that his face looked flushed and handsome: for the first time, he struck me as sexy, as a man in his prime, while below him, closer to the light, Sally was a dour lump. "She needs a place more like this one," Peter said, eyes aglow, and I thought then of Ted and Mary, how Ted must have looked exhilarated, wild, coming home from his visits with me—from even our chaste exchanges of Aury.

"I'm glad you're home," Sally said, lifting her chin to look at him, and I swallowed a hard knot in my throat, knowing that she'd reached me, that I'd think of that timid and beseeching gaze the next time I saw Ted.

SID'S NEW NURSING HOME had rocking chairs and plaques with messages in the lobby; the aides, instead of white dresses, wore ankle boots and white pants, their underwear showing through. When Sally and the kids and I arrived, Sid was being cleaned up; from the door to his room, I caught a glimpse of back and buttock, and an unmistakable whiff of stool. "Hold on a minute!" the aide called, pushing the door shut with her foot.

Ezra sighed and slid down the walll. "Bo-ring," he said, his new word. He found kindergarten bo-ring too.

The twins found an empty wheelchair and started pushing it around. Linnea screamed, possibly in happiness.

The door popped open. "He's all spruced up!"

We crowded into the room. The aide stood on the far side of the bed behind Sid, like a 4-H'er posing behind her prize chicken.

Barbara went to the head of the bed and peered at her grandfather's face. "What's that in his eye, Mommy?" she asked. There was a bit of sleep on an eyelash; the aide wiped it away with a wet washcloth.

"I'm Rose," the aide said to Sally. "I was on nights, but I'm new on days."

"Nice to meet you," Sally said. "Any problems?"

"Oh no!" said Rose. "He's a real doll baby."

Joshua had clambered up onto a chair beside Sid and, before anyone noticed him, tossed a small rubber ball aimed at Sid's open mouth. Gabriel screamed with laughter.

"Oh no no no," Sally said in a horrified tone. "This is your grandfather, Joshua. Oh, we would never hurt your grandfather." The ball had glanced off Sid's cheekbone and bounced to the floor.

"A real doll baby," Rose repeated. "He don't give us no trouble at all. Nice and quiet. What did he do?"

Sally, mouth open, didn't speak for a second, so I obligingly rushed in. "He was a magazine distributor," I said.

"Oh." Rose smiled. "Those little trucks. I heard you all were from L.A."

Sally and I both nodded.

"He has a nice face," Rose said. "Nice smooth forehead." She patted it. "Not a lot of worries these days, eh, Sidney?" She straightened up and turned to Sally, her voice proud. "We turn our people every two hours. No one ever gets bedsores here."

"It's a very caring facility," Sally assured her. "As nice as his place in L.A."

The aide beamed.

ANOTHER EVENING AT HOME with Sally, the big kids in bed—something about the mountain air, they slept gloriously—the baby nestled on Sally's lap and Linnea, who couldn't fall asleep without Sally, sleeping on the floor beside the rust-colored sofa. Sally was going on and on about the thing I least wanted her to mention. Me. Ted. Adultery. Pain. She'd lit the candle again, and for some reason, I was remembering Sid's house in the Malibu hills, the house that clutched the hillside with its view of the ocean. Ben's tooth had sat in the little box on the Biedermeyer chest. I had the tooth with me now, in its little plastic bag in the enameled pillbox in the jewelry sack in the pocket of my suitcase.

"Look, Sally, what about me?" I finally objected. "Ted makes me feel alive! We have great sex! We're a unit together! And we were married before he ever met Mary."

"Oh." Sally waved her hand dismissively. "Sex is overrated. The best thing about sex is it makes babies."

Hadn't she said something like that before? The best thing was the joy, the connection. The best thing was wanting it. The best thing was feeling totally alive, in the moment, your genitals swelling so big they blotted out the rest of your life.

I suddenly recognized the reason I'd thought of Sid's house. The smell from Sally's candle was the smell on Sid's old deck. "What is this?" I said, pointing at the candle. "What scent?"

"Rosemary," Sally said. "For clarity and spiritual renewal."

"Your father had rosemary growing on his deck in Malibu, remember?"

Sally smiled dreamily, stroking little Shoshana's fuzzy head, and I knew she was thinking of the old daddy, not the shell we'd seen today.

"He hurt you a lot, your father," I said. To say sex was overrated. Never.

"Oh, no," Sally said, "Daddy never hurt me. Never. Not me." She paused a moment, considering. "He did hurt Ben."

Should she know? Could she? "What do you mean?" I said, unable to mask the urgency in my voice, and my mind was already taking the trip upstairs to the guest bedroom, opening the suitcase, and slipping that tiny pillbox from its soft fabric pocket.

"Daddy thought Ben was weak," Sally said. "He thought Ben's problem with his sexual identity was weakness, and that using drugs was weakness. And Daddy wasn't"—she paused, made a fist—"Daddy didn't like weakness. He was definite." She was speaking in the past tense.

"That's true."

"He knew what he wanted."

"Definitely."

"He was unafraid."

"I think he would do anything," I said. "I think in the right circumstances he was capable of anything."

Sally looked up from Shoshana, and in her gaze was both a sharp puzzlement and some of the old snap that had driven her to buy Ben his Happy Families, that had won her every trial. "What are you saying?" she said. "Daddy had scruples. I know you never liked his business, but you have to admit he had scruples."

Her husband was out walking again tonight. She had six children.

"His whole insistence on condoms," Sally said. "Don't you think that was a scruple?"

She was my best friend. Who was I to destroy her innocence, even for her own good?

"You're right," I agreed. "The condoms were a scruple."

I GLANCED OVER HER shoulder at the monitor. Endless words. A far cry from the monitors in Sally's old locked room.

"What is this?"

"He calls himself the Web Reb. It's a rabbi in New York who answers questions. He's interesting."

"Do you write him?"

"Uh-huh. He's traditional, he's Lubavitcher. The Lubavitchers believe the Messiah's coming any day now. Some of them thought their leader could be the Messiah, but he died back in June."

"They thought their leader was the *Messiah*?"

"They believed in him. They had faith in him."

"Crazy," I murmured. Then: "You don't believe the Messiah's coming, do you?"

Sally shrugged. "Oh, I doubt it. This rabbi's one of several I write to. He's not the only rabbi on the Web."

WE DROVE THE LONG gravel driveway down the mountain, through groves of pine trees and past outcroppings of rock to the main road, where we turned north toward town. We passed an elaborate gate on the right, stone columns supporting a metal arch over a paved road that took off across a field and disappeared in the bare trees beyond. SNAKE-BYTE RANCH, read the letters on the arch. On the distant hillside shone the glittering windows and brown roofs of some enormous complex. "Is that a resort?" I asked, gesturing at the roofs; I'd heard there were resorts in Idaho.

"Laurie's house," Sally answered with a tight smile. "Peter's little friend," and before I had a chance to express my astonishment, she directed my attention to a hovering line of gray on the far end of the field. "Look. The landing strip. The mogul flies in on weekends." Her left hand gripped the steering wheel tighter. "When I'm lucky."

I COULD HEAR BRITTANY'S VOICE, more excited than I'd ever heard it, as I walked up the stairs to Aury's room. "Her daddy killed her mommy. My mommy said she never thought she'd ever know a murderer, but Mr. Crossburn was a murderer."

"Mr. Crossburn killed somebody?" Aury's voice was incredulous.

"He killed Lindsey's mommy. It was on the news."

I opened the door to see Aury with her hands over her ears. "Brittany," I said, "Aury doesn't even watch TV. Please stop talking to her about these terrible things. It's time for you to go home."

"ANOTHER CONSULTING DOCTOR?" a woman's weary voice said. I brushed past everyone in the hall and walked into the patient's ICU room. She was unconscious. I examined her, looked through her chart, walked out. This patient was a bigshot, a lawyer's widow, ex–Garden Club president. Her adult children, two men and a tight-lipped woman, appeared from three sides to form a wall around me.

"That's our mother. And your name?"

I told them who I was.

"I assume you're a specialist."

"I'm an internist."

"Our family doctor is an internist!" one of the sons protested.

The daughter took charge. "We just want to know what's really going on."

I went into my spiel. A pneumonia, a strange pneumonia, not a bacteria or a virus but a parasite. I could feel their interest reluctantly pick up. "The pneumonia suggests a disorder of the immune system. Her body's simply not fighting this infection the way it should."

"Is she going to die?" the daughter interrupted sharply. I looked at her. A muscle between her eyebrows was twitching convulsively, a small machine with a life of its own. "Our father died almost two years ago, you know, of a strange infection. Tuberculosis in his bowels, the pathologist told us. In his bowels! Who's ever heard of that? I asked them to send the specimen to the Mayo Clinic."

"He did volunteer at that drop-in center," the blond son said earnestly.

"And Ralph, our handyman," the other son interrupted, "don't forget he'd been treated for TB."

"I thought my father's infection was very peculiar," the daughter said firmly, eyeing me with wariness. I fervently hoped she was older than me. "Very peculiar." She cast a defiant glance at her brothers.

"What did the Mayo Clinic say?"

"They never got the specimen! Always some excuse. You know how hospitals cover for their own." The daughter gave an angry snort. "Back to Mom: Is she going to die?"

I'd underestimated the daughter. "She may die."

"The antibiotics aren't working?"

"There're working some. But the effectiveness of antibiotics is limited when someone's immune system isn't doing its job."

The daughter exhaled sharply. "Thank you for telling us," she said. "We appreciate your honesty." She glanced at her brothers as if to confirm this, but they were blinking hard and looking at the floor.

"There's something else you should know," I said. "I was asked to see your mother because I'm a doctor who treats people with HIV. I'm sure you've heard of HIV. It gets into people's bodies and it—"

The daughter was ahead of me. "She has AIDS."

"Yes. Your mother has AIDS."

The daughter took a step back from me, from all of us, and stared, mouth open, past me to the metal edge of her mother's bed. I swear that at that moment I could read her mind. It was saying: I knew it would come to this, I warned her, I knew this would come to pass.

It's not such a strange story. The strange thing for me was to hear it from the daughter who, in 1975, during a trip with her college roommate to San Francisco, saw a patrician older man enter a bathroom behind a young man wearing jeans and a heavy leather belt. As the two of them disappeared behind the cinder-block wall, the daughter had a glimpse of the older man touching, in a shepherding sort of way, the younger one's shoulder, and at that instant she recognized, all at once and so mysteriously it was inarguable, her father's secret life.

"And I went to my mother," the daughter recounted, nostrils flaring, "and I said, 'Mother, I just really want to know what's going on.'"

PRISTINE CAPE COD on nearly 2 treed acres. Designer kitchen, three bedrooms, 2½ baths, large weather-treated deck. An oasis of privacy and charm. $220,000.

"I don't see why not." Cleve frowned. He was now my financial adviser as well as my accountant. "Even if you divested the drug stocks, you'd still be putting equity in the house. What can you get for your town house?"

I told him. "It's not a high-rent district," I said. "But the place will show well."

"What's the decor?"

"California modern."

He punched some numbers into a calculator. "You're planning to maintain your current level of income?"

I nodded.

"I wouldn't put down more than what you get on the town house. You'll need the yearly deduction you get on the interest. Excuse me, but for a doctor you don't make diddly."

I laughed.

"Every time I put through your co-pay I think, damn, I should pay this good doctor more."

THE BLOND SON APPROACHED through the ICU doors. "The church people are here," he whispered.

"The church people, did you hear?" The sister flung the words like a splatter of mud. "The homophobic, homo-hating church people. And you know what, Dr. Mann? I just want to tell them, tell them, tell them!"

"Well," I said after a moment, trying to sound reasonable, "would that help your mother at all?"

"I want to help me!" the daughter cried. She threw her head back against the cinder-block wall.

"I TOLD MARY," Ted said quietly.

"*What?*"

"I did, I told her about us. I had to, Clare. Otherwise the lure of you would be too strong."

It wasn't enough not to sleep with me. "Why?" I finally managed.

"We've got to stay stopped, and I knew if I told her, we'd have to." He bit his lip, nodded, looked away. "That's it. That's it exactly."

We were meeting at a freeway rest area. A nippy winter day, not frigid. "Clare! Clare!" Ted's other daughters were scampering up the incline from the picnic table where they'd shared some cans of pop. "Can Aury go see *The Secret of Roan Inish* with us?"

It took me a moment to gather my thoughts.

"Please," Aury said.

"It's not violent," Stephanie assured me.

"Fine, fine," I said.

"I wanted Mary to come with me today," Ted said, "but she didn't want to."

"Good," I said wildly. "Excellent."

"She respects our position."

"Good. That's nice, yes. Aury," I called, "come help me get your stuff out of the car."

She danced along beside me. "I can see *The Secret*? I can really see *The Secret*?"

"Sure," I said, "why not? Let's go mad."

We brought Aury's knapsack and doll carrier back to Ted. "So this is definite?" I said.

A smile crossed his lips. "I know how you like definites," he said.

"*Ted.*"

His gaze wavered, but his voice was annoyed. "It has to be, Clare, don't you see?"

I didn't want to stop looking at him. "Ted," I said. I loved to say his name.

"You'll be busy with your move." He flicked a hand and turned away from me. "We've got to go. Girls!" he called, "I want everybody climbing in the van like nice little monkeys!"

"We're not monkeys!" all his girls squealed merrily, and then they clambered in the van and drove away.

FRANK HAD VISITED BAXTER. Baxter had a new friend living with him at the cabin, but the afternoon Frank visited, the friend felt sick and never emerged from his bedroom.

"You didn't even meet him?" I said. "Wow. How'd our family end up so goofy?"

"We're not goofy!" Frank retorted hotly. "I'm married, Eric's married, you're a doctor. So Larry Lumberjack has a shy roommate, does that make our whole family goofy?"

"You don't think Baxter's—" but I didn't have time to finish.

"You are absolutely obsessed with perversion!" Frank burst out. "Can't a fellow be a bachelor anymore?"

I WAS SLIPPING OUT the ICU doors when the daughter marched up to me. "Okay. Now that everybody knows, now that everything's out in the open, my brothers and I believe we should get the AIDS test too."

I was due at the closing in twenty minutes. "Your odds of picking up HIV from a family member without sexual contact are infinitesimal."

"But we're talking about our father and our mother, we shared a bathroom when we visited, we ate together—"

"You don't catch HIV by casual contact." I looked at her skeptical face. "If you insist on getting the blood test, your best bet is the health department downtown."

"Can't you write an order and we'll go to the lab here?"

"I can't write an order for something you don't need. And the testing should be anonymous. You can go to the health department. Getting involved in this whole thing would be"—I smiled apologetically as I backed away—"a waste of time for me."

"I can't believe this."

"I'm sorry, but I'm running late to a meeting. If you're really against going to the health department, why don't you call your family doctor?"

"Never mind. I'm sorry I asked you. I understand."

"I'M CALLING FROM the new house! It's beautiful, we love it. It's a great day here, feels like May instead of March, Mom's sitting out in the backyard and Aurelia's on a glider beside her reading *The Hobbit*. Yeah, yeah, new start in life, you know about that. What are you doing? You're on the computer? Oh no! You're talking to the Web Reb again? At least your modem has a dedicated phone line, otherwise I'd never be able to get through. How are you? I haven't heard from you in ages. Are you okay? You don't sound like yourself, you sound like—you're kidding. He left? He moved in with his girlfriend? What's a grown man like Peter doing abandoning his wife and six children? Has he gone totally insane?"

I hesitated a moment. "Sally, you still have me. Do you want me to come visit?"

I didn't get there till late June—problems with getting infectious disease to cover my patients—and Aury, with all her swim meets, had to stay home in Ohio. It was 1995. My second visit to Idaho.

"Listen to this." Sally opened a book of poetry. "'The one who waits is always the mother'—here's the line I love: 'all her fingers jammed in the automatic doors of the world.'" She looked up to be sure I'd gotten it. "I love that line! I love it!"

Linnea made a sound, picked up her bowl of cornflakes, and over-turned it on her head.

"Linnea, that is not appropriate." Sally picked up the bowl and went to the sink for a dish towel, which she brought back and laid on the table in front of her daughter. "Wipe off your head, please."

Linnea did as she was told, swabbing her hair, at Sally's prompting picking out the soggy cornflakes from behind her ears and laying them in Sally's palm. To me, Linnea was an eerie child: she was two and a half years old and seemed intelligent, yet she didn't utter a word.

"You think the husband's going to let Laurie go just like that?" Sally snapped her fingers. "Fat chance. They've got a prenup! She won't get the house, income, nada. That scares me. You think she'll want to stick around here and live with Peter? Does Peter want to stay around here? He says he does, but I don't want him running off and leaving our kids without a father."

"Sally, plenty of kids grow up without a father."

"No offense to you, but don't you think Aury's more balanced since she's been seeing Ted? On the phone, she sounds much happier, even though it's made things more complicated for you. Peter's not a bad man. He's a foolish man, but he's not a worthless father."

This surprised me, because I had always thought Peter was worth-less as a father. His eagerness to please seemed to extend only to adults. He never changed a diaper, read a story, or spooned food into a wait-ing mouth. "He never took a really active role with the kids," I haz-arded.

"No, but he was there," Sally answered quickly. "And he'll be bet-ter now. Not having the kids with him all the time, he'll realize what he's given up."

"Hmmm," I said, unconvinced, and it hit me what a web of illu-sions Sally lived in. I thought of Ben's tooth. I'd taken to bringing it with me. Was I as deluded as she was? Were there obvious things I couldn't see? Would I want someone to tell me?

Sally turned away from me with a fierce look. "Maybe I'll offer him alimony. Contingent on his staying near here."

I'D LOOKED UP FROM the letter, my mouth dry. "She says I was very attentive to her mother."

"Her mother was unconscious," Mr. Kapstone, the medical center president, snapped. "She needed you to be attentive to her."

"I didn't handle it properly," I admitted. "I should have ordered the HIV tests for her and her brothers. I was wrong."

"We can't afford wrong in this medical center. Not with people of this caliber."

"Not with people of any caliber, I hope."

The air between us seemed to bristle.

"I'll tell her you admit your mistake," Mr. Kapstone said. "That's something."

"DID I TELL YOU that the principal said Ezra was too bright for school?" Sally's voice, mocking the principal's, took on a prissy whine. "'We're lacking the staffing to give him opportunities to challenge himself.' Bitch. She had the gall to suggest homeschooling. Look, I said, I could homeschool him, it'd be fine, he and I would have fun and he'd learn what he needs to know but that's not the point. The point is a parent will not be around forever, and I want him to know how to get along with other teachers, other kids, everybody! I said to the principal, my dad's a vegetable, my mom is dead, my brother is dead—what if I were helpless in the world? I'm training my kids to survive after I'm gone." She jabbed the air with her finger. A thrill ran through me: Had she really called Sid a vegetable? "Then I said listen, my kids are all bright, and they know about good things, and half the reason they're turning out okay is they don't watch TV. TV is a scourge. It's hideous!" I suddenly saw her as she'd been twenty years before, pacing our dorm room, railing about the idiocy of Anaïs Nin. "Why are you smiling? You know it's true. It's just something you can't voice to people, they'll think you're sanctimonious."

"Aren't you?"

She couldn't stifle a small smile, but then she erased it. "Is sanctimony bad? At least it's honest. At least it's trying for some kind of purity of feeling. And that's the problem with TV, it's not honest. TV takes everything—death, passion, perversion—and turns it into a show. It turns pain into entertainment."

I made some kind of neutral, soothing face.

"It makes us all voyeurs," Sally said, her voice firmer. "We're supposed to sit and watch."

I nodded ever so slightly.

"I should know!" Sally said, biting off her words. Her tone softened now, her message completed: "I should know. I made sex into a spectacle, didn't I? Just like my father." She threw her gaze angrily around her house. "And look where it got me."

It was the same lovely rustic house. Her kids were the same animated children. She still had enough money that she would never need to work. The only difference was that Peter was gone. And the old Sally, in a way, was back.

"OH NO, NO, we're not vegetarians," she was saying later. "It's that we've been eating meat in a sacramental sort of way. Like in 'She'll Be Coming Around the Mountain': 'Oh, we'll kill the old red rooster when she comes.' 'When she comes' is a meaningful event. To kill the rooster is an honor attended *her*. So you're the lady in the song."

"You're going to kill a rooster for me?"

Thankfully, Sally laughed. "We're not that literal yet. We went to the supermarket and bought chicken. For chicken cacciatore." Her tone sobered. "Maybe someday we'll be that literal. I am trying to observe the Shabbos, did I tell you that?"

"I did that once." We looked at each other and laughed.

"Oh, that reminds me," Sally said. She went to a desk in the living room and reappeared with something in her hand. "Look what I found." It was a photo of the two of us from my first visit to California, taken outside on the patio of the house off Mulholland, the espalier behind us. I remembered Sid taking it, his knees apart and flexed, his face hidden. "Big future!" he had said to make us smile.

"I'm going to frame it," Sally said.

I didn't look like Joni Mitchell. I had her hair but not her cheekbones; my eyes were less intelligent and more avid than hers. But Sally, just as I remembered, looked like a pretty farmgirl. It was a surprise to think that face came out of Los Angeles. There in the photo was our amazing unformedness, our round faces peering—in something like flirtation—at the world. We looked as innocent and unknowing as two tomatoes. We thought we knew so much. Yet what did we know then, really? We knew we planned to grow up and find love. We knew we adored our fathers. We knew we were best friends.

I looked up to see Sally making her way slowly across the kitchen, arms laden with peppers and onions, a canister of salt tucked under her chin and a cauliflower in her hand. "Good grief, Sally," I said, relieving her of the cauliflower and salt, "haven't you heard of a cry for help?"

She fell apart one night on that visit. I was teasing her about a neighbor whose wife had moved to Manitoba, and she rose up in anguished fury.

"He's not a potential partner for me, Clare. First off, he's not Jewish, and I'm going to all the trouble of dealing with Salt Lake to get a Jewish divorce, and secondly, I couldn't take another partner now, Clare, I'm, I'm—" Suddenly, inexplicably, Sally began to cry. "I'm scarred, Clare, I'm horribly scarred."

Everybody then was talking about childhood sexual abuse, and the thought flew into my mind that Sid, dirty awful Sid, had forced himself on his daughter. Perhaps she was just now remembering. The trauma of Peter's leaving had squeezed the memory out. She could finally call him a vegetable. "Oh, Sally," I said, "I'm so sorry." I could tell her now, I realized, what Sid had told me about Ben. Let her know how irredeemable her father was.

She was still sobbing. "I miss them so much," she said, sniffing. "So much." She hesitated and sniffed again. "Last week I was out walking toward town with the kids, and we went near this development they're building, and...there were cranes and dump trucks. The kids got all excited watching them, and I walked up and asked one of the construction guys what they were doing, and"—she sniffed again—"they were digging a pool!" She broke out in fresh sobs, almost keening.

"A pool? You mean a fishing pond?"

"A swimming pool." Sally sniffed.

"You found that sad." Somehow I never imagined a swimming pool in Idaho.

"I know it sounds ridiculous, it just hit me. I told the kids something had blown into my eye. But I was thinking about the house off Mulholland, and how when we moved in, the pool wasn't built, and later I remember the cranes and the dump trucks and how excited Ben was, he must have been about two, and he ran around the family room saying, 'Tuck! Tuck!' And Daddy put him on his shoulders and carried him outside to watch, and Mommy and I stood in the door to the garage. That's what I remembered. It hit me then that my family is gone, really gone, and even though I have all these kids, they'll never know my family, so in a way they'll never know me, because they don't know me with my family. I don't have a context for my children."

"That's not true. They'll see you in the context of your family's absence," I said, reasonably. But I knew instantly what a bad thing I'd said.

"I only see him twice a week now," Sally sobbed. "I'm not a bad daughter, I just can't. I can't."

"I'm sorry," I said. I envisioned Sid carrying Ben on his shoulders, the little boy shouting, "Tuck! tuck!" Gone, gone, they were all gone. An orgy of loss. Sally loved her father; he would never abuse her.

"We were normal," Sally said. "We were a normal family." She set down her mug of tea with a thwack and looked at me. "I've got to stop grieving. I've got to keep myself together for my children. I have no choice."

For the rest of my visit, she was fine.

"YOU'RE SCARED?" Ted had said sharply. "What in the world are you scared about?"

A gas station at a busy exit. It seemed to be our collusion, that we would meet to exchange Aury at progressively less welcoming places. The woman behind the counter was smoking, so we moved outside to stand by the tires.

"I don't know, I feel like I crossed some political line. I know the medical center's technically a nonprofit entity, but there's a lot of pressure on all the clinics to be cost-effective, and I'm not sure my clinic is. So a letter like this..." I shrugged. "It gives them an excuse."

Ted frowned; it scared me that he didn't argue. "Medicine's becoming extremely money-driven," he said.

"Nothing but a goddamn business," I said bitterly. I was forty: Where would I work if my clinic closed?

Ted's eyes clouded; I thought he might be blinking back tears. A white car with dirty tires pulled in front of us, spattering our legs with mud. "You don't deserve to have your practice treated like a business," Ted said thickly, and I thought of my clinic, its upholstered chairs with peeling arms, its big sample closet from which I filled recycled plastic bags with free pills, my scene in the waiting room earlier this week with the "user" who wanted an early script for more AZT, having sold his previous pills on the street as amphetamines. In what heroic landscape did Ted picture me working?

ANOTHER DAY DURING THAT trip to Idaho in June, we had a confrontation by the river. Two men, with big boots and lots of equipment, wanted to fish in the river from Sally's shore. Sally told them they weren't allowed.

"We've always fished here. We've fished here for forty years. My dad used to bring me here."

"I understand that the river holds memories for you, and I respect memories, but I respect life too, and fishing is a way of taking life. One of many ways."

The men eyed each other. It struck me that they suspected Sally was some kind of nature freak. "Fishing's natural," the younger one said. He looked at Shoshana in the carrier on Sally's back. "The Indians used to fish."

"It's a final decision. It's my property, and I'm unswayable."

"That's too bad," the older man said, "your little boys would like it." Ezra was teaching the twins and Barbara his version of karate, which involved a lot of grunts and hopping, as Linnea the silent rocked herself in the grass.

"My girls might like it too," Sally countered quickly. "And they'll grow up and decide for themselves, I'm sure. But it's not an experience they're getting under my auspices."

"Your boy go to school?" the older man said, nodding at Ezra.

"No, I homeschool him." Sally's answer startled me, because it was untrue. Later she said she'd told him that so he would think she was some hippy-dippy type not worth his efforts to pester.

"I don't think he'd pester you," I objected. "He seemed nice."

"They all seem nice. Listen, I'm a woman alone in the country with six kids," she reminded me. "I've got to protect them."

I hadn't thought of it like that.

FRIDAY NIGHT I DREADED, with all the hints Sally had made about their observing Shabbos, the Sabbath. But it was fine. A few mysterious prayers in Hebrew, some candles, and—considering six children were involved—a relatively peaceful dinner. Before dusk,

Sally turned the lights off in the bedrooms, turned the lights on downstairs and in the bathrooms, and that's the way things stayed until Saturday night. Turning lights on and off counted as work, and observing Shabbos meant no working.

The next morning, Barbara wanted to go to Wal-Mart. "We can't go today, lambie," Sally said. "It's Shabbos." The twins wanted to help their mother bake cookies. "Not today," she said, "it's Shabbos."

"I can see some advantages to this Shabbos business," I said. It was surprisingly warm, although there was snow on the mountains, and we sat on the front lawn in lawn chairs looking out over the valley. Shoshana was asleep on a blanket beside us, the other kids scampering in and out of a grove of trees.

"We Jews are practical," Sally said with a wink, the gesture so unexpected I felt myself blush.

"How much is that house the mogul owns?" I asked, twisting around in the direction of the path.

Sally lifted her hands above her head and stretched out on the lawn chair. "Millions. It's advertised in *Town and Country.*"

She reminded me of Sid, stretching out like that, and suddenly I missed him. The old Sid, the Sid before Ben was dead, the Sid who asked if his business was worse than building the better bomb. A question I'd never wanted to answer. Maybe not. Probably not. Not.

He was big, that Sid. He was a force, a character, and I wondered fleetingly if Sally and I would ever seem as big to our offspring as Sid had seemed to us.

Ezra was running toward us. "Mommy, Mommy! We found a bunny nest! We found baby bunnies!"

Sally was on her feet instantly. "The little kids aren't touching them, are they?" She hurried off behind her oldest son.

I sat for a moment and looked out over the valley, the patches of green trees and snow, the rocky outcroppings, the long view to the mountains in the distance. "I love her," Sid had said. "We've always had this special bond, Sally and me." He was never, in essence, an evil man. For the first time I understood this. Even if he did just what he told me, when he did it, he was not in his best mind. I won't excuse him by saying he wasn't in his right mind, only that he wasn't in his best. He was losing control, he was panicked, he had made himself so adept at rationalization that he forgot that there were things a thinking human cannot, without consequences, do. But in the end he was a thinking human. On the altar of Sally's big future, he sacrificed not just Ben but himself.

I heard the sound of a sharp spank, then a wail. The whole group was coming back, Linnea trapped and writhing under Sally's arm. "Never never never touch a bunny," Sally scolded. "I just hope that bunny-mommy comes back."

In a moment Ezra was wailing too. "Mommy, I want the bunny-mommy to come back!"

"It will, honeybear. It will. We'll just leave the babies alone now."

Ezra gave a long, quivering sob. "Can I go make sure the bunny-mommy comes back?"

"No, lovie, you need to stay here with me. If that bunny-mommy has any brains, she'll come back."

"I don't think she has brains," Barbara announced.

"What about the bunny-daddy?" Ezra sobbed. "If the bunny-mommy won't look after them, what about the bunny-daddy?"

"Oh, sweetie. Bunny-daddies aren't around much."

"I hate Daddy," Joshua annnounced suddenly.

"Oh, Joshua," Sally said. "We all know that's not true."

Barbara gave her mother a smirk. "I know a people-daddy who's not around much."

"Linnea, ouch, honey, let go of my arm. I'm going to set you down, but you've got to stand here, okay? You can't go back by the bunnies."

"How do you keep a people-daddy around if a bunny-daddy hops away?" Barbara was grinning.

I recognized the tilt of Sally's chin, the firmness in her voice. "Our people-daddy is never leaving. Understand, Bubbles? Never. Not if this people-mommy can help it."

I GOT FIRED. My HIV clinic was closed, my patients' files transferred to the division of infectious diseases. "Idiots," Sally said. "Unbelievable. You could move out here. You could practice regular medicine. You wouldn't even have to practice medicine. You could live here with me and the kids and care for us."

Sally paying the way. Paying the way with her blue movie money.

No, that wasn't fair. Paying the way with her botched face-lift money, her lumpy liposuction money. Paying my way.

"It's beautiful here! You should see my roses. And we have plenty of room. Aury would love it. Even your mom! Your mom would love it. You could give her the whole annex." The annex was the small cinder-block house beyond the vegetable garden, where Sally and Peter had first lived when they were building their house. There was nothing new with the divorces; the mogul had fired his financial adviser and was shopping for a new divorce lawyer, and Sally wouldn't make any move toward letting Peter go until she could guarantee he'd stay close.

"I'll visit. I'm staying here. We have this new house. And my mom's happy here, Aury's got her friends and her swim team, we're only a few hours from Ted, and I know it sounds hokey, but I couldn't leave my patients. I have contacts. I'll set up something in town."

"Can you get by financially?"

"I'll be okay. I have some money saved up, actually. That account-ant Cleve's been helping me."

"I admire you."

"Thanks. I kind of admire myself. I want to stay in the fray," I said, closing my eyes. "Even if I don't stay at University, I want to keep up my practice with AIDS."

"In the fray," Sally echoed softly, respectfully. "I guess that's where we both belong." I knew some people would say Sally had left it, but they were wrong.

There were days I admired myself, but other days I felt like a wisp, a nothing, a middle-aged woman who'd gone soft and useless, who couldn't even cook, an object of ridicule to Timothy Quiver and his infectious disease colleagues. On those days, I remembered Ben.

"STRANGE CALL FROM SALLY," my mother said. "We talked more today than we have in the last fifteen years."

"Sally called?" Aury and I had been swimming.

"She's moving."

How could that be? "She told you that? Not back to Los Ange-les—"

"She bought a house. It's around the mountain or somewhere. Where Peter and that girlfriend of his live now. Some computer mil-lionaire owned it. Sally wanted to buy it for Peter so he'd be close to their children, but the only way the millionaire"—my mother sneered over this word—"would sell was if Sally signed a contract saying she'd live there herself." I was surprised my mother had grasped this convo-luted story; I was having a problem grasping it myself. "Peter's appar-ently thrilled," my mother went on. "He and the girlfriend are going to move where Sally's living now. Sally says they're basically exchang-ing houses. She says in a way it's ideal because the houses are pretty close. There's a path. She says Peter designed the place she's leaving."

"Sally told you this? Sally and the kids are moving to the house with the airstrip?"

"An airstrip! She didn't mention an airstrip. She did call the place a palace. You know what that millionaire did? He played with her by driving up the price."

"I can't believe this. Sally hates that house."

"She's doing it for the children! I told her she should be proud. It's never wrong to do things for your children."

"SO YOU'RE GOING TO see possibles," Ted said with a sly grin. We were at our Burger King eating lunch and exchanging Aury—a dangerous treat—and she and the girls were off in the play area.

"I don't want to see possibles," I groused. Ted was leaning forward, as close as he would let himself get to me. "But I'm sure you're right, in private practice, I'll have to see the stupid possibles."

Ted held his palm out and separated his third and fourth fingers like Spock giving the Vulcan salute. "A chink in the wall of your unacceptance of ambiguity."

I scowled. "I don't know why I have to accept ambiguity."

"Oh, Clare," Ted said ruefully, sitting back in his chair. "When you're looking at me, what are you looking at except ambiguity? What am I? I'm a ball of ambiguities."

"Ball of ambivalences would be more accurate."

Ted's mouth dropped open; he looked at me in exasperated affection. "You're your daughter's mother, that's for sure."

"It is sure."

Ted, smiling to himself, looked down at the table. "Ambiguities, ambivalences. You're the sure one. And I'm nothing but a big ball of ambis."

"Don't you love me anymore?" My words popped out before I thought of them. He'd said he'd always love me, always, even if our physical relationship didn't continue. Had he been lying? Did his withholding his body from me mean he'd lost affection for me? I loved him more now that we weren't sleeping together. Not sleeping with him was pain added to love, a sort of sacrifice. I glanced around us, suddenly sheepish, but there was no one close enough to hear.

A spasm that looked like anguish crossed Ted's face. He reached over and briefly cupped my cheek in his hand, as if I were a child. "Of course I love you, Clare," he said. "When will you believe that?"

Now, I thought. Tears came to my eyes. Now.

I LOOKED IN CLEVE'S mouth, listened to his heart and lungs, poked at his belly. Nothing really new. So far, he was okay. Every day he took six capsules of AZT.

But he seemed edgy, uncomfortable. "I've been on the Internet," he said. "They're out there, protease inhibitors are out there." A new class of anti-AIDS drugs, soon to be tested in clinical trials. I was a little surprised Cleve had heard of them, but why should I be? Cleve kept up to date.

Cleve cast a glance around my new office: the plants, the pictures, the commodious exam rooms. I had to produce here—see enough patients to pay my salary, and more—or the group wouldn't keep me. I was seeing plenty of possibles.

"Get me one."

I didn't understand what he was asking. "Get you what?"

"A protease inhibitor."

I took a big breath. "Sure, I can try," I told him, "but since I'm not at University anymore, it might be harder to get in studies, and since protease inhibitors are study drugs, not drugs actually on the market yet, I might not—"

Cleve stared at me. "Then I'll go to the doctors at University." I recoiled. What was Cleve saying? I was his friend. "What good are you," he said, "if you can't get me something better than AZT?"

"You don't necessarily know it'll be better," I managed weakly.

Cleve shot me a skeptical look. And he was right, the Internet had told him, as my conferences had told me, that the buzz about these new drugs was wonderful. People with AIDS might live if they took protease inhibitors. Of course, there had been promising treatments before.

"I'll try, Cleve. No promises, but I'll try."

"I'm not going to sit here and let you let me die. Don't think you can get rid of me that easy."

Well, he was an angry man. I knew that. That was something I loved about him.

"I'll get some for you," I promised, not knowing how I'd do it. "I'll get it."

I flashed back to Sally and me driving down Rodeo Drive years before, dangling Ben's essential heroin in the little box of Chinese food.

"HE WON. I've never even met him, and the bastard won. He's a maniac, they say. Hires people Wednesday and fires them Friday. But he won, there's no question about it. You know what his lawyer told me? 'We've got you by the short and curlies, Mrs. Newcomer.' Can you imagine? It's actually a clever expression. But I have reasons to console myself. The kids are excited, they'll each have their own room. And of course there's a computer room, which is thrilling for them, or it will be when we have something to put in it. And the indoor pool will be great, although it's empty now and the doors are locked and I'm trying to hide it from Linnea until she's potty-trained. So it's not a disaster. I did it for love, I keep telling myself. I did it for my kids. I'm sure Peter won't leave Idaho now. He loves our old house. He designed that house. I think his dream was always to live there with Laurie. Oh Clare, when I think of living in a house with a cedar-shake roof... I never dreamed. Can you come out here?"

"I can't take the time off, not now."

"Should I send you and Aury a ticket?"

"Not now. Let me get a few months of steady billing, then I'll come."

But I saw her within weeks, at Sid's funeral.

He died on a Thursday afternoon in August 1995, several days after Sally's last visit. Rose, the aide, walked in to turn him and found him dead. Rose the aide found Rose the patient dead: everyone noticed this coincidence. When Sally got to the nursing home, he was propped up in his bed, a sheet smoothed across his chest, a crucifix stuck in his crossed hands.

"I wanted to throw it out the window," Sally said, "but I just laid it in a chair."

"Poor baby," Rose said. "Poor sweet baby."

Sally had the body flown to L.A., where the junior rabbi from Sally and Peter's former temple agreed to officiate at the funeral. She had me flown to L.A. too, so I was waiting at the airport Friday afternoon when she and Ezra and Barbara arrived; the younger children were in Idaho with Peter. We stayed in a bungalow at the Beverly Hills Hotel, certainly more hotel than we needed, but Sally had arranged the accommodations. "Daddy would want us to enjoy ourselves," she said. She seemed eerily calm, like someone on tranquilizers, although I knew she'd be shocked to hear this. We were within miles of Sid's old houses, of Sally's houses, but she said she had no urge to see them, and besides, we shouldn't drive on Shabbos. I felt as though we were on our own little island, far from anything we knew. We spent most of our two evenings together talking about my new practice. We got room service and played with the kids in the pool.

"What'd the rabbi say?" I asked at one point, after he had phoned.

"He asked me what Daddy's dreams were. I didn't know." Sally shook her head. "He wanted to be big, but in the end he got so small."

The funeral was Sunday afternoon, in a lavishly treed cemetery next to the graves of Esther and Ben. At the last minute Sally called up Teresa, who now worked for an old neighbor of Sally's, and asked her to stay at the hotel with Ezra and Barbara during the funeral. "I don't want to scare them," Sally said.

We drove to the cemetery in our rental car with the windows down, and I realized how happy I was to again be in L.A. I liked everything about the air: the warmth, the breeze, the brightness, even the smell of exhaust.

Aunt Ruby came, and Uncle Freddie, looking surprisingly well, and a man who turned out to be Uncle Freddie's brother visiting from Boca Raton, and a temple contingent of men in dark suits whom the rabbi had phoned to be sure there'd be ten men—a minyan—in attendance. I wondered if there'd been an obituary in the Los Angeles paper; if Virginia Luby (who should now be on probation, having served her months in prison; her son actually served longer, having been on probation before) knew, or the mysterious Buck. At the last minute, a tall woman with her face draped in a mantilla arrived: Sara Tweedles, corporate lawyer.

"Good to see you," Aunt Ruby said to Sally, squeezing my elbow. "Doesn't my Freddie look good?"

The service wasn't very long. We all stood. There was a lot of Hebrew, which meant nothing to me, and the rabbi flailed a bit with the eulogy, and then it was over and the rabbi was nodding toward the shovel and the pile of dirt, but Sally didn't move.

"Sally?" Aunt Ruby whispered. Sally ignored her. "Well, okay then," Aunt Ruby said, and she stepped forward, lifting the bottom of her skirt and mincing around the grave. She took a shovelful of dirt and dropped it on the casket, and the sound was as dreadful and final as I remembered from Esther's funeral. "Freddie?" she inquired, holding out the shovel.

Freddie dropped two shovelfuls, then Freddie's brother took a turn, and then there was an awkward pause—the temple men looking at one another—before Sally stepped to the far side of the grave. She wore a navy suit with a zippered front, really a very businesslike outfit, and she kept her face down and her lips set as she worked. She dropped in the first shovel of dirt—thud—and the second, then the third, and then she kept shoveling, over and over, one load of loose dirt after the next, until her forehead was gleaming with sweat and it was clear to even me, a nominal Presbyterian, that what she was doing was well beyond custom. The thuds began to sound less hollow once the top of the casket was totally covered with dirt—and more like splatters, or swishes, and I'm sure it wasn't only to me that their tone changed, taking on a quality at first rancorous, then deranged. "What is she doing?" Aunt Ruby said. "Has she been drinking?" The whole tiny congregation seemed to draw together in alarm and look to the rabbi for help. He seemed too wispy to have much authority, but when he crept up beside Sally and spoke in her ear, she immediately stopped.

"A KOSHER KITCHEN isn't hard if you're a vegetarian," Sally said. It was before seven A.M. on a late-October Sunday and she was bustling, celery and onions on the stovetop, rice steaming. The kitchen was the one room in her new house that seemed fully occupied. She always liked to be one day ahead on her meals.

"But you're not a vegetarian," I said automatically. Then I thought of the things Sally had turned out to be without my knowing it. "Are you?"

"Not totally, no," Sally answered. "I can't imagine Passover without brisket. But we don't need a lot of cookware for meat. One roasting pan, one casserole."

Passover? Brisket? Sally had never mentioned either to me, but now she spoke of both like inalterable traditions.

"You don't need a special dishwasher for the meatware?" I was being facetious. Sally, in her new kitchen, had separate cupboards for dishes to use with dairy products and dishes to use with meat. This was the essence of a kosher kitchen: separate plates, silverware, serving dishes, pots and pans, and utensils for meat and dairy dishes. Cookware apartheid, Sally called it. A rabbi from Salt Lake, she told me, had offered to come blowtorch her stove to make the kitchen truly kosher. "But that seemed too extreme," Sally had said.

"I'm glad you have limits."

"See, the reason you do this," Sally had said, "is to make a point of eating. If you keep kosher, you can't just grab something and pop it in your mouth. It makes eating an intentional act. A religious Jew does things with intention."

"And complication," I had added. Sally had plenty of room in this kitchen. There was a cupboard devoted entirely to children's toys. Despite its top-of-the-line appliances, the kitchen had a sort of virginity: Sally didn't believe the lower oven had ever been used. Laurie microwaved her meals.

"We wash the meat plates in the sink. We don't use the dishwasher for the meat plates." Sally wrinkled her nose. "I'm not sure that's technically necessary, but it's what we do."

"Oh, brother."

Sally turned to me, affronted. "It's tradition! I don't mock anything you do."

Tradition. How did you fit a dishwasher into tradition? "I'm not mocking you. I just wonder where this fervor comes from. You used to have a Christmas tree."

Sally frowned. "Used to, what's used to? People change! You used to sleep with a different guy every—" Sally stopped, seeing the insult she was heading into. "Year," she ended weakly. We both laughed.

Sally sighed and wiped the faucet with a rag. "Your needs," she said.

"Yeah, my needs. And you know what? Except for Dan Trimball—you remember Dan, the chemistry professor—and Mark Petrello, for about the first week we were married, I never really enjoyed sex with anyone. Never. Not until Ted came back."

"You two should have stayed married."

"I know. But we didn't, and it was my fault, and now it's too late. I sure miss sleeping with him, though."

"Mommy," came a small voice from the door, "my nose isn't working." Gabriel, in his blue footed p.j.'s, blanket clutched in his hand, was standing in the cavernous family room adjacent to the kitchen. His little voice echoed in the almost empty room.

"Oh, lovie," Sally said, "you don't know how to blow your nose?" It turned out to be quite a feat to teach him, and by then other children were awakening, and Sally and I were hurled into the day.

THE MOGUL HAD SENT a minion to do his closing, and two moving vans to remove every scrap of furniture from the house he had once, in a burst of expansive optimism, built for himself and his bride. There were nail holes in the walls where his valuable paintings had hung; furniture impressions lingered in the carpets. The living room was fronted with windows that towered to maybe fifteen feet, and from the gallery edging the living room, the state highway was barely visible through the trees. Weeds were sprouting through cracks in the landing strip. Sally had managed to put something in each room: a pool table in the dining room, a chair covered with an afghan in the library, a computer on a table in the computer room, a bed the kids could bounce on in the former exercise room. It wasn't the way I would have done it—I would have fully furnished one or two rooms and left the rest empty—but that was Sally's choice. She wanted, she said, to "inhabit" the house. There was an entire wing of bedrooms, enough for each child to have a separate room, but so far, the kids had dragged their blankets and pillows down the hall each night and slept on the floor outside Sally's room.

When you left the house in the evening, a light came on automatically over the front door, and as you walked down the sidewalk to the circular driveway, more lights came on, a sequence of beams that followed you as you moved, that made you feel like some movie star being stalked by photographers' flashes. "Ridiculous," Sally said, but the lights were wired into the security system, and she couldn't figure out how to shut them off. There were lights triggered by motion at the back of the house too, and when the kids came down the path from Peter and Laurie's, their homecoming was sequentially lit up. Sally would stand and watch for them from the kitchen, and I thought how Peter had once used that path, how Laurie must have waited for the lights as eagerly as Sally did. The driveway, Sally said, was heated: Laurie had never had to call someone to shovel. Presumably this still worked; Sally would find out this winter.

"And to heat this place!" she raved. "He could have put in solar panels. It really is an immoral house."

"How can you afford it?" I asked. The upkeep on my new house in Ohio was bad enough.

"It's a stretch. Maybe I'll sell it. But who would buy it? There's not a market here for houses this size. People who would spend the money want to build."

I imagined what Sally's living situation would sound like to an outsider: a retired lawyer, now divorced, living alone in a huge house with her six children. But that would be inaccurate, it would leave out the isolation, the bitterness, the headiness, the wasted extravagance of a driveway lighting up like Christmas (sorry, Sally) when someone walked outside to see the stars. One day I walked into the living room at dusk and saw a shadow flit behind the couch, the only piece of furniture. For a moment I thought it was a ghost, haunting this glassed and vacant room, but it was only silent Linnea, staring at me with her unreadable eyes. Autism is a diagnosis that comes to mind, but what do I know about children? Sally doesn't buy it. She thinks Linnea is biding her time, that one day she'll look at the piece of toast on her breakfast plate and say, "Mommy, I much prefer eggs." The pediatrician did suggest a specialist in Boise. Someday. Maybe. "And what if she is autistic?" I asked, desperation welling inside me, an inchoate fear that Sally, like her father, could simply throw a child away.

"Then we'll deal with it," Sally answered. "But I won't start dealing with it unless I'm sure it's there." She walked away, as she often did, grumbling happily. "Damned mogul," she might say. "Stick me with with this house." Or: "And he enjoyed it, he enjoyed it! I was never even allowed to talk to him, but every lackey I talked to let me know that he enjoyed it."

I GOT CLEVE HIS PILLS. I actually got lots of patients pills, because the drug company needed a doctor who didn't want a blinded study, who would agree to give each patient the real thing and not a placebo. Timothy Quiver and his ID consorts, bless their fuzzy little heads, took months to convince themselves an unblinded study would "fit" their academic setting. So any patient in town who wanted something new came running to me.

Cleve's libido was returning, he told me; he'd gotten out his video collection.

"Bathhouse Fantasy?"

Cleve bunched his fingers together and kissed the tips. "Your friend's father was an artist."

THAT SUMMER WHEN AURY went to Colorado, my mother and I drove to the Smokies so she could see bears.

"Do you think I did something wrong with Baxter?" she asked. "I don't care about his lifestyle, but why can't he find love? Frank and Eric did."

"Oh, Mom," I said. "That's just his nature. He's a hermit."

She shook her head. "At least you have Sally."

"HE WAS A FUNNY GUY. He never did anything without thinking. He always said"—Sally tapped the side of her head—"'You need a plan.'"

The kids around the kitchen table grinned. They'd heard these stories before. "My grandpa had a huge business," Ezra announced to Aury. "He sold things. But he didn't give people what they needed, he sold them what they wanted."

"Ezra's going to sell people things they need," Sally explained. "That's more in keeping with Torah."

"Grandpa didn't keep kosher," Barbara's voice rang out. "Grandpa ate *lobster*!"

"He was a wonderful man to his family," Sally said, summing up, "but he wasn't much of a Jew."

"I can see where it's nice to have Torah," I said. "Cuts out all the ambiguity."

"That's not true. The whole Talmud is nothing but arguments over the interpretation of Torah."

I sighed. "You think you'll be this religious ten years from now?"

Sally grinned. "Maybe more."

"How can you be more? Will you blowtorch your stove? I can see the point of religion, but I can't see the point of all these rules."

Aury's eyes were wide; we'd had a long talk on the plane about what to expect.

"What's the point, kids?" Sally asked. "We all need meaning in our lives. This gives us meaning."

I was startled by her putting it this baldly, but Sally was always direct. "Even if it's"—I cast about for the word—"goofy meaning?"

Sally made a face for her children, as if I'd just said something even the baby would know was ridiculous. Her voice dropped. "It's not goofy. It's old. It's time-honored. It's the way my father's father lived, and his parents before him. Judaism is three thousand years old! How can you not respect something that's lasted that long? There I was out there, I had my kids; they're forward, but I had nothing behind me. Nothing. When your personal history is gone, you have to start looking for something else. So I looked to tradition."

"Do you flush the toilet on Shabbos?"

"Only dirty. We don't flush if it's pee. But we do that all week long, it's environmentally responsible. Right, kids?"

"If it's brown, flush it down!" Gabriel shouted with zest. Aury winced.

"Flushing a toilet wastes water," Barbara said solemnly.

I guffawed. "Washing your hands wastes water."

Barbara cast an inquiring glance at her mother.

"That's sanitation," Sally said. "Washing your hands helps stop the spread of germs. In a family this size, we can't afford germs. You need to wash your hands, honey."

She's going to have a bunch of weird kids, I thought. No TV, no videos, limited toilet flushing, kosher. All this and Idaho too.

"Ezra," Sally said firmly, "save some cacciatore for Aunt Clare." It was a new sort of cacciatore, mushroom and tofu. Still, Sally made it especially for me.

"Mommy," Joshua said, "can Jews eat pizza?"

"You can eat cheese pizza, honey. If Laurie offers you pizza, tell her you only eat the plain cheesy ones, okay?"

"I hate Laurie," Joshua said; Sally didn't correct him.

Where was Peter in this? I thought. What did Peter think? But I'd never know.

"Oh, I don't know," Sally said, refilling my plate. "Maybe this is just a phase. Maybe ten years from now, I'll be using the meat-dish shelves to store canned hams or something."

We couldn't stop giggling.

PERHAPS SID ROSE DID, as he said that morning at the Beverly Hills Hilton, buy Sally her future. Although that is unthinkable.

I don't want to be an optimist. An optimist believes things always turn out okay; that, as my Sister Mary Klein said, all things work together for the greater good. Aunt Ruby was an optimist. If she fed Freddie, she'd make him well; if Sally knew about Sid's business, she'd be a better person; Sid had loved his kids so much he'd never, ever hurt them. I don't have that kind of faith. Things happen that should never happen. I think of Roger at his end, picking at his hospital bedsheets, his brave grin when the woman at his door was only me and not his mother. Or Ben walking up that hill in Mexico, huffing a bit, not looking back; Sid following, the gun in his pocket thunking on his leg. How could I say these things work for the greater good? Even considering it mocks their useless tragedy. And that's the essence of tragedy: it's useless. In 1993, my worst year, I lost thirty-three patients.

On the other hand, an optimist can go on.

"You know, we have to live with it," Sally said. "In many ways, it's a great house." Her cheeks were shiny, red; her new and cheaper health insurance didn't cover prescriptions, and a medication for her rosacea would be, in her current circumstances, a ridiculous extravagance. "It's bracing to not have money for every whim. Like I tell the kids, it's not the end of the world."

But I can't forget that memorial, that tooth. I've brought it out to Idaho. I've moved it from the pillbox to the pocket of my jeans. Someday, maybe, now that Sid is truly gone, there'll be a time and place to tell her.

"**DID YOU PLAY THAT** new Maccabees game on the computer, Barbara?"

"Yup."

"Was it fun?"

"It was great, Mommy. I killed Ezra, I killed him."

"Bubbles. Say something else. Say you beat the pants off him or something."

"Yeah, right," Barbara scoffed. She looked at me and rolled her eyes. I smiled at her gently, trying to show her she should be grateful. I was grateful.

Later, Sally was picking up children's clothes from the floor and talking. "And then we can't go outside on Shabbos after dark, because we set off those stupid lights."

"Good grief. Sal, you're not turning them on. They're automatic."

She nodded, but not miserably. "They still go on because of us."

"Have you talked to the Web Reb about this?"

"I've talked to several Web Rebs. Opinions vary. If you view going outside as being the agent of turning the lights on, then of course going outside is forbidden. But if you consider the lights simply the response to a movement in the air independent of you, then you can go outside. I kind of prefer the stricter interpretation."

I stopped in my tracks, gave her a warning look. "Sally, you're a maniac! Do you realize you're becoming a maniac?"

"Opinions vary. Do you have anything you need washed? I'll do a load of darks."

We clambered downstairs to the basement laundry, under the bedroom wing, our arms filled with clothes. "You're not asking me, but if you want to know one of the things I treasure most about Judaism, it's the prayers, and my favorite prayer is the shehecheyanu."

"The sh-what-ee-ah-noo?"

"Shaw-heck-ee-ah-noo."

"Oh. Well, why? What's remarkable about it?"

"In English, it's 'Thanks be to God for giving us life and sustaining us and enabling us to reach this season, amen.' It's a prayer of thanks for being alive and staying alive. You say it on special occasions. We just said it during the High Holy days." They had gone to Salt Lake City for Yom Kippur and stayed in two hotel rooms with all the lights on.

"That's interesting."

"It's a lovely prayer. People have said it for thousands of years on their most important days. I've gotten to a point where, when something really special happens, I call it a shehecheyanu moment."

"That is nice. I like that."

Sally was going through pockets. I remembered her on the dorm hallway phone, moaning in Spanish to Patricia about how difficult it was to separate darks from lights. Now she was forty and a laundry expert.

"What's this?" she said, holding up a little plastic bag. She glanced at the jeans draped over her left arm. "It's from your pocket."

I couldn't speak.

"It looks like . . ." She frowned. "What is this, Clare? It looks almost like a tiny piece of cheese, but it's hard."

I opened and closed my mouth. Finally I got it out. How could I not tell her? "It's Ben's tooth. It was lying in a box on that big chest of drawers at your father's house in Malibu. I found it when I went over there to clean things up, after your dad went into the nursing home."

She looked at me in astonishment. "And you've had it all this time?"

I nodded.

"How do you know it's Ben's?"

"I'm assuming it is. Your father told me he had a piece of Ben's tooth as a remembrance of him."

Sally's voice cracked. I couldn't look at her. "Daddy told you?"

"When he and I went out to breakfast, remember? At the Beverly Hills Hilton. After Ezra was born."

"Daddy told you?"

"He told me he had Ben's tooth. You know"—I searched for an analogy—"like a lock of hair or something."

Sally's eyes were wide, her body frozen. The tooth lay on her palm. "Oh," she said, glancing up at me. "A memento."

"You should keep it," I said. It wasn't a normal tooth. It wasn't intact. It was a splinter of a tooth, really, but Sally made no mention of this. "I brought it out to give you. I was going to give it to you yesterday, but I forgot. I feel terrible that I left it in my pocket like that. I'm sorry."

"That's all right. I'm happy to have it." Sally looked at me with a quick smile, slipped the tooth back in its bag, fingered the bag into the pocket of her shirt. "Did Daddy talk to you about Mexico when you two went out to breakfast?"

"You mean being down there with Ben? No, not really. He was just sorry that he hadn't done more for Ben. He felt guilty he hadn't done everything."

"That's all he said?" Sally went through more pockets, finding coins, the stick from a lollipop, an eraser shaped like a Jewish star.

"He wasn't very specific. I had a feeling he . . . felt a lot of guilt. That he hadn't done everything to save Ben." I was going to get through this, I realized. I could survive without telling her what Sid had told me.

"That's all he said?" She nodded at the detergent sitting on a shelf; I scooped out a cupful.

"Basically. He wasn't very specific."

"Okay. I can live with that." She touched my arm reprovingly. "You should have given this to me before, Clare. As a memento." She patted her pocket, right over her heart. Then she bundled all the clothes into the washer and I poured in the detergent. Neither of us said another word about Sid or Ben.

SATURDAY IT RAINED all day. At nightfall, at the end of Shabbos, Sally called the kids for a short ceremony, with prayers and a cup of wine and a braided candle and the passing of a small box—the Havdallah box—filled with aromatic spices. The scent of this, Sally said, was supposed to remind people of the "sweetness of the Shabbos."

Sally's Havdallah box was the small hinged box I'd noticed years before on top of the Biedermeyer chest at her father's house in Malibu, the box that had contained the tiny plastic bag enclosing Ben's tooth.

"Smells okay," Ezra said, sniffing perfunctorily.

"Let me smell it!"

"Mommy, Joshua's going to drop it!"

"I will hold it," Sally said. "No arguments. Now you line up and you can each come sniff it. Gabey, hands off. You don't open it. Come on, Aury. Linnea, did you smell it?"

Satisfied, the children drifted away. Sally doused the candle's flame in the cup of wine, and I walked to the switch by the sink and flicked lights off and on, off and on. Sally laughed.

"Come here," she said. "I want to show you something."

The Havdallah box was lying open on the table. Inside it, unsheathed from its tiny plastic bag, nestled among the curls of spices, was Ben's fractured tooth. "Look at that," I breathed, my voice cracking in wonderment.

"I'm not sure it's kosher," Sally said, "but it seemed right."

I WAKE UP in the dark with a lurch, and it comes to me very clearly: Sally knows.

I don't know what she knows, exactly, what Sid told her, but I know she knows the truth. All those months Sid spent in her house, those sweet and terrible months, as Sally called them (and her adjectives are precise): on one of his lucid days, I'm sure, Sid told Sally something true. What he did to Ben, what Ben did to himself—I don't know what he told her, but something.

Secrets and noise.

The darkness in the room lifts slightly, but I don't roll over to check the clock. I lie there and think my thoughts, and it comes to me that ever since her father went into the hospital, maybe even before, Sally has been on a quest. For years now, steadily and not without missteps, Sally has been setting her life right. Having all her children, leaving Los Angeles, writing to the Internet rabbis, counseling me about Ted, extricating herself from Peter, buying this enormous house, koshering her kitchen, celebrating Shabbos, reclaiming Ben's tooth—weren't all these things, in their essence, attempts to make things right? Even taking on her father's business had been done out of a confused sense of duty. An outsider wouldn't understand this, but none of Sally's acts have been acts of whim. They've been calculated, considered, planned as carefully as one of Sally's old cross-examinations. Intentional, she told me: a religious Jew does things with intention. She has set out to remake her life. To call up a response this vigorous, whatever she had learned about her father must have been bad. Not bad; terrible. Her own word.

She made no reference at all to Ben's tooth being broken. As if that chip were all that she expected. As if her mentioning its fractured state might lead me to questions she had no desire for me to ask.

It's getting brighter. I can see on the long chest of drawers my open suitcase, Aury's bookbag, the framed photo of Sally and me in our youth, with our innocent tomato faces.

She grew up to be a hero, my friend Sally. A blooming hero. There's no one else alive who would recognize this. It wasn't what Sid would have dreamed of as Sally's big future, but she, in her own odd way, has created a large life.

I think of my own foolish self. Sid's real business, my father's embezzlement, the identity of Aury's father, the precariousness of my job: I have a long history of realizing things late. I'm not what you'd call a woman quick on the uptake. As Aunt Ruby said, Gullible's Travels. But ultimately (and this may be my strength), I do realize.

A beam of light slips over the hillside and shoots into my room. Bits of dust dance in the air. Soon the children, Aury among them, will stir from their heap in the hallway outside Sally's door.

LATE THAT MORNING we go for a walk; away from the path to Peter and Laurie's, away from the airstrip, the long driveway, the house with its banks of windows. The sky is huge and blindingly blue, the deciduous trees patched yellow and red against the pines. "I love this time of year and the combination of the colored leaves with the green," Sally says. Shoshana is asleep in the backpack. "And I love the pine needles and the leaves crunching underfoot. Kids! Isn't this a great time of year? Aren't you glad we live in Idaho now?"

They don't answer, tearing off ahead of us, but they all seem happy. Even Aury is almost running, slipping on the path and laughing.

"I'm glad I brought Aury," I say.

"Are you kidding? It's like she's another sibling. I love to see her with my kids."

Are you kidding? Sid's phrase.

Joshua runs back to ask for his shoes to be tied, then Gabriel unties his shoes so Sally can retie them, too. Ezra asks if they can turn toward the river when we reach the bottom of the hill, "so we can do some fishing with our hands." Surrounded by the other children, even silent Linnea seems normal.

"My God!" I say as the children run off again. "Your kids won't leave you alone one minute!" Then it worries me that I've offended Sally by using the Lord's name in vain.

"I guess they love me!" Sally, to my relief, laughs.

I'm not sure many people love me. Ted does, or so he says when he's not wallowing in his ambis, and my daughter does in her precise and carefully calibrated way, and my mother does because she's my mother, and my brothers do, I suppose, although what that means they probably couldn't say. I don't feel like the center of anyone's world. The day I was fired, it crossed my mind that I could load up the car, grab my mother and daughter, and vanish from Ohio and the most this act would invoke in anyone was mild curiosity about what salacious secret had driven me away.

"That's absurd," Sally says. "That's the most ridiculous thing I've ever heard. What about your patients?"

Well, that's true. My patients would miss me. They whisper to their loved ones and point at me as I walk down the hall. Only a few stayed with the division of infectious diseases. But the thing is, as I point out to Sally, all my patients are going to die.

"Not anymore!" Sally teases, because I've told her about the possibles I'm seeing.

"Mommy," Ezra whines, dropping back beside us, "Joshua threw a stick at me."

"Joshua!" Sally snaps. "Put that stick down!"

He gives an elaborately innocent shrug. "But it was an accident!"

"I don't believe in accidents. Put it down. Gabriel! Barbara! Get back on the trail. You want to fall off that rock and get squished like a bug?" She turns to me. "These kids are too intrepid."

I love your adjectives, I think. Your defining adjectives.

In the meantime, it's struck me that, yes, in the past it was true that all my patients would die, but now who knows? I've seen two of them for eight years.

"You've been a great friend to me," Sally says, shifting the straps of the baby's pack.

I replay the word in my mind: *great*.

"Oh," I say, a trifle belatedly, "You've been a great friend to *me*."

"I'm an okay friend," Sally says. "The biggest part of my energy these days goes to the kids."

And your religion, I think, but I don't say that. "That's how it's supposed to be. I'm different, I'm not a very motherly mother."

"You don't have to be. It's like Aury popped out fully grown."

We look at Aury now walking carefully down the path, hands in her pockets, head down. "Amazing," I say.

"Exactly," Sally answers.

"Remember back in college when you met that couple on the plane and you wanted to be part of a unit like that?" I ask, suddenly inspired. Sally nods. "Well," I point out, "we're the unit." We are walking into a clearing, and I squint.

Sally looks at me sidelong for a moment. At first she smiles with a trace of sadness, then she winces a little and turns away. "Complicated," she says.

She doesn't realize that I know. She thinks there's a secret between us, a sort of stain, although I know there's not.

We walk in silence for a few moments.

"Daddy wasn't a good father to Ben. I know that," Sally says suddenly, talking into the air. The mournfulness of her voice unhinges me. I have one of my flashes of telepathy, I can sense she's ready to make a confession, that she would tell me at this moment what she knows. But I don't want to hear it, I don't need it, I want the field of father-talk between us to be clean, unbesmirched and unbesmirchable, as she must wish her memory of her father were.

"But he was good to you, Sally!" I burst out. "He was good to you!"

She stops and looks at me, her eyes startled and grateful, and I'm wearing an impossible smile, something I'm struggling to keep from a grimace, but some muscle in my face relaxes and I succeed. We both know. We recognize Sid's tragedy, that a person can be possessed of wondrous gifts—verve, imagination, drive, even the ability to love and be loved—and still make a glittering slag heap of his life.

"Remember how you bought him a set of textbooks so he could follow along in your courses?" I say.

Sally smiles back. "He always wanted to learn."

"Remember how he called Mr. Gifford a 'poofessor'?"

"Not very politic, Daddy. I hope you don't quote him to Cleve."

"Cleve would have liked him. He loves his movies."

Ahead of us, the children are entering the river's grove of trees. "Stay on the path!" Sally bellows. "No climbing on the rocks! No one in the water!"

In response, Barbara's tanned hand shoots into the air and, fingers spread, bobbles back and forth.

"Aury will keep an eye on them," Sally says, as if to convince herself. "She's responsible." But I notice her steps speed up.

Our children's voices rise up from the path in front of us. "Was I mad to have all these children?" Sally says. The words might be lighthearted, but in her voice there's a splinter of fear.

"Not yet!" I answer, and we both smile.

But our smiles are masks. Who knows what risk and joy and madness lie ahead, as our children tug us into the inscrutable future?

acknowledgments

Thanks to my teachers Stuart Friebert and Diane Vreuls; my agent, Harriet Wasserman; and my superb editor, Cindy Spiegel, and her assistant, Erin Bush, all of whom pulled my writing into the light of day and helped me, in ways big and small, to improve it.

Thanks to my patients, who've made me proud to be human.

Love and special thanks to my husband, the wittiest and kindest man I know.

Martha Moody is a physician living in Dayton, Ohio, with her husband and four sons. *Best Friends* is her first novel.